THE LINDEN WALK

Elizabeth Elgin is the bestselling author of *All the Sweet Promises*, *I'll Bring You Buttercups*, *Daisychain Summer*, *Where Bluebells Chime*, *Windflower Wedding*, *One Summer at Deer's Leap*, *The Willow Pool* and *A Scent of Lavender*. She served in the WRNS during the Second World War and met her husband on board a submarine depot ship. A keen gardener, she has two daughters, five grandsons and a great-granddaughter, and lives in a village in the Vale of York.

D1092890

By the same author:

Whistle in the Dark
The House in Abercromby Square
The Manchester Affair
Shadow of Dark Water
Mistress of Luke's Folly
The Rose Hedge
All the Sweet Promises
Whisper on the Wind
I'll Bring You Buttercups
Daisychain Summer
Where Bluebells Chime
Windflower Wedding
One Summer at Deer's Leap
The Willow Pool
A Scent of Lavender

WRITING AS KATE KIRBY:
Footsteps of a Stuart
Echo of a Stuart
Scapegoat for a Stuart

ELIZABETH ELGIN

The Linden Walk

HarperCollins*Publishers*

HarperCollins*Publishers*
77–85 Fulham Palace Road,
Hammersmith, London W6 8JB

www.harpercollins.co.uk

This paperback edition 2004
1 3 5 7 9 8 6 4 2

First published in Great Britain by
HarperCollins*Publishers* 2004

ISBN 0 00 717084 X

Set in Sabon by Palimpsest Book Production Limited,
Polmont, Stirlingshire

Printed and bound in Great Britain by
Clays Ltd, St Ives plc

For Ian Sommerville, friend and editor

Dear Reader,

You don't need to have read the previous four 'Sutton books' to enjoy this book. *The Linden Walk* is a novel in its own right, though you might be forgiven for calling it an indulgence on my part because I too wanted to know what finally happened to the Clan, those six younglings who grew to maturity during the long years of the Second World War: Tatiana and Andrew, the Kentucky cousins Sebastian and Kathryn – we knew them as Tatty, Drew, Bas and Kitty – and Daisy and Keth, of course.

There were things to be explained, too, loose ends to be tied. Would Drew love again after losing Kitty? Would Keth return to France to find the grave of the young girl shot whilst helping him to reach safety in England? Would Tatty ever meet the half-brother – or sister – she knew to exist?

I have untangled these mysteries and, in doing so, have had the joy of creating a new Clan who will know the delights of growing up at Rowangarth as their parents did, and running free as my first Clan, whilst the sombre and empty Pendenys Place moulders away, unwanted and unloved.

I hope you will enjoy reading this book as much as I enjoyed writing it for you.

Love,
Elizabeth.

The Pendenys Place Suttons

The Rowangarth Suttons

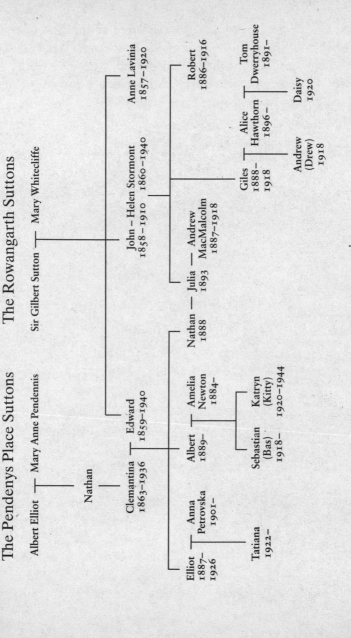

The Rowangarth Suttons

Sir Gilbert Sutton — Mary Whitecliffe

Anne Lavinia 1857–1920

John 1858–1910 – Helen Stormont 1860–1940

Robert 1886–1916

Giles 1888–1918 — Alice Hawthorn 1896–

Tom Dwerryhouse 1891–

Andrew (Drew) 1918

Daisy 1920

Nathan 1888

Julia 1893 — Andrew MacMalcolm 1887–1918

The Pendenys Place Suttons

Albert Elliot — Mary Anne Pendennis

Nathan

Clemantina 1863–1936 — Edward 1859–1940

Elliot 1887–1926 — Anna Petrovska 1901–

Tatiana 1922–

Albert 1889– — Amelia Newton 1884–

Sebastian (Bas) 1918–

Katryn (Kitty) 1920–1944

ONE

September, 1948

'Well, that's the christening over and everyone gone but me.' Lyndis Carmichael got to her feet. 'Care to walk me home, Drew?'

'I seem to remember,' he said softly, 'you asking me that once before.'

'Yes. Before . . .'

'Before Kitty,' Drew Sutton supplied, gravely.

'Mm. I asked this sailor to see me back to Wrens' Quarters. We'd never dated before – not him and me alone, exactly. Usually his sister was there, too.'

'But that night?' he prompted.

'That night, Wren Carmichael made a complete fool of herself. She asked that sailor if he would kiss her goodnight – as in properly, and not the usual brotherly peck on the cheek. And when he did, that stupid Wren offered her virginity on a plate; told the sailor she was in love with him. Best forgotten, wouldn't you say?'

'But I just remembered it!'

'Well, so now I'm remembering you once told me about this Linden Walk and the seat on it and the scent of linden blossom. I asked if I would ever get to smell the blossom and you said if I was a good little Wren, I might. But good little Wrens didn't have a lot of fun, did they? Still, I've got to see your Linden Walk at last, though I can't smell anything.'

'You're too late. The trees flower in summer.'

'Ha! The story of my life! Not only do I miss the blossom, but when I eventually get to sit with you beneath your trees, all I get for my pains is a frozen behind. That seat is hard *and* cold!'

'I'm sorry. So which way shall we go – the long way round or the short cut through the wood?'

'Whichever,' Lyn shrugged, hugging herself tightly because not only was she cold but she was shaking inside. And that was because if something didn't happen tonight to clear the air, she was packing up and going to Kenya. Too damn right she was!

'What is it, Lyn?' He took her arm, guiding her towards the stile at the near end of Brattocks Wood. 'I watched you in church today. You looked so sad. Want to tell me about it?'

She remained silent for all that, because they were passing Keeper's Cottage. She had stayed there often with Daisy, her friend, fellow-Wren, and Drew's half-sister, but in another life, it seemed.

'What's wrong? We're old friends – we get on fine, you and I.'

'Oh sure, Drew. And every time I come to stay with Daisy and Keth, you and I meet and chat like old friends and you kiss me goodnight as friends do – a brotherly peck, like always. Friends! That's all you and I will ever be!'

2

She walked ahead, shoulders stiff, and because the moss at the side of the path was damp with dew, she slipped and would have lost her footing had not Drew grasped her elbow, and steadied her.

'Careful.' He was still holding her. 'I'm sorry the way you feel about you and me. Can't you tell me?'

'About why I looked sad in church? Hadn't thought it showed but yes, I *was* sad – or maybe it was self-pity. That baby is so beautiful I wanted one of my own. I envied Daisy and Keth; wanted to conceive a child, you see, with a man I loved. I wanted all the morning sickness and the pain of heaving and shoving that baby into the world! And every time Daisy puts Mary to her breast I go cold, I'm so jealous! That's what I've become. An untouched, unloved woman who aches for a child!'

Unspeaking, he let go of her arm and there was such a silence between them that she could hear the thudding of her heart and the harshness of her breathing. Above them, a cloud shut out the last of the sun and a flock of birds wheeled overhead, cawing loudly as they settled to roost.

'Rooks!' she murmured. 'Daisy tells them things, doesn't she, and her mother, too. Rooks keep secrets, I believe, so how if I tell them one? Want to hear it, Drew Sutton?'

She walked towards the elm trees, heels slamming, not caring about the slippery path. Then she stood feet apart, hands on hips, looking up into the green darkness.

'Hey, you lot! You listen to things, don't you? Then get an earful of this and hear it good, because I'll not

3

be passing this way again! I'm leaving. Off to Kenya to Auntie Blod because I can't take any more!' She sucked in a deep breath, holding it, letting it go noisily, but it did nothing to calm her.

'There's this man I fell for – a real hook, line, and sinker job – first time we met. I thought he might have had feelings for me, as well, so what d'you know, rooks? I offered it with no strings attached – except that perhaps he might have said he loved me, too. But he didn't say it because he knew I wasn't his grand passion. He met her not long after, his cousin from Kentucky and you can't blame him for the way he fell for her. He'd loved her all his life, only he hadn't realized it!'

She stopped, shaking with anger and despair, and her words swirled around her and spiralled up to where the rooks roosted. And she covered her face with her hands and leaned against the trunk of the tallest tree, because all at once she felt weary and drained. The tears came then; straight from the deeps of her heart and they caught in her throat and turned into sobs that shook her body.

'Don't cry, Lyn. Please don't cry.'

He reached for her and because she did not turn from his touch he took her in his arms, cupping her head with his hand so her cheek rested on his chest. 'Ssh. It's all right. Let it come . . .'

'Drew, I'm s-sorry. That was bloody awful of me.'

'It wasn't. But if it was, I deserved it.'

'No you didn't. Can I borrow your hankie please,' she whispered.

'Be my guest.' He pushed her a little way from

him, dabbing her eyes, then giving her the handkerchief, telling her to blow her nose.

'Good job it's getting dark,' she said sniffily. 'I must look a mess.'

'Yes, you must. Your mascara, I shouldn't wonder, is all over your cheeks – and my shirt front, too – as well as your lipstick.'

'It isn't funny, Drew. I meant it. I did love you. It's why I'm going away.'

'But you *can't* go away. What about Daisy? What about your house?'

'I'd pack in my job for a couple of months – see if I liked it. Then if I did I'd come back and sell up.'

'But you didn't like Kenya, you said so; never wanted to go back, you once told me.' He said it softly, coaxingly, as if reasoning with a child.

'I didn't – don't. I'd stay here if just once you'd say you love me, even though you didn't mean it. And if sometimes you would kiss me properly like that night outside Wrens' Quarters, when Daisy wasn't there . . .'

They began to walk, then, climbing the boundary fence to stand at the crossroads beside the signpost. Away from the trees, it was lighter.

'You look just fine – your mascara, I mean,' Drew said.

'That's okay, then. Daisy won't be asking questions, will she, when I get back to Foxgloves.'

They walked slowly, reluctantly, as if both knew there were things to say before they got to Daisy's house, though neither knew where those words would lead.

'I'm sorry, Lyn, that you were hurt so much. Those brotherly pecks we've been having lately – I thought it was what you wanted. I didn't realize that – well, that after Kitty you'd gone on carrying a torch for me, sort of. And that morning I rang Daisy to tell her I'd got engaged, you spoke to me, too, and sounded glad for me. You said you hoped we'd both be happy.'

'Yes, and then I sat on the bottom stair and cried my eyes out. The entire Wrennery must have heard me. You thought I was a good-time girl, Drew? It was the impression I liked to give, till I met you.'

'It would still have been Kitty,' he said gently. 'She knocked me sideways.'

'I know. And I wasn't glad about what happened to her. When she died, all I could think was that it could have been Daisy or me, in the Liverpool Blitz. It was damn awful luck. I tried not to think about you and how terrible it would be when you got to know.

'But I *was* sad about Kitty. I had to bottle everything up because Daisy was in such a state, kept weeping and wanting Keth, but there was only my shoulder for her to cry on.'

'There's a seat a bit further down – I think we've got to talk, Lyn.' He took her hand and they walked to the new wooden memorial bench. 'When I came back from Australia and got my demob, I didn't go straight home to Rowangarth.'

'I know you didn't. We ran into each other, in Liverpool. Remember? It was blowing, and raining icicles. You seemed lost, as if you were looking for something.'

'I was. Or maybe I was convincing myself that Kitty really wasn't there and never would be again. So I stayed the night, then caught the first train out next morning. But she wasn't at Rowangarth either, nor in the conservatory nor the wild garden. All I could find of her was a wooden grave-marker with her name on it. It was like a last goodbye.'

'It must have torn you apart, Drew. Are you ever going to forget her?'

'No. She happened and I can't begin to pretend she didn't. But at least I've accepted the way it is. Mother told me she wasted too many years raging against the world after her husband Andrew died. She begged me to try not to do the same.

'When finally she went to France to his grave, she had to accept he was dead, she told me. So I was luckier than she was. At least I was spared the bitterness. All I have to contend with now is the loneliness.'

'And I've just made a right mess of it, haven't I?' Lyn whispered. 'My performance in the wood must have shocked you. Sorry if I embarrassed you.'

'You shocked me, yes, because I'd never really realized how you felt. Even after the war was over and you started visiting Daisy and Keth and we met up again and –'

'And walked, and talked!'

'And walked,' he laughed, 'and talked like old friends.'

'All very nice and chummy, till I put the cat among the pigeons.'

'Among the *rooks*! But are you really thinking of going to Kenya?'

'Thinking, yes, but I won't go. And Drew – before the soul-searching stops, this is your chance to cut and run; give me a wide berth next time I come to Foxgloves. Because I won't change.'

'You must have loved me a lot,' he said softly.

'I did. I do. I always will. And if you can still bear to have me around after tonight – well, you don't have to marry me. If sometimes we could be *closer*, sort of. It's just that I'm sick to the back teeth of being a virgin, still.'

'Lyndis Carmichael.' He laid an arm across her shoulders and pulled her closer. 'What on earth am I to do with you?'

'Like I said, you don't have to marry me . . .'

'Oh, but I do! You *can* love twice, Mother said, but differently. So shall we give it a try, you and me? Knowing that Kitty will always be there and that sometimes people will talk about her just because she was Kitty and a part of how it used to be, at Rowangarth?

'Knowing that every time you and I walk through the churchyard or down Holdenby main street, we shall see her there? And can you accept that every June, Catchpole will take white orchids to her grave and that she was my first love? Knowing all that, will you be my last love, Lyn?'

For a moment she said nothing, because all at once there were tears again, ready to spill over, and she wouldn't weep; she *wouldn't*!

'That really was the most peculiar proposal I ever had.' She blew her nose, noisily. 'Come to think of it, it's the *only* proposal I ever had! It – er – *was* a proposal?'

'It was, but I think I'd better start again. I want you with me always, Lyn. Will you marry me?'

He still hadn't said he loved her, she thought wonderingly, as a star began to shine low in the sky, and bright. But he *would* say it. She could wait, because now tomorrows were fashionable, and people could say the word without crossing their fingers.

Their lips touched; gently at first and then more urgently, and as she pulled away to catch her breath she looked over his shoulder at the star; first star – wishing star. So she closed her eyes, searching with her lips for his, wishing with all her heart for a child with clinging fingers that was little and warm and smelled of baby soap. Two children. Maybe three.

'I think,' she said shakily, 'that if you were to kiss me again as in properly and passionately, I'd say, "Thanks, Drew. I will."'

It seemed right, somehow, and very comforting that as they kissed again, a pale crescent moon should slip from behind a cloud to hang over Rowangarth's old, enduring roof as new moons always had, and that from the top of the tallest oak in Brattocks Wood, a blackbird began to sing Sunset.

As it always would.

TWO

At the house called Foxgloves where Keth and Daisy lived off the Creesby road, all was quiet. Bemused, Lyndis gazed into the fire. It had really happened, Drew asking her to marry him and she saying yes. A very calm yes, considering she had been dry-mouthed and shaking all over. She still couldn't quite believe it. The wayward little pulse behind her nose still did a pitty-pat whenever she thought about it and to bring herself down to earth, she would close her eyes and cross her fingers and pray with all her heart that nothing would happen to prevent it. Because it had happened before, though lightning didn't strike twice in the same place – well, *did* it? Fate couldn't do it again to Drew. Not when Kitty had been killed by a lousy flying bomb when everyone thought the war – in Europe at least – was all but over.

Kitty had been one of the Clan. Special, that Clan. Still was. Before, when they'd met up twice a year, it was as if they had never been apart. Bas and Kitty, the cousins from Kentucky, were Pendenys Suttons, really, though drawn always to Rowangarth and Drew and Daisy and Keth. And Tatty, of course. Half Pendenys Sutton, half Russian, she had been the awkward one, the defiant one. Kitty, the naughty one, had been beautiful and headstrong and a show-off. No wonder Drew had been completely besotted by her. Poor Drew. Thousands of miles away with the Pacific Fleet when it happened, and not even able to say one last goodbye at her graveside.

But that war was over, now. Six damn-awful years it had lasted and she and Drew two of the lucky ones. Kitty had not been, though she would never be dead. Not completely.

'Right!' The door flew open. 'That's the baby fed and in bed so give, Carmichael. Tell *all*!'

'Daisy – surely not at this hour? You've had a big day. You must be asleep on your feet.'

'Blow the hour! Mary is asleep, Keth is marking homework in his cubbyhole upstairs so he'll hear if she cries. No excuses. This is Wren Purvis-from-the-bottom-bunk. Remember our heart-to-hearts, Lyn?'

She dropped to her knees to stir the fire and lay another log on it.

'Mm. Good ones and bad ones . . .'

'Yes, and I put up with all your bad ones which makes me entitled to hear the best bit of all, so let's be having it. From the beginning.'

'But you know about it. Drew and I are going to be married. You were right. "*Do* something," you said. "Go in at the deep end and if it comes to nothing, then at least you tried." And the deep end it was – feet first.

11

I can hardly bear to think of it. Hands on hips in Brattocks Wood, yelling my head off at those rooks!'

'Lyn – will you never learn? You don't yell at the rooks. You don't even *talk* to them. You put your hands on the tree trunk – connect yourself to it, sort of – then you send them your thoughts.'

'Thoughts? It was for Drew's benefit, don't forget. He isn't a mind-reader. Poor love. I yelled like a fishwife.'

'He needed a shove. My brother has always been a tad too placid.'

'Well, he got the message in the end.' She clucked impatiently then went to sit at Daisy's side on the sofa opposite because it would help, she all at once realized, if she didn't have to look her in the eye when she told all.

And tell all she did; was glad to. Told every word, gesture and sniff. What she had said; what Drew had said.

'And Drew so serious and kind about it. Yes, *kind*, actually. Me offering it on a plate – *again*! Telling him I was sick of being a virgin, still; that he didn't have to marry me. I must've sounded desperate. But it worked. I got what I wanted, what I've always wanted since the day I met him.'

'What we all wanted, love. I wanted it, Mam wanted it and Aunt Julia wanted it, too. She most of all. So what did she and Nathan say when you arrived at Rowangarth with the news?'

'Drew's mother let out one yell then hugged me and hugged Drew, and Nathan beamed all over and raised his eyes to the ceiling and said, "Thank God for that!" And Drew's mother said she would go to the bank first thing in the morning and get the jewels out so I could choose a ring, but I had to tell her I was going back to Llangollen in the morning.

'And Drew said, "She'll be back on Friday. Get them out for then. And no, Mother! No champagne! We've got to go and tell Lady and Tom – and Keth and Daisy. Save the champagne till I've got the ring on her finger!"'

'You'd think there was still a war on. I mean, you can't get anything half decent at the jeweller's. Best you have a family ring, Lyn.'

'Your mother said that, Daisy. "You'll be having one of Grandmother Whitecliffe's rings I shouldn't wonder. She left all her jewellery to Julia, you know." Your folks were pleased, when we told them.'

'Well, of course they would be. Mam especially. She's been wanting Drew down the aisle for years.'

'I still can't help thinking I did it a bit sneakily, Daisy. I practically put the words into his mouth. And for all that, he never said he loved me. Just that he wanted me with him always. He'll probably have changed his mind in the morning.'

'Not Drew. And the I-love-you bit will come. It did happen rather quickly, after all. Maybe he *thought* he said it. Who cares? You're engaged. So when is it going to be?'

'Haven't a clue. We didn't talk dates. Like I said, it all –'

'I know. Happened so quickly. It'll be here at Rowangarth, of course. You'll be having a white wedding? What are you going to do about a dress?'

'Lord knows. Clothes are still rationed. I haven't seen wedding dresses in the shops, yet. Mind, I haven't been seriously looking.'

'Then you'd better start, Carmichael. Of course,' she said obliquely, 'you could use mine. Mam would be tickled pink if you did. And she'd alter it around a bit.'

'No! I mean, no I wouldn't want it altered, but yes I'd love to wear it. It's the most beautiful wedding dress I've ever seen. D'you remember when your mum had got it almost finished? You and I were on a crafty weekend after a week of nights and you stood on the kitchen table so she could see to the hem. So cosy. I sat on the brass stool beside the fire and watched, and envied you like mad. Long time ago, that was. Before, I mean, when I was head over heels in love with Drew, and . . .'

'You're talking about Kitty coming over to join ENSA? Before he realized she was the one. Is that what you're trying to say?'

'Suppose I am. I was going to be your bridesmaid, then I chickened out.'

'Because by the time Keth and I finally got ourselves down the aisle, Drew and Kitty were engaged and you couldn't bear, you said, to see them together.'

'A bit childish of me, wasn't it?'

'Yes, but understandable, in the circumstances. Anna Sutton – *Pryce* – gave Mam two ball gowns; a rose one and a pale blue one. Mam made them look a bit more bridesmaidy and saved no end of clothing coupons.'

'I should have worn the blue one, but Kitty stood

14

in for me. They looked lovely on your wedding photos, she and Tatty.'

'Well, there are still two bridesmaids' dresses in store at Rowangarth. Mam went to a lot of bother over them. She'd love to see them on show again. A June wedding, might it be . . . ?'

'I don't know, Daisy – I honestly don't. I still can't believe any of it has happened. Suppose I'll feel a bit more engaged when I get a ring on my finger.'

'Ooh, Lyndis Carmichael!' Daisy jumped to her feet. 'For someone who has just said yes to the man she's been in love with for years, you are being very nonchalant about it, if I may say so! Anyway, I'm going to make a milky drink – want one?'

'Please. And Daisy – nonchalant isn't the word. I'm stunned. I can't seem to take it in. Keep thinking I'll wake up soon, and find I've dreamed it.'

'Well you haven't, old love. There's going to be another Sutton wedding and Mam and Aunt Julia are going to have the time of their lives. You *will* be married from Rowangarth, Lyn? It's such a lovely place for a wedding.'

'I'd like nothing better, and will you be my matron of honour, Daisy, wear one of the dresses?'

'You know I'd love to – and could you nip upstairs and ask Keth if he wants a drink, too?'

When Lyn had tiptoed downstairs, she knew that her, 'Yes, please, and a biscuit if there's one going,' wasn't necessary. Already the milk pan was on the stove and three mugs and a plate of scones set on a tray.

'See, Lyn. Cherry scones from this afternoon. Tilda

always makes cherry scones for special occasions. She gave me some leftovers. You'll have to get used to Rowangarth's little habits and cherry scone days, and suchlike. You'll have to get used to being lady of the house. You and Drew will have it all to yourselves, once the Reverend and Aunt Julia have moved into the Bothy. She hopes to be in there by Christmas. It's going to be just wonderful, isn't it? So much to look forward to. Tatty and Bill having a Christmas wedding. And then there'll be yours and Drew's and by then Gracie will have had sprog number two and she said she wants it christened at All Souls, by Nathan. I shouldn't wonder if Bas and Gracie don't come over in the summer, once you've set a date, Lyn. The Kentucky Suttons used to come over twice a year, regular as clockwork at Christmas and for a month in the summer. That's when the Clan were all together and *oh, no*!' She ran to the stove as the milk began to froth and boil, removing the pan. 'Now look what you almost made me do! All this wedding talk!'

They laughed, and Daisy spooned Ovaltine into the pan and whisked it, pouring it frothily into the mugs.

'Take ours through will you, Lyn, and I'll take Keth's up to him and have a peep at the baby. And by the way,' she said when they were settled once more beside the sitting-room fire. 'I'm not going to be your matron of honour. If Bas and Gracie are over at the time of the wedding, I think Gracie should be asked. After all, she *is* family and she'll be decorating the church for you. She's smashing with flowers. Served her time as a gardener-cum-land girl at

Rowangarth. In Catchpole's time, that was. Have a scone. They're delicious.'

'Okay. So I ask Gracie, but who'll wear the other dress?'

'You should ask Tatty. She'd love to do it. Mind, she might be pregnant, by then. Told me they're going to be very careless about things 'cos they want a family right away. Still, if push comes to shove, I wouldn't see the other frock go to waste. And had you thought, Lyn? You and me almost next door to each other. Just like it was when we were Wrens. Doesn't seem like five minutes since I arrived at Hellas House running a temperature, and you looking after me. We've come a long way, since then. We'll be sisters-in-law.'

'*Half*-sisters-in-law, if you want to be nit-picky. And Daisy – would you mind if I took my drink upstairs? I've got to be up early tomorrow – get the first train out. I'm doing afternoons at the hotel and if I miss that train I'm going to be late for work. Sorry, old love . . .'

'And would that be so very awful, considering you'll be giving notice anyway? Why don't you pack in working and stay with me till the wedding?'

'Nothing I'd like more, Daisy, but right now I'm high as a kite. This isn't the time for decision making. I'll think about it, though. It'll all depend on Drew. Can't wait to see him in the morning – ask him if he really, *really* wants to marry me.'

'Idiot,' Daisy grinned. 'A Sutton doesn't go back on his word. Now get yourself off. I'll follow you when I've seen to everything down here. Getting a bit tired myself. But hasn't it been one heck of a day, Leading-Wren Carmichael?'

'One absolute corker of a day, Wren Purvis-from-the-bottom-bunk. And I'm glad we're going to be sisters. I truly am.'

Lyn lay in bed, looking through the uncurtained window at the moon, high in the sky and shining gold now; the same paler moon that was witness to what happened tonight. Because it *had* happened. Drew *had* asked her to marry him and she had said yes. Disbelievingly almost, she said, 'Thanks, Drew, I will.' Said it nonchalantly, as if she had proposals of marriage every day of the week, and had got rather blasé about them.

She was always doing that; hiding her feelings for fear of being hurt. Because she *had* been hurt. If worlds could end, then hers would have ended the morning Drew phoned Daisy to tell her he and Kitty were engaged; had met up on a Liverpool dockside and *wham*! The two of them had spent the night at Kitty's theatrical digs and the next morning Lyndis Carmichael smiled brilliantly into the phone, wished them both all the very best, then wept as if her heart would never be whole again – nor had it been, until tonight.

So why was she wide awake and tossing and turning? Why could she not believe that what she had longed for since the first time she and Drew met had happened? Why had she said – albeit jokingly – that she couldn't wait to see him in the morning, ask him if he really wanted to marry her?

'You're a fool, Lyn,' she whispered to the moon. Of course he wanted to marry her. A Sutton didn't go back on his word, Daisy said. Yet she was afraid, still, and she knew it was because she would always be second best; second choice. Drew would never forget Kitty. He'd said so. Kitty would always be there because she had been one of the Clan – that *bloody* precious Clan she'd always envied because she could never be a part of it.

Mind, Gracie had never been part of the Clan and it had worried her not one jot. Pretty, happily married Grace Sutton who expected her second child at Christmas. Lyn liked Sebastian Sutton's wife, just as she liked Tatty. Born to a Russian countess, Tatiana Sutton was as English as London Bridge. No one would know she was half-Russian, spoke correct Russian fluently, and conversed with the sombre Karl in his native Georgian, too. Tatty had taught Kitty to swear in Russian and in return Kitty taught Tatty to spit like a stable lad. Maybe Gracie's baby would be born on Tatty and Bill's wedding day. A cosy, family wedding in the little Lady Chapel it was to be and no white dress nor virginal veil Tatty stressed because she and Tim – her first passionate love – had been lovers from the start. Like Drew and Kitty, she supposed, because air-gunner Tim had been killed, too.

So why wasn't Tatiana making a big production of her wedding to Bill and why did Bill Benson seem to happily accept the way things were – that the woman he would marry at Christmas had loved before; just as Drew had loved before – Drew's mother, too.

'Oh, *dammit*!' She flicked on the bedside light, padded across the room to draw the curtains, checked that the alarm at her bedside was set for five in the morning, then whispered, 'Goodnight, Drew. And it *will* be all right, my darling, I promise it will.'

She loved him – enough for both of them – and one day he would tell her he loved her too.

She closed her eyes and began to count each solemn second as it ticked away on the clock beside her, but it did nothing to help her fall asleep.

They waited on the platform at Holdenby Halt. Drew looked at his watch then said, 'Any time now you'll hear the train. The driver always gives a hoot just before the bend – a little past Brattocks. Then soon it'll arrive, and you know what, Lyn? This station hasn't changed one iota since ever I can remember.'

'You don't have to come to York with me. I'm quite capable of getting myself onto the Manchester train.'

'Of course you are, but mightn't it just occur to you that maybe I want to. For one thing, it'll give us an extra hour together and for another, I want us to talk – plans, dates and all that. There's always an empty compartment on this early train, so we can natter all the way to York. Have you had any thoughts on the matter, Lyn?'

'Nope. All I could think about last night was had it really happened and when the heck I was going to get to sleep!'

'You, too? Mind, it did happen quite suddenly. Takes a bit of getting used to. No second thoughts?'

'No, Drew.' *Oh, liar Lyndis Carmichael!* 'Had you?'

'Plenty, but no doubts. Wondered why we hadn't got around to it before, as a matter of fact, and then I thought you might have decided that you didn't want to be Lady Sutton, after all.'

'Oh, my Lor', Drew, *Lady* Sutton. I hadn't thought . . .'

'Comes with the job, I'm afraid. You'll get used to it.'

'Y-yes . . .' The little train – the Holdenby Flyer, may God bless it, Lyn thought fervently – saved her the embarrassment of a reply. 'It's coming,' she said. 'Right on time.'

'Usually is,' Drew smiled, picking up her case, scanning the carriages as they slipped slowly past, pleased at the number of empty compartments. 'The front of the train.' He took her hand. 'Plenty of room there.'

He helped her aboard then slammed the door firmly shut, pulling up the window.

'There now, let me check. All present and correct. One case, one grip and one fiancée.' Satisfied, he sat beside her, pulling her arm through his, smiling down at her.

'That was nice, Drew.' Lyn's cheeks pinked. 'You calling me your fiancée, I mean.'

'Well, you are, aren't you?' he grinned. 'Unless of course you've changed your mind.'

'I am, and I haven't. So let's talk plans,' she smiled tremulously as the whistle blew and the train jerked to a start. 'Whatever you want is fine with me.'

'Right! We'll have the banns read starting next

Sunday, then we'll get married about the middle of October – that suit you?'

'Just fine. But it wouldn't suit Daisy nor her mother and it certainly wouldn't suit *your* mother! White weddings take a lot of planning, don't forget. Besides, I'll have to give my parents in Kenya fair warning and plenty of time to get themselves organized and over here. And Daisy is insisting on a summer wedding. Bas and Gracie should be over by then and wanting their new baby christened. Your sister has got it all worked out. We had quite a long session last night.'

'And?' Drew quirked an eyebrow.

'Well, I'm to ask Gracie to be one of the bridesmaids and if Tatty isn't pregnant, she says, I ought to ask her – to wear the other dress, I mean. And I shall wear Daisy's wedding dress. She offered and I couldn't say no – it's so beautiful. That was as far as we got, I'm afraid.'

'Might Tatty be pregnant?'

'No, of course not. But they do want a family so there'd be no point in waiting I was given to understand.'

'And what else did Daiz come up with? Did she – er – mention how many children you and I will have?'

'She didn't get around to it, actually. Nor did I.'

'But you want children, Lyn? I mean – everything seemed to happen so suddenly. You said you did after the christening but . . .'

'Don't worry, Drew Sutton. I want children, too. As many as the Good Lord thinks fit to send us. You and I were only-children. I'd like it if we had a couple, at least. Three would be nice.'

'Be happy to oblige,' he laughed, then all at once

serious he cupped her face in his hands, saying softly, 'You *are* sure, Lyn?'

'I'm sure, Drew, but had you realized that not since you called for me at Foxgloves have I had so much as a kiss. Almost half an hour ago, that was!'

'Again – happy to oblige.'

He tilted her chin and kissed her. Not with passion but with tenderness, Lyn thought; a reassuring, comforting, it'll-be-all-right kiss and for the time being the niggling doubts left her.

'I'll call at Denniston when I get back – tell them about us. Bas and Gracie are leaving for Rochdale tomorrow to stay with Gracie's folks for a week before they go back. They're sailing, by the way. Better than flying, I suppose, all things considered. Mind, Mother will have been on the phone, spreading the news – nothing so certain. First she'll be on to Daisy's mother at Keeper's and by the time she has finished ringing around, the entire Riding will know. There'll be no need to put it in the *Yorkshire Post*.'

'The announcement – it won't go in just yet, will it?'

'No. Not until you and I have talked about it and what we want putting in; we haven't got a date yet, have we? But it's like Nathan said last night. He doesn't know what gets into normally well-balanced women when the words wedding or new baby are mentioned. He said it'll be murder, the to-ing and fro-ing between Rowangarth and Keeper's Cottage. Is it going to be a surprise to your folks, too? And before we can really announce it, I suppose I should ask your father's permission, Lyn?'

'Drew! Don't be so stuffy.' She gave his arm a little punch. 'This is the middle of the twentieth century. Our generation has just fought a war, earned a bit of independence. It'll be fine by them. Dad will be relieved that I'm off the shelf at last and Blod – *Mother* – will say, "Ooh, our Lyndis. There's lovely . . ." I can just hear her. I'll write to them, airmail, tonight.'

'And you'll tell them you're very happy?'

'I'll tell them.' Because she was. Crazily, ecstatically, *unbelievably* happy. So happy, in fact, that if the Fates got wind of it they'd be jealous, and that would never do. 'And here's York and we haven't settled anything.'

'We have, sweetheart. We've talked wedding dresses and bridesmaids and decided – almost – on a summer wedding. And three children.'

'And that we're both happy about us?'

'Happy. A bit bewildered still, but happy, Lyn. *Very* happy. Don't ever forget it, will you?'

THREE

'Who on earth have you been talking to, all this time? I've tried to ring you three times, and you're always engaged!' The back door of Keeper's Cottage was opened without ceremony by a breathless Julia Sutton.

'Sorry,' Alice smiled, 'but it isn't every day our son gets engaged.' *Their* son. She, who had reluctantly borne and birthed him, Julia who reared him as her own. Dwerryhouse. At two years old, Drew hadn't been able to pronounce her name. Mrs Lady he had said instead and she had been Lady ever since. And, thank God, she had come to love him deeply. 'Isn't it going to be grand? Lyn wants to wear Daisy's wedding dress. She'll have to try it on, next time she's over – see if it fits.'

'It will, near as dammit. Who else have you phoned, Alice?'

'We-e-ll, Daisy, of course. And I mentioned it to Winnie at the Exchange and I rang Home Farm to tell Ellen and I'll be nipping out to tell Polly. Not that she won't have heard, of course. I'm so thrilled. Can't seem to settle to anything, this morning.'

'Nor me. In the end, Nathan asked me if I'd mind getting off the line; that he's got parishioners who might want to get through. "Why don't you pop along to Keeper's," he said. "Have a good old natter with Alice." All of a sudden, he's taken on a hounded look, poor love; something to do with women and weddings, he said.'

'Tom's exactly the same. Men can be very peculiar. But let's have a sit-down, and talk about things.' Alice set the kettle to boil. 'By the way, did you phone Denniston House?'

'I did. Told them Drew would be calling when he's back from York. He'll be wanting to say goodbye to Bas and Gracie. They're going to Gracie's folks for a week, then off back to Kentucky.'

'And a Christmas baby for them. So much to look forward to. Tatty's wedding, as well. We've been lucky there, haven't we?'

'Drew and Tatty, and them not getting together, you mean?'

'Exactly. It could have happened, Julia. I mean, Drew losing Kitty and Tatty losing her Tim. Drawn together, they could have been. What would we have done? How would we have told them?'

'I don't know, and that's the honest truth. But it isn't going to happen now, Alice. Remember when we told Drew that you were his real mother?'

'I do. Our Daisy acted up like a right little madam. Flounced off in one of her tantrums. Couldn't accept there'd been another man in my life.'

'Two men, did she but know it. Elliot Sutton who raped you and my lovely brother, who married you and claimed the child for Rowangarth. We were more than lucky, considering the lies we told and –'

'White lies, Julia. Heaven must have approved of what we did. Drew was born fair as all the other Rowangarth Suttons; not dark like *him*. No need for Drew ever to know about his getting. There's few living, now, who know.'

'Just you and Tom. And Nathan and me. No worries that it's ever going to get out, now.'

'And Giles. He knew. So badly wounded. Never have a son for Rowangarth he said to me one night, when I was nursing him. He was in pain, and couldn't sleep and we were talking. And I told him that that was ironic, because I had a child inside me I didn't want. A rape child. Natural, him being the gentleman he was, to offer to marry me. I was grateful to accept, and why not, when Tom was dead, or so they said. That was a terrible war. I'm glad Giles lived long enough to know I'd had a boy.'

'Poor dear Giles. Survived his war wounds to die of that awful 'flu. That 'flu took more people than were killed in the war. But what has got into us, getting all nostalgic and raking up the past! Let's be having that cuppa, and get down to the present and Drew's wedding. June, wouldn't you say?'

'It'll be up to the pair of them, but I reckon next June would be as good a time as any. And the white orchids will be flowering, don't forget, for another Rowangarth bride.'

'Mm. Mother carried them to her wedding, and I did. And Kitty should have.'

'Kitty. We aren't going to be able to forget her, are we, Julia?'

'No. And we don't want to. Kitty is still a part of what was. Natural we should keep her with us.'

'Yes. Let's hope that Lyndis will accept it, and understand . . .'

'She will, Alice. Given time, I'm sure she will, so don't let's spoil this lovely day? Let's be glad that everything has worked out so wonderfully well. And I'm not interfering, truly I'm not, but wouldn't a June wedding be great? Plenty of flowers – roses, as well as the white orchids. And a marquee on the lawn. When I told Tilda and Mary the first thing they said was that thank goodness we could have a wedding that was almost normal. Food-wise, they meant. Tilda has been wanting something like this to happen. She remembers the dinner parties at Rowangarth, before the war.

'"Such goings-on, and all of us running round like mad things. But it was right grand," she said. "Mind, that was in Mrs Shaw's day, and I was only kitchen maid, then." I think she's going to look forward to the challenge, now she's our cook. And I know food rationing isn't over yet, but we needn't feel quite so guilty about getting a bit on the black market – just the once. It isn't as if merchant seamen are risking their lives, now, getting food to us across the Atlantic.'

'Mm. Just this once. It's a pity, hadn't you thought, that Lyn's mother is going to miss all the fun – the planning, I mean. Sad she's so far away.'

'There's nothing to stop her coming over and joining in. She'd be very welcome. Drew has met her –

just the once – and he says she's a lovely lady. There'd be loads of room for her. Bedrooms and to spare. I think Lyn should suggest it to her, when she writes.'

'Oh? But you won't be living at Rowangarth for very much longer, will you? Be in the Bothy by Christmas, you said.'

'Okay. So she can stay at the Bothy with Nathan and me. Lyn's father, too. Who cares? But even with me not there, Drew will be able to manage on his own for a few months. There'll be Mary and Tilda to look after him – and anyone else who might want to stay there.'

'Mary and Tilda are both married and live out, don't forget. They wouldn't be on call twenty-four hours a day.'

'Alice! You're looking for trouble. Drew isn't help-less. He had six years in the Navy, don't forget. It'll all work out, in the end. I suppose that all I can think of right now is that we're going to have a Christmas wedding in the family and a Christmas baby, given luck. And another wedding in June. Makes you giddy, just to think about it.'

'It does. And coming back to Lyn – I'll bet you anything you like that as soon as she gets back to Llangollen, she'll send a cable to her folks, *Drew and I engaged. Letter follows*. Hope she manages to get back all right. She's got to change trains at Manchester and Chester, don't forget. Hope she hasn't got her head in the clouds and ends up in Liverpool, instead. And y'know, Julia – Drew and Kitty wasn't to be, but he and Lyn will make a go of it, I know they will.'

'They will, Alice. As long as we all remember – without being in any way disloyal to Kitty's memory – that it's Drew and Lyn, now.'

'Drew and Lyn,' Alice held high her teacup. 'Bless them both. And may they be very happy together.'

She wiped a tear from the corner of her eye, then smiled brilliantly at Julia.

Her dear friend, Julia. Her almost-sister who knew all about first loves and last loves. She would, Alice decided, make a very good mother-in-law.

'Well, look who's here!' Tatiana Sutton had seen her cousin's approach and run to the door to greet him. 'If it isn't the blushing bridegroom himself. Come on in, do!'

'Hey up, Tatty. I've hardly been engaged a day, yet. Give a man a chance!' He took her in his arms, hugging her tightly. 'I'm still a bit bemused. Never thought she'd have me.'

'Have you? She's been crazy about you for years! You'll both be very happy, I know it. Hang on, and I'll call Bill. He's in his garret, painting. Won't be a tick.'

'No, Tatty. Give it a couple of minutes, if you don't mind. You see, I feel really good about Lyn and me. Is that wrong of me? You'll understand – Tim, I mean. How do you feel about marrying Bill, or is it too personal a question?'

'Coming from you, Drew, no it isn't. And I'm very happy about Bill and me. He knows that Tim and I were lovers. Bill and I haven't been. He would rather wait, he said, till we were married. But it isn't a problem, not even when I talk about Tim, once in a while. Tim is a part of my past and you can't wipe out what has been – just accept you've got to live with it, be it good or bad.'

'Thanks, Tatty. I hoped you'd say that. I won't ever forget Kitty, Lyn understands that.'

'I like Lyn, Drew. You'll be great together, like Bill and me.'

'And Mother and Uncle Nathan, too. A different kind of loving, Mother told me, but good.'

'Exactly. So let's sit in the conservatory and talk weddings. Yours and mine.'

'Y'know something, Tatiana Sutton? You were such a brat when you were little, but you've grown into a lovely person – and beautiful, like your mother.'

'Why thanks, cousin dear. And there's another happy second-time-around. My mother and Ewart Pryce. She's stupidly happy with him but she wasn't, with my father.'

'How do you know?'

'I just do, that's all. No one would talk to me about my father. Elliot Sutton. For all I knew about him, he was just a name on a gravestone. I even asked your mother to tell me, and she's a most reasonable lady and broad-minded too, but not one word would she ever say. She just went all vinegar-faced then said, rather apologetically, that she didn't remember a lot about him because he was always gadding about, somewhere or other. And then she said, "Mind, if you were to ask me about Nathan . . ." Why does she so obviously love my father's brother, yet hates my father?'

'Don't know, Tatty. All I know is she goes all po-faced about him. Lady, too. I've learned to keep off the subject.'

'Well, *I've* found out, Drew, but keep it to yourself, mind. Uncle Igor told me, swore me to secrecy, though. I got quite close to him. Used to visit at Cheyne Walk when he was there alone living in the basement, and the Petrovska here at Denniston because of the bombing on London. And I'm sorry. I shouldn't have mentioned bombs on London.'

'Tatty, bombs *did* drop on London. Nothing's going to change that. But are you sure you want to tell me?'

'I'm sure. Quite simply, my father was a womanizer. He didn't love my mother but she had a title. Countess, actually, which meant very little in Russia and still less when you are a penniless White Russian refugee. But he married her to please his mother because she was a bloody snob and wanted a title in the family, and was desperate for a grandson. Grandmother Clementina thought her money could buy anything. I think had my little brother not been stillborn, my father could have gone his own sweet way with his mother's blessing and his pockets lined with cash.

'But my father overstepped the mark. Whilst Mother was pregnant he seduced a housemaid, here at Denniston. She was very beautiful, I believe. Spoke no English. Natasha Yurovska. She came with them to England when the Communists took over in Russia.'

'So what happened to her?' Drew felt bound to ask.

'When my brother was stillborn I was told that the Petrovska and Uncle Igor took my mother and the housemaid back to London; both of them away from my father. I don't know what became of the girl. It was all hushed up, the Petrovska saw to that. Had to be. Natasha Yurovska was pregnant.'

'And does my mother know this, Tatty?'

'About Natasha? I don't know, but I don't think that's why she hates him. I reckon Uncle Nathan knows, though. Mother was once deeply religious – used him as her confessor I believe, but priests never say anything.'

'And are you thinking what I am thinking . . . ?'

'That I have a brother or a sister – well, half so. It was one of the good things about finding out about my father, but I shan't try to find him – or her. Needles in haystacks, and that sort of thing. But somewhere out there, someone belongs to me. I've asked my mother but she told me she didn't know when or where Natasha Yurovska's baby was born. Nobody would tell her. I sometimes think that even Uncle Igor wasn't told. The Petrovska refused to say. But this is neither the time nor the place to lay souls bare. I'm sorry, Drew. I shouldn't have gone on about it, especially when you are so happy – and me, too. We should forget about my father. He's gone, and we shall talk about weddings and about being happy – and that it's all right if sometimes we mention Tim and Kitty because people can love twice, but differently. Uncle Nathan and Aunt Julia are living proof of that.'

'Well, it's your turn first, Tatty. Are you excited?'

'N-no. Not starry-eyed, breathlessly excited. More a warm sort of contentment and having someone at long last I can trust and who will always be there for me. And of course, it'll be good going to bed with him,' she said without so much as the blinking of an eyelid. 'With Tim it was a kind of snatched, there's-no-tomorrow loving. Things are different, now the war is over. We can plan ahead; have kids. And *kids* I said. Not an only child, fussed over by its mother and not wanted by its father. How many will you and Lyn have, Drew?'

'Haven't a clue.' He laughed, disarmed by her frankness. 'Lyn wants children, though. She told me so.'

'Good. That's settled, then. And you are both to come to my wedding. It'll be the week before Christmas. No formal invitations, or anything. That okay?'

'Accepted soon as asked. There's Bill, crossing the yard.'

'Mm. He's an old love. Doesn't want to sleep with me before we are married on account of someone getting his mother pregnant then shoving off and leaving her. Very puritanical, in some ways. So I told him that that being the case, he could stay in his studio over the stables till the wedding. He'll be wanting a hot drink. Let's go to the kitchen. Karl will have the kettle on the boil. And forgive me for blethering on, Drew, but I'm very happy this morning. Suddenly, it's all happening for the Suttons.'

'The *young* Suttons. For the Clan.'

And they smiled into each other's eyes, because

34

they understood each other and the way things were for them. And that it was going to be fine.

Lyn Carmichael sighed and laid down her pen. Already she had sent a cable to Kenya then bemused, still, had taken her place behind the hotel reception desk without a word to a soul. But it would all seem right when she had written to her parents, she told herself; had written it word for word so she could read it out loud and know it really had happened.

She sighed again, wriggled herself comfortable in Auntie Blod's sagging old chair that stood beside Auntie Blod's fireplace in the cottage she had left two years ago. And now that thick-walled little house was Lyn Carmichael's, or would be in eleven years' time, when she had paid off the mortgage. Four hundred pounds she had paid for it and nothing in it had changed, except that with the war over it had been wired for electricity. So she had stored away her oil lamps and promptly put her name on waiting lists for everything and anything that would plug in. A vacuum cleaner, a cooker, a toaster, a fridge and – there was posh! – a washing machine. And this far, she had been able to buy nothing to plug in, though she was climbing the lists nicely, she was assured, when every once in a while she checked.

Yet soon she would have no need of such things. Soon, by summer probably, she would live at Rowangarth; have no need for the little four-roomed cottage. And that would be a pity, because she loved the safe, warm little house.

How many rooms at Rowangarth? She had no idea. Fourteen bedrooms, she thought, if you counted the attics. And loads of bathrooms. More than three hundred years of Sutton history, too. Being a Sutton was going to take a bit of living up to. Kitty would have taken it in her stride, because she had been born a Sutton; been used to living in a big house and having money. Loads of it and even more when Clementina Sutton, who once lived at Pendenys Place, died. Apart from Denniston, half her fortune had gone to Kitty's father, Albert; the other half to Nathan, parish priest of All Souls and married to Julia. Happily married.

Lyn longed to hear from Drew. Pity there was no phone, here. Auntie Blod had never bothered, so that was something else Lyn was on a waiting list for. Not that it mattered much now, and Drew might ring her at work tomorrow if he could remember which duty she was on. She hoped he would. Just to hear him say, 'Hi, Lyn,' might rid her of the peculiar feeling of being suspended between delight and disbelief, because being engaged to Drew Sutton took a bit of getting used to. She had been sure enough about things this morning when they had kissed goodbye at York station. She had closed her eyes and clung to him and not cared at all who saw them. His lips had been warm, his kiss firm and lingering. It had been all right this morning, yet now she was alone, and desperately longing for bed.

Yet first she must finish her letter – the most important one, she supposed, she had ever written – and seal it in the pale blue airmail envelope ready to take to the post office to be stamped and sent flying on its way.

So having picked yourselves up from the floor, isn't it the most marvellous news? Drew asked me to marry him and of course I said yes. Everyone was wonderful about it, Daisy most of all. I am to wear her beautiful wedding dress and be married at All Souls by Drew's Uncle Nathan. Sometime in the summer, I think it will be, with you to give me away, Dad. I can't wait for you both to see Rowangarth and as soon as we have fixed a date, you must put a big red ring around it on your calendar.

She laid down her pen again. This was not a letter from a young woman crazy with joy, because there was no joyousness in her words. Relief, more like, and gratitude, yet overshadowed by the niggling remembering he had said those words before to Kitty, and that he said, 'Marry me, Lyn' without saying he loved her.

'Bed!' she said out loud. She was weary for sleep. Today had started early with the five o'clock jangling of the alarm and she had travelled home by train then hurried to the hotel to take her smiling place behind the reception desk. It was past eleven, now; had been dark these past two hours. Her eyes pricked with tiredness. Very soon, her cablegram would arrive in Kenya. The letter could wait until tomorrow. One day more would make little difference.

She got to her feet, placed the guard over the fire,

checked the front and back doors, then walked slowly upstairs to the little room with the sloping ceiling and the fat feather mattress that called her.

She slipped out of her clothes, leaving them to lie where they fell and wriggled into her nightdress. Then, without washing her face, even, she pulled back the cover to slip into bed.

And next morning when she awoke, she could not remember switching off the bedside lamp. Nor whispering goodnight to Drew.

'Of course, Tilda,' Mary Stubbs remarked, 'Mr Catchpole is sure to do the florals – for the wedding, I mean.'

'Well, of course,' Mrs Sidney Willis, nee Tilda Tewk, conceded. 'I grant you there's no one in the Riding to touch Jack Catchpole when it comes to bouquets and sprays and buttonholes.' She almost included floral tributes, but decided against wreaths when weddings were the topic under discussion. 'My Sidney would be the first to acknowledge it, him being Parks and Gardens before he took over at Rowangarth. But he *is* an expert on orchids and will see to it that all's well in the orchid house in time for the wedding.'

Rowangarth's famed collection of orchids was back to its pre-war glory now it was no longer considered unpatriotic to heat the orchid house, which they had done with unrationed logs and a sneaky shovel or two of craftily acquired coke, when no one was looking.

'There'll be Tatiana's wedding to consider, an' all,' Mary reminded. 'Quiet wedding or not, the lass will want her bouquet and the guests,' such as there would be, she thought not a little ungraciously, 'are going to want sprays and buttonholes.'

'Sidney has the matter in hand. He says there'll be chrysanths in plenty, but little else for Mr Catchpole to work with. Mind, the church'll be decorated for Christmas.'

What would be lacking in florals, Tilda considered, would be more than compensated for with holly and ivy.

'But Tatiana isn't having the church. She wants the Lady Chapel,' Mary felt bound to point out.

'My husband is well aware of the fact. He'll be decorating the chapel for Christmas, an' all. I shouldn't wonder if he doesn't pot up a little spruce – for Tatiana, I mean. Would be nice for her to have a tiny tree, he said. Tastefully decorated, mind.'

'I wonder why the lass wants such a quiet do. It isn't as if she has to get wed,' Mary frowned.

'As long as her Uncle Nathan says the words over them, Tatty won't care what she's wearing or that the chapel will be as cold as charity and there'll be few presents.'

'I'm bound to agree with you there,' Mary conceded, she rarely agreeing with Tilda on debatable points if only to remind that she was Rowangarth's parlour maid when Tilda had been but a kitchen maid. 'But the lass has money enough in her own right, so her won't worry overmuch about wedding presents. Her grandfather saw to it she wasn't left short. And that grandmother of hers left Denniston House to her don't forget, and the contents, though what made the old cat do such a thing I'll never know.'

The late Clementina Sutton of Pendenys was never noted for her generosity; rarely made a kindly gesture.

'Probably did it when she was half sozzled. She hit the bottle hard after her precious Elliot died. Folk reckoned he'd had a drink or two an' all when he crashed his car and went up in smoke. Was seen in the Coach and Horses in Creesby with a woman who wasn't his wife, though talk had it he left alone, later, an' him so fuddled with drink that he couldn't crank up his car.'

'Well, he's gone now, so don't speak ill of the dead in *my* kitchen, dear.' Tilda felt it necessary to remind Mary from time to time that she was now Rowangarth's cook, and happily – *thankfully* – married to Rowangarth's head gardener.

'Wasn't speaking nothing but fact.' Undaunted, Mary set the kettle to boil. All Creesby and his wife knew what a wrong 'un Elliot Sutton had been. Indulged by his mother until he thought he could do no wrong. And when his wrongdoings sometimes surfaced, the foolish Clementina straightened things out, because most folk – even those badly done to – had their price. 'They won't be wanting tea upstairs. The Reverend has gone to see the Bishop and Miss Julia is at Keeper's – talking weddings, no doubt. Her went to the bank, yesterday, and we all know what about. Drew's girl will be choosing a ring, I should think. I've often wondered, Tilda, what became of Kitty's ring. Opals and pearls, she chose, and may I never move from this spot again if I didn't think at the time that opals were bad luck and pearls brought tears.'

'I reckon it went with her to her grave. Miss Julia wouldn't want it back – not if every time she opened that box and saw it, it reminded her of Kitty. She loved that lass.'

'A right little minx, but no one could help loving her. And so beautiful. Her and Drew would have had lovely bairns.'

'Lyndis is beautiful, an' all. Kitty's opposite, in fact. Maybe as well,' Tilda sighed. 'And there's cherry scones left over from the christening in the small tin. They'll be past their best if we don't eat them soon.'

Tilda sat in the kitchen rocker and closed her eyes and thought about how it had once been in Lady Helen's time when that lovely lady, God rest her, came out of mourning for her husband and gave her first dinner party in three years. A simple meal, yet Mrs Shaw – once Rowangarth's cook and God rest *her*, too – had been days and days preparing and cooking and garnishing so that everything might go well at her ladyship's first timid footsteps back into society.

Well, now there would be Drew's wedding, and with food not nearly so hard to come by Tilda Willis would be able to show the folk hereabouts how well Mrs Shaw had trained her up to the status of cook. Mrs Shaw's standards, Tilda thought smugly, would be maintained as that dear lady would have expected.

'Butter on your scone, or jam?' Mary interrupted the reverie.

'I think it might run to butter – though only a

scraping, mind.' Butter was still rationed. 'And I'll have the first pouring, please.' Rowangarth's cook did not like her tea strong. 'And don't forget Miss Clitherow. Jam *and* butter on hers.'

'Very well.' Miss Clitherow had come to Rowangarth as housekeeper when Helen Stormont married Sir John. Old, now, she spent her days in a ground-floor room, dozing and remembering – and being grateful to Miss Julia and young Sir Andrew for letting her live out her time with the family she had served through good times and bad. And through two terrible wars, an' all. 'Jam and butter it is, poor old lass.'

Yet she still had her wits about her, Mary was forced to concede, in spite of being nearer ninety than eighty and a little unsteady on her feet.

'And there's Drew, an' all,' Tilda reminded.

'*Sir* Andrew,' Mary corrected primly, 'is at Foxgloves, with Daisy. Be talking about the wedding, I shouldn't wonder. I suppose there'll be nothing, now, but wedding talk. Wonder when it'll be?'

'Your guess, love, is as good as mine, though I hope they'll wait for summer.'

Summer, Tilda thought. A June wedding and Rowangarth garden in all its glory. Flowers everywhere, warm sunny days, a marquee on the lawn and the special white orchids flowering. And herself rushed off her feet and loving every minute of it.

Tilda Willis was a very happy and contented woman. She'd had a long and anxious wait, mind, but Mr Right had turned up in the form of an Army Sergeant who was guarding whatever went on at

42

Pendenys during the war, though no one would rightly ever know, she sighed. But yes. A *very* happy woman.

'I phoned Lyn, last night. Managed to catch her before she went home from work.'

'And does she still love you, bruv?' Daisy smiled. 'It's still on, then?'

'Love me? I – I suppose she does. Actually, Daiz, I didn't ask.'

'Didn't *ask*, you great daft lummox; didn't tell her you loved her?'

'Actually – no. But she knows I do.'

'Maybe so, but a girl likes to be told. Often!'

'Sorry. Just that it's going to take a bit of time getting used to it. It happened so suddenly. One minute I was escorting the lady home and the next, there I was, engaged.'

'Hm.' That hadn't been Lyn's version, Daisy considered, but what the heck? 'She'll have written to you?' Letters could say more than words.

'She has. In the post. I should get it tomorrow. And she's written to Kenya, too. Sent a cable first, of course.'

'I wish she was on the phone. I've got to wait for *her* to ring *me*. There's so much we have to talk about.'

'Then it's going to have to keep till Friday, Daiz. That's when she's coming. Lyn was owed a shift by one of the other receptionists, so she's called it in. I'll be meeting her at York in the afternoon. Mother is going to the bank to get the rings out, on Thursday. Reckon we'll both feel a bit more engaged when Lyn has got a ring on her finger.'

'So you don't feel very engaged at the moment, Drew?'

'Of course I do. Only it's like I said, everything happened so suddenly. I still can't believe it – that I was so long in asking her, I mean. But we can talk about things at the weekend. It'll work itself out.'

'Yes. When you've had time to get used to it! But Lyn's had all the time in the world to *get used to it*, as you say. The girl has been in love with you since the year dot! What's the matter with you, Drew Sutton? Why aren't you throwing your cap in the air? You aren't having second thoughts, because if you are –' her narrowed eyes met his across the kitchen table '– then all I can say is . . .'

'Daisy, I am *not* having second thoughts! I'm going to marry Lyn, only it's a bit up in the air at the moment. But we'll talk about the wedding and by the time Lyn goes back to Llangollen, she'll have a ring on her finger and we'll have fixed a date.'

'Oh – well – that's all right, then,' Daisy conceded. 'A summer wedding would be lovely. Keth and I planned a summer wedding. The day after my twenty-first birthday it would have been, but for the dratted Army sending him back to Washington without so much as a by-your-leave or a quick forty-eight hours' leave pass for us to get married. You and Lyn shouldn't hang about.'

'Daisy, love, there isn't a war on, now. There's all the time in the world for us to make plans. As a matter of fact, I *do* think a June wedding would be fine. Mother thinks so, too. But it'll be what Lyn wants. She might want it to be soon – have a quiet

44

wedding like Tatty and Bill are having. Mind, I hope she won't. Pity no one is allowed to go abroad, yet. A honeymoon in Paris would have been great.'

'Hard luck, bruv! When Keth and I were married Paris was occupied by Hitler's lot. We made do with Winchester. But I don't think *where* is important. Being together – married – is all that matters.'

'Agreed. So are you going to put the kettle on? Tilda told me there were cherry scones left over from the christening. You wouldn't have one left?'

'I am, and I would. And you can have a couple. You used to adore cherry scones when you were little. I remember Mrs Shaw making them, and you nibbling the scone away till there was just the cherry left in the middle.'

'You used to nibble too, Daiz. We all did, except Bas. He used to eat his cherry first so Kitty wouldn't pinch it – and, oh dear . . .'

'Yes. Kitty. You said her name, then looked all embarrassed and it's got to stop. No one should be afraid to say her name, Drew. Kitty happened and she's still with us because she was one of the Clan. She was a part of our growing up, and nothing can change it.'

'Granted. And it was fine talking about her, until now. Lyn, I mean.'

'You think she'll be jealous? But why should she be? Tatty talks about Tim, still, and Bill accepts it as perfectly normal. Why should Lyn be any different?'

'Sorry. You're right, Daiz. Lyn isn't the jealous sort, is she?'

'Are you asking me, or telling me? Actually, she

could be quite jealous of the Clan. She called it "Your precious Clan". And once I caught her looking at the photo of us all – the one Aunt Julia took the Christmas before war started. She had quite a funny look in her eyes as if she wanted to be a part of it, yet was glad she wasn't. Maybe she envied our closeness. Or maybe it was our growing up together. We did have a charmed life, you've got to admit it, Drew.'

'I know. Wonderful days. But surely Lyn can be a part of it, now? Married to me, she'd qualify.'

'No, she can't. No one can. Kitty's leaving it doesn't mean there's a vacancy. The Clan was our youth. No one is ever lost to it, and no one can ever join it. Not now. It was something – well, unique . . .'

'And precious. When I was overseas and sometimes at sea for weeks on end and the heat unbearable, I'd think about the Clan, and where we used to meet.'

'Mm. In the wild garden. And in summer we'd lie in the grass under the trees and talk and talk. I used to think about the Clan, too. I remember when Liverpool was blitzed, night after night. Lyn and I were two of the lucky ones. We were three floors underground, and protected by reinforced concrete. The safest place around. But when we saw the devastation it was horrifying, and we all had to shut our minds to it. Thinking of the Clan helped a lot.'

'So am I allowed to nibble my scone – just one last time?'

'You are,' Daisy laughed, glad that they were back on an even keel again. 'And I won't pinch your cherry.'

'Good old Daiz.' Drew laughed with her, then said,

'That's the baby crying. Go to her – she sounds upset.'

'It's all right. Probably only just wind. I'll bring her in and you can put her over your shoulder and pat her back. It's quite rewarding when you get a burp out of her and you've got to learn how it's done, Drew Sutton.' She hurried out to return with a red-faced baby who had all at once stopped crying. 'Ooh, the little madam. She only wanted attention. Here you are. Give her a cuddle.'

And Drew took his goddaughter who felt incredibly small and fragile in his arms and thought about the children Lyn so desperately wanted, and how good it would be, making them together. Tenderly he patted the little back and Mary Natasha nuzzled his neck then obliged with a burp which made him feel immensely proud and think that maybe after all, Lyn could be quite right. Having a baby – babies – might not be half bad.

'I'll keep her for a few minutes, get her to sleep for you whilst you have your tea and scone, Daiz.'

And Daisy wrinkled her nose at him and said, 'Thanks, bruv,' and thought how very much she loved him – and wanted him to be happy.

As happy as she and Keth.

FOUR

'Want to know something, Bill Benson?' Tatiana Sutton kicked off her shoes with a cluck of contentment, tucking her feet beneath her, snuggling closer.

'So tell me,' he smiled.

'If you kiss me, I will.'

He kissed the tip of her nose. These days, he was always careful not to indulge in petting sessions because he knew exactly where they could lead. More than once he had admitted – to himself, of course – that keeping lovemaking until their wedding night had been a decision he should never have made. His own fault, always having been a bit holier-than-thou about taking liberties with the opposite sex, because someone had taken liberties with his mother, which had landed the resulting bairn – himself – in an orphanage when only one month old. Too much of a burden, he had been told later, for a bit of a lassie hardly into her sixteenth year to shoulder alone.

So he had accepted, very early in life, that that kind of behaviour wasn't on and that no bairn of his would be born out of wedlock because no matter how kindly an orphanage he'd been brought up in he had always envied the kids in school who had two parents living under one roof, even if legitimate fathers were known to leather small boys' behinds or sometimes come home the worse for drink on pay days.

'You got your kiss – now tell me,' he demanded.

'Oh, just that I'm happy. It was lovely having Bas's lot to stay, but it's nice having the place to ourselves again with no one to interrupt us.'

'There's Karl . . .'

'Karl doesn't count. Grandmother Petrovska insisted he stayed on here when mother married Ewart Pryce and I was left alone in "*that beeg place without a chaperon and heffen only knows what might happen to an innocent girl alone*" Tatiana mimicked. 'And don't let him fool you. Karl understands English even though he won't speak it – well, only to me.'

'I often wonder about him – his background, I mean. I sometimes miss Scotland, but at least I know I can go there whenever I want. Karl can't go back to Russia.'

'True. Him once being a Cossack and loyal to the Tzar, it wouldn't be wise. But he never speaks about his past. He attached himself to our family when they were trying to get out of Russia, and Mother told me they wouldn't have made it without him. That's why he's still with us. We owe him.'

'He's very protective of you,' Bill frowned.

'I know he is, but you needn't worry. When we are married I shall ask him if he wants to go back to London to Grandmother Petrovska and Uncle Igor.'

'And if he doesn't?'

'Then he stays here, at Denniston. He's no trouble, and he does all the gardening, remember.'

'I'm no' complaining.' Bill Benson's philosophy was to live and let live.

'Good. So tell me, who rang you this morning?'

'London. The agent I got in touch with wants me to go down there with my portfolio, and if he thinks I'm any good he'll take me on. Mind, he'll take ten per cent of all I make but he'll earn every penny of it – do the selling and see to contracts and that sort of thing. He'll haggle about price, too, something I'm not much use at.'

'Of course he'll take you on. You're good. When shall you go?'

'Soon . . .'

'Then if you intend staying overnight, ask Aunt Julia if you can stay at Montpelier Mews. No point paying hotel bills when there's a bed for the asking, for free.'

'I thought it was we Scots who were meant to be mean! You Russians are every bit as canny.'

'I'm *not* Russian – well, only half so. And born and bred in England. Do you mind, darling, that grandmother is a countess and that, as the daughter of a countess, mother is entitled to the courtesy, too. At least, that's the way it used to be, in Russia. Mind, I shall be happy to be Mrs Benson. Are you looking forward to our wedding?'

'Of course I am. It'll be winter, soon, and gui' cold in that studio of mine. Can't wait to move in here.'

'It was your own choice to stay put, so don't

moan. Let's face it, here we are almost alone, and you still go on about waiting till our wedding night. It's not a lot of fun when things get passionate and you start counting to ten. You're always the one to put a stop to it and it ought to be the girl who says no.'

'You're joking, Miss Sutton.'

'I'm joking, darling. But I'll be glad when we're married. December is a good time for a wedding. Short days, long cold nights. If this coal rationing lark goes on for very much longer, bed will be the only warm place.'

'Tatiana!' He let out a laugh. 'Have you no shame? The granddaughter of a countess, reared by a nanny, taught by a French governess, with Karl always hovering to make sure the wind didn't blow on you! Whatever happened to that ladylike lassie?'

'The war happened, Bill,' she said softly, eyes sad. 'Oh, I know wars are immoral, but that one gave a whole generation of women their freedom. This ladylike lassie was away like a shot to London, translating.'

'And you met a lot of wounded airmen . . . ?'

'Yes. And I met you, Bill.'

'But what made you do it, darling? Escorting airmen with their faces burned away – didn't it embarrass you, showing them around London, with people looking away and –'

'No, it didn't. I did it for Tim. And your face wasn't as badly burned as some.'

'No. I was blind,' he offered without rancour.

'Yes, but you aren't now. Tell me, Bill –' She changed the subject quickly, so she needn't think about Tim.

'– are you always going to paint flowers and florals?'

'Why not? It's what I do best and it brings in the shekels. I'm not going to live off my wife!'

'No one wants you to, so don't get all Scottish prickly about it! Just because I'm not short of a pound or two doesn't mean you're a kept man.'

'Not short! The way I see it you're filthy rich!'

'I've been lucky. Mother didn't have to marry money, exactly, but it seemed fortunate at the time that she fell in love where money grew on trees. And because of it, a lot of it came my way, through my father. Us Petrovskas hadn't a bean. Left it all behind in St Petersburg – sorry, Leningrad.'

'Aye, and when your granny died she left you this house, an' all.'

'True. But Grandmother Clementina, as I have often said, probably did it when she was tanked up on brandy. She hit the bottle in a big way, when my father was killed. And she didn't leave it to me, exactly. Denniston House was her wedding present to my parents and she left things the way they were. If you want to split hairs, it was Grandfather Sutton who willed the money to me. He was a darling; didn't deserve to be married to Clementina.'

An absolute old love, who had understood about Tim. The only grown-up, it had seemed, she could trust with her secret.

'But Tatty – why should the old lady have taken on so? She had two other sons.'

'Yes, but they weren't her precious Elliot!'

'That's a gui' peculiar way to speak of your dead father.'

'*Why* is it? He didn't like me. I was a girl. Why should I like *him*?'

'Dislike a man you don't even remember,' Bill said softly, heeding the narrowed eyes, the disapproving mouth.

'I *do* remember him. At least, I remember *memories*. Always unhappiness, and my mother sobbing . . .'

'Then one thing I promise. I'll not make you cry, sweetheart. And I'm in danger of getting sentimental and sloppy so I'd best be away to my celibate garret,' he grinned. 'Besides, I need to be up early – get the morning light. I aim to have the watercolour finished tomorrow – want something half-decent to show to the agent.'

'Must you go, just yet?' Tatiana teased her finger-tips over his face. 'It'll be cold in the loft and you haven't any paraffin left for your stove . . .'

'Aye! We won a war and three years on we're still rationed! Four-page newspapers, ninety miles of petrol a month for cars, a shortage of coal and the RAF airlifting food to Berlin instead of bombing it!'

'Never mind. At the end of this month we'll be allowed to use gas and electric fires again, so on October first you'll be able to plug in and warm up.'

'So I will. But why is this country in such a mess? It's like we're still at war. They've even rationed bread, now, and bread was never rationed, as I remember it, even though most of our wheat was brought here in convoys!'

'Darling! I love it when you get on your soapbox – especially when you have a dig at Mr Attlee, and you a red-hot socialist! The war cost a lot of money

– I suppose it's got to be paid for, now. And you've got your National Health Service at long last. Free false teeth, free spectacles, pills and potions and operations for nothing. And no doctors' bills coming in every month! So kiss me goodnight and go to bed. Would you like a hot-water bottle?' she asked, eyes impish.

'So what do you take me for – a jessie, or something?'

They were laughing now, and kissing, with Tatiana murmuring, 'I love you, Sergeant Benson. Can't wait for December.'

'And you, hennie darling, will get your bottom spanked if you don't stop your teasing! So one more kiss, then throw me out, eh?'

At the door he turned.

'Oh and by the way, Miss Sutton, I love you, too. Even though you're a filthy capitalist, I love you a lot!'

'There now. The Whitecliffe jewels.' Julia Sutton arranged lockets, necklaces and rings on the coffee table beside the fire. 'I'll leave the pair of you to it. Take what you want, Lyndis.'

'They're so beautiful.' Lyn took a heavy gold locket containing a lock of pale yellow baby hair. 'Who did this curl belong to?'

'Haven't a clue, though I'd like to think it was my mother's hair,' Julia smiled. 'Mother was very fair. Glad you like them. Didn't think you young ones would go for old-fashioned stuff like this.'

'Old-fashioned, Mrs Sutton? But they're family

history. Much more special than going to a jeweller's and asking to try on the third one down on the left of tray twenty-six.'

'If there were decent rings in the shops to choose from, don't you mean, Lyn? *Why* is this war lasting so long – the shortages, I mean. Do without. Export or die, the government tells us. Tighten your belts. Though I suppose it's better, now, than it was after *my* war,' Julia frowned. 'At least war heroes aren't being thrown on the scrapheap this time around, and forced to beg or sell bootlaces on street corners. It was an obscene war.'

'Don't, dearest.' Drew took his mother's hand and squeezed it tightly. 'Your war and my war – they're both over, now. It's just that it's taking longer than we thought to clear up after this one, and – I'll get it,' he said, as the phone began to ring.

He hurried into the hall and it gave Lyn the chance to say, 'Look – I'm not being awful, or anything, but is – well – is Kitty's ring amongst these? I wouldn't want to choose hers and upset Drew.'

'No, Lyndis. Kitty's ring was opals and pearls and she – we-e-ll – it went with her.'

'Good. I'm glad. I mean, I'm glad she was – was –'

'Wearing it at the end,' Julia said, matter-of-factly. 'And you might as well know the whole of it. She wore her wedding dress, too. Amelia – her mother – sent one over from America for her. It was hanging here at Rowangarth with a sheet draped over it, waiting till they could be married.'

'Then I'm glad she wore it, but so sad . . .' Lyn whispered.

'Sad. I told Drew when I wrote to him after the funeral. He agreed with what I had done. He was in the Pacific . . .'

'I remember.'

'Of course you do! You and Daisy were Wrens together. Sorry, Lyndis. Shouldn't have said what I did.'

'But I began it, asking about Kitty's ring. Just because Drew and I are going to be married doesn't wipe out all memory of her. They were deeply in love, and I accept it.'

'So were Andrew and I. Passionately. But love can come again – remember that if you have doubts. Tell yourself that love can happen twice, though differently. It did for Nathan and me. Kitty was, is, and always will be. It's going to be up to you, Lyndis, how you handle it, but never forget that I do understand and if ever you want to talk to me about anything –'

'Talk about what?' Drew stood in the doorway. 'Secrets between you already?'

'Idiot! Of course not. With her mother in Kenya, I offered to stand in if Lyndis wanted to talk about – well, you know – *woman's* things. Anyway, who was that on the phone?'

'Daisy. She insists we go over so she can admire the ring – she wants to have a wish on it, she says.'

'It took you a long time to say that,' Julia smiled, relieved the awkward moment had passed.

'Not really. I had a word with Keth, too. About cars.'

'So now you can have a word with your intended

– about rings. And make sure you've got your key with you when you go out. I'm going to meet Polly at the Bothy at eight – okay? And like I said, Lyndis – feel free . . .'

And with that she was off, banging the door behind her, taking the stairs two at a time, as she always did.

'Have you chosen?' Drew asked softly.

'N-no. I haven't even looked, properly. I feel embarrassed, sort of; don't want to pick out the biggest and best.'

'Why ever not? It wouldn't worry Mother. She's never been one for jewellery; keeps giving pieces of this lot away. She gave Lady pearl eardrops for her twenty-first and Daisy got a sapphire and diamond brooch as a christening present. There are a couple I like, though.' He laid two rings on his hand; one a sapphire, one an emerald. 'Mother would want you to have something decent. Feel free, like she said.'

'I like them, too. They're both beautiful,' Lyndis whispered, wishing her cheeks didn't burn so. 'I think you should choose, for all that.'

'Then the emerald it is. It matches your eyes, Lyn. Try it on.'

'Tell you what – the ring that fits best must be the one.'

'Then it looks like it's the emerald,' Drew smiled when the square-cut stone set with diamonds slipped on easily, whilst the sapphire refused to budge past her knuckle.

'The emerald it is. And anyway, Daisy has a sapphire ring. Wouldn't want her to think I was copying hers. Will you put it on for me, Drew, and kiss me? And then we'll put everything back in the box and give it to your mother, before she goes out. She'll want to know which one I've chosen. And will you tell me why I feel so light-headed and floaty? I can't seem to take all this in.'

'We-e-ll, I ought to say it's because of the wonder of the moment, but it's probably because you arrived late and didn't want any supper. Now give me your hand, Lyn Carmichael, and bless you for saying you'll have me. I promise we'll be happy, *cariad*.'

'Drew! Who told you the Welsh for darling?'

'Who do you think? The adorable Blod, of course, that time we stayed with her. Have you heard from her, yet?'

'About us? No. She won't have got my letter, though I think she'll cable me back when she's had time to get over the shock.'

'You're happy about us, Lyn?' He tilted her chin, kissing her gently.

'I'm happy. I'm *very* happy, Drew.'

'Fine. So let's return the sparklers, then go and see Daiz . . .'

It was as they walked hand in hand to Foxgloves that Drew said, 'By the way, if we decide on a summer wedding, how about June the eighteenth? Entirely up to you, mind – will it be okay for you date-wise? The curse, I'm talking about.'

'I – I – yes. Fine,' she gasped, cheeks blazing, taken aback by the nonchalant reference to her periods. Drew had always been so quiet; never had a sister of his own. Not a live-in sister to talk to about such things. He'd been in the Navy, of course. There would have been talk on the mess decks, she supposed.

Yet the explanation was simple. Drew and Kitty had been lovers, would have discussed such things. They'd have had to, though Lyn was as sure as she could be that Kitty wouldn't have cared if she got pregnant, wouldn't have –

'Penny for them?' Drew smiled.

'I – oh, nothing of importance, really. Dates, I suppose. I ring them round as soon as I start a new diary, so I'm sure the eighteenth is fine.'

The ease with which she spoke amazed her; the laugh, too.

'That's settled, then. Daiz will be glad about that. She's been going on about it all week. And might I ask what you find so funny?'

'You and me, Drew, that's what. Sorry. I didn't mean to laugh about something so important, but think – a week ago we were friends, yet now we're all at once – well, *personal*. So can we,' she said breathlessly, 'whilst we're on the subject of things personal, talk about children, too?'

'Fine by me. You want some, don't you? I know I do.'

'I want children, Drew, and I'd like to have them before I'm thirty, or at least have made a start. So if you don't mind, I'd like us not to worry about – well . . .'

'Being careful? A honeymoon baby?'

'Exactly,' she whispered, taken aback once more by his directness, knowing that almost certainly he had talked this way before.

'Okay. Point taken. Where are we going for our

honeymoon, by the way? Abroad is out, thanks to the government's stupid restrictions. Paris would have been great. And there's Daisy, waiting for us.' Quickly, he kissed her cheek. 'Impatient as ever.'

And though it was almost dark, Lyn could hear the smile in his voice and was grateful for it. And love for him washed over her and made her glad. Happy, she supposed, or as near as made no matter. If Kitty wasn't so often there to remind her, that was.

'Hi there, Purvis,' she called and ran into Daisy's welcoming arms.

'Let's be seeing it then,' Daisy laughed, holding up her cheek for Drew's kiss, shoo-ing them into the sitting room. 'Oh, my goodness, Carmichael. What a beauty!' She held out her hand for the ring, slipping it on, closing her eyes as she turned it three times on her finger. 'And don't ask me what I wished for 'cause I'm not telling.'

'Just a minute, ladies, before you start oh-ing and ah-ing over rings and weddings and things,' Keth laughed. 'Would you mind telling me why the pair of you still use each other's surname? You aren't in the Forces, now.'

'True, Keth. But we both did a fair stint in the war, and using surnames was the order of the day. We're bound to revert, sometimes, to the old ways. Daisy will always be Wren Purvis-from-the-bottom-bunk to me.'

'And I was so glad to be Purvis – remember, Lyn? Dwerryhouse was such a drag of a name. The times people said, "Dwerry-*what*? How do you spell it?" So now you know, darling, and why don't you two pop upstairs to the cubbyhole whilst we talk about rings and weddings and things. You said you had something you wanted to talk to Drew about. And don't wake the baby,' she warned as they disappeared, fugitives from wedding talk. 'And I shouldn't tell you what I wished for, but do you want two or three . . . ?'

'Three, please,' Lyn laughed, 'though four would be marvellous. That house is big enough for *ten* children. And oh, Daisy, you're such a love. Did I ever tell you so?'

'Often. But only because it's completely true.'

So they laughed again and it was as if they were Leading-Wren Carmichael and Purvis-from-the-bottom-bunk again and lived in a billet called Hellas House in bomb-shattered Liverpool, and worked underground in a hot, airless Communications Office. Because they knew they would never completely forget their war, nor would they want to. Good times *and* bad.

'Well now. This is a lovely surprise. Do sit down, Miss Lyndis.'

'Thanks. But could you call me just Lyndis or Lyn, Miss Clitherow? Drew said you wanted to see my ring.'

'Well, not really. I have seen your emerald before. What I really wanted was the chance to wish you much happiness. It makes an old lady very glad to see it all coming right for Sir Andrew, you know. And could I presume to ask you to open the window a little? Can't abide a stuffy room. Most kind . . .'

So this was how it was to be, Lyn thought as she

unscrewed the window catch. Sir Andrew and Miss Lyndis. A far cry from the sailor on a minesweeper and she and Daisy meeting him when his boat docked.

'How's that? Feel a draught?'

'That is fine, thank you. I wouldn't have asked, but it's my hands. A little arthritic. Fiddling catches . . .'

'Miss Clitherow! If I can't open a window without –' She bit back her words, knowing at once it was the wrong thing to have said. Agnes Clitherow was a servant of the old order and did not ask the woman who was to be lady of the house to open windows. 'And I'm pleased we can have this chat,' she rushed on, 'because you have been here so long, know so much about the Rowangarth Suttons. I'd be so glad if you would sometimes talk to me about them. My ring, for instance. You said you had seen it before. When, exactly?'

'When Sir Gilbert Sutton gave it to his wife, Lady Mary – Sir Andrew's great-grandmother – on their tenth wedding anniversary. I was housemaid to the Suttons, then.'

'And you came to Rowangarth . . . ?'

'I came here with Lady Helen as a bride. By the time she was married I had been trained up to parlour maid. It seemed natural for me to accept when she asked me to come here to Rowangarth with her – as housekeeper, mind. Such a promotion, and me only four years older than Miss Helen. But I put my hair into a bun and tried to look severe, so no one quite knew how old – or young – I really was.'

'But, Miss Clitherow – that means you were born in 1856 and that you are –'

'In my ninety-second year, Miss Lyndis, and you are one of the few who knows it.'

'Then I won't tell. Promise.'

Come to think of it, there was a lot she would not tell, Lyn brooded, like the future Lady Sutton being illegitimate. Strange that for so long she had never known who her real mother was. Such a shock – a *wonderful* shock – to discover it was really the woman she had always believed to be her aunt. Blodwen, who had given her all the love she had ever known, and taken over her upbringing when as a young girl she was put in charge of the ship's nurse at Mombasa, en route for school in England. And never, had she but known it, to return to Kenya. Myfanwy and Blodwen. Twin sisters. Chalk and cheese. Myfanwy, her name changed to Margot, looking forward at her wedding to Jack Carmichael to a lady's life in Kenya; Blodwen, two months pregnant with Jack's child, loving him so much, yet saying not one word about it until it was too late. And Lyndis, their indiscretion, being grudgingly taken to Kenya by Jack's wife.

'Did you know I'm to wear Daisy's wedding dress, Miss Clitherow?' *Forget the past, Lyndis! Her father and her real mother happy at last, even though they are miles away, in Kenya!* 'It's so beautiful. I think it's better, even, than Princess Elizabeth's.'

'Ah, yes. A fairytale wedding. Such a glorious gown. It was right and proper the princess should be given an extra coupon allowance for it.'

'Hm. I wonder, at two clothing coupons for one yard of material, just how many that wedding dress gobbled up. And I still think Daisy's dress is the nicest

I've ever seen. So soft and full and floaty. She offered it to Tatiana, you know, but Tatty wants a quiet wedding.'

'Miss Tatiana has grown into a lovely person. It's sad her father didn't live to walk her down the aisle. And sad she never had a brother. Things would have been very different at Pendenys Place if that little boy had lived.

'But you wanted to know about the Rowangarth Suttons, about how it was. Lady Helen and Sir John. *Miss* Helen she was then. Helen Stormont and hardly out of the schoolroom when they met.'

'Tell me,' Lyndis smiled, 'was it romantic?'

'Oh my word, yes! Her coming-out ball. I was in service, then, with the Stormonts as parlour maid and they had rented a house in London for the social season. I was one of the lucky ones they took to London with them. I remember seeing Miss Helen before she went off to that ball. Dressed in baby blue silk, trimmed with white lace, and white rosebuds in her hair. It was that night she met Sir John and fell head over heels in love. Sir John was smitten, too; but then, the Rowangarth Suttons have always been lucky in love.

'Miss Julia was twice lucky. Doctor Andrew, her first husband, was a fine gentleman. Lady Helen adored him. And the Reverend has made Miss Julia happy, too,' the old woman smiled, eyes misty with remembering. 'And now Sir Andrew is to be married. I pray I'll be spared to see that day.'

'Miss Clitherow – of course you will. June the eighteenth, next year. Not long to wait.'

'I suppose not. The poor young man has waited long enough. But for that dreadful bomb, he and Miss Kitty would have – Oh, I am *so* sorry. Shouldn't have said that. Whatever was I thinking about? Getting old, you see. Sometimes I don't think.' Her voice trembled, tears filled her eyes. 'Forgive me?'

'Miss Clitherow, don't be upset. Please, please don't cry.' Gently Lyndis wiped away the tear that ran down the wrinkled cheek, then took the agitated hands in her own. 'I know how much everyone loved Kitty. I held Daisy in my arms and we both cried for her when she was killed, and for Drew, too.

'Kitty will always be remembered because she was such a special person. I know that and I won't ever try to take her place in the Clan. But I know how much you care for Drew and I promise always to love and care for him. There now – does that make you happy?'

'It does, Miss Lyndis. And bless you for not taking offence where none was meant. I think you will do very nicely for Sir Andrew. Just then, when you dried my tears and spoke so kindly and gently to me, you reminded me of Lady Helen. Oh, yes, Sir Andrew will be twice happy, just as Miss Julia has been.'

'Thank you. And I think you are tired. Shall I go, now, and let you have a little sleep?'

'Most kind. Yes, I generally have a little nap about this time.'

'Then close your eyes. I'll tuck your rug around you.'

But Agnes Clitherow did not hear. Already she was asleep, breathing softly, a small smile on her lips.

'I'll make Drew happy, I promise.' Gently, Lyn kissed her cheek then quietly closed the door behind her. 'But oh, Kitty Sutton from Kentucky, you are going to be such a hard act to follow . . .'

For just a moment, doubt took her and she wondered how she would cope, and if she had been wise to say yes to Drew. Because the man she had loved since first she laid eyes on him already had two other loves to lay claim to him – Kitty and Rowangarth, and if Lyndis Carmichael was to have any chance of happiness she, too, must learn to love them both. They were a part of Drew and nothing could, or would change it.

Her eyes, as she walked slowly up the stairs, met those in the portrait of a long-ago Sutton – the one, was it, who fought at Balaclava? He wore a splendid red jacket, braided with gold, and was not one bit like the sailor whose cap she retrieved when Daisy, in her excitement, had thrown herself into his arms and sent that cap rolling along the pavement in wartime Liverpool.

She stood for a while, head high, eyes accepting the challenge.

'I will make him happy, I damn well *will*!'

A light shone from the kitchen window at the Bothy and Julia opened the front door and called, 'You there, Polly?'

'I am, Mrs Sutton,' Keth's mother, Polly Purvis, smiled, from the top of the stairs. 'I've been having a good look round. Upstairs is ready for the carpets and curtains, now.'

'Y'know, Polly, I never thought I'd say this, but thank heaven for Pendenys Place and all those carpets and curtains going to spare.'

'And thank heaven the dratted moths didn't get at them. Six years in storage is a long time.'

'There isn't the moth flying,' Julia grinned, 'that would *dare* eat Aunt Clemmy's carpets.'

Only the very best for Clementina Sutton's father who had built Pendenys Place for his only child as a wedding dowry, then furnished it with ostentatious bad taste.

'Curtains came back from the cleaners yesterday. I hung them on the line outside to sweeten. Will Stubbs said he'd make a start on getting the curtain poles put back if someone will tell him what height they're to go. I'll see to it, if you like.'

'You're a treasure, Polly. I'm glad you are coming to work for Nathan and me and you'll know that as a Sutton employee you won't have to pay rent on your almshouse any longer. Starting October first, I think it should be.'

'Why, thank you I'm sure.' She flushed with pleasure to think of five shillings a week saved.

'And see Tom if you want the odd rabbit or two, don't forget. Rowangarth perks, Polly.'

'Then I've got to be honest and admit that he slips me a rabbit every week.'

'Well, he would,' Julia laughed, 'your son being married to his daughter. But it's official, now. And a load of logs at Christmas.'

'I'm obliged, Mrs Sutton.'

Life, Polly Purvis thought, seemed only to get better

with each year that passed. Rowangarth had been good to her after what had happened in Hampshire and a far cry away from the night she accepted she was a widow, with a child to rear and only ten shillings a week to manage on. Rowangarth – and the Suttons – had given her more than she ever dare hope for. Now, she was contented with a son who had married his childhood sweetheart, Daisy – aye, and given her a granddaughter, too. If only she could go back, just the once, to the little house called Willow End they once lived in, and on to the village and the church-yard, where Dickon lay.

But Hampshire was a long way away, and senti-mental journeys cost money, so she had contented herself with the photograph of the grave that Keth and Daisy took when they honeymooned in Winchester. Dickon was resting sweetly and out of his pain and shame, Polly brooded, and if there was a heaven then he would know how often she thought about him and missed him, still.

'I'm going to miss Rowangarth.' Julia's voice called Polly back from her rememberings. 'Was born there, lived all my life there, too. But Nathan and I will be very snug here, and it's only right and proper that Drew takes over Rowangarth. After all, it belongs to him. Come to think of it, it's been his since he was two hours old.'

'Then if the Fates allow, his children will be born there, too. And here's Polly Purvis coming to work for you and the Reverend when you move into this Bothy. It'll be like coming home to me. All those years I was cook here in the war, and looking after those land girls who lived in it. Happy days. You and me, Mrs Sutton, are two very lucky ladies, all things considered.'

And Julia Sutton smiled and agreed that they were. Very lucky ladies.

FIVE

A new car, Keth Purvis was bound to admit as he drove to school, was something most men wanted; the more so since manufacturers were at last being allowed to make them again. No more military vehicles. Cars for private use was now a tantalizing pipe dream, the new models being flaunted to the skies, then immediately exported to help the economy drive. Even if the garage in Creesby did manage to get a few to sell to the public, Keth frowned, there would be a waiting list for them a mile long. And what was he bothering about, anyway? He couldn't afford one – simple as that.

Yet his wife could. Daisy had money, a fact few people were aware of. Not even Lyn knew. All those years she and Daisy had been together as Wrens and knowing the way women chattered, it still amazed him that his wife had been so tight-lipped about her fortune.

They had talked about new cars that morning – or rather, Daisy had. Sitting on the edge of the bath as he shaved, actually.

'We've got to talk, Keth. Seriously,' she had said. 'About cars. You know there's going to be a motor show in London?'

'Yes. The first since 1939,' he had said, casually as he could, staring into the mirror. 'Was talking to Drew about it. I think he'd like to go. Said there'd be some new models on show.'

It had been a mistake, mentioning new cars.

'So why don't you go with him, and get one?'

'Darling girl. New cars are for export. There won't be any released for the home market.'

'It said in the paper there'll be *some*, and I'm sick of you driving that old boneshaker. It isn't safe. It needs new tyres, for a start.'

'But no one can get new tyres. They're like gold dust.'

'So get a new car, then. I want you to have one.'

'Daisy Purvis.' He kissed the tip of her nose which was tilted dangerously high to match the set of her mouth, and such signs were best not ignored. 'Look – can we talk about it tonight? Don't want to be late for school.'

'I *want* you to have a car,' she had repeated, tight-lipped. 'A new one. And okay, we'll talk about it tonight, but if you say one word about the money there'll be ructions.'

The money. Daisy's money. A small fortune.

'Tonight,' he had said. 'Promise . . .'

His foot touched the brake. The road ahead was full of children. Watch out for the little blighters, Keth. They could dart in front of you with never a glance to the left or right. Children of all ages who called him Sir and to whom he taught mathematics.

He slowed almost to a crawl, thinking about his own child. A month old and already a dark-eyed, dark-haired beauty who smiled often, now. Mary, more precious than any new motor.

Carefully he parked in his allotted space. The old car had a few more miles left in it yet – but how to convince Daisy? Deliberately he pushed the problem from his mind and thought instead how lucky – how *damned* lucky – he had been to survive the war, and all at once cars didn't seem important.

Not until tonight when he got home that was, when it would all start again.

'I'll be making bramble jelly today.' Alice Dwerry-house poured her husband's ten o'clock drinkings into the large cup that had once been Reuben's.

'Came by some crafty sugar, did you?'

'Indeed I did not!' Even now, she was apprehensive about black market dealings. 'It's the sugar the government allowed for jam-making in the summer.'

Allowed, she thought peevishly. Sugar should have been taken off the ration by now, and butter and lard and bacon. And good red meat!

'Very nice.' Tom was partial to bramble jelly. 'You'll be over to Foxgloves with a jar for Daisy this afternoon?'

'No. I'm going to Creesby to look at material. I've got eight clothing coupons put by, and I want to make myself something nice for Drew's wedding.'

'But lass, it's months away! Next summer!'

'I know it, but I don't want to be all last-minute

rush. I might have to look around quite a bit before I find something that goes with my best hat.'

The Best Hat. A magnificent creation and very expensive. The one she had worn to Daisy's wedding and would be brought out many more times if Alice was to get her value out of it.

'Aye. The hat.' Alice had looked a treat in it. 'I suppose Polly will be wearing her wedding hat, an' all – if she's asked.'

'Of course she'll be asked. Oh, Tom, I'm so looking forward to it. Can't wait to see my lad married.'

Her lad, Tom brooded. Born when Alice was wed to Giles Sutton, then left at Rowangarth for Julia and Lady Helen to rear, Drew being of substance and title before he'd hardly drawn breath. But Alice had come to love her son in the end; had forgiven his getting.

'Your tea is going cold. You were miles away.'

'Mm. Thinking about the birds in the far cover,' he said offhandedly. 'They're thick on the ground, this year. Won't be long to the first.'

The first day of October when pheasant shooting would start. No need to remind a gamekeeper's wife. Mind, it wasn't the same as in the old days, Alice thought longingly, when there had been weekend shooting parties for Sir John's friends. Giles, who took over the running of Rowangarth estate when his father died, hadn't been one for pheasant shoots; didn't hold with killing. Never had. Yet he'd enlisted in the Great War for all that, but as a stretcher-bearer because stretcher-bearers and ambulance drivers and medical orderlies weren't called on to fire guns, take

73

life. Life had been sacred to Giles Sutton. All life. Pheasants included.

'I said I was thinking about game birds in the far cover, and you didn't hear a word of it.'

'Sorry, Tom. I was miles away. In France, if you must know.'

'Lass, that war is over. We've had another since. They're even calling them World War One and World War Two now.'

'So they are.' But that first war, hers and Tom's, would always be the Great War to those who had fought in it. Great only because it was obscene and bloody and uncaring. Patriotic slaughter. Alice Dwerryhouse knew, because she and Julia had been there. 'I was a young nurse at the Front and now I'm a grandmother. Things change.'

'Aye, they do.' Tenderly he touched Alice's cheek. 'They do, thank God. And you're still my lass.'

'And I love *you* Tom Dwerryhouse, but I've got things to do, so drink up that tea and be out of my kitchen from under my feet!'

Alice, Tom thought contentedly as he made for the far end of Brattocks Wood, dogs at his heels, who regularly ordered him out of her kitchen with a sharp word, but who loved him with her eyes every time she looked at him. Dear, precious Alice, his first and only love. How much better could life get?

Lyn Carmichael smiled at the ring on her left hand, then at the letter that lay on the table in front of her. It had been the first thing she saw when she opened her front door, last night. An envelope bearing an airmail sticker and a Kenyan stamp. From darling Blod; Blodwen Carmichael, who for years had been her aunt and was now her mother. Her real mother; birth mother. The news of it had shocked, amazed and delighted Lyn. When she had given it time to sink in, that was; when her father had written to tell her that her mother – the woman she *thought* was her mother – had been killed in a car accident. It was only then Lyndis learned the truth; that she really belonged to the dear person she called Aunt Blodwen and had been given to her twin sister to rear in Kenya, half a world away. Given to Myfanwy, who spoke with an English accent and had never, Lyn supposed, completely forgiven her husband and sister.

Lyndis looked at the generous, rounded writing and was glad that everything had come right for Auntie Blod and her father; glad they had married the minute the war was over and sailings to Kenya available to civilians once more.

. . . Can't wait to see you again, and talk things over with my girl, Auntie Blod had written. *In fact, your dad and me got a sudden yearning to spend Christmas in Wales. You could put us up if we decided to come, couldn't you? I said to your dad that I couldn't wait to see that little cottage again and he said that was all right by him and anyway, we'd both have to meet Drew's family and talk about the wedding because your dad is determined to pay for the lot, he said, and you are to let him, because he isn't short of a pound or two as well you know.*

Lovely girl, I'm so happy for you. I know I have said it twice already in this letter, but I shall go on saying it, because your happiness is all that matters in this world to me – apart from your dad's, that is.

Christmas in the little house near Llangollen and the three of them together as a real family for the first time in her life, Lyn realized with delight. So long since she had seen her father. She had been a schoolgirl of twelve when they said goodbye the day she sailed alone for England, and boarding school. Stay with your Aunt Blodwen for your holidays, they said, with no mention made about when she would go back again. And anyway, the war had prevented her return to the country she was brought up in.

Maybe they would all be asked to Rowangarth for Christmas. A good idea, that, because sooner or later the parents would have to meet and there was room enough for twenty Christmas guests in the house she was soon to share with Drew.

Lyn Sutton. Lady Lyndis. Mistress of Rowangarth, and she not knowing the first thing about belonging to the aristocracy and living in a big old house where money was no problem and everything she could see when she looked out of any upstairs window, belonged to the Rowangarth Suttons.

All at once Lyn wanted to see her parents at Christmas; no, dammit, *needed* them with her because there was so much to tell them, so much she was unsure about. Now, it was important she talk to Auntie Blod – to her *mother* – and tell her of the doubts she sometimes had about marrying Drew. Not that she didn't love him. She did; loved him with all her heart and mind and wanted no other. But she and Drew were chalk and cheese and the life Drew had been born into and accepted as normal would take Lyn Carmichael a lot of getting used to, even with Daisy nearby to open her heart to.

Drew and Kitty, now, had been another matter. Kitty was a Pendenys Sutton whose parents were richer, even, than the Suttons of Rowangarth. Kitty would have fitted in well; would have slipped into her role as lady of the manor with no trouble at all because a manor – or its Kentucky equivalent – was what she was used to. And though a flying bomb had snuffed out that young eager life, Kitty would always be at Rowangarth, sleeping away time beside Drew's grandmother, beneath a white marble gravestone.

Kathryn Norma Clementina Sutton
KITTY
1:11:1920 – 18:6:1944

Lyn jumped to her feet, pulling in her breath, holding it, then letting it out in little calming huffs, closing her eyes, whispering, 'I'm sorry, truly sorry . . .'

But sorry for what? That Kitty would never carry white orchids at her wedding, the flowers every Rowangarth bride carried; those same special orchids Jack Catchpole laid at the white gravestone every June, on the anniversary of that tragic death.

And there was something else. She recognized it,

truth known, the moment Drew suggested the eighteenth of June for their wedding. Yet she had stubbornly pushed it to the back of her mind, even though she knew it was the anniversary to the day, almost, when he and Kitty should have been married; and a year later, on that same June day, when a bomb took Kathryn Sutton's life.

'*Damn!*' Lyn reached for her coat, not caring that it was late and that they might be in bed, not even caring that the ringing of the phone might awaken Mary. She had to speak to Daisy *now* because if she did not, it would be Drew she would ring and heaven only knew what might be the outcome then.

She slammed the door shut behind her, then wheeled her cycle from the shed, determined to pedal to the crossroads and the telephone box that stood there.

All right, so it was a long-distance call and she couldn't be sure, even now, that she would get through straight away, but she had at least to try. For the sake of her peace of mind she must face the doubt that had nagged her since the night Drew asked her to marry him and Daisy, dear Purvis-from-the-bottom-bunk, was the only one who could help, give the comfort Lyn was so in need of.

How could Drew not have remembered, she fretted. And even if he had and was determined to put it behind him, did he expect Lyn Carmichael, much as she loved him, to walk down the church path to her wedding and ignore the white gravestone beside it, which bore the name *Kitty*?

Surely July would have been a better month, or

May, even? Did it have to be June because the white orchids would be flowering and because Rowangarth's gardens would be at their beautiful best, and days long, and warm? Did it have to be the anniversary month?

She was glad, when she reached the crossroads, that there was a light inside the phone box; relieved, too, she had put her door key and purse in her pocket, though she had no recollection of having done so.

She leaned her cycle against the phone box, heaved open the creaking door, then whispered, 'Please don't be asleep, Daisy?'

'Well, now, look who's here so early in the morning,' Alice smiled. 'Nothing wrong, is there?' There was, of course. She hadn't been Daisy's mother all these years, and not know. 'Bring Mary in, and let me have a cuddle?'

'You can get her wind up, an' all,' Daisy shrugged. 'I came here in such a rush that I didn't bother, after her feed. It's Lyn, Mam,' she said when they were settled in the safe familiarity of Keeper's Cottage kitchen. 'She phoned last night in a right old state.'

'Problems? Surely not about the wedding?'

'Sort of. Said she was sorry for ringing so late, but she had to speak to someone. To put it in a nutshell, she thought a June wedding wasn't right.'

'But I thought it was all agreed?'

'Seems not. Lyn isn't having doubts, exactly, but I know her only too well. When Drew asked her to marry him and even when she'd got the ring, there weren't a lot of stars in her eyes. Not like there should have been. Something was bothering her, I knew it.'

'So why isn't June right? A lovely month, but surely it can be changed?'

'Of course it could be. Lyn knows it – we all know it. It isn't just the date Drew suggested, though now that I think of it I can understand why Lyn has got herself so upset. June is the anniversary month, she said. Even over the phone, I knew she was near to tears, and you can understand it. She said she accepted that Kitty was and always would be a part of the order of things, but I know that a June wedding apart, Lyn has always had doubts about following Kitty. I don't think she's ever going to be sure that Drew will forget her entirely.'

'Well of course he won't! He wouldn't be the Drew Sutton I know, if he does. But there are all kinds of love, surely Lyn's got the sense to know that? She isn't the lass I thought she was if she's going to start putting obstacles in the way. She's always been mad about him. Why the doubts, now?'

'We-e-ll, knowing Carmichael, I'm pretty sure it's because she hasn't ever – I mean, to put it bluntly, Mam, that for all her supposed sophistication, Lyn is still a virgin and she's always known that Drew and Kitty were close. *Very* close. Lyn, it seems to me, is worried about not measuring up – and not knowing what to do, either – making a mess of her wedding night.'

'And why should that worry her? A woman isn't supposed to know anything about – well – things like that. It's taken for granted that the man –'

'Mam! There's been a war on, had you forgotten? Things change.'

'All right. I'll grant you that, our Daisy, and that couples might have taken liberties, from time to time. But does she have to be so nervous about it? I'd have thought that anyone who was in the Armed Forces as long as Lyn was would have been a bit more relaxed about such things, even if she hadn't exactly –'

'Dabbled a toe in the water,' Daisy supplied. 'Done it. And to save you mentioning it, like Keth and I did!'

'I'm sure no such thought entered my mind, Miss!' Alice flinched at her daughter's directness. 'But is there some reason for Lyn feeling the way she does? Was she brought up strictly? Prudish, even?'

'Lyn went to boarding school, don't forget. She said you learn a lot in a dormitory of curious girls. And Auntie Blod wasn't the least bit prudish. I don't know why Lyn should have doubts about marrying Drew. It was all she ever wanted, from the minute she laid eyes on him, yet now, when he's asked her, she's got a fit of the inferiorities! It's as if she's waiting for something to go wrong – and it won't! I told her there's no reason for her doubts. Kitty and Lyn are totally different. Drew won't always be comparing one with the other. He wouldn't do such a thing.'

'Of course he wouldn't and I hope you managed to convince Lyn. Are you going to have a word with Drew about it? Did Lyn ask you to? Because if she didn't, I think you should be very careful what you say, Daisy.'

'She didn't ask me. I think she was unburdening, sort of. But I think I should tell Aunt Julia about it. Lyn seemed pretty desperate and it was me she rang,

81

don't forget, not Drew. I'm hoping Aunt Julia will be able to sort something out – tactfully, I mean.'

'Oh, Daisy Purvis! Your Aunt Julia *tactful*? More like you should have a word with Nathan, if you're determined to interfere.'

'*Mother!* I can't talk to the Reverend like I can talk to you, old love though he is. I can't tell Drew about it, either. Don't want him to think me and Lyn have been talking about him, now do we?'

'You're right. And I think I'll put the little one in her pram, then you and I can decide what's to be done. Mind,' Alice said from the doorway, 'it might be best if it were me had a word with your Aunt Julia, work it out between us what's to be done. If anything needs to be done, that is, and you're not making a big drama out of it.'

'No drama, Mam. All I know is that Lyn phoned late last night and she was worried. And she shouldn't be. This should be one of the happiest times of her life and it isn't. I know it.'

So what was wrong? Alice thought as she tucked in her sleeping granddaughter. Surely nothing that couldn't be sorted, one way or another? Trouble was, that it was no one else's business but Lyn's and Drew's. And Lyn had chosen not to tell Drew.

Ah, well. Tom would be home soon for his morning drinkings. Best set the kettle to boil and warn Daisy not to say one word about Lyn's call in front of her dad. The less people who knew the better, in Alice's opinion, because she did so want to see Drew married. She wanted it so much it worried her that Lyn might be having second thoughts.

Trouble was that Lyn couldn't make it to Rowangarth next week. Her duties at the hotel, she had said, prevented it. And Drew and Keth were talking about going to the Motor Show in London the weekend after, so the poor girl was going to be alone in North Wales with her doubts for the best part of three weeks, and that would never do. Oh, my word, no!

SIX

'Alice! Am I glad to see you!' Julia called, striding across the grass to the wild garden and the stile Alice was climbing. 'The place is so quiet. Nathan's having forty winks – Miss Clitherow, too. And Mary and Tilda have gone to Creesby . . .'

'Aye. And Drew off to London, with Keth.'

'Bill Benson is with them, too. Going on business. They're all staying at Montpelier Mews, by the way. I asked them to light a fire and open windows – air the place a bit.'

'Montpelier. Dear Aunt Sutton's little white house. Do you ever remember, Julia? I mean, do you ever allow yourself to remember?'

'The time you and I stayed there? The time we went to a Suffragette meeting?'

'Aye, and got into a fight. And me supposed to be there to chaperon you, yet I turned a blind eye when you slipped out to meet Andrew.'

Should they be talking about Andrew? Alice brooded. Didn't he belong to the past and wasn't Julia happy with Nathan, now? She must watch what she said, even though it was years and years ago.

'Doctor Andrew MacMalcolm. Oh, Alice. Think of Andrew and we are both young again. You were only seventeen and being so bossy about me meeting him. And don't look so embarrassed. I can think about Andrew, talk about him too, and it doesn't hurt any more; just makes me glad that I met him and married him, even though the war only let us have ten nights together.'

'That war was – was *obscene*, Julia. Try to forget it.'

'Forget. And I've got Nathan, now, bless the lovely man. Newly ordained yet he assisted at our wedding. Blessed Andrew and me, even though he was in love with me himself. Hadn't realized, he once let slip, that until I told him I had met a young doctor, that he'd been in love with me all his life, practically, and hadn't known it until it was too late. It's the same for Drew, now. He can talk about Kitty and accept that she has gone. Not that he'll ever forget her, of course.'

'None of us will, Julia. She was the naughtiest of all the Clan. Poor Bas was terrified of his Grandmother Clementina, yet Kitty didn't care one bit about offending her – said the most awful things.' She took Julia's arm. 'But let's go in the back way? There'll be no one in your kitchen and it's always so snug, there. And we won't be disturbed. I want to talk to you. Been trying to for a couple of weeks, now.'

'Sounds interesting. Gossip?'

'Far from it.' The warmth of Rowangarth kitchen met them as they opened the door. 'Wasn't sure I should mention it, then talking about Kitty did it, I suppose. Shall I put the kettle on?'

'Please. And what about Kitty?' Julia settled herself at the table, chin on hands.

'It's more about Lyndis. The poor lass is getting herself into a state.'

'Wedding nerves? But it's months away.'

'In a state about Kitty, it seems.' Alice busied herself setting a tea tray as she had done so often in this kitchen in the past – in another life, it seemed. 'It was Daisy told me. I've been wondering if I should tell you, especially as it should be something between the two of them. Drew and Lyn, I mean. To put not too fine a point on it, Julia. Lyn opened her heart to Daisy and to my way of thinking, it should have been to Drew.'

'Oh, Lord. She's not having second thoughts?'

'Not about loving Drew. As far as I can see, she's got a thing about Kitty – thinks she'll never be able to take her place. And you've got to admit, Julia, that Kitty is a hard act to follow. She and Drew were besotted.'

'That war has a lot to answer for, Alice.'

'Like our war. But you and I managed. Things came right, in the end. And don't think I haven't thought long and hard about telling you, because I have. Drew and Lyn's business, really, but Lyn confided in Daisy. That's why I think you should know. But we'll wait till I've seen to the tea.'

'Fine by me.' Julia dipped into her coat pocket, bringing out cigarettes and lighter. 'And don't go on about me smoking. I know I promised Nathan faithfully I would give them up when the war ended . . .'

'Then why don't you? You'll end up with bronchitis and it'll be too late, then.'

'Oh, all right. I'll give up smoking when Drew is married – will that suit you? And pour us a cuppa, old love, then tell me what's bothering you.'

Alice repeated the conversation she had had with Daisy, word for word, then said, 'You can see Lyn's point of view, can't you? And I haven't liked telling you, but it's far better you and I try to help things along, rather than our Daisy blurting the whole thing out to Drew. I told her to leave it to you and me. It's a rum do, isn't it?'

'Not really. I always thought Drew and Kitty were lovers, and good luck to them, I said. I mean – think of the times I wanted Andrew and me to jump the gun. I was desperate to get married, if only to sleep in his bed! Drew and Kitty only did what I wanted to do.'

'Couldn't agree more. But Lyn thinks she's going to mess up their wedding night; thinks of herself as second best, it seems to me.'

'So are you going to tell Daisy you've told me, Alice?'

'I think I should. And I'll tell her that me and you both sympathize with Lyn and we're on her side. And I'll tell her to let the matter rest; not to say anything about it unless Lyn brings it up.'

'Of course. Shall I mention it to Nathan?'

'Best not. I'm glad I've told you, for all that. Lyn's such a grand lass and very much in love with Drew. And he's in love with her, an' all – but maybe differently. Happen she'll come to see that, in the end.'

'Yes, but what I'm mystified about, Alice, is Drew setting a date for June of all times. Either he's forgotten about Kitty – and I know he hasn't – or he's decided to meet things head-on and –'

'And go with the flow, you mean, because haven't we all said that June is such a lovely month for a Rowangarth wedding? Said it often, and it is. Even the white orchids will be flowering and June is the time for marquees on the lawn and, oh, everything. Trouble is, we none of us thought.'

'You're right, of course. It's the one thing I can't stand about you, Alice Dwerryhouse. You usually are! And I suppose May would be just as nice a month as June – if Willis can bring the white orchids forward in time. I suppose, with Jack Catchpole to help him, he should be able to produce enough for a bouquet.'

'A bouquet? But there's a bouquet of orchids goes on Kitty's grave every eighteenth of June – and will do, an' all, as long as Jack Catchpole draws breath. Happen now might be the time to break with tradition. Maybe Lyn would like to carry roses. There'll be enough of them about, in May.'

'I see what you mean, but it would be so wonderful if the tradition could be kept up, though I suppose it wouldn't do to make a fuss and bother about it. Not really. I'm just thankful the two of them are getting married. Wouldn't care if they had a quiet wedding like Tatty and Bill. I just want Drew to be happy again, that's all. Lyn is such a capable girl, really. Apart from Kitty, I can't think of anyone better to look after Rowangarth when Nathan and I leave.

And I've done it again, haven't I? "Next to Kitty," I as good as said. Y'know, we must be extra nice to Lyndis next weekend when she comes to visit. Wish she were on the phone. There's nothing I'd like more, right now, than to give her a ring and have a good old chat. Pity there's a waiting list for phones, too. You'd have thought, after all this time, that things would have got back to normal!'

'Well, at least the war is over, Julia love. At least we can look forward to things getting better. We've got a lovely twelve months ahead. Tatty's wedding and Bas and Gracie's baby. And them coming over to have Nathan christen it. And then *the* wedding . . .'

'Yes. Whenever it is, and whatever date they fix, Drew's wedding is something I've lived a long time to see, Alice. And they'll surely have children. Lyn did say that she didn't care how soon.'

And hope and pray, Julia thought soberly, that nothing goes wrong; that Lyn accepts what is past and looks to the future. In time, she was sure Lyn would. Maybe when she held her first baby in her arms it would happen. Maybe when she gave a son to Rowangarth, or a lovely little fair-haired daughter. Or one with chestnut hair!

'And share the joke, will you?' Alice demanded. 'You were grinning like the Cheshire cat.'

'Was I? Then if you must know, I was thinking about a granddaughter with hair the colour of Lyn's. Now wouldn't that be just something?'

And Alice agreed that it would. Really, really something!

* * *

'I love my daughter to bits, but it's so nice to have a mother and mother-in-law close at hand to baby-sit.'

Daisy sat on the hearthrug, her arms on Keth's spread-eagled knees, toes curling from the heat of the fire.

'And it's nice to be home from London,' Bill Benson grinned. 'Last time I saw it, I was blind – if you get what I mean.'

'Y'know, I'd never thought of that, sweetheart – that when you were in London you couldn't see anything, I mean. Did it live up to your expectations, now you've had a look at it?' Tatiana wanted to know.

'I'd prefer Glasgow. Folk'll give you a smile, there, and the time of day. But I liked the wee house fine.'

'Aunt Sutton's house in Montpelier Mews? It's a snug, tucked-away little place. When I was tiny, there was a lovely lady called Sparrow used to caretake it for Mother.' Drew had been fond of Sparrow.

'She looked after me and Kitty,' Tatiana smiled, 'when we lived there during the war. She wasn't half bossy, but we adored her. I remember –'

She stopped, looking down at her hands. What she remembered should not be talked about in front of Lyn – or Drew, for that matter – but she and Kitty had been very happy being bossed about by Sparrow. Until the flying bomb, that was.

'Go on, Tatty – what do you remember?' Keth unthinking urged.

'Oh – we-e-ll – I – I suppose it was when the siren used to go,' Tatiana said, disliking herself for not being more careful. 'That house had once been a stable, belonging to one of the big houses in the Square. Then, when cars became all the rage, stables were made into garages.

'Aunt Sutton's house still had the inspection pit. No one had bothered to fill it in when the garage was made into a house. Sparrow made a shelter out of it. A bit of a squash, but we survived. There was a searchlight and an ack-ack gun in the park nearby, and when the searchlight lit up we all got into the pit. Mind, we were very near Hyde Park. The bombing wasn't so bad, there. Not like they got it in the East End and oh, damn, damn, *damn*!'

She covered her face with her hands. What had she said! They had been in Hyde Park the day the flying bomb dropped. Kitty had crossed the road to post a letter to Drew.

'Look – I'm sorry. It was just that – Oh, dammit, I didn't think. Me and my big mouth. Sorry, Drew. Sorry, Lyn.'

'That's all right,' Lyn said so softly that her words came in a whisper. 'It was a terrible thing to have happened. Daisy and I were lucky, in Liverpool. It could have been either of us. And I've just had the most marvellous idea,' she rushed on without stopping to draw breath. 'We can't go abroad for our honeymoon, so why don't we stay at Montpelier Mews? Would your mother let us, Drew? Tucked away, you said . . .'

'Darling. What a good idea.' Drew reached for Lyn's hand, holding it tightly, sensing her distress. 'Why didn't *I* think of it?'

'Lyn, you'll love it! But let's not get on the subject of honeymoons!' Knowing what she did, Daisy was eager to talk about something else. 'Now that we're all together, I wouldn't mind hearing about the Motor Show. All I could get out of Keth was that the three of you had a good time out on the loose in London!'

'Well, *I* had a great time,' Bill enthused. 'Not only did an agent take me on his list, but the show was fine, an' all. New models, all sleek and shiny. There was a little job; a Morris Minor. Jeez, I'd have killed for one of those. Trouble is, I can't drive.'

Which made them all laugh and the tension in the room to ease, and Tatty, desperate to make amends, said, 'Why don't we have a cup of tea and a piece of cake? I stood in a queue for ages in Creesby, this morning, but I got a cream cake. *Cream*, would you believe!'

So everyone said cream cake would be just marvellous, because they all knew things had got a bit dicey for a while, and each of them thought, as Tatty hurried to the kitchen, that Lyn had taken it pretty well, all things considered.

And they wondered, too, if ever the time would come when they could think about Kitty and speak about Kitty, and not feel disloyal to Drew. And to Lyn, as well, for that matter . . .

Daisy and Keth had left Denniston House early, because of Mary's ten o'clock feed, and as Drew and Lyn walked back to Foxgloves alone, Drew said, 'You're quiet, darling. Tired? Sure all this coming and going between here and Wales isn't getting a bit much for you?'

'N-no. Of course it isn't. I'm fine. Just fine.'

'Then is it about Montpelier Mews? Have you changed your mind about us going there, in June? Something is wrong, Lyn, I know it.'

'Look, Drew – Montpelier is fine. If you must know, it's June that isn't. I'm sorry, but June seems to be an anniversary month, sort of. The month you and Kitty should have been married. The month she was killed. And white orchids on her grave, always, in June. I – I'm sorry, but I don't think I can cope with it. Not then. Some other time. July, perhaps . . . ?'

Her voice trailed off in a trembling whisper.

'Sweetheart.' He gathered her into his arms. 'Why didn't you say something? How long have you been bottling it up?'

'Don't know. Since the night I tricked you into marrying me, I suppose.'

'*Tricked*, Lyn? What are you talking about? I *asked* you to marry me.'

'All right. So you did. But only after I made a fuss, yelled like a hoyden at those damned rooks, put the words into your mouth, practically.'

'Lyndis Carmichael – what am I to do with you?' He tilted her chin, kissing her gently. 'Didn't I tell you that I thought you were a career girl, had bought your own home and was happy with your life the way it was? I hadn't the gumption to realize, I suppose, that you might still care for me like once you did. I thought, you see, that you hadn't minded at all when Kitty and I got engaged. Not till you told me not so long ago that you'd sat on the stairs in the Wrennery, and cried your heart out. I *want* us to be married, Lyn. I want you and me to live in Rowangarth and bring up our kids there. Hand on heart, I *do*.'

'And I want to marry you, Drew, but please not in June? It's the best month for weddings I know, but the war is over now, and we can pick and choose when we marry.'

'So when would you like it to be, darling? Do you want a quiet wedding, like Tatty and Bill are having? Shall it be at Christmas, too, in the Lady Chapel? I don't care at all where or when. I just want us to be married.'

'Christmas?' She gave a shaky laugh and he felt the tenseness in her lessen a little. 'Not Christmas, *cariad*. I haven't got around to telling you, but Auntie Blod and my father would like to come to Wales for Christmas.'

'Auntie Blod? When are you going to call her Mother, Lyn?'

'Never, I suppose. And it doesn't matter what I call her as long as I know she's my real mother. But what do you think about them coming for Christmas? I think Auntie Blod is getting homesick for Wales. Wants to see the little cottage again, she says. I really think, though, that she wants to meet your folks, and see Rowangarth and talk about the wedding. I don't think I'd like it, either, if my daughter was getting married and I was stuck miles and miles away. And I miss her, Drew. I want her to be with me, when we get married.'

'Of course you do. Seems to me that neither of us has got used to the idea of being married. It did happen a bit – sort of quickly.'

'I can't argue with you on that point.'

'So let's take a deep breath, and think things out?'

'Come down off our pink cloud, you mean?'

'Not if you don't want to. Pink clouds are fine by me. But let's suggest your folks spend Christmas at Rowangarth? Mother would be in high old delight with all the wedding talk. And let's you and me settle now – right now, here on this spot – when you'd like us to be married.'

'All right. I'd like us to be married in April, like Daisy was. That suit you, Drew?'

'If it can't be soon, like Christmas in the Lady Chapel, then April sounds a good month to me. Agreed, then?'

'Agreed. And we'll fix a date when I've had a peek in my diary.'

'The date. Of course. Very important. Now, shall we kiss on it and shall I take you back to Foxgloves? With a bit of luck Keth and Daisy might still be up and we can tell them the news.'

'They'd better be up. I haven't got a key!'

So laughing, and hand in hand, they ran as quickly as they could in the darkness to Foxgloves with the news.

November, and the government, in its magnanimity, lifted control on the manufacture of cutlery, fountain pens and jewellery. A small step towards normality, some said, but wouldn't it have been better by far if food rationing had been done away with, or at least the present miserable rations doubled.

In that month, too, a son was born to Princess

Elizabeth, and if you wanted to put not too fine a point on it, another infant to help swell the baby boom, because that was what the amazingly large number of babies being born in the United Kingdom was called.

But by far the most startling event, and the most startled teacher of mathematics ever, was the arrival home of Keth Purvis on the last Friday in November – he would never forget the day – to find the path at the side of his house blocked by a car, which gleamed in his headlights and was shiny black and very new.

'Well, I'll be damned!'

He got out of his own much less shiny motor and walked around the intruder, squinting inside to see gleaming upholstery – it couldn't be leather, surely? And the *thing*, as far as he could see, had key ignition, indicator lights that flashed left and right and heaven only knew what else.

The back door opened and Daisy stepped out with Mary, swaddled in a shawl, in her arms.

'Happy birthday, darling.' She took his hand, wrapping his fingers around a small key.

'My birthday is in July,' Keth said, dry-mouthed. 'You know it is.'

'Well then – Happy Christmas! You do like it? It's a Morris Minor, the new model.'

'Like it? Daisy Purvis, I don't know what to say. I mean, where did you get it? *How* did you get it? I don't believe it!'

'Then you better had, because it's yours. And I got it from Creesby Motors by writing out a cheque.'

'But wife darling, what was the magic word, for heaven's sake!'

'The magic word was Purvis. I went to see them just before you and Drew went to London, and the man said there was no chance at all. Three new cars was all he'd ever had and they were gone straight away. So I asked him if he would put your name on his waiting list. And when I said Purvis, Mr Keth Purvis, he asked me if you were the schoolie who taught his boy maths at Creesby Grammar. And I said you were.

'"Then in that case, Mrs Purvis, your husband has a fair old chance of getting one of the next new motors I get in," he said. You see, darling, it seems his son is a bright enough lad, but had a mental blockage when it came to maths. Was making the boy's life a misery. Then you started teaching there and his son came on in leaps and bounds, and all because of you. "Good at sums he is now," I was told.'

'It gets queerer by the minute,' Keth laughed. 'The boy isn't called Colin Chambers, is he?'

'Our Colin? Sounds like him.'

'But Daisy love, schoolteachers – schoolies – don't have the kind of money to buy new cars. At least, this one doesn't.'

'So are we going to get onto The Money subject?'

'No, darling. No, of course not. But –'

'No buts. Either you like it as much as I do, or it can go back to Creesby Motors. Keth – just think? When the better weather comes, you'll be able to take your mother to Hampshire. She's never seen your dad's grave since we left there; only the photograph we took of it when we were on our honeymoon.'

'But petrol is rationed. How am I to get to Hampshire and back?'

Keth was laughing, now. With disbelief Daisy supposed, but laughing, for all that.

'The nice man threw in a full tank of off-the-ration petrol. In gratitude it must have been.'

'Daisy Purvis!' He kissed her soundly. 'You are a witch! Mary Natasha Purvis, your mother is a witch!'

'Mm. Mummy's got a magic name,' Daisy laughed. 'And Mary is getting hungry. Go on, then. Open it! Get inside!'

'I love you,' Keth whispered, but already the kitchen door had banged behind her.

He ran his hand over the shiny, slippery bodywork, then said again, 'I'll be damned.'

His hand shook as he pushed the key in the lock, then he sat in the unfamiliar seat, sniffing the newness smell, wondering how any one man could be so lucky. And not just car-lucky. Lucky to survive the war, to get out of France. Lucky to have Daisy and Mary Natasha. And of course he would take his mother to West Welby to see his father's grave. Hampshire was a long way away, but somehow he would get petrol; on the black market, if he had to. But he would take her there, stay overnight, make a real outing of it – if you could call a visit to a grave an outing.

He ran his hands round the steering wheel, then wiggled the gear lever. Tomorrow, he would take it on the road. He wondered what the boys at school would say on Monday when Sir arrived in a brand-new car;

wondered what Drew and Bill would say. Drew would know whose money had paid for it; Bill would not. The Money. Daisy's secret.

And there was another grave he would visit. He had thought to do it for a long time; now it had become a must. He must go to France, to Clissy-sur-Mer and find the grave of a sixteen-year-old girl – if she'd been given a decent burial, that was. But at least he would go to Tante Clara's house, perhaps see the lilies in the back garden, ask at the bread shop for news of Madame Piccard and a girl called Hannah Kominski who had become Elise Josef on a forged passport. Codename Natasha. He had called his daughter for her and for the people in Clissy-sur-Mer who had died so he could get a package back to the stone house, in deepest Argyll. He drew in his breath, tapping his forefingers on the wheel, remembering Castle McLeish and a submarine – the *Selene*. And a tipsy-winged plane called a Lysander that flew him and the package to safety, the night Natasha died. Daisy knew little about France. He had not been able to tell her. Signing the Official Secrets Act made sure he did not.

'Why Natasha?' she asked when he had chosen it as Mary's second name, and all he had been able to tell her was that it belonged to a sixteen-year-old girl who had died.

Well, he was going to France just as soon as the government lifted the ban on travel abroad, and if it meant telling Daisy every single word of what happened there, then he would and damn the trouble he might get himself into. Daisy would understand, once she knew. Knowing her as he did, she would insist that he make the sentimental journey that would help ease his conscience. When a man was as lucky as Keth Purvis, it was the only way he could tip his cap to Fate, and ask that he might be allowed to keep what was so precious to him. Nothing to do with the car. The car had only brought things to a head. Too much luck. He had to make amends.

He got out of the car, locked it, then opened the kitchen door. Daisy was sitting there, Mary at her breast. It was a sight he never tired of because it made Daisy even more beautiful. She looked up, and smiled.

'All right, now? Got over the shock?'

'I think so. Thank you, darling.'

He bent down to kiss her. Later, when Mary was asleep and they had eaten supper, would be the best time to talk.

'Sweetheart,' he whispered. 'There's something I've got to tell you. I'm not supposed to, but I don't care.'

'About the war, Keth – *your* war?'

'Yes. But you half knew, didn't you, that I didn't spend all the war code breaking.'

'Sort of. France came into it, and someone called Natasha. That much you admitted to, and then you clammed up.'

'I had to. I'm still bound by the Official Secrets Act. For thirty years, I was told. But let's see Mary off to bed and have our supper. Then I'll tell you.'

'You don't have to, Keth, though I would like to know; clear things up, kind of. And Mary's finished, now. Can you get her wind up for me, then I'll make a start on the meal.'

Keth held out his arms for his daughter, loving the

milky, baby-soap smell of her, loving her so much it made him afraid.

'The new car, darling.' He kissed the nape of Daisy's neck as she bent over the cooker. 'I still can't believe it. How do I begin to say thank you?'

'By winding Mary and getting her to sleep for me.' She turned, kissing him provocatively. 'And that's just for starters.'

'I love you,' he said softly. 'But I don't have to tell you that, do I?'

'Yes, you do. Every day. There'll be trouble if you ever stop. Now get from under my feet, Keth Purvis. I'm busy!'

'You sound just like your mother,' he laughed, then laid his daughter over his shoulder so she could snuggle her little soft face into his neck. Then he began a heel and toe rocking movement. It always got her to sleep. He laid a hand protectively over the back of her head, wondering how any woman could find the strength to give away her child.

'I'm adopted. I don't know anything about my mother, except that she wasn't married and couldn't keep me. I only know that I was born in Paris and that she was called Natasha. That's why I took it as my codename,' Hannah-Elise had told him.

Give his little girl to another woman then turn, and leave her? Give Mary away, never knowing that before she reached womanhood she would die, be killed?

'I think she's asleep,' Keth whispered chokily.

'Then take her up, will you? The cot's ready. Careful, now.'

101

Daisy switched on the hall and landing lights, watching her husband carry their child to bed, thinking how lucky she was; always had been. And how grateful she was to be so loved.

SEVEN

'That's it, then.' Tom Dwerryhouse unfastened his brown leather leggings, then eased off his boots. 'No more shoots till the New Year. Can't say I'm sorry. It's hard work, organizing those syndicates. Most of the guns haven't got a dog with them, and wouldn't dream of using a loader. Not like shoots used to be, Alice. And before you say it,' he hastened, 'I know that leasing out the shooting keeps me in a job, but some of that lot need an eye keeping on them. Think they're still in the war, and taking pot shots at anything that moves.' He held his hands to the fire, then gazed at the table top and the paraphernalia of dressmaking spread there, instead of a white cloth and cutlery. 'Supper a bit late, is it?'

'Unless you've lost your sense of smell, only by ten minutes. It's all in the oven, ready to dish up. Pheasant casserole. By the time you've washed your hands I'll have cleared this lot away. Told you, if you think back, that I didn't want to be last-minute with my dress for the wedding, and I was right. Wedding brought forward, now, to April.'

'Aye, lass, but that's still near on five months away.'

'I know that. And I'm glad I didn't buy anything flimsy, with June in mind. Must have known to buy something a bit more substantial. April can be cold, sometimes. Can't go far wrong with a nice bit of fine wool, though heaven knows why I chose this colour – apart from it going nicely with my hat, of course.'

'I like it. You'll look bonny in it. What colour would you call it, Alice?'

'Apricot, and it'll never be out of the dry-cleaners, if you want my opinion.' Carefully she gathered swathes of material and the pieces of paper pattern pinned to them. 'But never mind. April is the best month for weddings. Our Daisy's was perfect. So get out of your best suit and put something comfortable on. Five minutes, and supper'll be on the table.'

Pheasant, with carrots and baby onions and jacket-baked potatoes. Casseroling was all she could do with the old bird Tom had brought home yesterday but welcome for all that, when meat was as hard to come by as it had been in the war.

But the war was over, and Daisy and Keth and Drew safely back from it; Lyndis, an' all, thanks be. She heard Tom walking overhead and the creaking of the wardrobe door. Nasty old month, November, but Keeper's Cottage was snug and warm, and there was a good play on the wireless tonight. And with a little new Sutton due and Tatty getting wed next month, and Christmas to follow, it wasn't a bad old world, Alice was bound to admit. Better by far than the day Daisy had left for Dunfermline to be a Wren, and the war looking like it would go on forever.

Yet it had been over these three years gone and herself a gran, and Daisy living hardly a cock-stride away. Aye, and Keth with a new car and half of Holdenby green with envy.

'Aaaah.' She billowed out the tablecloth then let it fall to a sigh of contentment, smiling at her husband more comfortable now in corduroy trousers that had seen better days, and the sweater she knitted for his last birthday. His fifty-seventh and him as good to look at, still, as the day she'd first met him in Brattocks Wood.

'So what have you been doing with yourself this afternoon?' Tom sat in the fireside rocker, filling his pipe then laying it aside in the hearth to be smoked when supper was cleared away and Alice sitting opposite him, knitting.

'Doing? Well, apart from laying out the pattern, I've been to the Bothy. Polly was there, and asked me in for a look round. You'd hardly know the place, Tom. That little room you slept in has a carpet on the floor that stretches from wall to wall, and very posh curtains. All from Pendenys, of course. I reckon Julia will be doing a forage in Rowangarth attics before so very much longer. Nothing ever thrown away, there. Lady Helen used to say, "Keep a thing for seven years, and you'll find a use for it." Shouldn't wonder if Julia doesn't find most of what she needs up there to furnish the Bothy. Remember when you slept there, Tom, with the garden apprentices and the stable lads?'

'Aye, and ruled with a rod of iron by Jinny Dobb . . .'

'Who did Rowangarth's washing, an' all, and told fortunes. Then the Great War came, and there was no one there to be looked after; all gone to fight. Then we left Hampshire, came home again to Rowangarth. Left Dickon behind in the churchyard, and Beth and Morgan in Beck Lane with a stone over them so people would know, and not disturb them . . .'

'And Polly and Keth came with us, too, and Polly took over at the Bothy, grateful for a job and a roof.' Tom stared into the fire. 'And her glad when the government commandeered it and put land girls in there for her to cook for, when another war came. Memories, Alice. Good ones and bad ones. But it worked itself out in the end, and if you don't mind, love, I'm ready for my supper.'

'Was there ever a time, Tom Dwerryhouse, when you weren't? And shift your feet so I can get at the oven!'

So he smiled and got out of her way, and if she hadn't had a very hot dish in her hands, he'd have pinched her bottom as she bent over. A very nice bottom, come to think of it, for a grandmother who would not see fifty again!

Lyn had been sure all day that a letter from Kenya would be there when she got home from work. And it was.

She put a match to the fire, changed her wet shoes for slippers, then carefully slit open the envelope.

Hullo, lovely girl!
This is a quick one to tell you that your dad has got us a passage home, and we should dock

*in England a week before Christmas. We have
a cabin on a cargo ship from Mombasa to Cape
Town where we embark on the* Stirling Castle
*– newly refitted after being a troopship in the
war.*

*I'm a bit nervous about flying, so your dad
said it was no problem. By sea was much nicer,
even though it's going to take a lot longer.*

*Will give you all details – sailing times, cabin
numbers, etc, as soon as we have them
confirmed. Now that I know we are almost on
our way, I can't wait to see my girl again. And
I'll remember to pack warm clothes. I haven't
been so long gone that I have forgotten how
cold it can be in Wales, in winter.*

Will write again, soon.

With love,

Mam X X (and Dad)

Home! Her mother – her darling Auntie Blod –
was coming home for Christmas! Only then did Lyn
realize how much she had missed her, needed her.
Eighteen months since she had seen her; eighteen
years, near as dammit, since she saw her father.

Christmas, and them together in the little cottage
in Wales – or would they be asked to Rowangarth?
And how long would they be staying, once they knew
that the wedding had been put forward to April? She
wouldn't care if they never went back. They would,
of course, but just for a while she would be part of
a family, with her father walking her down the aisle.

Her father, Jack Carmichael, was little changed it

would seem, from when she last saw him. Still straight-backed and slim; still the thick, dark hair with hardly a streak of grey in it. Handsome, even yet. No wonder Auntie Blod had fallen in love with him and stayed in love with him.

All at once Lyn felt a strange contentment, because she wasn't alone; stupid of her ever to have thought she was. Soon, she would have her mother to confide in, to tell of the uncertainties she still sometimes felt. And her mother would understand because she knew, didn't she, what it was like to love a man, to lose him and then, in the end, to marry him.

'There's stupid, our Lyndis. Worrying about your wedding night, are you? Then get yourself into bed with him, girl. Try before you buy, why don't you? I did!' Lyn could almost hear the words.

'Yes, and look where it got you. It got you pregnant with me,' Lyn smiled to the face in the mirror over the mantelpiece.

All at once she was hungry. Nothing like good news to give you an appetite. She would boil the brown egg Daisy's mother had given her and slice into the loaf Daisy's mother had baked, then spread it thickly with bramble jelly. Sheer bliss. Eating home-made bread and jam was almost as good as being in love, especially when you were getting married in April. The second Saturday in April. It had a firm ring to it. Daisy had been married in April.

'I always associate my wedding with windflowers,' she once said. 'The little white, wild anemones. They were flowering in Brattocks Wood.'

And she had added, pink-cheeked, that she associated their honeymoon with bluebells because they had gone back to the place she and Keth grew up in, made a sentimental journey to Beck Lane in Hampshire, where the woods were thick with bluebells. And they had been lovers there. Lucky Daisy and Keth who had wanted no other. They were still at school when they realized they were in love. No complications for those two; no doubts.

The fire had begun to blaze and crackle. Outside, the night was dark, but this snug, thick-walled little house with curtains pulled across the windows and lamps burning softly, was a good place to be. If she couldn't be in the winter parlour at Rowangarth with Drew, that was. And the two of them making plans in the fireglow or even – crazy thought – making love?

But no, not now. She had lived these many years a reluctant virgin and would stay so until her wedding night. And instead of thinking about wedding nights she thought about a boiled fresh egg, and bread and jam and Drew, who loved her, even though he had never said so. Never actually said the words.

'I love you, Drew Sutton,' she whispered to the brown egg she lowered carefully into the pan. 'I always will . . .'

'So it's to be an April wedding?' Mary Stubbs sniffed. 'Why the change of plan? I'd have liked June much better.'

'Aye, but it's not for you to say, is it, since it's not you going to wed Sir Andrew.'

'Don't talk so daft! I'm well suited with the man I've got, thanks all the same.'

Well suited with Will Stubbs, once stable lad at Rowangarth, then promoted to groom and, since motors had replaced horses, now as apt a motor mechanic as any in these parts. Because Will had been astute; had learned about motors and their innards in the Great War, because horses, he had decided, would be on their way out once that war was over with. And he was right! He was very often right, Mary Stubbs was bound to admit; was what people might call a self-educated man though Tilda, in a fit of rage, had once called him a right know-all; she at the time being on the shelf with little hope of ever getting off it, and prickly about those who had.

Then the government had commandeered Pendenys Place and the Place Suttons thrown out of it and Sergeant Sidney Willis, together with a battalion of Green Howards, came to guard it. Very lucky Tilda had been, meeting her Sidney.

'We'll be invited to the wedding,' said Tilda, seeing the need to change the subject. 'And no problem with what to wear. You and me both have wedding outfits and decent hats.'

'So we have, but I'm going to have to ask Alice Dwerryhouse to let mine out – just a little . . .'

'Middle-age spread, Mary?'

'No, Tilda dear. Just contentment and the love of a good man. And I'll be off to look in on Miss Clitherow, make up her fire, then see if there's anything Miss Julia or the Reverend wants when I'm in Creesby, this afternoon.'

'You could call in on that grocer of ours, ask him if he's got anything under the counter. That man is too smug for his own liking, ladies always flattering him for handouts. That one needs to be reminded that food won't always be rationed and that in the old days, Rowangarth was one of his best customers!' Tilda longed for the day when, telephone to her ear, she gave her order to the grocer and the butcher and what was more, had them delivered! 'But everything comes to she who waits,' she nodded with a narrowing of her eyes and a rounding of her mouth. 'Oh my word, yes!'

'Then I think you'll be in for a long wait, Tilda. What with that lot in London rationing bread and everyone on waiting lists, still, for the necessities of life!' (Mary Stubbs longed for a refrigerator.) 'And with the Royal Air Force dropping food that by rights should be ours for those Germans in Berlin, I don't know what the world is coming to. Our lot *did* win the war, Tilda? Correct me if I'm wrong!'

'We won it.' Tilda smiled. 'I think it's just peace that we can't get used to.' Wars weren't all that bad; not when they had landed a battalion of Green Howards on her doorstep. 'And will you tell Miss Julia that I got a jar of coffee powder the other day, and would she and the Reverend like to try it for elevenses?'

'*Powdered* coffee,' Mary gasped. Whatever was the world coming to!

Olga, Countess Petrovska sat beside the fire in the small, ground-floor room at the back of the house in Cheyne Walk. She did not like sitting in what had once – in another fairytale life it sometimes seemed

– been the housekeeper's room. But now they had no housekeeper, no servants and anyway the small room was more easily heated. She closed her eyes and drifted back to the house beside the River Neva where fires warmed all the rooms, and servants enough to keep them constantly burning.

It would be bitterly cold, now, in St Petersburg. The river beside which she once lived would have started to freeze, but she would have been making plans for Christmas, which lasted well into January, with parties and balls and friends calling each afternoon to gossip about who was with whom at the ballet, last night, and who would get himself talked about if he were foolish enough to have more than two dances with the Sudzhenska girl. Talked about, or compromised into an engagement if he wasn't careful and thought less about her father's wealth and more about her sullen, spotty face!

'Mama. You were daydreaming again!' Igor's clicking fingers demanded attention.

'Yes. I was in my salon with my friends, drinking tea from china cups.'

'And putting St Petersburg society to rights!'

'Tittle-tattle. Gossiping about anything and nothing, my only worry to find wives for my sons and thinking about whom my daughter might marry in two, three years' time . . .'

'When you ought to be thinking about your granddaughter's wedding!'

'Tatiana has a mother to worry about her; a mother who right from the start was determined to do exactly as she pleased. First she insisted upon marrying Elliot

112

Sutton, then she went to work – a Petrovska, working! And now she has chosen to marry a doctor and become one of the middle classes!'

'Mama! My sister was young and foolish and you did nothing to stop her marrying Sutton.'

'He was wealthy . . .'

'He was a brute! He wanted only to breed from her!'

'Igor! Watch your tongue when you speak to your mother! I will not have such coarseness in my home! But you are right, I suppose,' she shrugged. 'He wanted a son. His mother *demanded* a son. Such a loud woman, that Mrs Clementina, but breeding will out!'

'Shall we talk about Tatiana?' he said softly, coaxingly.

'Who is to marry a man with no background.'

'A man who cares deeply for her, Mama. And don't forget you said you quite liked him, when you met.'

'I – I suppose I did, though he wasn't an officer. But he did look me in the eye when he spoke to me. My granddaughter will be happy enough. She has a house, and money. She has forgotten she is Russian.'

'*Half*-Russian, and as English as they come. I am fond of Tatiana, was touched when she asked me to give her away. You'll be coming with me to the wedding?'

'I think not, Igor. I dislike English trains and it is even colder in the north than it is here. And I have nothing to wear.'

'You have your sable, Mama. December is a month

for furs, and yours will be the finest in the North Riding! Now – where will you stay? At Denniston with Tatiana, or at Rowangarth? Julia Sutton would be glad to have us. Or shall you, perhaps, stay with Anna and Ewart?'

'Why did I sell the tiara?' Olga Petrovska demanded petulantly.

'Why, Mama? We needed the money. You sold it after Anna had worn it at her wedding to Elliot Sutton. You got a good price for it.'

'Yes. The money helped. If only we had been able to get more out of Russia, we wouldn't be beggars, now.'

'My father and Vassily were killed, trying to get *more* out of Russia. Be content, Mama, that you got out with your life. And the tiara did not bring happiness to Anna. I think it is best that Tatiana cannot wear it.'

'Of course she couldn't wear it, even had I not been forced to part with it! Tatiana will not be wearing white. She is determined to be married in ordinary clothes. I doubt she will carry flowers, even. But it will matter not much, I think. She is marrying out of her faith.'

'Tatiana will be married by her uncle, an Anglican priest. He is a good man and will speak the words with love. So will I ring my niece? Will I tell her that her grandmother looks forward to her wedding? It would seem ungracious if you were not there. She will want your blessing.'

'Since you seem determined to put an old woman to such trouble – yes, ring Tatiana. Tell her her grandmother will stay at Denniston House, and will remain there, over Christmas. It will make a change, I suppose, from cold, bombed London.'

'London is a better place to be in than Leningrad – than *St Petersburg*, Mama. Think of the desolation there. Remember that you said you were proud of the way the Communists fought the Nazi armies for Mother Russia.'

'I remember. What is left of my St Petersburg, the people there deserve.'

And why did she always think of her house beside the River Neva when things, here in exile, got bad; when there was no coal to burn in the grate, when rations ran out? In her heart she knew she was being foolish, that almost certainly her beloved house had been blasted into ruins in the long, bitter siege or, at the very best, was now in a sad and run-down state with a family living in each room, using Olga Petrovska's most modern water closets or doing their washing in her baths, with the shining taps turned green with neglect. Best she forget about the days when Peter, her husband, and elder son Vassily had been alive; when her children were young and they spent their summers at the farm at Peterhof, not many miles away from the Tzar, God rest him, who spent summers there, too.

They had run through the fields, her children, like barefoot peasants; had fished in the stream and helped in the hay meadows. Life had been good then, had she the sense to know it. But happiness is always ahead, or behind you. She had never once thought, 'Today, I am the most fortunate, the most contented woman in all the Russias,' and more was the pity. She pulled her shawl more closely around her shoulders then closed her eyes, to shut out the present.

And her son sensed her withdrawal, and said nothing, because these days, the only time she smiled was when she thought about the time before the revolution when life had been tranquil. So he, too, closed his eyes, pushed his feet closer to the small fire in the small grate, and thought not of the house by the River Neva, but of his niece and her wedding and how pleasant it would be to see her happiness. Had he had a daughter of his own, Igor pondered, she would have been exactly like Tatiana; would, if that daughter were very lucky, be blessed with his niece's beauty, and with not a little of her independence and courage.

But he had not married, for who would want a penniless White Russian even though he was, if everyone claimed his own, Count Igor Petrovsky. And which woman, with one iota of sense, would have taken him when he came burdened with an autocratic mother who was only happy when she could escape to her beloved house beside the River Neva?

He sighed, and thought instead of his niece, the amazingly well-balanced outcome of a disastrous marriage who was to marry, soon, in the little hundreds-of-years-old chapel.

And there was a smile on his lips, too.

'You can't mean it, Keth Purvis. Take me all the way to West Welby in that car of yours?'

'Of course I mean it. I always said I would take you back there one day, to see Dad's grave.'

'But how will you manage it, boy, when petrol is rationed and, anyway, when are you to get time off school?'

'At Christmas – when driving all the way to Hampshire wouldn't be a lot of fun, and at Easter, when I had thought to go. And don't look so dumbfounded. You know you'd like it.'

'And does Daisy agree with all this, then?'

'She does. You and I were to go, she insisted, and you know what Daisy is like when she sets her mind on anything. And as for petrol – well, Creesby Motors threw in a full tank of it when we bought the car and don't ask me how they were able to do it, because I don't know. All I do know is that there was five months' petrol rations in that tank, so I'm hanging on to my coupons –'

'Your *legitimate*, above-board coupons, Keth?'

'Whatever. So I'm well in hand, petrol-wise, and should be able to get you there and back when the better weather comes.'

'And I appreciate it, son, but will you tell me one thing? Will you tell me how much that motor cost? And this is your mother, asking.'

'If you must know, it cost two hundred and seventy pounds.'

His cheeks flushed red, because he knew who had paid for it, and his mother, mistaking his shame for anger, said she was sorry, that it wasn't any of her business; that she had only asked because she didn't want to think of him getting into debt to pay for it.

'It's all right, Mam. It swallowed up my Army gratuity and all of my savings, but I managed it.'

He was ashamed of the blatant lies that came too easily, but his mother had never been told about Daisy's money. The fewer who knew, the better, Daisy had always insisted. Even Lyn thought the fortune her cabin mate had inherited on that twenty-first birthday was a mere thousand pounds, and only told because it had been necessary to find an explanation for Daisy's visit to the solicitor at Winchester. What that inheritance had grown into over the years until Daisy came of age was obscene, almost. His fiancée had become richer than Drew, truth known. Amazing, really, how someone so flouncy and quick-tempered as Daisy could have kept all that money so secret.

'Hullo, son,' Polly Purvis smiled. 'You've come back to earth, then? Where were you?'

'As a matter of fact, I was thinking about West Welby.' His cheeks flushed red again because he was not a good liar. 'Was thinking, as a matter of fact, that you might be a bit disappointed when we go to see Beck Lane. Daisy and I found it a bit run-down and neglected. No one living in either Keeper's or Willow End.'

'It wouldn't matter, Keth. I couldn't go all that way and not walk down Beck Lane, now could I? And I'd want to take a look at Morgan and Beth.'

'Of course you would.' Keth took his mother's face in his hands and gently kissed her forehead. 'And maybe, if we are lucky, the bluebells will be out in the beechwood and if the piggy-bank runs to it, I'd like us to stay the night somewhere; make a real outing of it. And at least there are films for cameras in the shops again. We can take lots of snaps. But I want you to promise me you won't get too upset, Mam.'

'Just a little sad for my Dickon, allow me that. But I'll count my blessings. I've always known that you take what life throws at you and that nothing lasts, neither good times, nor bad. And I shall look forward to going to Hampshire and staying overnight. Sure you can afford it, son?'

'Sure – or I wouldn't be asking you.' He smiled, loving her very much, knowing he had lied again, that it was Daisy who insisted on paying for the trip. 'We'll have a look at the calendar – make sure it doesn't clash with the wedding.'

'Aah. The wedding.' Polly smiled then closed her eyes and thought about the dress she had worn to Keth's wedding and the fine hat Daisy had bought her in the swankiest shop in Harrogate. Polly Purvis had plenty of good times for the counting. Oh, my word, yes!

'So tell me, Keth?' Daisy slipped her arm into his, snuggling close, knowing she must tread carefully. 'About France, I mean – if you haven't changed your mind, that is?'

'You've got to know, darling, then maybe when you do, you'll understand why I've got to go back to Clissy.'

'To France?'

'Yes. To Clissy-sur-Mer when I became Gaston Martin and had a codename *Hibou*.'

'So I was right all along,' she whispered. 'It *was* cloak-and-dagger stuff! You were in terrible danger, and I never knew.'

'Not dangerous for me. I wasn't the one who took risks, not *real* risks. I was taken there by submarine, rowed ashore then met and handed over to someone who told me her name was Natasha. I remember thinking at the time that it had come to something when a child was the best they could manage. I didn't think that being out after curfew was a stupid – and dangerous – thing to do. She took me to Madame Piccard's house. That house was all I saw of Clissy. Never went beyond the back gate; never saw the village.'

'In what they called a safe house, were you?'

'That's it. I took the identity of a French soldier Gaston Martin, officially posted missing at Dunkirk; unofficially taken off the beaches with our lot and was then living in Ireland. He was deaf – caused by explosions. Lucky for me, that, as long as I remembered when a stranger came along, that I couldn't hear a word they said.'

'And did they? Come along, I mean.'

'Once. One of the occupying German soldiers and the local gendarme with him. Routine check. Looking back, knowing what I know now, I think the gendarme was in on it – or at least sympathetic to anyone he suspected to be in the Resistance. I had supposedly gone to Clara Piccard's house to dig her garden. I had a forged work permit with me and she made no bones about her hired help. Luckily, I knew how to dig.'

'But Natasha – where did she come into it?'

'Natasha – her real name Hannah Kominski – was adopted. Her parents were Russian refugees who

120

lived in Paris, next door to Madame Piccard, who worked as a nurse there, before she retired to Clissy-sur-Mer. The Kominskis – they were Jewish – realized it was only a matter of time before they were arrested, so they made sure Hannah was safe. Madame Piccard had retired to Clissy by then. Her husband was killed in the Great War, so she'd gone back to nursing. They sent Hannah, with forged papers, to her for safe keeping. There were a lot of good forgers around in our war, Daisy. Hannah became Elise Josef and worked as a courier, sometimes, for the Resistance. She took the codename Natasha, because it was all she knew about her birth mother.'

'And the Kominskis?' Daisy whispered, all at once sad.

'There were a few letters from Paris, then nothing. Tante Clara – that was what Natasha called her – said they must have been deported and we all know now that meant to a concentration camp.'

'But how did Hannah survive? Why wasn't she picked up, too?'

'Because she was dark, but not Jewish; didn't have the Jewish nose. Do you know, darling, that the Nazis had an instrument for measuring noses? Natasha's real mother had given her a tip-tilted nose. It saved her life, I suppose.'

'So can you tell me why you went to France? Did you even once consider the risk you were taking?'

'I did. It was the only way for me to get back home from Washington. I was stuck there and I nagged them until they said okay, that I could go back to the UK as soon as a passage could be found for me.

But there were conditions attached, they said.'

'Conditions like you owed them one, sort of?'

'That's it. Because I was a mathematician, I worked in the cipher department at the British Embassy in Washington. They knew I had knowledge about – well – a certain machine. Very secret, really.'

'Mm. Talk had it where Lyn and I worked in the war, there was a secret machine there, too. So secret, in fact, they had an armed Marine sentry always outside the door. I didn't see it. Wasn't even allowed near the *door* . . .'

'Sounds as if it could have been like the one I'd been sent to collect. They called it Enigma, and because I'd worked on a similar one in Washington, they thought I was the best bloke to collect the special one from France. Special, because our lot could only break German Army messages and their Luftwaffe messages. We needed to be able to break their naval code. It was urgent. We were losing too many merchant ships in the Atlantic.'

'I know, Keth. I spent my war in Liverpool, don't forget, and I know that the underground bunker I worked in looked after ships in the Western Approaches and the Atlantic. Looked after! Half of every convoy was sunk!'

'So you'll realize the importance of the naval Enigma I was sent to collect. And don't ask me how it was come by. All I know is that when I got it back, I was told they'd only recently acquired another. I hit the roof. Asked the fellow there if he wanted a matching pair for his mantelpiece, or something, and did he know that a kid of sixteen had been shot, getting

122

me and his precious bloody machine onto a Lysander to fly it back to England?

'But he only said that things like that happened when there was a war on and that sailors had been killed, too, getting the other one. A right swine, he was. Hard as nails. I thought I'd blotted my copybook good and proper and that he'd send me back to Washington, out of spite. But he didn't. I was debriefed, warned to keep my mouth shut, or else' – he pulled a finger across his throat – 'then sent back to Bletchley Park.'

'So you were in England for a time and I never knew it, Keth?'

'That's right. I couldn't even phone you. I was told to write letters as if I were still in Washington and they doctored them to look as if they'd been posted there. That's why I shouldn't be telling you this. It's why our little girl is called Mary Natasha and why you must never speak of it to anyone but me.'

'And it's why you need to go back to Clissy-sur-Mer?'

'Yes. To try to find Natasha's grave – if they gave her a decent burial, that is. And I need to know – or at least my conscience needs to know – what happened to Tante Clara and Denys and Bernadette, too. Bernadette was a wireless operator for the Resistance. I never knew what Denys did, only that he and Natasha took me to a field at the back of the chateau and put down landing lights for the Lysander pilot to see. Two minutes was all that pilot was allowed to land, get me on board, then take off. I try not to think of it . . .'

'But you do, Keth, all the time, and it's why you must go back to France just as soon as restrictions are lifted. You and I have so much, darling, and I want you to go, if only to say a thank you, and a thank you for me, too, to those people who hid you and got you safely back. I owe Natasha, as well. I wish there were some way of letting her know. And I won't say a word. You know I can keep secrets.'

'Like your money? I know you won't talk about it, ever, though one other person knows. Y'see, when it was all over and done with and before I went back to Bletchley Park, I was given leave.'

'Yes. I got leave, too. We wangled a night together. But who did you tell, Keth? You were taking a risk, weren't you?'

'Not really. It was Nathan Sutton I told. I felt so bad about it and that I was safe back in England when a whole lot of people at Clissy were almost certainly arrested and interrogated. Maybe even shot. I couldn't square it with my conscience until I'd told someone. Nathan was a priest. We went for a walk to the top of the Pike and he got the lot. I felt better for telling him and I knew he would treat it like a confession – sacrosanct. Knowing Nathan, he wouldn't even tell your Aunt Julia.'

'No. Not him. But can we talk about it again, when it won't be quite so bad for either of us? There's so much I want to know, but my mind's in a spin. It's a shock, knowing we might never have married, or had Mary; that you might never have got back.'

'Sobering thought, isn't it? And worse than that, even, was Natasha getting the bullet that was meant for me. A bit of a lass, and far braver than I was.'

'So that's why you'll go back, darling. And I want you to. Just you and your conscience and your thoughts. It'll help. I know it will.' She lifted his hand, kissing his palm then closing his fingers around the kiss. 'And do you know how much I love you, Keth Purvis?'

'As much as I love you, Daisy love. And thanks for understanding, and that it's best I go alone – maybe after the wedding, in the Whit school holidays.'

'Whenever, darling. But right now, will you kiss me, then hold me tightly and tell me you love me and that you'll never do anything so stupid again.'

'I won't. I promise.' He kissed her gently, then again, passionately, and she kissed him back. 'Have we got time, darling? Before Mary wakes for her ten o'clock feed?' she said softly, lips against his ear. Then she kissed his eyes, the tip of his nose, his mouth. 'Have we?' she whispered huskily.

EIGHT

'That wouldn't be coffee?' Ewart Pryce raised an eyebrow to the percolator that slurped lazily on the stove.

'It *would*. Real grounds. Got a quarter of a pound, yesterday. Things are looking up. Time for a cup?' Anna lifted her cheek for her husband's kiss.

'Please. Not many in the surgery this morning, and only three visits. So what's news?'

'Not so good. Two bad bits in the paper. National Service increased from a year to eighteen months and the King and Queen aren't going to Australia. Seems the King isn't very well. Any idea what the matter is?'

'Haven't a clue, darling. Buckingham Palace haven't consulted me.' His eyes lit on the envelope and the large, old-fashioned writing in black ink. Always black ink. 'Your mother . . . ?'

'Mama has decided to come to the wedding, but must decline my offer of a bed. She will be staying at Denniston House, she says, and has written to tell Tatiana. Ewart, *why* can't she stay with us? Tatty is going to be busy enough without two house guests – even if they are family. Igor won't be any trouble, but Mama will complain. She always does.'

'She's an old lady, darling, and she misses Russia.'

'So do I. So does Igor, but we don't go on and on about it. To me, Russia is a long way away and a long time away. My daughter is as English as they come, and as for myself – well, I'm happy being the wife of a country doctor, even if Mama thinks I've lowered myself into the middle classes.'

'The old get bewildered, Anna. She lost her husband and a son in the uprising.'

'Yes, thirty years ago, but she's still in mourning. She likes being unhappy, but I'm glad she'll be there to see her granddaughter married. Karl will look after them when Bill and Tatty leave for their honeymoon, and I'll keep an eye on things – tactfully, of course. And I've got to fly, or I'll miss the bus. Going to Creesby for a final fitting and to pick up my wedding hat.'

'You're looking forward to it, aren't you, darling?'

'I am. And if Tatty's half as happy as I am with my middle-class marriage, she can consider herself lucky. Heavens! Is that the time! See you, Doctor dear!'

With a banging of doors she was gone, and Ewart smiled fondly, whispering, 'And I love you too, Anastasia Aleksandrina Pryce,' then poured himself another cup of coffee.

'Letter from Lyn?' Julia asked. 'Everything all right at her end?'

'Complications, actually,' Drew frowned. 'Her folks are arriving on the fifteenth of December.'

'So what's complicated about that?'

'Nothing at all. She's looking forward to seeing her mother – and her father. Be interesting, that, since she hasn't seen him since she was a schoolgirl. Trouble is though, what with one thing and another I won't be seeing Lyn till Tatty's wedding. Seems she's swapping her shifts around so she can get time off for that. Not a lot of good, this long-distance courting.'

'So why must it always be Lyn who comes here? Hasn't it ever occurred to you to shift yourself and go to her place? And if it's going to use up too many petrol coupons, get yourself on the train, for heaven's sake, like Lyn does.'

'I'd thought about that a couple of times but decided against it. After all, Lyn lives in a little village. There'd be sure to be talk.'

'Andrew Sutton, I don't believe it! Girls don't need chaperoning, now! And why are you suddenly so holier-than-thou? I'm sure Lyn wouldn't mind losing her reputation – even if nothing happened.'

'Now it's my turn not to believe it! Are you suggesting a dirty weekend or something, and you a priest's wife!'

'Drew! I'm beginning to lose patience with you. Dirty weekend, indeed! You make it sound sordid, and it shouldn't be. Not between you and Lyn. And did I suggest you sleep together? I merely said that *you* should go and see *her* once in a while. Why should Lyn do all the running about?'

'I think she comes here because that's the way she wants it.'

'You're sure? Has she said so?'

'N-no. Not in so many words, but wouldn't she ask me if she wanted me there?'

'She's your fiancée, Drew. Does she have to ask you?'

'I suppose not, but – oh, hell, Mother, I don't know. Sometimes, I just don't know!'

He got to his feet, walking to the window, hands in pockets and Julia knew, from the set stiffness of his shoulders, that now was the time to ask.

'Don't know what? That everything isn't as it should be, that you made a mistake? Is that what you're trying to say, Drew?'

'Of course I haven't made a mistake. I want to marry Lyn. But does she think the same way? And I ask that because I know something isn't quite right. She's gone on the defensive, kind of. It's as if she's all at once shy with me. It was better between us when I used to take her out, in Liverpool. When Daisy was on leave, I mean, and the two of us got on just fine.

'Lyn was fun, then. She laughed a lot and we did mad things; ate fish and chips out of newspaper and went to Charlie's, on the Pierhead, for a mug of tea and a cheese sandwich. Wads, we called them.'

'Yes, Drew, but that was before Kitty. If what I heard is to be believed, Lyn was in love with you even then; had hopes that someday, things between you might develop, sort of.'

'I've asked her to marry me. Surely that's development enough? But I don't think she's as sure of

129

her feelings, now. Oh, outwardly things are fine between us, but there's a wariness in her eyes. I can see it.'

'Look, Drew – I've got letters to post. Walk with me, to the village?'

Out of the house, Julia thought, it might be better. Outside, neither of them would be able to show anger, annoyance.

'Okay. Could do with a breath of fresh air.'

'Then shall we go through Brattocks and down the lane, the long way round? Might be as well, if we did. Get things into the open, sort of. And I know you need to talk to me – talk to someone, Drew – though heaven only knows why it can't be to Lyn. You were always easy in her company. What's gone wrong?'

'I wish I knew.'

'Mind if I make a suggestion? Could it be that suddenly Lyn is worried that she can't follow Kitty? Have you and Lyn been lovers?'

'No, we haven't.' He closed the door behind them with an unnecessary bang. 'Once, we might have been but not now, it seems.'

Not since the night, outside Wrens' quarters, that Lyn had told him she loved him, wanted him. Offered it, actually, though nothing happened because he hadn't been quite sure. Of himself, that was. It was as if he'd known, even then, that he was waiting for Kitty. But he couldn't say that. Not to his mother. Not to anyone. There were things you just didn't talk about, and that was one of them.

'Once? Before that night you met up with Kitty? You were very sure, about *her*.'

'Very sure. She knocked me for six. I'd loved her all my life, and I hadn't known it. We spent the night together and it was so easy, so right. Are you shocked?'

'Shocked? And what makes you think that only you and Kitty knew about love? I loved like that, once. When Andrew and I were apart, all I could think of was soft, sinful double beds. And I would have, even before we were married, but Andrew counted to ten for both of us! I know what it's like to love desperately in wartime, so don't think I'm uptight about you and Kitty. I was young, too, don't forget.'

'Then you married Nathan, Mother?'

'Yes. I married him because I loved him. Differently, I'll grant you, and the only mistake I made was not doing it sooner. I can talk about Andrew now with affection, and Nathan accepts that. Does Kitty have to come between you and Lyn, Drew, because it seems she is!'

'Not as far as I'm concerned, she isn't. But there was a war on when Kitty and I were together. No tomorrows, remember . . .'

'I remember. God Himself knows I remember, but if you can't convince Lyn that it's her you are marrying, then things aren't going to get any better. You've got to be sure – *both of you*.'

'I'm sure, Mother, but I know Lyn isn't. Not entirely. She wanted the wedding changed from June to April. I don't think she wants to carry white orchids, either. She said that June seemed to her to

131

be a remembering month; that it was in June Kitty and I should have been married and another June when Kitty was killed. And it's every June that Jack Catchpole puts a bouquet on her grave. Can you blame Lyn for getting the jitters?'

'No, I can't,' Julia said softly. 'But I blame you, Drew, for letting her have doubts. Don't you think it's about time you sorted things between you?'

'So what do you suggest I do?'

'*Do?* You get yourself over to Wales this next weekend, show willing for once. Lyn can't come to you, so you must go to her! And I don't mean you should both leap into bed. Far from it. It seems Lyn is unsure enough, without you making it worse. Just be with her, Drew. Talk to her, because she sure as anything wants to talk to *you*! Be nice to her and if you've got to, eat fish and chips out of newspaper!'

'You're right. You usually are, dearest. But in what way do you think Lyn is unsure? Might help a bit, if I knew.'

'I'd bet anything you like that she's unsure about herself; unsure because she's a virgin, still, and she's afraid you'll compare her to Kitty.'

'Oh, no. I can't accept that! Lyn was always very blasé; completely sure of herself.'

'Well, for what my opinion is worth, she isn't so sure about things now. Lyn is a woman in love and she's afraid of losing you. I think she fell in love with you the first time you met and nothing has changed, I'm pretty sure of it.'

She dropped the letters in the pillar box, then turned for home.

'My, but it's cold. One good thing about late November is that there are very few people about. No one stops you for a chat! Let's go to the kitchen, and sweetheart a pot of tea out of Tilda?'

And Drew smiled and said, 'Y'know, for someone who isn't a mother, you've made a pretty good job of being mine. And I'll go to Llangollen this weekend – surprise her.'

'Yes, and get something sorted out, eh? Clear the air, why don't you?'

'Clear the air,' Drew nodded, though how, exactly, he wasn't sure. Play things by ear, should he? Alone together in that little house, things just might be different. He would have to go carefully, for all that, because he didn't want to lose Lyn; would never forgive himself if he said the wrong thing and got his ring thrown back at him for his pains.

Dear Lyn, who had always loved him.

Drew stowed away his bag, then laid the flowers carefully on top of it, thankful he was on the last leg of his journey. Change at Manchester, change at Chester for Wrexham; bus from there to Lyn's place. And she had done it every weekend she could get away, bless the girl.

But he was bearing gifts. Tom had given him a young pheasant, plucked and ready for roasting. Alice had sent a new-baked loaf and Tilda had scraped enough rations together to make a baking of cherry scones and wrapped four in greaseproof paper, with her love. And Willis had sent chrysanthemum blooms because he feared frost, soon, and those he couldn't dig up and plant again in the shelter of the green-house, he had cut for folk deserving of them.

'There's ten tawnies for your intended, Sir Andrew. Match that hair of hers,' Sidney Willis had chuckled. 'Sent with compliments. And mind you don't knock their heads off between here and there. Very top-heavy those big blooms are.'

Tawny, to match her hair. Lyn was very beautiful; had the green eyes and porcelain skin of a true redhead. And in summer her face freckled – on her cheekbones and across her nose.

He had thought often, lately, about her body and how it would be. Her naked body, that was. He had never seen her anything but well covered. At first in thick black stockings and shirt and collar and tie; latterly in civilian clothes, true, but only in his imaginings had he seen her naked, in bed, in his arms.

The conductor of the green bus interrupted his thoughts, asking where to, and a return or a single, was it? And Drew handed him the correct money and was told that in five minutes he would be at Croes-y-Dwfr, which he knew to be the crossroads near the hamlet in which Lyn lived. Only a few more minutes and she would open the door and say, 'Hullo, sailor!' like she used to and he would wonder how he could ever have thought things weren't right between them.

But she didn't say it. She just stood there, eyes wide, and whispered, 'Drew? What is it? Why have you come?' then stood aside to let him in.

'Come, idiot? To see my girl!' He laid bag and flowers on the floor. 'Don't I get a kiss?'

'Of course you do!' Laughing, she was in his arms,

eyes closed, lips parted. 'It was just that I didn't expect you – didn't think I'd see you for ages.' Her cheeks pinked, her eyes shone. 'Oh, Drew *cariad*, there's lovely to see you!' she laughed breathlessly when they had kissed and kissed again. 'And how did you know I'd just put the kettle on?'

And Drew was all at once certain that given a little time together sitting close in the firelight and kissing sometimes, and laughing too, things would be as they had once been when he kissed her a passionate good-night on the stone steps of Hellas House – and she had told him she loved him.

'Flowers,' he said, giving her the chrysanthemums. 'From Willis.'

And Lyn thanked him and told him to take off his jacket and get himself to the fire, for a warm. Then went in search of a vase.

They shared a tin of tomato soup and a tin of baked beans for supper, eked out with thick slices of the Keeper's Cottage loaf.

'There's no one bakes bread like Daisy's Mum,' Lyn said.

'You are speaking, if I may say so, to the converted. We used to smell baking day from the other end of Brattocks, then swoop on Keeper's for bread and honey. Like a swarm of locusts, we must have been.'

'We? The Clan?'

'Yes, but I'm not here to talk about when we were kids, darling. I came because I wanted to see you and to talk about you and me.'

'Like . . . ?'

'Like – we-e-ll, the wedding, for one thing.' Dammit, she was icing up again. 'And for another, I want to know what happened to the girl I asked to marry me. There now, Lyn, I've said it. I'm looking, I suppose, for the Wren who was good at passionate goodnights.'

'That Wren was demobbed ages ago. The war's over, Drew, and I'm going to wash the supper things.'

She got to her feet but he caught her wrist and held it tightly.

'No! The washing up can wait. Sit down – please?'

'Very well.' She positioned herself awkwardly on the edge of the sofa, so he was obliged to lay an arm around her and pull her closer. 'But it seems to me, Drew, you're making a drama out of nothing.'

'I don't think I am.' He could feel the tenseness in her shoulders, see the defiant tilt of her chin. 'Something's upsetting you, something isn't quite right between us and I want to know what it is. I've a right to know.'

'So what do you want to hear?'

'That you haven't changed your mind, that you still want to marry me.'

'You know I do! Oh, hell, Drew . . .'

She let go a sigh and closed her eyes and he knew she was fighting tears.

'Don't get upset, Lyn? Please don't cry? Just tell me what it is and I'll understand.'

'You want to know? You really want to know, Drew Sutton?' She pushed him away from her, then faced him defiantly, cheeks flushed. 'I'm jealous of Kitty, I suppose. And I know I'm being stupid, but that's what it really boils down to. I've never been with a man before and I'm going to mess up our wedding night because I don't know how to do it!'

'Most brides don't know, either,' he said gently.

'Oh? Daisy knew, didn't she? And Kitty knew.'

'Yes, and I thought Lyn Carmichael was pretty curious, too. What happened to the passionate redhead? You were eager enough, then.'

'I know. We were pretty good together, once. I thought you felt as I felt and I wanted you Drew, and to hell with what might happen. I didn't care if I got pregnant, that's how much I wanted you. But you patted my behind and steered me towards the Wrennery door. After I'd said I loved you like some silly little bitch, you didn't want me.'

'I'm truly sorry I hurt you, Lyn, but why have you changed?'

'Because that night, it would have been all right between us. Neither of us would have known what we were doing. I knew you were a virgin, too, and that the first time might have been a bit of a fumble, but we'd have understood. It's different, now. For me, it is.'

'I'm sorry you feel like that. Don't you think it's about time we put all this behind us and started out afresh – like we both felt the night you said you'd marry me? And does it matter when our wedding night is? Do you want us to be lovers before April? I don't care, Lyn, about all that virginity lark. There's been a war on and people are more broadminded about things like that. I thought you were a very modern woman; that you'd understand.'

137

'Oh, yes? Lyn Carmichael should know all about sex before marriage, is that it? Auntie Blod stood by whilst the father of her unborn child married her twin sister! Carrying on should be bred in me, should it?'

'Oh, God, Lyn!' He threw up his hands despairingly, then brought them down with a slap on his knees. 'You told me just as soon as you found out that Auntie Blod was your real mother and it didn't make one blind bit of difference then, and it doesn't now. I liked your mother – your Auntie Blod – the minute I met her and I still like her. I'm looking forward to seeing her – and meeting your father, of course.'

'Me, too. Years since I saw him, but he seems to have aged very gracefully, if snaps are to be believed.' She grasped the get-out. Talk about anything, Lyn, but the fact that Kitty and Drew were good together, once. 'I had a letter this morning; written the day before they left. They should be well on their way, now. It's going to be a wonderful Christmas for me. My parents married at last, and staying with me. One of their cases, I believe, is packed full of unrationed food.'

'So will they go back to Kenya? Well, the wedding is in April – will it be worth two journeys?'

'I don't know what is happening, Drew. I only know that in less than three weeks, they'll be here.'

'Would you all like to come to Rowangarth for Christmas? The mothers are going to have a lot to talk about.'

'Sorry, Drew. New Year, maybe? It's just that I think that Mam would like Christmas here – with

138

her husband. She's so happy, now. I should be mad at my father for getting her pregnant then marrying her sister, but I can't be. And anyway, it wasn't entirely his fault. Auntie Blod didn't tell him till it was too late. But I really am going to wash the supper dishes, and tidy the kitchen. It's a routine I've got into, so you'd best give me a hand.'

'Okay. But only if you kiss me.'

He held out his hands, drawing her to her feet, gathering her to him, holding her close. Then he kissed her long and hard and felt her body relax against his.

'Don't, Drew,' she said huskily, pulling her head away.

'Why not? I like kissing you. You're very good at it, when you put your mind to it.' He kissed her again, all at once wanting her. 'Leave the dishes, Lyn? Let's go upstairs?'

'No, Drew. Remember the night we got engaged – it was me put the words into your mouth, wasn't it? And now you think I want to sleep with you because I reminded you I'm still a virgin and not sure how it would be between us, on our first night? Well, you're wrong, and if you came all the way here just for *that*, then you'd better pack your bags and take your flowers and your bloody pheasant with you, and shove off. Sorry, sailor, but that's the way it is, so stop patronizing me if you know what's good for you!'

She ran across the room and he heard the urgent pounding of her feet on the stairs and the angry closing of the upstairs door. And worse than that, he heard the unmistakable slamming home of a door bolt.

'So what do you do now, Drew?' he asked of the empty room that for all that seemed full of her anger. Coming here hadn't been such a good idea after all. Or had it, and was it he who had loused things up? Didn't Lyn have every right to say no to him? After all, he'd done just that to her, once. Maybe it would be all right in the morning – honours even, sort of? Maybe tomorrow they could kiss and make up and things would start to come right between them? He hoped so, because if it didn't . . .

But best leave it. Tomorrow was another day, wasn't it? Yet surely tomorrow never came? They had said that, in the war. Tomorrow was a word they tried not to use.

But the war was over; over, but not forgotten it would seem, so best put the whole stupid mess behind him and get himself off to bed. He knew where the little spare room was, had slept there in the war, when once he and Lyn had hitched from the Pierhead to the crossroads that led to Auntie Blod's place. No problem, there. Pity he couldn't turn the clock back to that long ago weekend.

But time couldn't be turned back, and anyway did he really want to? Did he want to wipe out the months spent with Kitty and their urgent and unashamed loving?

Of course he didn't. Kitty had happened and he would never forget her. It would be wrong of him to try. And the hurt he felt when the letter came, telling him, was behind him now. Kitty was sleeping away time in the churchyard at All Souls; sleeping beside Gran. Kitty was gone, except for the small, secret corner of his heart that would always belong to her. And he was going to marry Lyn. In April.

He put the guard over the fire, then walked to the stair bottom, turning out the lamp, making his way carefully to the little back room. There was no light beneath Lyn's door. She had shut him out completely; no use knocking.

He lay, hands behind head, for a long time, fighting sleep, willing her to come to him, wanting to lie close to her, soothe her doubts, kiss her fears away, take her gently and with love. But when the downstairs clock chimed once, he knew that tomorrow had come and there would be no opening of the door, no one whispering, 'Drew? Are you awake . . . ?'

'So, Drew – how did it go? Got things sorted?' Julia asked. 'We can talk, now. Nathan won't be back from Evensong till eight, at least. No one will interrupt us. And if you don't want to tell me,' she added hastily, 'I shall understand, of course.'

'There's nothing to tell, Mother. Lyn was pleased to see me when I got there and I tried to get her to tell me what was bothering her; because I knew something was, I told her. And it all came out, eventually. What it boils down to is that she's jealous of Kitty – of Kitty's memory, I mean. And that she and I were lovers. That's what I think hurts Lyn most. I tried to sort things; tried to get her to talk, but –'

'But you made a mess of it?'

'I'll never earn a living in the Diplomatic Corps, that's for sure. I asked her to go to bed with me and

141

that was it! Door slammed in my face. I waited a bit; didn't know what to do. Was hoping she would come to me, but no such luck. Anyway, things were better in the morning. I thought she had got over whatever it was, even though she didn't seem to want to look me in the eye.

'So I said, "Doesn't a man get a decent good-morning from his girl, then?" and she smiled, and kissed me and said she was sorry. What for, mind, I had the sense not to ask. It was a decent day. I walked with her to the hotel, then went back to the cottage. She had left the pheasant doing slowly in the oven and instructions about basting it and to take it out if I thought it was overcooking. She was back at four. I'd peeled the potatoes and sprouts and put apples in to bake.'

'Good for you. Didn't know you had it in you,' Julia grinned.

'Mother! I did six years in the Navy, below decks. We all had to muck in, especially on the *Maggie* where everyone had to help out. But we had a good meal and I washed up and Lyn dried, then we listened to the wireless. There was dance music on, but we didn't dance.'

'Why not?' Julia demanded sharply.

'No room.'

'Drew! You don't need a ballroom! Dancing, when people are in love, is holding each other, even if you've only got a hearthrug to dance on. Better, that way. Andrew and I often danced without music, without moving, even. Very romantic . . .'

'Mother! You don't have to tell me how to romance

142

a girl! Of course I wanted to hold her; we danced a lot together, once. But I was scared she'd slam down the blinds again, so I behaved myself. I kissed her goodnight, and this morning she was working ten till four, same as yesterday, so I left her at the hotel and got the first bus out. Not what you'd call a successful weekend, but at least I know now what's bothering her.'

'And you know how best to deal with it? Given it some thought, have you then?'

'I have, but it isn't going to be a lot of good, is it, when we aren't going to see each other till Tatty's wedding. She's looking forward to it. Says her folks will have arrived by then and she won't mind leaving them on their own for a couple of days. They'll probably enjoy it, she said.'

'So, until the wedding, you're going to have to write to her a lot, tell her how much you love her. Pity she isn't on the phone. She should be, you know, alone in an isolated cottage. Can't you try doing something about it?'

'She's on the waiting list, Mother. Unless something happened like she was pregnant and there alone, she's got to wait, like other people.'

'When are we going to meet her parents?' Julia changed tack abruptly because she knew she might explode if they didn't talk about something else. 'And what does Lyn call her mother – is it Auntie Blod, still?'

'Most times it is. But I think when she sees them together and finally realizes they are married, *churched*, Lyn called it, she'll call her Mum, eventually. Churched, eh? Lyn's got a wicked sense of humour, you know. She's fun to be with, apart from being very – well, very attractive.'

'She's a lovely young woman and you're not half-bad, yourself. You'll have beautiful children, Drew.'

'Ha! *Children*, you said. The way we're going on, they'll be immaculately conceived!'

'That wasn't funny. You're going to have to learn to be patient with Lyn. I like her; have always liked her, and I won't be best pleased if you lose her through being stupid.'

'I won't lose her, Mother. I love her too much.'

'Then keep on telling her. Write lines and lines of it in every letter. And I'm sorry, son, for going on.' She ruffled his hair like she did when he was a boy. 'You see, I care for you both so much and I know you'll be happy together. I'm even having lovely little daydreams about a granddaughter with hair the colour of Lyn's. Stupid old woman, aren't I?'

'Stupid? Not you, dearest. And old – never! And I'll be patient with Lyn, don't worry.'

He would be, he thought later when he was in bed and thinking about the weekend, and Lyn. And about not seeing her until Tatty's wedding. And about telling her he loved her, because he did. He loved her a lot, even though he hadn't told her so.

And that wasn't on. Not asking a girl to go to bed with you and you not ever having said 'I love you'. It wasn't an accident, either. He wanted to say it, but every time he tried, the words wouldn't come. It should be easy to say, just as he was thinking it, now.

I love you, Lyn Carmichael. I love you, love you, love you . . .

Then why hadn't he told her so?

NINE

Drew sat in the winter parlour, Lyn's letter on his knee. She must have written it immediately he left on Sunday; at work almost certainly, since it was on hotel headed notepaper and folded into an envelope bearing the name *Riverstones Hotel, Llangollen* on the flap. It was as well, he thought, that he had written to her that same Sunday evening; that their letters had almost certainly crossed in the post.

My darling Lyn, he had written.

I am back at Rowangarth and wondering what happened this weekend, and why things were still up in the air when I left you.

I wish you would open your heart to me completely; we are going to be married, Lyn, and there must be no secrets between us, no doubts.

For my own part, I can't wait for our wedding day. If thoughts of a big wedding upset you, we can have a quiet one – just you and me and families, it truly doesn't matter one iota.

If, by asking you to sleep with me on Friday night, I offended you, then I am sorry. Fact is, that I wanted you very much; wanted to hold you close and, if nothing else, to awake in the morning with you beside me.

I know you are apprehensive about things and we must talk about it next time we meet which should be on Dec 17th for Tatty's wedding. How long will you be able to stay?

This is a muddle of a letter. What I am really trying to tell you is that I want you, only you, and that I love you very much.

I won't ask you to ring me; don't want you going to the phone box in the dark, but I will try to get through to you at work. And yes, I know private calls are not allowed to staff, but hard luck! I will still try to get through.

Take care of yourself, cariad. *Write to me soon.*

Always,

It had been easy to tell her he loved her; easy to write it down on paper, and next time they met the first thing he would say – after he had kissed her – would be 'I love you, Lyn Carmichael. I will always love you.'

He wished they were not so far apart, wondered at the cussed independence that made her want to work until a few weeks before the wedding. As far as he was concerned, she could hand in her notice tomorrow and come to Holdenby; stay at Rowangarth or, if she preferred it, with Daisy and Keth. He just wanted them to be together like two ordinary, normal people, planning to get married soon.

He picked up Lyn's letter to him, hearing her voice with an ever so slight Welsh accent, as he read it.

Dearest Drew,

You have gone, and I am wondering what it was all about; how we could act like a couple of idiots – you by asking me to sleep with you, me for refusing.

I will ring you on Tuesday when I finish work. Can you hang around between 4 and 5 p.m?

Why was I such a fool? Why do I love you so much, Drew Sutton?

In haste, and with love,

He sighed, relieved. She still loved him. Tomorrow night, with luck, she would be able to ring before it got too dark; from a phone box near the hotel, he hoped. She would be all right; had endured the Liverpool blackout for years, hadn't come to any harm. Now at least there were lights again in streets and on cars.

He did love her; was weary of being alone and having his aloneness magnified by Keth and Daisy and Tatty and Bill. He wanted to be the other half of a couple, needed Lyn beside him always. Lyn wanted children, and he was glad about that. Children at Rowangarth, wanted and loved. He wondered if his son would be fair as most Suttons were, or would come with Lyn's red hair. It would be good to be like

Keth and Daisy, have a child of his own. Wouldn't be long, now, before Bas and Gracie had another baby. Two or three weeks.

The phone rang and he hurried to answer it.

'Hi, bruv.'

'Oh, it's you, Daiz.'

'Were you expecting it to be Lyn, or something?'

'No. She's ringing tomorrow. What's news?'

'Bill and Tatty are here. I know you are on your own, so get yourself over to Foxgloves. Okay?'

Good old Daiz. She would want to know what had happened at Lyn's place and he wouldn't be able to tell her with Tatty and Bill there. Which was just as well, because all he was prepared to say was that everything was fine; that they'd had a good weekend. And what was more, she could make of it whatever she wanted, the nosy little madam!

All at once he felt good, felt that things would come right for him and Lyn and that the next time they met, all would be back to normal – or as near normal as he could make them.

On the notepad he wrote, *Gone to Foxgloves. Got a key. D.* Then he took a torch, shrugged into a warm jacket. With petrol saving in mind he decided to walk there; skirting the wild garden, over the iron fence into the lane, past All Souls and the vicarage, then onto the Creesby road.

There were two houses on that road; Ewart Pryce's house and surgery, and Foxgloves just off it. In all probability, Tatty had been visiting her mother and decided to call on Daisy, too.

The night was frosty, the sky full of stars. Drew

pulled his muffler up to his ears, and strode out. He felt good to be seeing Daisy and Keth and Tatty and Bill. With only three weeks to wait, Tatty would be all wedding talk; Keth would want to chat, still, about his new car and Daisy, who had turned into a mother, would either be ironing baby clothes, or talking about Mary. Life, when you looked it in the face, could be pretty good from where he was standing.

Daisy was indeed ironing when Drew got to Foxgloves; Bill sat in an armchair by the fire, Tatiana at his feet. On Keth's knee lay Mary Natasha.

'Hullo, Miss Purvis. Why aren't you in bed?' Drew smiled.

Mary could focus her eyes properly now, Daisy had said, and turn her head in the direction of sound, which she did, fixing Drew with a brown-eyed gaze.

'She's had a tummy ache, and awful wind. My fault,' Daisy shrugged. 'I ate too many sprouts yesterday. Seems Mary doesn't like them as much as I do. But she's fine, now; won't be long before she's asleep. Take a pew, bruv.'

Drew sat, head back, sprawling his feet in the direction of the fire.

'Guess what, Drew?' Tatty said. 'The Petrovska phoned. She's not only coming to the wedding, but she's arriving on the fifteenth and staying, would you believe, over Christmas and the New Year!'

'Oh dear,' Drew grinned. 'Serves you right for getting married!'

He fended off a flying cushion, then thought again how lucky he was to have all this; how good that

Lyn would soon be a part of it. Not a part of the Clan, exactly, but an honorary member like Gracie and Bill.

Yes, indeed. Life, from where he was sitting all comfortable and warm, was *very* good.

'Mind if we leave the door a little open, Mother? Lyn is ringing me after work – between four and five, it should be.'

'Hm. There were letters from her yesterday and this morning. Hope you are writing back promptly. Will you be going to see her next weekend, too?'

'No. We talked about it but she's working extra shifts, getting time in hand for when her folks arrive – and for New Year, too. She'll be spending Christmas with them, but I'd like it if they could all stay here for New Year. Is that all right with you, Mother?'

'We'll be in the Bothy by then, God willing. Do you want them to stay with Nathan and me, or would you like to put them up at Rowangarth? It might be as well if they stayed with you. Tilda and Mary like having people to fuss over. And Lyn has never stayed here. Might be a good time for her to start getting to like it.'

'She likes it already, though I don't think she's all that keen to be Lady Sutton. I told her she'd get used to it. And I don't think she'll ever be referred to as her ladyship, as Gran was.'

'Your gran was special – one of the old order. Not like – we-e-ll, not like some.'

'Like your Aunt Clemmy, you mean? Dearest, there *couldn't* be two Clementina Suttons. Wasn't she a dragon? Bas was terrified of her, though Kitty just loved to annoy her. Kitty was – oh, dear. There I go again!'

'Look, Drew, you can't go walking on eggshells all your life. We talk about your gran and Clemmy, don't we, without saying "Oops!". If Kitty's name is taboo, then Lyn's always going to have a thing about her. And I know what I'm talking about. I was that way about Andrew being killed. There was anger at first; vicious anger. Ours was a special love that had been wiped out by a land mine – and a week before the war ended. I wasted a lot of years being bitter. Kitty wouldn't want you to waste your life as I did. Lyn will accept her, given time – and understanding.'

'I know she will. If she wants, we can have a quiet wedding like Tatty and Bill. I told her so. Can't wait for April and there she is! Talk of angels!'

He hurried towards the phone, closing the door behind him. 'Hi, Lyn. Where are you?'

'In the phone box, idiot – at Croes-y-Dwfr. Thank you for your letter, darling!'

'Thank you for yours. Both of them. But what's news? Got anything to tell me.'

'News? I'll say I've got news! Got a cablegram from the folks! They're arriving at Southampton on the fifteenth of December – in two weeks, Drew! I can't think straight. I didn't know how much I missed Auntie Blod, but now they're on their way – well, isn't it just great?'

'Wonderful news, darling. I'll be able to meet your father, get to know him – ask him for your hand in marriage.'

152

'Yes, and I'll have to get to know him, too. Do you realize the last time I saw him was when he handed me over to the ship's nurse at Mombasa with never a mention that I wouldn't be going home to Kenya again. Mind, I might have gone back, sometimes, if it hadn't been for the war. And here is my home, now.' There was a small silence, then she said, 'I'm blabbering on, aren't I?'

'Just a little – because you're excited. But have you anything else to tell me, darling?'

'Yes, that I'm sorry for spoiling things at the weekend and that I love you very much.'

'And I love you, Lyn.'

'What was that? Couldn't quite hear you.'

'I said,' he cleared his throat, then said loudly, 'I love you, Lyn.'

'Good. That's what I thought you said first time. Great to hear you say it twice in the space of thirty seconds!'

'Do you want your bottom spanked, Miss!'

'Oh, *please*. I like it when you get bossy!'

'Lyn, be serious. Your folks arriving on the fifteenth – does it mean you won't be here for the wedding?'

'Of course not! I'm coming to Daisy's on the seventeenth. They'll have got themselves settled in, by then. Maybe they'll like being on their own for a couple of days.'

'Two days? Is that all you can manage?'

'Afraid so. I'm a working girl, don't forget. And I'd like to have Christmas in Wales with the parents, though if it's all right at your end, can we all have New Year at Rowangarth?'

'Good idea. Can just see the mothers – all wedding talk. Mother and Lady are at it all the time. Tom and Nathan are going to leave home, they say, if there's much more of it!'

'Well, Auntie Blod – *Mum* – will just adore it. And darling, I'll have to go. Got no more sixpences left. I love you.'

'And I love you – there now, that's three times I've told you! Take care, darling. Try to ring again, soon . . .'

'That was Lyn,' Drew smiled, holding his hands to the fire. 'That hall is like an ice house.'

'Well, of course it is. Coal is rationed, remember? Everything all right?'

'Fine. Lyn's folks are arriving on the fifteenth, but she's still coming to the wedding. Can only manage two days and I suppose she'll be staying with Daisy. But she did ask if they could all spend New Year here. I said she could. Is that all right, dearest?'

'I've already said it is. Rowangarth is your house, but the Bothy isn't far away. We can have some get-togethers and lovely long chats. I think your wedding will be Nathan's last. He wants to retire and Arthur Reid has been curate here for long enough. Nathan will be glad to hand over to him.'

'Couldn't agree more. But I'd like it if Nathan christened our children. Can he do that, if he's retired?'

'I suppose he can still do baptisms. After all, if a midwife thinks a newborn baby is in danger of dying and can't get a priest in time, she can baptize it herself. So there's no reason why a retired vicar can't do the odd christening. And I know that, because I was once –'

'Yes, Mother. Once a nurse. You still think about those days, don't you?'

'Sometimes. They were terrible times, but we got through them, Alice and me. I was proud to be at the Front – and terrified out of my life, sometimes. But we were young, then – it seems now it was another life.'

'How old are you?'

'I'm fifty-five, you know I am, and Alice is three years younger. And it isn't gentlemanly to ask a lady's age.'

'Yes, but you and Lady are my mothers – that makes it all right.'

'All right. Enough talk about *tempus fugit*. You and Lyn are going to have children, then? You've talked about it?'

'Of course we have. Two at least. Lyn wouldn't care how soon, she said. And Mary Natasha is such a little poppet. I quite envy Keth. And Bas, with almost two . . .'

'Then shall I tell you something?' Julia said softly, 'I'd like you and Lyn to have children. Alice is a grandmother and I want to be one!'

'We'll do our best, Mother – be a pleasure.'

'Good! That's something else settled. And Rowangarth is a lovely place for children to grow up in. Me not having a family – except you, of course – I used to encourage the young ones to come here.'

'We all liked it better than Pendenys. It was a peculiar house; not quite real, I always used to think when

I was little. But Rowangarth was old and higgledy-piggledy and the fires sometimes smoked, but no one nagged us to wipe our feet, or complained that we made a lot of noise. And Cook always seemed to have something nice to eat. Cherry scones and iced buns. I hope Tilda will bake scones and buns for my children . . .'

'Tilda is like me, Drew. She can't wait. But to hear you talking about my grandchildren makes me very glad – so go easy with Lyn, son? I can understand she might be a little apprehensive about well – *things*, but I know you'll be all right, the two of you. Just give it time?'

'I will. I wish Lyn were here, for all that. I feel at a bit of a loose end, sometimes.'

'Then if you're in need of something to do, you can come up to the attics with me. One or two things I want to sort out to take to the Bothy. And the painting of Rowangarth in the library, too. Aunt Sutton gave it to Andrew and me as a wedding present. I'd like to take that with me – okay?'

'Fine. Take anything you want. Are you going to miss the old house?'

'I suppose I will, sometimes. I was born here, don't forget. But Nathan and I aren't moving to Australia. We'll only be round at the back, so I suppose I'll be in and out all the time – well, until you're married, of course. I'll have to remember, then, that it's Lyn's house, and watch what I say.'

'Mother!' Drew took Julia in his arms, hugging her tightly. 'You'll treat this house as your own – always. Lyn won't mind one bit. I'll bet anything you like she'll appreciate a bit of interference until she gets the hang of things.

'So let's get ourselves upstairs and have a good old root around. I haven't got Tatty and Bill a wedding present, yet. I asked her, but she said there wasn't a lot they needed since she inherited Denniston fully furnished, as it were. Said I wasn't to bother. But if we find anything that might suit, I just might take it.'

'Like what? It's mostly junk up there, as far as I can remember. And don't you think your cousin is worth something better than junk from Rowangarth attics?'

'Yes, I do. But there's nothing at all in the shops, yet. You still need to get dockets from the Board of Trade. Even when a child outgrows its cot and needs a bed, you do.'

'Well, your child won't need to worry. There are loads of cots up there – if you don't mind them being a bit old-fashioned. And there are beds, too. I wouldn't mind a couple of singles for our spare bedroom, though I suppose the mattresses won't be a lot of good, now. But let's get on with it, shall we? And no deviating – like finding old photograph albums and getting sidetracked, looking through them! Time enough for that when you and Lyn take a new broom to the place and have a good old clear out.'

'Time enough,' Drew smiled, taking his mother's arm, switching lights on and off again as they climbed to the very top of the house. 'Let me get her settled in, first. And I think she'll be more interested in the nursery floor than the attics.'

'You think so, Drew?' Julia pushed open the creaking door, snapping on the light, sniffing the attic smell. 'Robert and Giles and I were the last to use the nursery. I didn't have a nanny for you. Didn't want to share you. Will you and Lyn be getting a nanny, when the time comes?'

'I'm pretty sure we won't. She's wanted children for so long that I know she won't give them over to someone else to look after. That being the case, I suppose we'll have to cast around for a bit more help in the house. But we'll worry about things like that as and when they happen. Right now, getting married is as far ahead as I can think.'

'Couldn't agree more. Take each day as it comes and it'll soon be April. And the sooner the better, as far as I'm concerned.' She looked round the untidy room, crammed with Sutton cast-offs, knowing she mustn't let herself get sentimental about some chance object that might set her off on the road to the past. 'Now, keep your eyes open for an occasional table, and a couple of footstools – and the beds, of course. Oh! Doesn't the place smell musty. Remind me, when the better weather comes, to open all the skylights and give these attics a bit of a blow-through.' She threw back her head and laughed. 'What I should have said is don't forget to remind Lyn to do it!'

And Drew laughed with her and for the first time in many weeks felt extremely contented, and impatient for his wedding day.

'Such a journey, Anna! No heat on the train, no dining car. If we hadn't got here soon, I don't know what would have happened to me. I will have caught a chill, I know it.'

'But Mama – have you had nothing at all to eat?'

'We have done very nicely,' Igor Petrovsky smiled. 'A flask of hot milk and one of coffee, and sandwiches and apples.' His mother did not like travelling on public transport – it was as simple as that. He took his sister in his arms, kissing each cheek, then kissing her hand. 'It is good to see you looking so well. I am looking forward to the wedding – and having Christmas at Denniston House. And it will be good to see Karl, too.'

'It is as well,' the Countess sniffed, 'that Karl will be there to look after us when Tatiana goes off on her honeymoon. December! What a time to get married!'

'Tatiana will be back long before Christmas, Mama. She and Bill are only going to London for a few nights; look at the sights, see a few shows, maybe. They are staying at Aunt Sutton's house.'

'Ah, yes. In a stable!'

'It isn't a stable, Mama, and you know it. It's a dear little house. Tatiana is going to be very happy with Bill. I hope you won't say anything to upset her.'

'Upset her? Why should I do that? I have no small regard for her husband to be. He seems an honest man and has a future I believe, as a painter.'

'As a commercial artist, Mama. There's a lot of difference. And he's very steady and cares deeply for Tatiana.' Anna Pryce almost used the word *love*; that he and her daughter loved each other very much. But she did not say it, nor would she to her mother, who

159

had always maintained that love and marriage were the recipe for disaster. Olga, Countess Petrovska, was of the unshakable belief that in the upper classes, respect, breeding and a good bank balance was of far more importance. Love was something for the foolish – and look where it got them! Look where it had got her daughter who had been so besotted with Elliot Sutton and his eager, social-climbing mother that the marriage was doomed long before Anna came back from her honeymoon; came back pregnant, at that!

'Is there a conveyance, Anna, or do we have to take that ridiculous little train to Holdenby Halt?'

'No, Mama. Ewart is at the hospital all day and offered his car *and* his petrol, so I hope you will remember to thank him. Now stay here with the luggage, and Igor and I will look for a porter. We'll soon be at Denniston and as warm as toast, so cheer up, Mama. You have come to see your granddaughter married and to give her your blessing, don't forget.'

'I will try my hardest. Never let it be said that a Petrovska does not know how to conduct herself on *all* occasions! And hurry, and find someone to help with the cases. This station platform is as cold as Siberia!'

And would that it could be, she prayed silently, fervently. Frozen wastes and all!

Karl waited in the window and when the car drew up outside Denniston House, he was already walking, erect as a Cossack, still, down the stone steps.

'Little Countess,' he said in Russian to Anna,

nodding deferentially, then opened the door so Olga Petrovska might struggle out, silently cursing small cars in general and her stiff old bones in particular.

Then she hitched straight her furs and stuck out her chin offering her gloved hand to the old retainer. And he bowed low, brushing it briefly with his lips before clicking his heels and standing to attention, in a salute to Igor Petrovsky.

'Karl, old friend, it's good to see you!' he replied in Russian, holding out a hand. 'You do not change.'

'Uncle Igor!' Tatiana skipped down the steps, holding wide her arms, kissing her mother's brother soundly. 'And if you do not mind, Grandmother, we will speak in English. Russian only on saints' days is the rule, and today is not a saint's day!'

Then to soften the reprimand, she bobbed a small curtsey to the older woman, then kissed each cheek.

'And you are cold! Come inside, do! We have been saving coal and paraffin like mad and Karl has been sawing logs. The woodshed is full. We'll be nice and warm for the wedding and for Christmas, at least.'

'And where is your intended, Tatiana?'

'In Harrogate. Gone to collect a picture he's been having framed. And you're not to ask about it. It's a surprise. And are you coming in, Mother?'

'Sorry, darling. Got to go to the hospital to pick up Ewart. I'll ring, later. 'Bye, Mama!'

'It surprises me,' said the Countess as the car crunched down the gravelled drive, 'that your mother seems to have petrol and to spare, Tatiana.'

'No. The petrol she used today coming to York was a part of Ewart's personal allowance. As a doctor,

161

he is allowed extra. But there is no petrol to spare, so you are very honoured to be met. Now please come inside and let's shut the door. We are letting all the warmth out. Is tea ready, Karl?'

'Is ready, little one,' he said in reluctant English.

'Good. Then welcome, both of you, to my home.' She had learned, in dealings with the Countess, to establish territorial rights from the word go, and Denniston House was Tatiana's, lock, stock and barrel and the elderly woman was being subtly reminded of the fact.

She winked at Igor Petrovsky and he winked back, the many chats they had had in Cheyne Walk remembered. He had grown to like his sister's child in spite of her parentage; admired her courage in working in London and staying there, in spite of the Blitz. He had willed her the deeds of the house in St Petersburg and the farm at Peterhof. Not that she would ever inherit, but father and elder brother had died returning for those deeds and the gold and valuables they had hidden. He, Igor, had bought his way out of Russia with a ruby ring and a jewelled pendant, hidden in the rough peasant tunic he wore. And the deeds, of course. Tatiana's, one day, to remind her of what might have been.

'I will never understand why you must choose a cold, miserable month for your wedding,' said the Countess, her feet in warm slippers, a woollen shawl around her shoulders and fortified by tea. 'Your cousin has decided on a more civilized date.'

'Drew will be having a big wedding. It's the custom,

at Rowangarth. The whole village will be there.'

'And you are going to spend your honeymoon in that little stable-cottage in London when you can afford a decent hotel?'

'We are staying in Aunt Julia's little mews house because that's what we both want, Grandmother. We'll only be there a few days; I want to be back here for Christmas. It's Bill's birthday on the twenty-fifth – his twenty-fourth.'

'And you are having no attendants, nor wearing a veil?'

'No, Grandmother, because I'm not wearing white.'

'And I suppose you won't even carry a bouquet.'

'Ah, but I will. Catchpole is making me a bouquet of white flowers. He'll be making a spray for you and a buttonhole for Uncle Igor.'

'Can't you afford a proper florist, child?'

'Why on earth should I do that when Catchpole is so good at florals? He's always done Rowangarth weddings and christenings – and funerals. He'll be doing Drew and Lyn's wedding, too. He'd be very upset if we got an outside florist.'

'I suppose Lyn will wear white – have attendants, too?'

'She will. There are two lovely bridesmaid's dresses at Rowangarth and she's wearing Daisy's wedding dress, clothes rationing being what it is. Gracie and Bas should be over from Kentucky. They'll have their second baby by then and will want Uncle Nathan to christen it at All Souls. There are three of us about a size; the bridesmaid's dresses won't be a problem. Either Daisy or Gracie or I will wear them.'

'*You* Tatiana? If you are anything like your mother you'll be well pregnant by April!'

'That might be nice,' Tatiana beamed. 'But I'm not one bit like my mother.'

'You are, child. Like her, you are very beautiful, though you may not think it.'

Igor, eager to have the conversation on a less personal level, interrupted. 'And I think your friend Lyn will be getting excited. When will her parents arrive?'

'They should have docked at Southampton late last night. They could be in Wales, now. And Lyn *will* be excited. She hasn't seen her folks for eighteen months, at least.' She chose not to explain Lyn's father's prolonged absence – not to the Petrovska.

Now, weeks later, Lyn Carmichael was not just excited; more, she was delirious with joy and disbelief. And not a little tearful. She had seen the cottage lights when she turned into the lane.

'Blod!' She was here! Her mother and father had arrived! And done it sneakily, too, to surprise her! She began to run, flinging open the door, calling, 'Auntie Blod! Mum!'

Then all at once they were hugging and kissing and the months between wiped out.

'Hullo, lovely girl. Thought we'd surprise you!'

'But couldn't you have popped your head into Reception to let me know you'd arrived safely?'

'Like your mother said, Lyndis, a surprise.'

Her father was standing there, head tilted, a small smile on his lips. And he was little changed. Still slim

164

and straight and hardly a grey hair to show for his years.

'Dad,' she whispered. It was then the tears came. 'It's been so long.'

'Too long. Am I forgiven, Lyndis?'

'Nothing to forgive.' She laid her head on his shoulder, holding him close, doing what she had wanted to do as a child and had not because, even so young, something had warned her not to. 'Glad you made an honest woman of Auntie Blod.' She sniffed, inelegantly. 'My, but this is going to take a bit of getting used to. I just can't believe it!'

'Well, you better had, girl, because me and your dad are here to stay. And you'd better start trying to call me Mum. I like it better than Blod.'

'I'll try. And *stay*, you said? How long?'

'We-e-ll. Me – I'm stopping. Full stop. And after New Year, your dad is flying back – quicker, see – and seeing an agent and selling up. He's retiring.'

'And you're coming to live in England?'

'No. In Wales, *merchi*. I got homesick, see. Oh, Kenya is a wonderful country, but I missed my girl and when you told us you were getting married I said to Jack, "There now! I'm stuck here, missing my grandchildren."'

'Mum! Let us get down the aisle, first!'

'Missing my grandchildren, I said, and us with enough in the bank, and you with a comfortable pension. And to be truthful, girl, I wasn't happy living in our Myfanwy's house. Got homesick for my little cottage.'

'But it's my house, now.' Lyn laughed shakily, eyes

bright with a mixing of tears and mischief. 'Cottages in Wales are worth a pretty penny, these days. And I've had electricity put in, and done all sorts of things to it.'

'So would a thousand pounds buy it back?' her father raised an eyebrow.

'We-e-ll – I won't be wanting it after April.' She laughed, then held out a hand. 'Done! And I'm so glad I'm going to have parents again – near at hand, I mean. Well – nearer than Kenya. It's a fair old train journey from here to Holdenby, mind. And you're sleeping in the front double, you two. I'm in the single and oh, it's all getting just a bit too much!'

She flopped onto the sofa, covered her face with hands that shook, and gave way to sobs.

'Ooh, our Lyndis – whatever is the matter – shock you, did we? Ah, well, you were always a one for getting yourself into a right old state.' She sat beside her daughter, pulling her into her arms, patting her back as if she were a child again. 'Now, what say we have a cup of tea, eh, Jack? That's what we all need. And then we can talk about things calmly. We haven't put you out, our Lyn? You won't be missing Tatiana Sutton's wedding?'

'No, Mum. I'm leaving here Friday and I'll be back late Sunday evening. Knew you wouldn't mind. I'm looking forward to seeing Drew.'

'Well, of course you are. By the way, there's a case in the kitchen and be careful – it's full of tins – not half heavy. Tins of fruit and tins of butter and, oh everything. When we can think straight again, we'll unpack it and get it all put away.'

'Thanks, Mum. And you do look wonderful. You're slimmer and your hair is just great.'

'Well, I've been eating properly, lately, and I can afford to go to the hairdresser, now. Had it done on the ship, coming over. Real posh. Shops and everything on that liner. And you look wonderful, too, our Lyndis. See what a change love makes? And here comes your dad with the tea.'

And they laughed and took deep breaths, because they were all high as kites. And Blodwen Carmichael raised her teacup and said, 'Well, here's to the three of us, eh?'

'A real family again,' her husband smiled.

But Lyn said, 'Oh, will you stop it the pair of you or you'll have me in tears again. A girl can only take so much happiness, you know.'

'Oh, I do know, *cariad*. I *do* know,' Blodwen said, and smiled at her husband. 'And me and your dad are going to be like Darby and Joan in this little house – if you're sure we can have it?'

'I'm sure,' Lyn smiled.

Sure about being happy; sure that she wanted to marry Drew; sure about everything, now. Well – *wasn't* she?

TEN

Drew waited on the platform from which the train to Holdenby would leave. The Holdenby Flyer they called it and he had many memories of it. Some happy, some sad.

Waiting as a small boy on the platform, his insides wriggling as the black, clanking monster hurtled into the little station. It was so big, so noisy, that he would cling to his mother's hand and close his eyes and wait for the shaking and trembling and the noise to die down, when there would only be steaming hisses and doors banging open and the station master shouting that this was Holdenby Halt.

Then sitting safe inside it, always a window seat, looking out so he might not miss passing the far end of Brattocks Wood, and wondering when he would be big enough for his feet to reach the floor of the compartment and not stick out so awkwardly.

Sometimes, the Holdenby Flyer took them to join an even bigger, much noisier train with at least ten carriages behind it, which would carry them miles and miles to Southampton, and then to West Welby where Tom would be waiting with Mr Hillier's pony and trap to take them the last few clip-clopping miles to where Daisy and Lady waited with Morgan the spaniel, and Tom's three black Labradors barking to welcome them.

Drew kept his gaze on the footbridge Lyn would cross, because though trains were better at time-keeping since the war ended, you could never be quite sure when, and at which platform, they would arrive.

He returned his rememberings to Holdenby Halt and the sad times; times when he was returning to his ship, leave over; the time when he knew that Kitty was in North Africa, entertaining troops and that when she got back to London, Leading-Telegraphist D/WRX 805 Sutton A R G would be on a troopship taking him – though he had not known it – to Australia to join the Pacific Fleet. That had been the saddest of his departures from Holdenby Halt.

Or perhaps the absolute sadness was when he returned to Rowangarth when the war was over, and the certain knowledge that when he stepped off the little train, Kitty would not be waiting for him, nor ever would be again.

Yet now he was waiting on York station for Lyn. He had not seen her for almost three weeks and he was impatient to hold her, kiss her and tell her he loved her. Most important, saying I love you.

People began to hurry over the footbridge; those eager to be home or to catch a connection, followed by those who walked more slowly, hampered by luggage. He saw Lyn, and smiled. She was easy to pick out in a crowd. You looked for that glorious hair.

He walked towards the bottom of the stairs, wanting to meet her, knowing it would be like swimming against a tide of people. She walked carefully down the last few steps and he knew her case was heavy.

'Darling. Let me have that.' He took the case, then grabbed her hand, hurrying towards the waiting Flyer. 'Lordy – what have you got in this?'

'Bricks! And hullo to you, too!' she gasped, teetering behind him on high heels.

The guard was standing, green flag at the ready, whistle poised. They made a dash for the front of the train where there was a better chance of finding an empty compartment. Drew found one, slammed shut the door, and pulled up the window. Only then did he take her in his arms and kiss her.

'Hi, Lyn,' he said softly. 'I've missed you.'

'Missed you, too,' she said huskily, lifting her lips for another kiss. 'And don't try to sling that case on the rack; you'll do yourself a mischief. It's mostly full of tins. Mum brought them with her from Kenya. No food rationing there.'

A whistle sounded, the train juddered forward then stopped and juddered again, throwing them off balance so they were obliged to sit down.

So they leaned back against the buttoned, faded upholstery and Lyn whispered, 'Tell me, please?'

'I love you, Lyn Carmichael.'

'And I love you.'

'No more worries, darling?'

'No more worries – we-e-ll, maybe just a few. Little ones, like will it rain on our wedding day, and – and . . .'

'And our first night together? That, sweetheart, is the very least of your worries, so don't give it another thought. And I came by train to meet you not just to save petrol, but so we could have this half-hour together, though thank goodness the car is at the station. I don't fancy walking to Rowangarth carrying that case. Tins, you said?'

'Mm. A tin of butter each for your mother and Daisy's mother. And a tin of peaches each and thick cream. And a bag of sugar. I've never seen my store cupboard so full. And talking about Aunt – about *Mum*, she isn't going back to Kenya. Dad is going, after New Year. Flying back to do the business and pack what they want to bring back. Selling the rest – and the house.'

'But that's marvellous, Lyn. Aren't you glad?'

'You bet I am. They seemed so far away, before. They're going to buy back my little house. Everything has worked out very well.'

'And your father? How was it, between you?'

'Just fine. It's good to see them both so happy together – at last!'

'Glad we'll all be together at New Year. Polly is going to baby-sit Mary Natasha, so Keth and Daisy can come to the party, and Tatty and Bill will be there and Anna and Ewart Pryce and maybe Uncle Igor. The Petrovska has declined, though. She and Karl are to see New Year in at Denniston. They'll be talking about the old days, no doubt, and wishing they had a few slugs of vodka to knock back. Mother's looking forward to meeting your folks. Maybe, if there's paraffin for the stoves, we'll be able to have a few dances in the conservatory.'

171

'Mm. Lovely.'

She thought of a photograph on Daisy's locker in Cabin 4A, at Hellas House. It had been one of the Clan, taken in the conservatory and obviously at Christmas because, in the room beyond there had been a tree that not even the black and white of the photograph could spoil. And they were all there; Kitty, Daisy and Tatiana in pretty dresses and dancing pumps and Drew, Bas and Keth in their Sunday best.

They stood together, the Clan, arms linked and smiling. Daisy said Kitty had been teaching them to dance the tango. Always Kitty, who could climb trees faster and higher than anyone else; could spit farther than any boy and who could swear in Russian.

And at New Year they would all be there again, except Kitty. Perhaps to dance Drew said, with she, Lyn, taking Kitty's place. And because of it, Drew's mother wouldn't even think of taking another photograph of the Clan because it wasn't the Clan any more. Never could be.

'So tell me?' A hand passed in front of Lyn's eyes. 'What you were thinking about, I mean.'

'I was thinking about Tatty's wedding.' The words came glibly, so she warmed to the lie. 'I've brought my best suit with me – reckoned it might be cold in the little chapel.'

'It most certainly will. And it's damp, too, so it will smell a bit. But it's a good smell, if you know what I mean.'

'Think I do. An old-as-time smell – mixed with musty books and dusty hassocks. The chapel at home smells like that. I used to call it the God smell.'

'It'll be warmer, in April – and we'll be in the main church. I remember Daisy's wedding. April the seventeenth, forty-three.'

'I know. Tatty and Kitty were bridesmaids. You seem to forget that I got that wedding word for word when Dwerryhouse got back from leave. In between her dissolving into tears and wanting Keth, that was.'

'Do you remember a lot about your war, Lyn?'

'Not really.' She was telling lies again. 'I think maybe that when I'm much older I'll remember every little thing about it. They say that when you get old you can remember your youth in Technicolor, but you can't remember where you put down your reading glasses an hour ago.'

She was doing well. She had said Kitty's name and the world had not stopped spinning. The word had slipped naturally from her tongue and the conversation had not faltered. She slipped her hand in Drew's, twining her fingers in his, moving closer, hearing three toots from the engine ahead, which meant they were running alongside Brattocks Wood. And then, around a sweeping curve and less than a mile ahead, would be Holdenby Halt.

'Almost there,' Drew smiled. Then he tilted her chin and kissed her gently. 'One more minute . . .'

He got to his feet, pressing his knee against the seat as the train braked and jerked, holding out Lyn's coat. And she slipped her arms into it then turned to face him.

'This has been one heck of a week, so far, and it's going to get better,' she whispered, and before she could kiss him back the Holdenby Flyer stopped with

173

a jerk and a judder and threw them back on the seat.

'Holdenby Halt!' the station master was calling. 'All alight, for Holdenby!'

'Much, much better.' Drew tugged on the leather strap and let down the window, reaching through for the door handle. 'And here we go, then. Full speed ahead to Tatty's wedding.'

And though they did not know it, there was wonderful news to come. From Julia, that was, who heard the car and ran into the stableyard, smiling widely.

'Drew! Lyn! It's arrived. Read this!' She thrust an envelope into Drew's hand. 'Gracie's baby's here.'

Eleanor Sutton arrived at 1 a.m. 16th December.
7 lbs 4 ozs. Mother and baby well. Letter follows.
– Amelia Sutton

'A little girl,' Lyn breathed. 'And nearly on Tatty's wedding day. I like the name.'

'Mm. No one knows where they got it from. Probably just a name they both like. And I do remember Gracie once said she would never use family names. Too much risk, she said, of upsetting people. One of each, they've got. That was clever.' Julia stuffed the small envelope in her pocket then reached for Lyn, kissing her cheek. 'And come inside, the pair of you. It's freezing out here! Get yourselves to the fire!'

'Are you going to see Tatty?' Julia asked when supper was over.

'Best not. She'll be washing her hair and doing

things to her nails, I shouldn't wonder. Lyn has tins – food – in her case. Some for you and some for Lady.'

'Mm. And next time I come I'll bring some for Daisy. Mum brought a whole load of food. We had buttered toast this morning for breakfast. Sinful. My case is in the hall – I'll leave the tins on the table and if you don't mind, Mrs Sutton, I'd like to get to Foxgloves, now. Could do with an early night.'

'It's a long fiddling journey for Lyn,' Julia said when she and Nathan were alone. 'Drew should go there more often.'

'He can't, now, sweetheart. Her parents have the spare room. Be nice to meet them, get to know them.'

'And talk about the wedding. It'll be April in no time at all and Lyn hasn't tried on Daisy's dress, yet.'

'She will, when we've got Christmas and New Year over with.' He picked up the evening paper, reaching for his reading glasses. Hiding behind a newspaper was the only way to avoid wedding talk, and even with Tatiana and Bill safely joined tomorrow, there would be at least three more months of Drew's wedding to contend with.

Women were delightful. They coped with wars and rationing and babies and cleaning; did most things far better than men. Admirable creatures until a wedding was in the offing, then something turned them all at once into prattling monsters.

'Think I'll have a look at what Lyn has brought, bless the girl. Half for me, half for Alice, it'll be. Might just pop over to Keeper's with them. Alice will be alone. Tom goes out for a drink, Fridays.'

'A good idea. You'll have plenty to chat about,' he said, eyes teasing.

'Loads. I still haven't made up my mind about what to wear in April and Alice is going to want plenty of time if she's to make it for me. Sure you don't mind if I pop out for half an hour?'

When the front door had banged, Nathan removed his spectacles, folded the paper and dropped it to the floor at his side. Then he stretched his legs, feet to the fire, folded his arms and closed his eyes.

Half an hour? He'd bet on at least two!

Tatiana Sutton was neither washing her hair nor doing things to her nails. She was in Bill's room, over the stables, watching as he packed a case.

'That's it then,' she smiled. 'You've slept in your garret for the last time. When we get back from London you'll be able to move all your stuff into Denniston.'

'Aye. Mind, the light is good, here. Maybe I'll still use this as a studio – at least when the weather gets warmer. You won't want the conservatory cluttered up with my painting.'

'I won't mind at all. From tomorrow on, Denniston is your home. Stupid of the Petrovska to insist you and I mustn't see each other on the day of the wedding till we meet at the church. Good of Mother to put you up. You and Drew can meet at the church. I'll give him a ring, later, though he'll most likely be at Daisy and Keth's with Lyn.' She walked over to the paraffin stove to stand, back to him, holding her hands to the warmth. 'And I've something to tell you, Bill.'

'That you went to the top of the Pike, this afternoon?' he said gently. 'I saw you go – thought you would.'

'I had to.' She turned to face him.

'I'm glad you did.' He reached for her hand. 'I know you so well, you see. You had to tell Tim . . .'

'Yes. And say goodbye to him. Leastways, that's what I thought. But he wasn't there. Always, when I've been there before, stood at the place his bomber crashed, I knew I had only to talk to him – from my heart, I mean – and he would hear me. But this afternoon, he'd gone. Nothing there but the emptiness. Not even a curlew call.'

'That would be because he knows about us. I told him.'

'You *told* him? When? What did you say?'

'I went up there on Wednesday – when you'd gone to Creesby. Wanted him to know, I suppose, that you'd be all right with me to take care of you.'

'You *spoke* to him? But you don't know how. There's no bond between you.'

'There is, hennie, darling. We were both tail-end Charlies, both of us Scots. And we both of us love you. Best he should know the way things are. I stood up there, thinking what a lucky so-and-so I was, how lucky to be alive and to have you. And then it felt like I was on his wavelength, that he could home in on my thoughts. So I told him we were going to be married, that you would never forget him and that I didn't want you to.'

'And then what?' Her eyes were wide, her words a whisper. 'Tell me, Bill?'

'Then a curlew called. I saw it, right above me, like it knew I was there.'

'It probably did. Drew once said it was naval superstition that seagulls had the souls of sailors who had died, and when I went up the Pike – quite often, once – I always heard the call of a curlew. Perhaps, I thought, curlews had airmen's souls. I wanted to think that that was how it was; Tim letting me know he was still there.'

'Aye?'

'Do you think I'm mad, for believing such things?'

'Not if you don't think I was mad, going up the Pike the other day.'

'I don't. I'm glad you went and I'm glad we're going to be married tomorrow. I'll always love Tim because you can't stop loving someone just because he's dead. But I love you too, Bill Benson. Can you understand that?'

'Of course. Your mother loved twice; Drew has loved twice – what's so different about you and me?'

'Nothing at all – except you and I have had better luck than Aunt Julia's doctor, and Kitty and Tim had. Let's you and me never forget that, Bill?'

'We won't, I promise you. So let's away over to the house and you can ring Foxgloves and see if Drew is there.'

'And if he is, you can leave your case at Mother's, then we'll pop next door, and catch up with the news. And I forgot to tell you – Aunt Julia phoned. Gracie has had her baby. A little girl. Eleanor. Everything's fine.'

'I'm glad about that. You like the name?'

'Yes, I do. It's very old. We had a Queen Eleanor oh, ages ago.'

'Then let's make a bargain, and shake on it. When you and I have our children, you shall name the girls and I'll name the boys. That okay?'

'Fine by me.' She reached for his hand and placed a kiss in its upturned palm. 'And let's get ourselves over to Daisy's. I'm getting quite sentimental and it wouldn't do to break our duck at this late hour, now would it?'

Tatiana saw the lighted window at Foxgloves and tapped on the glass. She never rang the doorbell after dark, for fear of awakening Mary Natasha.

'Tatty. Hi.' Keth opened the door. 'Drew and Lyn are here – where's Bill?'

'Next door at Mother's, leaving his case. He's staying there overnight. And have you seen the sky? Very clear, and full of stars. A sign of a good day, tomorrow. The sun just might shine on me, for luck. But can I come in? I'm frozen.'

She hurried in to the warmth and held her hands to the fire and it was like coming out of a long, lonely tunnel; as if she had said goodbye to the past and was ready to start afresh with Bill, who was good and kind, and who wanted her.

'For someone who is getting married tomorrow, you seem amazingly blasé, Tatiana Sutton. I was sure you'd be at home, doing things to your face and hiding your case away so no one could stuff confetti into it.'

'I haven't packed yet, Drew. We're only away for

a few nights. We'll have a proper honeymoon later, when there aren't so many travel restrictions. And I shall enjoy tomorrow. Uncle Nathan will marry me and Uncle Igor will give me away and there'll only be the people I love most there – we-e-ll and the Petrovska.'

'Tatty! You don't mean that!'

'Not really. When she gets obnoxious I tell myself she has lost her husband and a son and a way of life she thought would last forever. And she's old, and I am young. Sometimes, Uncle Igor told me, Grandmother just sits, staring through the window, and he knows she's back in St Petersburg, and happy for a little while. It's sad, really . . .'

'Are the flowers seen to?' Daisy asked. 'What will your bouquet be?'

'Haven't a clue. Catchpole said I was to leave the florals to him, and I'm glad to. I only asked that it's something in white because I'm wearing my grey suit and an apricot blouse, which is a lovely warm colour. And a matching apricot hat with a wisp of veil. And that chapel will be freezing. I shall be wearing my fur-lined knickers, too! And I think we'd better stop talking about what the bride is wearing. I think that was Bill, tapping on the window. I'll go and let him in.'

She hurried to the door, because she wanted him to kiss her. She felt most content and she wanted a warm, contented kiss. Tomorrow, they could be as passionate as they wanted.

'You didn't stay long, Bill.'

'Your mother had people there, but she gave me

a key and said to tell you she'll be at Denniston at first light tomorrow.'

'Good. She can deal with things if the Petrovska gets stroppy. She might well, you know. Say hi to Bill, folks.' She guided him to a chair, then settled herself on the floor at his feet. 'The Petrovska has loads of excuses for getting out of things. "My poor head is achink. My sable isn't fit to wear. My feet are too cold in your Yorkshire weather. Aye do not approve of weddinks not in the Orthodox church . . ."'

'Well, if her fur coat is past it, I wouldn't mind giving it a home,' Lyn laughed. 'I've heard about sable coats but haven't actually seen anyone wearing one. They cost the earth!'

'Not in Russia,' Tatiana said matter-of-factly. 'And Grandmother has taken good care of hers. She puts it in cold storage every summer. As soon as there isn't an R in the month, off it goes to the furrier.'

'My mother,' Lyn giggled, 'would steal it off her back. She has always longed for a fur coat. Mind, there wasn't a lot of need for one in Kenya, but now she's back home for good, Dad says that as soon as there are furs in the shops again and clothes rationing ends, they'll go to Leeds and buy one.' Lyn was happy. She had missed Drew a lot, though her parents' surprise announcement that they intended to live in Wales had made her giddy with delight.

Drew was happy, too, that Lyn seemed more sure about April. He would still have to tread carefully, but the wedding tomorrow would be a good way for her to discover that the Suttons were just ordinary people when you got to know them, and stopped being in awe of the big houses they just happened to live in.

He smiled across at Daisy who sat on the floor at Keth's feet, elbows resting on his knees. Daisy seemed *very* happy, smugly so. She had a husband she adored and the most beautiful baby; money, too. Daisy was richer than he was, if push came to shove. Daisy's money was mostly in pounds, shillings and pence. His own fortune, Drew had to admit, was in property and land and he and Lyn would live on rents, and an income from the tea plantation the Suttons had once owned in India.

But money, possessions, didn't matter. Just getting through the war alive had been the most important thing you ever thought of. By comparison, nothing was better than being alive. Mother's first love, Andrew, was dead, and Tatty's first love, too. And soon it would be Lyn he would marry; would walk to his wedding past the white stone that bore Kitty's name.

'What are you thinking about, bruv? You had a distinctly soppy look on your face.' Daisy put paid to his rememberings.

'I was thinking about weddings,' he said glibly. You had to tell the odd white one. 'And how much I'm looking forward to Tatty's – and then my own. But I'm going to break up the party. I know Lyn is tired, and I wouldn't mind getting my head down. Got to be bright-eyed and bushy-tailed tomorrow to do my best-manning. And don't get up, darling.' From behind her chair, he kissed the top of Lyn's head, his hands lingering on her shoulders. 'See you in church, folks. G'night, each.'

Drew's leaving did indeed break up the gathering. Bill said that if he didn't shift himself he would be there till midnight, and that would never do, so how about walking Tatty home to Denniston? And Tatiana said that would be very nice, thank you very much, provided he kissed her goodnight on her doorstep.

And Keth smiled and thought how much Tatty had changed. Once the brat of the Clan, her every movement watched over by an anxious mother and a possessive nanny, she hadn't started to blossom until Mam'selle came to take over her education. Mam'selle had been a good sort. He wondered if she had returned to France when war came, and if she had joined the Resistance or become a Jerrybag and fraternized with occupying soldiers.

And then he thought again of Natasha and Tante Clara which made him all the more determined to return to Clissy-sur-Mer as soon as the government allowed. Because his conscience would never be easy until he had made the pilgrimage there; because his own contented life could not be justified until he had at least found a grave and the little house outside the village with, hopefully, arum lilies still growing in the back garden.

'I got a cake in Creesby this morning,' Daisy said when she and Lyn and Keth were alone. 'Had to queue for it, but it was worth it. And now that they've all gone, it's just the right size to cut into three. Tea, everyone?'

'Cake and tea would be lovely,' Lyn smiled, and Keth said need Daisy ask, and should he put another log on the fire?

'I've put a hot bottle in your bed, Lyn,' Daisy said as she handed out large mugs of tea and small pieces of currant cake. 'Er – everything all right?' she murmured, to which Lyn replied that things were better than all right, thanks for asking.

'I'm looking forward to New Year, though it'll be strange staying at Rowangarth. Never slept there, before. Mum is tickled pink to be meeting Drew's mother. Mum looks marvellous. Much slimmer, and she's had her hair cut shorter. Doesn't screw it up into a bun, now. Married life suits her.'

'She waited long enough for your father, that's for sure. I'm looking forward to meeting her again and showing Mary Natasha to her,' Daisy smiled. 'All things considered, Carmichael, life is pretty good, these days.'

And Lyn took a large bite out of the queued-for cake and agreed with her friend. Absolutely.

The simple beauty of the Lady Chapel more than compensated for its coldness. In the small, low windows stood copper vases of yellow chrysanthemums; on the altar candles burned warmly to show off the huge white chrysanthemums Sidney Willis said would have won a first at the Yorkshire show. Beside the simple altar stood a tiny Christmas tree in a terracotta pot, dug from Brattocks Wood only yesterday and decorated, as befitted a chapel, with variegated ivy, wisps of cotton wool to imitate snowflakes and topped with a Christmas star. Beside it stood a fat red candle, the flame flickering each time the door was opened.

In the front pew, Olga Petrovska sat unmoving, her coat collar pulled high, her matching sable hat so low on her forehead that only her eyes were visible. Tom, in his best keeping tweeds, and Alice, in her winter best, were handed buttonholes of tiny chrysanthemums. Jack Catchpole, handing out pins, was muttering that Christmas was no time at all for a wedding, the floral situation being what it was.

Julia entered, bowed to the altar then smiled brightly at Alice.

'I'd better sit with the Countess,' she whispered. 'Poor thing – she looks so old and alone.'

Alice agreed with her, though had it not been the season of goodwill as well as Tatiana's wedding day, she might have whispered back, 'Old and alone my foot! It's the way she chooses to be because her granddaughter is marrying out of her Church and into the *meeddle clarses*!' But Olga Petrovska would never be happy until a Tzar ruled Russia again.

'Hi,' said Drew who had been waiting at the door for the bridegroom. 'You all right, Bill?'

'Fine. I walked here.' He inspected his shoes for mud. 'It's a good sky, Drew. Looks as if the sun will shine for the bride. Are we too early?'

'No. Tatty will arrive on time, that's for sure. Shall we go in?'

They lifted the iron door sneck. It echoed like a pistol shot and made those inside turn sharply. In step, they walked down the aisle, looking neither right nor left, all at once feeling wrapped round by the white walls and the sense of time past and time to come.

Nathan strode in, in a flap of surplice and cassock,

turned to smile a greeting to those present, then whispered, 'Good. You're here. All right, the pair of you? And I won't say it, Drew . . .'

'You better hadn't. Mother checked it was there before I left home.' He slipped his hand into his pocket. 'The ring – okay?'

'Just making sure.' Nathan winked at Julia, then inclined his head in the direction of the Countess. 'And Tatty promised not to be late – so cold in here . . .'

'She won't be, Sir,' Bill said softly, knowing exactly what she would be doing now.

Tatiana Sutton checked that her gloves, her uncle's gloves and the posy of snowdrops – brought forward especially by Jack Catchpole and Sidney Willis, because not for anything was a Sutton bride carrying chrysanthemums! – lay on the hall table. Then she glanced around the conservatory and the extra chairs they had carried there, made sure the drawing-room fire was guarded, then made for the kitchen, followed by Igor Petrovsky.

'Five minutes before we need to leave.' She held out her arms to Karl, hugging him, then kissing his cheek, causing his eyes to fill with tears. 'I've come for your blessing,' she said, in Karl's native Russian.

'And I give it gladly, little one.' With his thumb he traced a cross on her forehead, then reached for her hand, kissing it gently. 'Go to your man with happiness.' He looked at Igor. 'For this one, there will be no tears.'

'No tears, and we must be going, Tatiana. Come with us to the door, Karl?'

On the doorstep Tatiana turned, eyes toward the Pike, smiling softly. Then she walked to the white-ribboned car that waited to take her to her wedding. To the man she loved.

'I was so proud of you, darling. You look so beautiful. Are you happy with your Bill?' Anna asked her daughter.

'You know I am. Wasn't it a lovely service? Didn't Uncle Nathan do it just beautifully?'

'Nathan is a very special person,' Anna smiled. 'He ties a very special knot. And, darling – go and rescue Bill from your grandmother. I wouldn't be at all surprised if he isn't getting chapter and verse about the Tzar-God-rest-him and the wicked Bolsheviks who looted her house.'

'She enjoys being sad, Mother. Let her have a little sadness today? After all, it's her only grandchild's wedding.'

But she went, nevertheless, to the fireside where Olga Petrovska sat with her hand on Bill Benson's arm, in time to hear, '. . . and you must be the man in your own home, Sergeant. I love my granddaughter dearly, but she can be headstrong and needs, sometimes, to be disciplined.'

'*What* did I hear you say, Grandmother?' she asked.

'Your granny said you're a mettlesome filly, and should have your bottom spanked every Wednesday,' Bill grinned.

'Then will you tell my *granny* from me that if ever you do that, I shall give you a fourpenny one straight back! And Karl is coming round with drinks, so look after Grandmother, will you? See you later, darling, when I've done my circulating.'

She blew a kiss and was away, happy and smiling, to talk to Miss Clitherow who sat in a wheelchair, sipping sherry.

In the conservatory Julia said to Alice, 'This is a good sherry, you know. Wonder how Anna managed to come by it.'

'I think Igor got a few bottles in London – from a contact.'

'Mm. I'll have to be on the hunt for a few bottles myself, for April. Do you remember this conservatory?'

'In our war, you mean? Oh, my word, yes! Soldiers were on the mend when they came to sit in here. It used to leak when it rained.'

'And do you remember the staff nurse – Ruth Love? And Sister Carbolic?'

'Yes, and me pretending I was a year older so I could go to France?'

'We had our first taste of war here at Denniston. Remember the stableyard when they brought all those wounded from France?'

Alice remembered. Some with a purple cross on their forehead to show they had been given morphine; some with the mud of the trenches still on them and covered with lice. They'd had to wear special aprons and rubber gloves and undress the men in the cold yard before they were allowed into the comfort of the ward.

'We never lost a patient, though. All the time you and I were here at Denniston, Julia, they all pulled through. But let's not think back. Today is Tatiana's and Bill's. Let's be happy for them.'

'Mm. And think forward to Drew's wedding – count our blessings, eh? And we'd better have a word with Anna – and, I suppose, the Countess. What time are the bride and groom leaving?'

'They're getting the six-fifteen from Holdenby Halt. Drew told me. Igor got a black market petrol coupon in London so he's giving it to Anna for taking them to the station in Ewart's car.'

'Seems there's a lot to be had, in London. Wouldn't mind a trip down there myself, when the weather gets better. It's ages since I've been to Montpelier Mews.'

'Well, the young ones are using it, now. Your Aunt Anne Lavinia would be glad about that. She was fond of young people – and horses. I wonder why she never married?'

'She never said, so we'll never know, now. But there's Karl with drinks. Do you suppose we could have another, Alice?'

'I don't see why not. Anna said there was champagne for the speeches and toasts, by the way, so we'd better watch it.'

'Don't worry, old love. The walk home in the cold will sober us up.'

And they smiled, like two women who had been sort-of sisters for a very long time, and who were enjoying Tatiana's wedding because they had seen her grow up from a Pendenys Sutton into a beautiful young woman who had gone her own defiant way. And who, today, had found happiness at last.

* * *

At the York Hotel there was a tap on the door and a muffled, 'Room Service.'

'Hullo there!' Bill opened the door to a smiling waiter carrying champagne and glasses, compliments of the management, and enquiring if they would be eating in the dining room. And Bill said firmly that they would not, but would appreciate sandwiches, if that wouldn't be too much trouble, and a large pot of tea.

'I agree entirely,' Tatiana smiled when they were alone again. 'And we must keep the cork from the champagne bottle – a souvenir. Are you happy, darling?'

'You know I am. I think it was a lovely idea to carry snowdrops. Where are they, now?'

'In water, I hope. I asked Aunt Julia to put them on my little brother's grave when she goes to church, tomorrow. You've seen the tiny stone with his initials on it. Uncle Nathan baptized him so he could have a Christian burial; called him Nicholas, for the Tzar. He's a lovely man. I wish he'd been my father – Uncle Nathan, I mean. But let's eat our sandwiches when they come, then get into our pyjamas? We can be thoroughly decadent, and drink champagne in bed. Let's not come down to earth until we have to?'

'*Pyjamas*, Tatty? I thought brides wore virginal white.'

'Reckon they do, at that. But I had only five clothing coupons left, so I blew them on my wedding blouse. Sorry, Bill. Mind, I needn't wear them.'

'Oh, but you will!'

'If you say so.'

'I do say so. I'm not forgoing the bridegroom's privilege of taking them off!'

And she laughed, wrapping her arms round his neck, telling him she loved him, and wasn't it marvellous that tonight – and every other night – neither of them would be counting to ten, ever again.

'Enjoyed yourself, Lyn?' They hurried home to Rowangarth, huddling together against the cold. 'Didn't Tatty look happy? It's obvious that Bill adores her.'

'And I adore *you*, Drew Sutton. Wish it had been us, today, though I suppose we can't deny the mothers their fun, arranging it all. And in April it'll be warm enough for a marquee on the lawn.'

'Yes, and talking about weddings – have you tried on Daisy's dress, yet? And what about the bridesmaids, Lyn?'

'Daisy and Tatty, though if Tatty isn't able, then I shall ask Gracie.'

'Why shouldn't she be able?'

'Daisy said Tatty hopes to be in the throes of morning sickness by April.'

'Good grief! *That* soon?'

'Why not? Do you realize it would make you the only one of the Clan who's still childless?' Lyn teased, still high on wedding euphoria.

'That's because I'm still a bachelor. I'll bet Gracie is feeling very pleased with herself, now. Can't wait to see them all. And you really should be thinking about the dress, Lyn. Mother was talking about you wearing a veil, the other day. Daiz didn't wear one. I think Mother rather hoped she would wear my grandmother's veil. I believe it's still in pretty good nick.'

'If that's what you want . . .'

'Up to you entirely.'

'Then I'd like to wear the veil, but I think I'd like roses for my bouquet – Rowangarth roses. Would that be possible?'

'I don't see why not. Catchpole and Willis can bring plants forward, or hold them back. Gardeners do it all the time for flower shows, and the like. There used to be two roses on the wall of one of the glasshouses. We'll have to pay the kitchen garden a visit. They might have been pulled out in the war when growing food was all the thing, but I don't think Catchpole would do that if there was any way he could save them. After all, he kept the orchid houses going – and orchids need fuel. Don't know how he managed it. Was always a bit worried the people from the Ministry of Food would order him to grow tomatoes, instead. But he got away with it.'

'I don't want to carry orchids, Drew. Somehow, they aren't – well – me. I'd like a coloured bouquet, if that's all right with you.'

'You can carry dandelions, if that's what you want.' They stopped in the shelter of the stableyard wall, and he took her face in his hands, and kissed her mouth gently. 'Your nose is cold, Lyn.'

'That's because I have a warm heart. And do let's hurry before the rest of me is frozen.'

They clasped hands and ran towards the Linden

Walk, then across the lawn, skirting the wild garden, making for the front steps.

'Y'know – it's suddenly struck me that the marble seat in the Linden Walk would be a lovely place for a wedding photograph,' Lyn said when they were warm in front of the winter parlour fire. 'Will the leaves be out, then?'

'I don't think so, but if we have a mild spring, they might well be budding. I think Daisy's best wedding photograph is the one where she's sitting on the stone steps beside the far lawn, and Keth putting her shoe on.'

'I remember that one. Your mother took it, didn't she? Daisy's dress billowing around her on the grass. It was so romantic, but Daisy said romantic her foot! She was wearing borrowed white shoes and all at once they started to pinch. She said that what she was doing, really, was giving her feet a rest. I haven't got wedding shoes, Drew. Suppose I'll have to splash out five clothing coupons for a pair – and only to wear once! Tatty wasn't stupid, having a quiet wedding. She told me the only thing she wore new was the apricot blouse, and it took her last five clothing coupons. But at least she'll get her wear out of it. I wonder when things will be back to normal, and rationing will end.'

'Haven't a clue, but you'd better check your passport. It will be out of date – or at least, the photo will.'

'The photograph was taken when I was twelve and came to school in England – well out of date. But why passports, all of a sudden?'

'Because the government just might do away with foreign travel restrictions, and we could get abroad for our honeymoon. Paris sounds good, to me. They say April is the best time to see it.'

'And you're sure' – she reached for his hand – 'that you're happy about us, that you still want to marry me? I know I keep asking, but –'

'Ask all you like, Lyn Carmichael – the answer will still be the same. Yes, I want to marry you. I happen to love you.'

'Mm. Tatty seemed very happy today, didn't she? Tim, I mean . . .'

'Darling. Ssssh.' He reached for her, holding her close, laying his cheek on her head. 'It's you and me, now – Drew and Lyn, always.'

Always, she thought, snuggling closer. A good word, always. Had a permanent ring to it.

'I love you, sailor,' she whispered.

ELEVEN

'So how do you like Aunt Sutton's little house, Bill?'

'I thought it was your Aunt Julia's . . .'

'It is, now. But it belonged to Drew's grandfather's sister, Anne Lavinia. She was a maiden lady, liked horses better than men. And I think she liked France better than England; spent all the time she could, there; died there, too.'

'Then since you ask, I think it's a great wee house and shut away, too. Fine for honeymoons. You'd never think you were in London.'

'It was better in Aunt Sutton's day. She was a real Edwardian; liked white paint and lots of potted plants, mostly ferns. Don't know where all the plants have gone; probably died from neglect now that no one lives here permanently. Sparrow used to look after them, when she lived here.'

'Sparrow was the housekeeper, wasn't she?'

'Kind of. Aunt Julia inherited her from Andrew, her first husband. Sparrow – Mrs Emily Smith, actually – once looked after Andrew's lodgings and kept his surgery clean. When he was killed, Aunt Julia asked her to move in here, keep the place aired. Sparrow looked after Kitty and me during the war when we lived here. Very strict, she was.'

She drew in a deep breath, wanting to remember, trying not to. She shifted her position, asking for a cushion to sit on because her bottom was uncomfortable.

'You Suttons are a funny lot. You seem always to sit on the floor. Your Aunt Julia does it, too. If your bottom's gone dead, come and sit with me. This armchair is big enough for the two of us.'

So she smiled and snuggled beside him, glad to be nearer. Because she always wanted to be near him, now. Since the wedding she seemed always to need to touch him, even if it was only linking her little finger in his when they walked.

'Mm. That's better . . .'

'Good. So tell me, why are you raking up the past? Had you forgotten that I know about this house and Sparrow and Kitty? It was Sparrow's niece Joannie who introduced you and I. Joannie organized people like you to take out people like me – wounded airmen with their faces burned away, get them used to facing the world again. I was blind, so I couldn't see the mess I was in – couldn't see you, either.'

'So did you approve of me, when your eyes got better?'

'You know I did. I knew you would be gorgeous, if ever I got to see you, that was.'

'Well you did, and we're married now.' The matter-of-fact Tatiana was in charge, again. 'And darling, will you do something for me? Before we go back, will you come with me to Hyde Park? Tomorrow, perhaps?'

'Surely. One of your old haunts, was it, when you lived here?'

'Sometimes we went there, if we were both off work at the same time. I – I haven't been there, though, for a long time. Since it happened, I suppose.'

'Ghosts to be laid?'

'Sort of. But I don't want to talk about it tonight. Tonight, really, we should be talking about the future, but I think we'll keep that for New Year's Eve, when we're home. Tonight, I just want to sit here, snuggled up and keeping warm. There'll be a programme of carols on the wireless, soon – let's listen and get in the mood for Christmas?'

'Good idea. Haven't thought about Christmas a lot. Couldn't get past the eighteenth, and if you'd turn up.'

'*Whaaat!* Me leave you waiting at the church, Bill Benson – now would I do that?'

'No, and you didn't, but I wasn't to know, was I? Thought it was all too good to be true. Was certain that something would go wrong, and I'd lose you. I love you very much, you see.'

'And I love you. I'm one very happy lady. And I'd like you to kiss me, please.' She closed her eyes and lifted her mouth to his. 'And let's not bother with the Christmas carols. Let's go to bed, darling?'

Tuesday morning was crisp and cold, the grass in the park still white with frost. Hyde Park lay just a step away; across the road to the Carriage Drive and on to Rotten Row then on again, to the Serpentine.

They walked, unspeaking, Tatiana knowing she must make the journey, Bill sensing her unhappiness, knowing she would tell him in her own time.

'It was a lovely day, then,' Tatiana whispered. 'Everywhere sunny and green. A Sunday. We'd taken sandwiches and Kitty had a letter to post. To Drew.'

'And neither of you thought – not for a minute . . . ?'

'Not for a minute. Why should we have? Why us? And the people in the Guard's Chapel – why them? They were in church. Sanctuary, it should have been. Do you know what I mean?'

'I think I do. I thought the same, once. Why was I the only one of that crew to parachute out? Why were the others killed and why, when I'd been so bloody lucky, was I blinded? All part of the scheme of things, hennie. I got my sight back, and I got you.'

'And I wasn't killed, but Kitty was. And all because she'd gone to post a letter to Drew. I watched her go, heard the thing coming over, and then it stopped. Fifteen seconds after the engine gives out, then that's it. I lived hours in those few seconds. Should I run to Kitty? I wanted to, but my feet wouldn't move. And anyway, I thought, it would drop on the other side of the park.

'I screamed at Kitty to get down, then I threw myself on the ground. It was under a tree . . .'

'Terrible things, those flying bombs.'

'Yes. They just fell, then exploded on the surface. Not like real bombs that left a huge crater. The fliers flattened everything around them. I think, unconsciously, that I'd been counting. I'd got to seventeen

198

before I heard the noise. No more, after that. I woke up in hospital.'

'Tatiana, darling girl. It's cold. It isn't a day for remembering. Let's away back?'

'No. Haven't been here since it happened. I'd thought about it, but I knew I wasn't brave enough to come alone. So bless you, Bill, for being with me. And can you wait here, for a minute? The tree is over there. I'd like to stand by it, on my own.'

'And say goodbye?'

'No. I wasn't at Kitty's funeral. Too ill. But I've said goodbye to her since in oh, dozens of places. And at her grave, too. I've got to stand under that tree, though, so I can realize how very lucky I am. All right, Bill?'

'Aye, lassie. I'll wait here. Do what you have to, but don't be too long, eh?'

He watched her go, never for a second taking his eyes from her. She walked straight-backed, head high, that granddaughter of a countess, with some of the aristocrat in her, still.

He watched as she reached the tree, looked up into the branches. Then she laid the palms of both hands on the bare, black trunk, and bowed her head. She was back, by his side, in little more than a minute.

'Got it sorted, did you?'

'Mm. I held my hands on that tree for a count of fifteen seconds, and it didn't take hours for me to realize that I was alive; that I had you. And I knew for certain that Kitty hasn't gone. Nothing could wipe out Kitty Sutton, like a duster across a blackboard. Kitty will never be gone. That's why I didn't say I was sorry that I was alive and she was dead, because she isn't dead. She was too joyous a spirit ever to be lost. She's somewhere, waiting, resting, wondering maybe.' Her voice fell to a whisper and she reached for Bill, drawing him close, resting her cheek on his chest. 'But she's with us, still. She *is* . . .'

'Aye, lassie.' He cupped her head with his hand, making little hushing sounds, begging her not to cry. But the eyes that looked up at him shone with love, not tears.

'It's all right, Bill. I know now why Kitty wanted me to come. She doesn't like being dead and because we were so close, I knew it at once. And darling, don't tell anyone about this? Don't tell anyone we came here? Promise you won't?'

'I promise, Tatiana.'

'Then let's go back to Aunt Sutton's little house? Let's go up west and see if we can get tickets for a show; see if we can find somewhere with a decent meal to offer? Tomorrow, we'll be back in Holdenby, Mr and Mrs Benson. Today, we are on our honeymoon, still, and tonight is our last night. Let's live it like there's no tomorrow?'

And he laughed, and took her cold cheeks in his hands and kissed her long and hard.

'But there is a tomorrow, wife darling. For you and me, there *is*!'

'I know it!' She threw back her head and laughed with joy. 'And aren't we the lucky ones!'

'So how does it feel – your first Christmas away from Rowangarth?'

'Rather nice, Nathan. Snug, and not so full of echoes as Rowangarth, but that's because the floors here are wood – except the kitchen, of course.'

'Hey! If you want to talk about echoes, don't forget Pendenys Place. When you walked anywhere, there, it was like being in a cathedral. But the Bothy will suit me nicely, Julia. Are you going to change the name?'

'Heavens, no. Bothy House, Farm Lane, Holdenby. That'll find us. And isn't it lovely, having fires in all the rooms? Decadent, sort of. Like when coal was one-and-six a bag, and not rationed. Weren't we lucky, there being some left in the coalhouse from the Land Army days.'

'And wasn't it lucky no one knew it was there, or it would've been burned long ago. When are we expected at Keeper's Cottage?'

'Daisy and Keth and the baby are there for Christmas dinner, but they'll be leaving before six, Alice said, because of the baby's timetable. She said we were to arrive at about six-thirty, for supper. She's doing jugged hare with the last of the Christmas port, mince pies and cheese for afters. Sure you don't mind having sandwiches for lunch? Polly said best I didn't try to cook Christmas dinner on that old iron range. Polly is used to it. I'm not. And the men will be here to fit the electric cooker, when the holiday is over. I shall manage very nicely, here, though it's a pity Drew couldn't go back to Llangollen with Lyn. It'll be strange for Lyn, having her parents with her for the first time ever.'

'Yes, but she'll be bringing them to Rowangarth,

for New Year. I'm looking forward to meeting them and talking things over with the lovely Blod.'

'Why do you call her that, Nathan?'

'Because that's what Drew always calls her. He's met her, don't forget. Before Kitty, wasn't it, when he and Lyn were close?'

'Yes. And they'll be even closer in April, thanks be. Wonder how soon they'll start a family. I'd like a grandchild. Alice is so smug about Mary Natasha that sometimes I could thump her.'

'Julia! Let Drew and Lyn get down the aisle, first! Just let's you and me sit here nice and snug and count blessings, eh? It's the first Christmas Day I've had off in years. I rather like being almost-retired.'

'*Almost*. Don't forget you've got Drew's wedding.'

'How could I forget?'

'And baby Eleanor to christen when Bas and Gracie come over in April. And you can't hang up your dog collar for a while, yet. There'll be Drew's children to christen, and Tatty's.'

'Tatty wants a family, then?'

'She certainly does. And she'll be a good mother, too. Denniston babies will have a lovely upbringing – not like Tatiana, poor child, when she was young. And we were right to move here. Rowangarth belongs to Drew. It's all his, now.'

'It's going to be a big change for Lyn, running that house.'

'She'll have Tilda and Mary. Those two come with the furniture and fittings. If I were Lyn I'd leave them to it, settle in gradually. I don't think Rowangarth will worry her. She loves the place. Being Lady Sutton, though, is altogether another matter. It bothers her a bit.'

'Can't see why. Drew has never bothered about having a title.'

'That's because he had one stuck on him when he was a couple of hours old, Nathan. People who watched him growing up referred to him as young Drew. Mind, after the war, they did sometimes give him his due and say, "Morning, Sir Andrew." But he's still mostly Drew. Lyn will get used to it. What worries me more is her having to follow Kitty.'

'Now why should it?' Nathan reached for his tobacco jar which was in exactly the same place as it had been at Rowangarth; on the small table beside his favourite chair, and always lined with a cabbage leaf. 'Lyn is a sensible girl. I think she's already come to terms with Drew's first love. I did it. Why shouldn't she?'

'Because you are you, and nothing flusters you. You waited years for me to come to my senses. You're as comfortable to have around as a pair of old slippers. Lyn is different and I'd bet anything you like that underneath there's a flash of temper to match that red hair. Drew is going to have to go carefully, at first.'

'Drew will be just fine. He's an old slipper type, too. And since it's Christmas Day, do you think we might have a sherry before lunch – just to christen the place, sort of?'

'What a good idea! And I know exactly where the decanter and glasses are. I'm not so disorganized as you might think.'

'I'll go and get them. Sideboard in the dining room?'

'No, darling. In the little back bedroom on top of an empty packing case, near the window. And be careful. I haven't got around to putting a light bulb in there, yet.'

And Nathan smiled and said he would be, and thought how lucky he was to be living in the Bothy, just he and Julia; lucky because it was Christmas and because Julia was his wife and he loved her very much.

At the door of the small bedroom he struck a match and held it high, whispering, 'And if you are only half as lucky as your Uncle Nathan, young Drew, you and Lyn will do very well indeed. Word of a Sutton, you will!'

Agnes Clitherow sat beside the drawing-room fire in her wheelchair, watching Drew pour sherry into two crystal glasses, because Miss Clitherow always insisted that the better the glass, the better the sherry tasted.

'Will I tell you something, Sir Andrew – as one who has watched you grow into manhood, I mean?'

'Of course you will! And I shall listen carefully, because you have so much to tell. How long have you been at Rowangarth?'

'Longer than I'm prepared to say! But this concerns you, when you were a little baby, just a few days old. Your father, the dear man, died the morning you were born because he was too ill and weak from his war wounds to fight that terrible influenza. And your mother, Lady Alice, lay there in a fever, because she had that 'flu, an' all.

'Miss Julia was looking after you and almost out of her mind, because your mother had no breast milk for you, and every time you were given a bottle of cow's milk, you threw it up. Hungry, you were, and crying all the time because your little empty stomach ached, I suppose.'

'Did I cry a lot, Miss Clitherow?'

'You did, and so would I have done if I were half starved. Anyway, Miss Julia – she was newly a widow, don't forget, and grieving for Doctor Andrew something cruel – said to me, "Miss Clitherow, I've got to find milk for this child! That war took too much from Rowangarth." Her two brothers it had taken and her own dear husband, you see. "And I'll not see it take this child from me!" She'd have called the doctor, but he couldn't have come. Too busy writing death certificates for folk round here who were dying from 'flu. Working night and day, he was.'

'But I got well, didn't I?'

'That you did, Sir Andrew, and all thanks to Jinny Dobb.'

'Old Jin? What had she to do with it?'

'Jinny Dobb knew all about hungry bairns. Her sister had had three lads all grown up tall and strong and reared on goat's milk, would you believe? Jin said Miss Julia should try it – a last hope, sort of. I remember it so well. You were in the kitchen, crying pitifully, your little feet to the fire and your toes spreading out to the warmth. And Jin mixed that goat's milk with water and brown sugar, and warmed it, and you sucked it from that bottle like a good 'un. And you kept it down! All you threw up was a big, contented burp of wind, then you settled down and slept. And stopped your crying, an' all.

'There's a sad end to it, for all that. Jin's sister's lads that had grown up so straight and strong were all taken in that war; all three brothers in one day. But this war – *your* war – was kinder to Rowangarth. Only took Miss Kitty, bless her. They say that God picks the fairest flowers for his garden. So sad . . .' Her head drooped, her eyes began to close. 'Oh, dear me. Nodding off, I was. Sherry always makes me nod.'

'Then shall I wheel you back to your room, Miss Clitherow, so you can have a little doze?' He took the sherry glass from her fingers. 'Is there anything you want?'

'I thank you – no. Mary Stubbs said she would come over and help me into bed at nine. And thank you for letting me share your Christmas dinner.'

'Thank you for coming. I was all alone. Good of Tilda to have brought it over for us.'

'The place won't be so quiet next Christmas. The new lady of the house will be having a party, I shouldn't wonder. Your grandmother, my dear Lady Helen, always loved Christmas; parties galore, and she loved young people around her. But I do feel a little drowsy. Thank you for your kindness, Sir Andrew.'

'And thank *you*.' He laid a rug over her knees, then bent to kiss her cheek. 'Happy Christmas, Miss Clitherow.'

He closed the door of the little room behind him, thinking how strange it was that the house was so quiet; as if it were waiting, almost. Waiting to be lived in again, and have children in it who would run wild at Rowangarth as the Clan had done. And he thought of Lyndis, wishing she were on the phone so he could wish her a Happy Christmas and tell her he loved her and couldn't wait for April.

Funny, for all that, that Miss Clitherow had mentioned Kitty. But everyone mentioned Kitty – all the time. And Lyn would get used to it; once they were married, it would come right for them both.

He raked through the fire and threw on more logs, then sat in the chair beside it, thinking of Kitty; thinking of the Christmas his mother had photographed them in the conservatory, all six of the Clan dancing to the gramophone, learning to tango. Taught by Kitty, of course.

He jumped to his feet, tired of the solitude, determined to walk in the cold air, wake himself up, bring the frostbite to his cheeks. And where better should he go than to the churchyard where the Suttons lay close together, the Pendenys Suttons on one side of the path, the Rowangarth Suttons on the other. It would be good to stand at Gran's grave, wish her a happy Christmas. And Kitty, too, who danced such an abandoned tango. Darling, beautiful, wilful Kitty . . .

'Are you warm enough, Grandmother?' Tatiana asked. 'Would you like your shawl?'

'No, I thank you. Today I am not feeling the cold so much. I must be getting used to your dreadful northern winters.'

'But surely it was colder in St Petersburg?' Tatiana

regretted the question as soon as she asked it. 'I mean –'

'In Russia it was a different kind of cold. Not like here. And in Petersburg we knew how to keep warm. There was coal and wood for fires and stoves and when we went out in sleighs or carriages, we had fur coats and fur hats. And blankets of fur, too, over our knees.'

'All right for some,' Tatiana shrugged. 'How did the peasants keep warm; your great unwashed? How was it for them?'

'Child, it is Christmas and I am a guest in your house, so I will not respond to your anger. And as for the people – I long ago decided they had a right to Mother Russia. Oh, they stole it from the Tzar, God rest him, but they fought like wild things when Hitler tried to take it from them. I have accepted that there will be no more Romanov, but I hope that some day you will be able to visit my beautiful city, and find your grandmother's old home.'

'We'll do that, if the Fates allow,' Bill smiled. 'That's a promise, Countess. Mind, there was a lot of bombing and people burned everything they could lay hands on during the siege to keep warm; furniture, trees . . .'

'Trees. Ah, yes.' Her eyes took on a remembering look. 'There were so many near my house. To look out of any window was a delight in summer.'

'Trees? Then don't you think it time for the Countess to have her Christmas present?' Bill smiled.

'I think maybe it is, darling. And Grandmother – I know I sometimes get uppity about your precious

Petersburg and your Tzar – but I do try to understand how it was for you, and how mad I'd be if
someone took Denniston House off me without so
much as a by-your-leave. I – Bill and I – thought you
perhaps would like a memento.'

She went to the conservatory and brought back a
large, flat package. It was wrapped round with brown
paper and string because Christmas wrappings were
still considered a luxury, and forbidden.

'This is for you, with our love. We hope you will
take it back to London and sometimes look at it, and
remember. And go on – open it!'

Slowly, the old fingers fumbled with the knots,
because even a countess saved string in post war
Britain. Then she shook off the paper wrapping and
held up a picture – a watercolour of a beautiful,
graceful building set against a summer-blue sky, and
with trees all around it.

'I – I hope I got it right. I took it from a picture
in a book. It's out of context, mind.'

'It is the Admiralty building, in St Petersburg.'
Olga Petrovska's voice was rough with emotion. 'And
yes, William, you have got it right – the column, the
statues, the beautiful spire. I lived near there, you
know.'

'You did? Funny, but I got the feeling you would
like it when I was looking for something to paint for
you.'

'You have it exactly right. Even the sunglow on
the dome is just as it was, in summer. I could see the
spire from my house. Do you know, William, that if
you could stand with your back to that picture and

look straight ahead, you would see where we lived, three houses down. It is most kind,' she whispered, eyes downcast. 'You could not have given me anything I appreciate more. Your husband, Tatiana, is a very talented painter.'

'But Countess, I'm no' a lot of good at such things. Flowers are what I do best. Are you sure you like it?'

'Very sure. I once painted – dabbled, really – but I was nowhere as good as you are, William. You have a feel for light and shadow. I suggest you continue to paint landscapes.'

'In watercolour?'

'Why not, if they are as good as this one?'

'Then you like it, Grandmother? You really do?'

'I *love* it. It makes me happy and sad, both at the same time.' She dabbed delicately at her eyes with a flimsy handkerchief. 'You know – sometimes in Cheyne Walk – I gaze through the window and shut London out of my vision. And I am back in my salon, looking through my window and down the Nevsky Prospekt. It takes me back to a time when I had a husband, and two fine sons and a daughter. Our future was secure. Sometimes I think that the only worry I had was who my children would marry – suitable spouses, I mean.

'But now my Peter is dead, and Vassily, too. And Igor is an old bachelor with no desire to marry and have a son to keep the name and title alive. And as for my beautiful Anastasia Aleksandrina –'

'Who made a disastrous marriage and who now is very happy with her middle-class doctor,' Tatiana

210

teased. 'Admit it, Grandmother! She is even more beautiful now she is in love at last!'

'Perhaps you are right. And you, child? I think you are happy, too.'

'I'm happy.'

'Aye. With her gui' talented husband who'll one day be a famous painter!'

'Do not joke, William. One day you *will* be famous – and rich, too. And since we are being so nice to each other, do you think we could have a glass of sherry, Tatiana? It is Christmas Day, after all. Let us drink to being happy, and then to my beautiful Admiralty.'

'Mm. And then we'll drink to the Tzar, God rest him,' Tatiana beamed. 'Had I better wake Uncle Igor and Karl?'

'No. Leave them to their so-English afternoon sleeping. There will be more for us, then. And who is coming up the drive? You have a visitor, Tatiana.'

'Aye. It's Drew, looking half-frozen. I'll away and let him in.'

'Do that, Bill, and I'll pour another glass. Poor love. He's all alone this afternoon.'

'That is not right. At Christmas and New Year in Petersburg, no one went alone and no hungry person was turned away from our door.'

'Well, Drew isn't exactly alone. He's going to Foxgloves tonight and on Boxing Day Aunt Julia and Uncle Nathan will be going back to Rowangarth for the day because the cooker isn't fixed up at the Bothy, yet. Don't worry about Drew. Lyn and her parents will be here for New Year, and then we'll all be counting off the weeks to the wedding.' She ran arms wide to greet her cousin, hugging him, kissing his cheek.

'Hi, Tatty. Happy Christmas. And may I say you look extremely good on married life?'

'You may. And before I get myself settled, I'll tell Winnie at the exchange that if anyone phones Rowangarth, she's to plug it through here. Then you can stay with us till you go to Daisy's.'

'Better hadn't. Miss Clitherow is on her own.' He smiled as the Countess nodded a greeting, and bowed as she would have expected, then kissed the hand she offered. 'And Happy Christmas to one and all,' he smiled, lifting his glass.

'Yes, and let's drink to next Christmas, as well, and that Rowangarth will be bursting at the seams!' Tatty beamed.

'It would make a change,' Drew smiled wryly, 'and I'll drink to it, gladly.'

'You and your fiancée will be married by then, Sir Andrew,' the Countess smiled. 'I hope my son and myself will receive an invitation to your wedding.'

'Of course you will. April the ninth. Write it in your diary. In ink!'

All at once the loneliness seemed to leave him, and he thought of Lyn and their wedding; wondered what she was doing now.

Happy Christmas, Lyn darling.

He sent his thoughts high and wide to a cottage at the end of a lane near Llangollen. Lyn would be happy, today. The first Christmas she had spent as part of a real family since she was twelve years old.

He would make her happy. As Tatiana said, next Christmas Rowangarth would be full of people. They would invite oh, just about *everyone* – if food wasn't still rationed, that was!

'You don't know how marvellous it is to have a mother and a father and all of us here together,' Lyn smiled.

'You've always had a father and mother,' Blodwen Carmichael snorted, 'except that now they're decently married!'

'Yes. I'm legitimate,' Lyn smiled dreamily, because she had had too much to eat and drink at Christmas dinner which left her feeling happy and contented.

'I like this house,' Blodwen said to her husband. 'It's such a nice little place. Where else would you find a house so right for us, with walls two feet thick. Cool in summer and snug in winter. You're sure, Jack, that you really want to come here to live?'

'If you'll be happiest here, lovely girl, then that's where I want to be. And I'll be near Lyn, too. The pair of us have a lot of catching up to do.'

'Mm. Nearly eighteen years, Dad. Mind, if you want to be even nearer, I can always ask Drew to bear you in mind when an estate house comes vacant. Do you fancy that, Mum?'

'It would have its points but I don't think it would be right, living so near to my married daughter.'

'Daisy only lives a few minutes' slow walk from her parents. No trouble, there. And handy for baby-sitting.'

'Y-yes. Very nice, I'm sure, our Lyndis. But I have a mind to live in my little cottage again. I've seen some lonely, unhappy times here so now I'm looking forward to living in it with your dad. And when we're settled in, he's of a mind to buy a car so we'll be able to come often to visit – when petrol comes off the ration, that is. You'll be happy with that, won't you, *merchi*?'

'Very happy, Mum.'

So happy in fact that it just wasn't true. Today, relaxed and warm, she felt wrapped round by her lovely pink cloud; felt that nothing, ever again, could make her unhappy.

But how would she feel in the morning? she demanded silently of the glowing fire. How would it be when she awoke tomorrow to windows frosted over, and the living room cold because the fire had gone out? How would it be when tomorrow she walked to the phone box at the crossroads and tried to get through to Drew – and no one answered, at Rowangarth?

Stop it, Lyn Carmichael! This was Christmas and soon it would be another year, and she and Drew would be married.

She took a cushion and hugged it, pulling her feet beneath her, wriggling into the soft sagginess of the chair to close her eyes and think about Drew, and how much she loved him. And, if she wanted a bonus for Christmas, how much he loved *her*.

'You've gone all quiet, our Lyndis. What are you thinking about?'

'Anything and nothing.'

'Are you, now? Thinking about nothing when your head should be full of your young man, and your wedding!'

'Actually, I *was* thinking about Drew . . .'

'And about your wedding, I hope. I must say that you're taking it all very matter-of-factly. You haven't even tried on Daisy's dress yet.'

'It'll fit. She and I are the same size. And now that Drew's mother has got the move behind her, we'll be looking at the family veil. Lady Helen first wore it.'

'Be a bit yellow, won't it?' Blodwen frowned.

'I believe not. Last time she checked it was all right. Daisy could have worn it, and didn't; Kitty wanted to wear it but . . .'

'Kitty. You're still worried about her, then?'

'I'm *not* worried, Mum! When did I ever tell you I was?'

'You didn't need to. I'm your mother; I know what goes on in that head of yours! And don't be shushing me and looking at your dad. He's been asleep these last ten minutes, so let's you and me have a talk, eh?'

'There isn't anything to talk about. Kitty was Drew's first love but it wasn't to be. Oh, sometimes I think about our honeymoon and me not – well, you know – me very inexperienced in that department.'

'So you haven't been lovers, yet? But you're normal, the pair of you; haven't you even talked about it?'

'Yes. A lot. But one of us usually has the sense to count to ten.'

'Well, I'm not suggesting anything, mind,' Blodwen said, matter-of-factly, 'but you are wearing his ring and I wouldn't be surprised if young people, especially engaged couples, didn't think it was all right to take the odd liberty. We've lived through six years of

215

war, and we're a bit more broadminded now, about girls being virgins on their wedding night.'

'Mum, there's nothing I want more than to marry Drew. And I don't care how soon I get pregnant, either! It's just that since we've behaved ourselves this far, it seems a few more weeks won't matter.'

'That's all right, then. God knows it was terrible that Kitty was taken, but she's at rest now, the poor young thing, and it's you Drew is marrying. So get that wedding dress tried on. You're a bit bustier than Daisy – it might want a bit of adjustment. And have a look at that veil – get yourself thinking weddings. And what about white shoes? Have you bought them, yet? And you'll need white stockings, too. You'd better be shifting yourself, our Lyndis!'

'Mum, I resent giving up five clothing coupons for a pair of shoes I shall only wear once! Daisy borrowed hers – I'll start asking around. And I don't fancy white stockings. They're a bit old-fashioned, now. I'll wear flesh-coloured ones.'

'Pity about those old clothing coupons. You'd have thought they'd have been done away with long ago. You could have had a lovely new dress, instead of having to borrow.'

'Mum! If wedding dresses were coupon-free, I'd still want to wear Daisy's. It's the most beautiful I've ever seen. And can we get off the subject of weddings for a bit? Thing is, I've been going every weekend I could to Drew's place; didn't think it right that he and I should be alone here. Might start gossip, for one thing.'

'Yes, and for another, you might have hopped into

216

bed, the pair of you and that would've been terrible, wouldn't it – being hanged for a sheep, I mean. Anyway, didn't you say Drew is on his own, now, in Rowangarth?'

'Yes. His mother and Uncle Nathan moved into the Bothy a week ago. And that's why I think it would be a good thing if Drew came here, for a change. As soon as Dad goes back to Kenya, I mean. I could share with you and Drew could have my bed.'

'Not a bad idea. I'm looking forward to seeing him at New Year. A long time since he came here with you. During the war, wasn't it? Daisy had gone home on leave, or something?'

'Mm. Drew's boat was in and I had him all to myself. Not long after that, Kitty happened . . .'

'And like I said, *cariad*, Kitty Sutton is at rest, now.'

'Yes. And I'm going to marry the man I've been mad about since the first time I met him, so don't worry about me. It'll all work out just fine, I promise.'

'Just fine,' Bronwen Carmichael echoed, yet she sometimes wondered about her daughter's attitude to her wedding. Drew was film-star handsome and loved her, of that there seemed no doubt. And Lyn loved Drew, so why wasn't the girl up and down like a yo-yo; buzzing around like a dizzy bee; over-the-moon happy? And why hadn't she yet tried on Daisy's wedding dress, nor bought her wedding shoes?

But maybe it was because Lyn couldn't quite believe her luck; that she wouldn't, in fact, believe it until she was walking down the aisle. And maybe the girl was right; it would work out just fine and it was only thoughts of her wedding night that was bothering her.

'Shall I put the kettle on?' she asked of the young woman who gazed into the fire; who should have had stars in her eyes, and hadn't. 'And you'd better give your dad a shake, ask him if he wants a cup, too.'

Ah, well. Not to worry, she thought as she set the kettle to boil. Things would work themselves out, given time.

Duw, but she hoped so!

TWELVE

'So, Drew – has it been a good birthday?'

They sat in the winter parlour, shoulders close, fingers entwined, feeling strange in the almost-empty house.

'It has. Never usually made a fuss on my birthday, it being between Christmas and New Year. I like the pullover you gave me, Lyn. Must have cost the earth.'

'It made a hole in my clothing allowance; long-sleeved pullovers cost eight coupons, so that shows how much I feel about you,' she teased.

'So you still love me, still want to marry me?'

'Yes to the first; eight clothing coupons I love you, and yes please to the second.' She held up her left hand so the emerald she wore flashed in the firelight. 'For a long time I was very conscious of my ring; like I was all left-handed. But I'm used to it, now. Can't wait to get the set.'

'Me, too. It's going to be good having the crowd here tomorrow night. I like your father, now I've met him, and as for the gorgeous Blod – she doesn't change. Still full of fun.'

'Yes, but slimmer and smarter and her hair is as

lovely as ever. And something has just hit me. What if we have a red-haired son? You Suttons are supposed to be fair, aren't you?'

'As long as he comes complete with his mother's freckles, I won't mind a bit. By the way, Tatty's mother won't be coming to Rowangarth to see the New Year in. She and Ewart are going to Denniston to keep Karl and the Countess company. Tatty said that not for anything was she being saddled with her grandmother tomorrow night; said having her over Christmas was bad enough!'

'But you told me the Countess was very affable on Christmas Day, that Bill had done her a watercolour of St Petersburg, and she'd been quite overcome.'

'She was. But she was her awful self again on Boxing Day, Tatty said. They had a good time in London on their honeymoon, I believe. Will you mind, Lyn, if we can't make Paris in April? Would Montpelier Mews be all right?'

'Anywhere will be all right. In April the parks will be green again and there'll be lots of blossom out. I think I'd prefer London.'

'But April in Paris would have been marvellous, darling.'

'So will April in London. Tatty said that staying at the little house was every bit as good as the bridal suite in the York hotel they spent their wedding night in. Loads cheaper, too.'

'Money doesn't come into it; not on honeymoons. But we'll have to wait and see if the government lifts travel restrictions. Quiet, isn't it?' He hugged her closer, then kissed her ear. 'You and me all alone, I mean.

Mary and Tilda gone home for the night . . .'

'And Miss Clitherow just two doors away, don't forget, so behave yourself! Just because your mother and Nathan have moved into the Bothy doesn't mean we can take liberties!'

'But you want us to, don't you, Lyn? People aren't so particular, now, about virginal weddings. Do we have to wait?'

'We don't have to, but I'd rather keep it for after we're married. Dammit, Drew Sutton, I've been hanging on for years for you – surely three more months won't make a lot of difference?'

'Of course it won't, but if just once both of us forgot to count to ten, it wouldn't be the end of the world, would it?'

'No. But I might be walking down the aisle three months gone, had you thought of that?'

'Actually, I hadn't,' he laughed. 'But you feel the way I do, Lyn?'

'You know I do,' she said softly, 'but I'd rather Uncle Nathan gave us the okay, first. He was so lovely when he married Tatty and Bill.'

'He ties a good knot, Daisy says. And there's no one in the world I'd want to marry us but him. You aren't going to get cold feet at the last minute – run away to sea, or something awful are you? You're truly happy about us?'

'I'm truly, *truly* happy, Drew.' She took his face in her hands and kissed him gently. 'But if we sit here much longer all relaxed and smug and *alone*, one of us is going to have to start counting! What you and I need is a walk in the cold air to sober us up, so why don't you take me back to Daisy's – the long way round. We can call at the Bothy to say goodnight to your folks and mine on the way. I wonder if your mother is missing Rowangarth. She's lived there all her life. Do you think it was a wrench for her, when the time came to go?'

'Not really. Nathan has as good as retired. He'll be handing over to the curate as from New Year's Day. He'll just be around the parish, if needed, except for our wedding and Eleanor's christening. Mother says there'll be a letter from Kentucky any day now, about Gracie's new baby.'

'Will I tell you something? I used to be madly jealous of Gracie. Daisy once came back from leave and said you and she and Gracie, and Tatty and Tim had all been to the aerodrome dance, and that you and Gracie danced together a lot. Did you ever think you might fall for her, Drew?'

'No. I liked her a lot and she was a good dancer, but Bas had made it pretty plain that he wanted Gracie. But if you're determined you aren't going to stay and run the risk of being ravished, then we'd better look in on Miss Clitherow and let her know we're going, and that I've got a key.' He drew her to him, kissing her long and hard. 'I love you.'

'And I love you, Drew Sutton, but let's get ourselves off to Daisy's? A few gulps of cold night air will do us both the world of good!'

And put paid for the time being at least, she thought, to all thoughts of *that*, no matter how delightful to contemplate!

* * *

'I was talking to Miss Clitherow. Getting to know the local history, sort of. Elderly she may be, but her brain is sharp.'

Alice and Blodwen Carmichael sat in the warmth of the Keeper's Cottage kitchen, drinking tea.

'Gossip?' Alice laughed.

'Kind of. What started it was that big old house. Saw it when Jack and I went for a walk. Pendenys Place. Terrible forbidding, it looks. Is it haunted?'

'Not that I know of. But the Army took it in the war – Lord knows what for – and it's been empty since they left. Nathan – Julia's husband – was born there.'

'But the Reverend is a lovely man! I was given to understand that the Pendenys Suttons weren't – well – out of the top drawer, you might say.'

'Miss Clitherow is a terrible snob, but she's half-right. Clementina Elliot married Edward Sutton. Edward was a Rowangarth Sutton, but the second son.'

'And second sons had to shift for themselves.'

'They did, indeed. Either the Army, the Church or marrying money. Mr Edward married Clementina's money. Mind, they were happy at first, but she had three sons in three years, then shut her bedroom door in his face, Mrs Carmichael.'

'Now didn't I ask you to call me Blodwen? We're going to be in-laws, so we'll have to drop the formality sooner or later. And I'd like it if I could call you Alice. Apart from being Drew's first mother, I feel I know you through Lyndis. She came here a lot, didn't she, when she and Daisy were Wrens. But tell me about that old house? Who does it belong to?'

'It isn't old – only built to look that way by old Nathan Elliot for his daughter, Clementina, when she married Edward Sutton. Mr Edward was a gentleman, deserved better than that one, in my opinion. But he spent as much of his time at Rowangarth as he could – it was still home to him, I reckon.

'Edward inherited Pendenys when Clementina died. She had intended that her first-born should have it. All she ever did – all her money – was for her precious Elliot. But he was killed and she never got over his death.'

'Elliot Sutton? His name came up yesterday, and Julia's face went like she was sucking a lemon. Didn't she get on with him, or something?'

'No one got on with Elliot Sutton, except Mrs Clementina. Not even his father. That young buck thought he could do as he wanted; knew his mother's money would get him out of trouble.'

'With women?'

'Yes. But it's all water under the bridge, now,' Alice said, firmly.

'Mm. Mustn't speak ill of the dead, I suppose.'

Blodwen knew when enough was enough, because it would seem that Alice Dwerryhouse hadn't liked the man, either. Funny, but a look of hostility had shown plainly on her face, too. Interesting, but the late Elliot Sutton was probably taboo, so best she leave it – for now.

'So Julia's husband is a rich man, Alice, and him with no son of his own to leave it to. Pity.'

'Nathan and Albert inherited the money – more

than a million between them – and Nathan was stuck with the estate. Eventually, it will end up with young Bas – Sebastian – Albert's son, in Kentucky. And he hates the place.'

'Is that Bas, who's just had a little girl?'

'It is. And Bas vows nothing on earth would get him to live there. The entail ends with him, and he says he'll pull the place down! He will, an' all, if I'm any judge of character,' Alice laughed.

'What a complicated lot our Lyndis is marrying into!'

'Nothing wrong with the Rowangarth Suttons, believe me. And I should know; I was one of them myself, for a time.'

'Ah. Lyndis told me about Drew having two mothers. You and Julia. You went to your Tom in Hampshire – left Drew behind. It must have been sad for you.'

'I was a Sutton widow; Drew belonged at Rowangarth. It was his inheritance. And I knew he would be fine with Lady Helen and Julia. We never lost touch. The first time Julia brought Drew to stay with us in Hampshire, he couldn't say my name; a big word for a little lad, so he called me Mrs Lady and I've been Lady to him ever since.'

Lies. But she could not tell Blodwen Carmichael the truth of it; of why it had not been hard to leave her son and go to her first love. But only Nathan and Julia and Tom knew, and they would never tell. And thank the good Lord that Drew had been born Sutton-fair and grown up in Giles's image, almost. Dear, gentle Giles. You couldn't speak his name and Elliot Sutton's in the same breath.

'Ah, there's lovely. And I know about giving up a child. I did it; gave Lyndis to my sister to bring up. My own fault, see? If I'd had the sense I was born with I'd have told Jack I was carrying his baby. But the wedding to our Myfanwy was all arranged and anyway, it would have caused a terrible scandal; you know the way people were about children got out of wedlock – still are, come to think of it.

'Anyway, it all came out in the end, and my sister agreed to take Lyndis to Kenya with them. I thought the child would be all right; after all, she'd be with her real father, I told myself. But I got Lyn back in the end. Our Myfanwy – called herself Margot, she did – must have got tired of looking at her husband's infidelity and packed Lyn back to England to boarding school. I got her for school holidays. Then war came and no chance of a passage back to Kenya, for her. It was wonderful, even though she thought of me as her Auntie Blod.'

'Well, it all came right in the end,' Alice smiled, glad the subject of the Pendenys Suttons had been sidetracked. 'You got your first love in the end, like I did. And Lyn waited a long time for Drew, when you come to think of it.'

'Drew is Lyn's *only* love. Shattered, she was, when Drew got engaged to Kitty. What was she like?'

'Kitty? I've got to say it, Blodwen. Kitty Sutton was – *is* – unforgettable. She was dark, with the most beautiful violet-blue eyes you ever saw. And such a tomboy. Always in mischief. D'you know, she would hide herself when she was staying at Pendenys and listen to what the grown-ups were talking about. Then she would tell it to the Clan – accents and all – and have them in stitches. So full of naughtiness, but you had to love her. A real actress, even then.'

'So that's what Lyndis is up against – a girl who is unforgettable?'

'No, Blodwen. Lyn isn't up against anyone. She knows about Kitty and that Drew – all of us, come to that – don't want to forget her. She's gone, now, and Drew accepts it. He loves Lyn, and I should know. Loves her differently, that's all.

'And since I'm being so frank and knowing him as I do, I think he's worried, sometimes, about Lyn's attitude. Not that he's ever said anything, mind, but it's my opinion that Lyn is making a stick for her own back for not facing up to Kitty. Drew is my natural son, and I want him to marry Lyn. Do you know, Blodwen, Lyn sat in this very room when I was doing a fitting for Daisy's wedding dress. Daisy was standing on the table whilst I fixed the hem, and Lyn was sat in the corner on that brass stool by the fire, though I don't suppose she ever thought she'd be wearing the dress herself, one day. She hasn't even mentioned trying it on, did you know? Mind, it'll fit just fine. The two of them are the same height and measurements, but she loves that dress. Even if clothing rationing ended tomorrow and she could go out and buy any dress she wanted, she would still want to wear Daisy's. She told me that herself.'

'So why, do you think, is she being a bit – *reluctant*, sort of?'

'I don't know. Daisy told me that sometimes Lyn seems worried that she's going to have to take Kitty's place. Mind, sometimes she seems happy as can be about it. Trouble is, it's a fair way from here to Wales and long-distance courtships aren't to everybody's liking. Things will come right in the end, and when we've got tonight over with and into another year, we can look ahead to the wedding – and to Bas and Gracie coming over with their new baby to be christened. The time will soon slip past to April. It can't come soon enough, as far as I'm concerned.'

'Yes. Brides do blow hot and blow cold, don't they? Only to be expected, a few mood swings. And don't forget, Alice, I'm not going back to Kenya. It'll be just Lyn and me on our own whilst Jack is settling things out there. If there's anything really bothering her, I'll soon get to know!'

'I've often wondered what made you come back here to live, Blodwen. You're going to have to get used to food rationing again – and the cold winters we have in the north.'

'There's cold winters in Wales, and it's Wales I've come home to. My Celtic blood, I suppose. Wales doesn't let go of you. Calls you back, sort of. There's a word we have for it. *Hiraeth*. A yearning, I suppose it is. And to be quite truthful – I wasn't best pleased living in what was once our Myfanwy's home. I didn't say as much to Jack, but he understood, bless him. I'm hoping he can get the house in Kenya sold and everything settled before the wedding. And that's another thing – Lyn said it was to be June, so what made her change her mind? She's never told me.'

Alice smiled. 'April is as good a month as any for

a wedding. I'll just pop outside for logs. Won't be a tick.'

She hurried out, leaving Blodwen to think that the more she knew Alice Dwerryhouse, the more likeable she became, and that once all the fuss of the wedding was behind her, Lyn was going to be real happy living at Rowangarth. Once she got used to being Lady Sutton, that was!

1949

'I've been thinking,' Keth said, 'that I'd better be making plans for the trip to Hampshire.'

'But it's only just February! Surely you're not going yet?'

'Of course not. I wouldn't want Mam to see the grave in rotten weather like it is now, but I want it all sorted out in my mind, for all that.'

'So when do you plan going?' Daisy frowned.

'Some time in March. I thought we might set off on a Friday, after school. The clocks will have been put forward by then, so we'll cover quite a few miles before it gets dark. If we stop for bed and breakfast along the way, we can be in West Welby by Saturday noon.'

'Which will give Polly time to see Dickon's grave and take a look at Beck Lane. She's bound to want to see it, Keth, though if it's still as it was when you and I were last there, she might get upset.'

'I'd thought about that, too, but she'll want to see the dogs' grave, if nothing else . . .'

'So are you sure you are doing the right thing, Keth?'

She went to stand behind his chair, bending to kiss the back of his neck, loving him as much as ever; still needing to touch him, kiss him, sit on the edge of the bath to watch him shave. She would never get used to the joy of their loving, never wanted to; and would never want to have someone taking her to see Keth's grave. Life without Keth would be unbearable. How had Polly accepted her widowhood the November night someone brought Beth back to Beck Lane in a sack? Beth, the retriever, reared and trained to the gun by Dickon.

'You'll take Polly somewhere decent to stay, won't you? If I can be of any help . . . ?'

What she really meant was that she would pay for the trip, but she had learned to walk carefully with the fortune she had inherited, and mentioned it as little as possible.

'You can get me a couple of petrol coupons – black market,' he grinned. 'That little car does about forty to the gallon, so I've calculated I'm going to need ten petrol coupons, there and back, to be on the safe side. I'm being careful, keeping my foot off the gas and coasting down hills, but I still need four coupons, at least.'

'Then I'm going to have to see the nice man at the garage we got the car from, aren't I?'

'Daisy, you're not to! I teach his son, for heaven's sake!'

'So you do,' she smiled, knowing the mathematics of the garage owner's son had improved beyond recognition since Mr Purvis had come to teach at Creesby Grammar. 'Maybe that's what gave me the idea.'

'Don't, Daisy – please? I reckon I'll be able to come by a few coupons somewhere or other.' It wasn't quite so unpatriotic, now, to sometimes dabble on the black market. 'Mam's looking forward to the trip, and I thought to do it before the wedding.'

'And once the wedding is over, you'll be making plans to go to France?' Daisy said flatly.

'Once travel restrictions are lifted – yes. Reckon it would be best if I drive south, then take the ferry over. I've heard that petrol is easier to come by, on the Continent. Shouldn't be a problem, there . . .'

'Of course it won't! Our lot only won the dratted war, didn't we, yet you'd never think so!'

'Darling, some way or other, I'll get the petrol. I'll have to, because I'm determined to go back to Clissy.'

'But *why*, all of a sudden? Since the baby was born you've gone on and on about it!'

'I have, because only when Mary Natasha was born did I really realize what a lucky so-and-so I was. I knew, then, that I had to make a gesture, if only to say a thank you over a grave – if I can find one, that is. The Gestapo weren't all that particular when it came to burying their dead!'

'Stop it, Keth!' She hurried to sit on the sofa beside him, taking his hand in her own. 'None of it was your fault. You and I were names and numbers and accepted we had to do as we were told for the duration. And if you can't find her grave, at least you'll have made the pilgrimage. I want you to go to that place. I owe it to Hannah – or is it Elise? – as much as you do.'

'Hannah? Elise? I shall always think of her as

231

Natasha who refused to be a child and was always reminding Tante Clara that she was sixteen and a bit.'

'Why someone so young got mixed up in the Resistance, I don't know. I've often wondered if this country had been occupied, how brave I would have been. Not very, I think.'

'Natasha got mixed up in things because Tante Clara was up to the eyes in it. I only found that out when I got back to the Stone House, in Argyll. Her husband was killed in the Great War, you see, and she couldn't forgive it. And Natasha, who was in her care, wanted to do more because I'm as sure as I can be that she knew she would never see her parents again.

'But sixteen is no age to die. Natasha had no childhood; only a few years with her adoptive parents, before the war started. It was a sin, in occupied France, to be both Russian and Jewish. And it won't be a sentimental journey, going back to Clissy; more like you said, a pilgrimage. You do understand, Daisy?'

'I do, darling. Do you realize that I've known you all my life? Mam said you used to stand by my pram when I was a baby, and make me smile. You took me to school, looked after me like a brother, put up with my tantrums . . .'

'You were very good at flouncing off in a huff, but it didn't stop me realizing that it wasn't a sister I wanted.'

'So – having established that I know you as well as I know myself, I wouldn't even think of trying to stop you going to France. You're going there because you're you, because a young girl was shot helping you to get out, and you'll never be quite at peace with yourself until you can see that village again – be near to where she lived.

'It's a pity Jin Dobb isn't alive, Keth. Jin could look into the past, as well as the future. What she told Mam and Aunt Julia came true, though neither of them wanted to believe her at the time, Mam said.'

'So what did she say to them?'

'They would never tell me, but I reckon Jin would have understood why you want to go; maybe help you sort things out in your mind. And we'll have to find a good excuse for you swanning off to France without me. The village will want to know why, and you won't be able to tell them; not even Mam and Dada.'

'We'll think of something,' he smiled. 'And bless you for understanding, darling.'

He pulled her closer and whispered kisses on her cheeks, her closed eyelids, her nose. Then he kissed her mouth and it was a kiss that said, *I want you*.

'Now that will be enough, Keth Purvis! It's only half past seven and I've got ironing to do and you've got books to mark. So get yourself into your cubby-hole and *behave*!'

Keth got to his feet, pausing in the doorway to smile. Then he winked, and took the stairs two at a time.

'Darling?' Daisy called softly so that he turned at the half-landing. 'I love you too – but later . . .'

* * *

'Aaah. That's better, our Lyn.' Blodwen Carmichael sat in dressing gown and fluffy slippers, her hair pinned up. 'Nice to get those old corsets off. I miss your dad, but at least I can relax a bit when he isn't around. I dread to think of the state I'd let myself get into when I was on my own. Having a man helps keep you up to scratch!'

'Will Dad be away long, do you think?'

'Shouldn't think so. There's a couple of buyers interested in the house. But whether it's sold or not, he'll be back for the wedding.'

'He'll have to. He's giving me away!'

'Getting impatient, are you, *merchi*?'

'I suppose I am, but it's hard to think about blue skies and apple blossom and me in a long floaty dress when there's a foot of snow outside. April seems forever away.'

'Well, it isn't. It's only nine weeks off – and you haven't even tried on that dress, yet. What's the matter with you, girl? Not losing interest, are you?'

'No, Mum, but all I seem interested in lately, is keeping warm. The weather is awful. But Drew won't be coming here, on Friday. I'm going to his place, instead. And you needn't worry about my dress. It's in the sewing room at Rowangarth. It's been there since Daisy's wedding and the bridesmaid's dresses, too. Hanging from big hooks in the ceiling with sheets draped over them.

'Daisy said in her letter that her mother is determined to get things moving, and that she and Tatty have already tried on the bridesmaid's dresses. There are two; an ice-blue and a rose one – made over from ball gowns Tatty's mother had no use for. Daisy has tried on the blue and it fitted perfectly, so it's pretty certain the wedding dress will be fine on me.'

'How can you be so sure, Lyn?'

'Because I'm the same size and height as Daisy. Mind, the rose one that Tatty tried on needs a bit of letting out around the bust, but that won't be a big job, Mrs Dwerryhouse said.'

'So can't you see ahead to April, lovely girl? Forget the gales and this awful snow; think apple blossom, and you being married at last.'

'What do you mean, Mum – *at last*? You'd think I've been on the shelf for years!'

'And so you have, waiting for Drew. And if he hadn't asked you, you'd still be there, because after him you never wanted any other man! So I'm glad you're going to Yorkshire on Friday, and don't dare come home unless you've tried on that wedding dress. Might make you feel a bit more bridal, if you did!'

'Mum, I *do* feel bridal. I want nothing more than to marry Drew. I fell for him the first time we met – nearly eight years ago, come to think of it – and nothing has changed.'

'So what's making you blow hot and cold, all the time? Because you are forever at it. One minute you're high as a kite and the next minute you're off on some other tack, like not trying on the dress and being blasé about everything. And don't say it's your female hormones! My generation never had female hormones, and we got along very nicely without them!'

'Mum, I do love Drew. I want to marry him and I really want to wear Daisy's dress. I don't care if all

Holdenby has seen it before, it's the one I want to wear to my wedding. And if I'm sometimes moody – well, put it down to the fact that I can't believe my luck, if you want an excuse. Because I can't! I keep thinking something will happen. Kitty was going to marry Drew, wasn't she?'

'Lightning doesn't strike twice in the same place. Drew isn't worrying, is he, so why should you be?' Blodwen urged. 'But is the truth of it that you're worrying about Kitty? Kitty is dead, poor young thing, and it isn't the dead you should bother about, Lyndis Carmichael. They'll never harm you. It's the living you ought to be looking out for – if look for trouble you must!'

'Kitty may be gone, Mum, but she's everywhere, still. She was one of that precious Clan, wasn't she, and the Clan won't ever let her go! Can you imagine what it will be like at the wedding? The Clan will be there, and they'll talk about Kitty as if that bloody bomb never dropped!'

'Now listen you to me, *cariad*. Come and snuggle up to your mum and let's you and me talk, eh? Brides always have wedding nerves, it's part and parcel of getting married. And why don't you make friends with Kitty?'

'*Mother!* What on earth do you mean?'

'Come you here, now.' She nestled her daughter close. 'And take notice of what I'm going to tell you. I lost the man I loved and I waited for him for more than eight years, so I do know what I'm talking about! Now tell me, have you and Drew been lovers, yet?'

'No, we haven't!' Lyn's chin was mutinously high. 'Oh, I know a lot of girls lost their virginity during the war. War made you want to. But I didn't, although I would have, if Drew had been in the least bit interested. Between you and me, Mum, Daisy and Tatty jumped the gun, and Drew and Kitty, too! In her theatrical digs, in Roscoe Street. So Drew is taking something on, isn't he? Not only do I have hang-ups about Kitty, I'm scared I won't be as good as she was in bed, and that's the truth of it!'

'We-e-ll, our Lyndis, there's two things you can do. First, you are going to have to forget counting to ten, because if you don't, you run the risk of spoiling your wedding night. Mind, I think there should be a law against it, on wedding nights. Your wedding day is going to be a big one and you'll be tired out even before you walk down the aisle. I reckon you should go to bed and sleep in each other's arms – get used to being together – because you'll feel better about everything after a good night's sleep.'

'But Mum, wedding nights – the first time – are special. It always happens. You know – confetti in cases, flimsy nighties, and – well – *that*.'

'I know. But you've got yourself into a state, our Lyndis, and it'll only get worse if you don't do something about it. Anyway, what's wrong with the morning after? But that's between you and Drew. I'm surprised you and him haven't at least talked about it.'

'We have, on and off, sort of. We've even agreed that we want children as soon as possible.'

'But you've never talked to Drew about the *intimate* side of things?'

'We-e-ll, no. I'll think about what you said, though. I will, honest. But you said *two* things. What else must I do?'

'You can straighten things out with Kitty, that's what!'

'Mother! Have you been at the gin, or something?' Shocked, Lyn sat bolt upright. 'How would I do that? It isn't possible!'

'It is possible, Lyn. You should have a word with her. I'll bet you've never been to her grave, even.'

'I – I've walked past it . . .'

'Yes. Eyes down. What about your Celtic blood, then?'

'The special powers we Welsh are supposed to have? Afraid you didn't pass your gifts on to me. I'm not like you are, Mum. I can't see into the future and I don't get *feelings* about things, the way you do.'

'How do you know? Have you ever tried, girl? Have you ever sat completely still, and opened up your mind and your heart?'

'To what, for heaven's sake?'

'To whatever you want. To Kitty Sutton, for a start.'

'Look, Mum, I know I've got to sort myself out and I'll do it – in my own time. I promise I will.' She got to her feet and made for the kitchen. 'I'm going to make a drink. Want one?'

'If there's any gin left, I'll have a drop in a tall glass with hot water and sugar, if that's all right.'

'It was tea I had in mind, but I think I'll join you. I feel like getting plastered.'

238

'Might be a good thing if you did, our Lyn! Maybe you'd let your hair down a bit more, lose your inhibitions. But let's have no more soul-searching and wedding talk, eh? Just tell me you'll bear in mind what I've said?'

'I will. I've already said so.'

She set the kettle to boil and took glasses from the shelf. Go to Kitty's grave, must she? Open up her mind and heart to her, talk to her? Oh, no. Kitty was at rest beside Lady Helen, and no way was Lyndis Carmichael going to start dabbling in things she didn't understand. Not in a million years, was she! So, sorry, Mum. Promise broken as soon as given, because Kitty has nothing to say to *me*! I'm not clairvoyant and that much I *do* know!

She reached for the green bottle, pouring out careful measures. Let her hair down? Lose her inhibitions? Too right she would! Trouble was that Drew was in Holdenby, so much good it would do her!

Defiantly, she sloshed more gin into her own glass. Get plastered? Why not!

'So what height heels do you plan to wear, Lyn? It'll make a difference to the length, you know.'

'Normal, Mrs Dwerryhouse – like now. I was in flat-heeled shoes all the war. Very high heels make me teeter, sort of . . .'

She could not take her eyes away from the froth of silk that still lay across the sewing-room table.

'That's all right, then. Now slip out of your skirt and blouse and I'll ease the dress over your head.

You're not wearing lipstick, are you? Don't want to mark it.'

Lyn said she wasn't, then closed her eyes and held up her arms. The silk made her skin tingle deliciously as it slipped over her head, then slithered and swished sensuously to her feet.

'Well, then – what do you think?' Alice could stand the silence no longer.

'I'd say,' Lyn whispered, opening her eyes, taking in the flush-cheeked girl in the long mirror, 'that if I could create something as beautiful as this, I'd burst out crying. Because that's what I feel like doing now. I'm going to float down the aisle in this. I loved it on Daisy, but to actually wear it is amazing. I'll take very good care of it, Mrs Dwerryhouse.'

'Tush, girl. Don't be bothering yourself about anything. Our Daisy got grass stains all over the back, but the dry-cleaners soon sorted it. And do you think you'll be able to manage the train? When it's over and you're at the reception, you won't want yards of silk trailing behind you. See, I'll show you how . . .'

She lifted the train to show, halfway down, a small circlet of narrow white ribbon.

'There, now. You just slip your little finger into that loop, and you've got your train lifted and under control. It's something I remembered from way back, when ladies wore long fancy skirts and wanted to keep them off the floor. You'll be wearing Lady Helen's veil?'

'I hope so. Drew's mother is going to get it out before I go back – see what condition it's in.'

'And have you decided, yet, what you'll wear with it?'

'Seems there'll be some apricot roses in one of the glasshouses that might be out in time. Mr Catchpole said Sidney Willis was giving them a lot of attention. He suggested a circlet of buds might look nice . . .'

'*Apricot*? You're sure, Lyn? I mean, with your hair they aren't going to look quite right. *White* roses, maybe? There'll be white roses, I'm almost sure of it.'

'No. I'm too pale for white. This silk is creamy, so it's all right. But if not apricot roses – then what?'

'Well our Daisy wore cymbidiums – they call them poor man's orchids – pink ones. And Kitty and Tatty carried tawny ones. We-e-ll, more pale green than tawny. Now *they* would go well with your hair.'

'Mr Catchpole never said anything about cymbidiums. Do you think that maybe he hasn't got any?'

'He'll have some, never fear! Mad about orchids and the like, him and Sidney Willis are. I'll have a word with them. If they're given good warning they can work miracles with flowers. Mind I'm not interfering, Lyn, but I think – ssssh! Someone's coming up the stairs.'

Alice ran to the door and put her weight behind it just as the knob turned.

'Who is it? Who's there?'

'It's me, Mam. Daisy.'

'That's all right, then. Don't want Drew seeing the dress before the wedding.'

'But he's already seen it. He was Keth's best man!'

'Maybe so, but he hasn't seen Lyn in it.'

'Funny, that. I called in at the Bothy on my way

here and asked Aunt Julia if she was coming to see Lyn in her wedding dress and she said she wasn't. "I don't want to see it until Lyn walks down the aisle in it," she said.'

'So what do you think, Daisy?' Lyn asked tremulously. 'Will I do?'

'Do? I'd like to think I looked as good when I wore it! You look absolutely gorgeous, Carmichael.'

'It isn't me. It's the dress makes me look good.'

'I've suggested she forgets apricot roses. Remember those flowers your bridesmaids carried, Daisy?'

'I do, Mam. Tawny green, sort of . . .'

'Yes, and exactly right for a bride with chestnut hair. I'll have a word with the kitchen garden about them.'

'Oh, why is everyone being so good to me?' Tears filled Lyn's eyes and she covered them with her hands. 'It's all so – so *wonderful*.'

'Watch it, Carmichael! Don't snivel all over my dress, or you're in trouble! And of course it's wonderful!'

'That it is. Weddings are grand for lifting people's spirits, and a spring wedding after this awful old winter is just what we all need. Now take off that dress, then off you go the pair of you and I'll clear up here and put the covers back on again. My, but it seems only yesterday I was sewing maid in this very room for Lady Helen,' Alice sighed.

'Mam's having a remembering do,' Daisy laughed as they walked downstairs. 'She'll be thinking about how she used to look out of the sewing-room window and could see the light on in Dada's bedroom at the

Bothy. Dada was under-keeper, then, and all unmarried male staff lived there in those days.'

'The Bothy isn't all that far from Rowangarth, is it?'

'No. You'll be nice and near to your in-laws,' Daisy teased. 'But it's quite light, yet. Shall we walk the long way round back to Foxgloves? We might find a few snowdrops in Brattocks.'

So they left by Rowangarth back door and made for the wild garden that led to the Linden Walk on the right and to Brattocks Wood, on the left.

'D'you know, Daisy, Mum told me I should try on the wedding dress; said I'd feel a bit more bridal, if I did. And she was right. I didn't want to take it off.'

'Been having words with your mother, then, about not feeling very bridal? Because you haven't been acting bridal, Lyn, if you don't mind my saying so.'

'I know. Stupid, aren't I? Mum straightened me out, though. Wedding nerves, she said. And then we got the gin bottle out. I'll tell you what, Purvis, the way I felt when I went to bed, I'd have dragged Drew up with me – if he'd been there.'

'So it's wedding *night* nerves at the bottom of it? Don't know why you're worrying. I didn't.'

'No, but you and Keth – well, you – er –'

'We'd been lovers before we were married,' Daisy said matter-of-factly. 'So what was so wrong with that? There was a war on. Mam found out, but she didn't tell Dada. Don't think she was best pleased about it, for all that.'

'And Tatty and her Tim were. And Drew and Kitty.'

'All right, Lyn. Like I said, we were at war. No tomorrows. Don't go on about it! Either have another good slug of gin tonight if that's what it takes, or shut up about it and walk down the aisle all coy on the ninth of April. Up to you, lovey. This is nineteen forty-nine. Queen Victoria has been dead a long time, don't forget!'

'I know. I'm an idiot. I promise to mend my ways. And thanks for everything, Daisy – and your mum. She was very bossy about the flowers.'

'She wasn't interfering, Lyn. She's just so glad Drew is getting married, that's all.'

'I know she is. I reckon she's loving every minute of it. And her idea about the tawny cymbidiums was brilliant. I hope I shall be able to have them.'

'You will. Catchpole will see to it. And look! There's Dada and Drew. Reckon they've been walking the covers.'

'Walking *what*?'

'Going round the game birds. The hen pheasants will be nesting, soon. The shooting went well this season, Dada said. A good thing; organizing shoots keeps him in a job, and a roof over his head.'

'I've a lot to learn about Rowangarth, haven't I, Daisy?'

'Not really. When Miss Clitherow is in the mood, she'll tell you anything, if it's etiquette you're bothered about. Mary Stubbs and Tilda will run the place for you and Dada will see to the shooting. And Drew knows already about running the estate. So all you've got to worry about, Carmichael, is learning to love Rowangarth, warts and all. And you will!' She raised a hand and called, 'Hi there, you two! Wait for us!'

Love Rowangarth, Lyn thought. But she already did. She only hoped that Rowangarth would love her, because she wasn't going to make a very good job of being lady of the manor, which was something else to worry about!

Then she remembered the silken magic of the wedding dress, and smiled.

THIRTEEN

Tatiana sat on the bench outside the station master's office and thought what a very special day this was going to be. Tuesday, March the fifteenth and Bill would be home in just a few more minutes.

She smiled at the hazel catkins and froths of white wild sloe blossom on the other side of the line, and at daffodils planted by the station master at the end of the war, which now had spread from clumps into a whole wave of gold.

Above her the sky was blue and the sun, if not yet warm, was bright and promising. Winter was over and there was so much to look forward to, so *very* much.

She heard three hoots. The train was passing Brattocks Wood. If she counted off a slow minute, Bill would be here; the man she loved more than she had ever thought possible.

Already, even at the count of thirty, she could hear the roar and clank of the train, the hiss of escaping steam as it braked; could sniff the train smell, warm, oily and sooty.

She smiled brilliantly at the daffodils, sharing her

happiness with them and the joy that bubbled inside her, turning to her right to see the big black engine rounding the bend.

'Holdenby Halt,' called the station master. 'All alight for Holdenby.'

He wore his bright new post-war uniform; it was the only thing that had changed at the Halt, Tatiana thought, her eyes raking the carriages for sight of her husband.

Then she was running to meet him, arms wide, holding her mouth to be kissed because kissing in public, started during the war, was taken for granted now.

'Darling! I've missed you!'

'Away with your bother, Mrs Benson. I've only been gone two days!'

'Two days and three nights! Have you missed me?'

'You know I have. I've got a present for you.'

'I've got one for you, too. At home.' They walked to the car park and Tatiana's small black Austin. 'It's about time you started learning to drive,' she smiled when they were heading for home. 'But tell me – how was London?'

'Just great. I reckon I did a good thing when I got myself an agent; especially one with a share in an art gallery.'

'So how was the exhibition, Bill?'

'Talent-wise, there were artists there better than me – but there were a whole lot I reckon I could leave standing. And I sold two of the four I took. The agent got a good price for them. Far more than I'd have asked. He told me to leave the other two at the gallery, that they'd sell in no time at all.'

'There you are! I told you you'd be rich and famous.'

'I don't know about famous but I'll settle, any day, for thirty guineas for two wee flower paintings.'

'Less ten per cent,' Tatiana corrected. 'What did you buy for me?'

'I got you two petrol coupons! You know, you can buy anything on the black market in London. Ten bob apiece.'

'Are they forgeries?'

'Hope not. And I stood in a queue and got you a lipstick. I felt a right jessie among all those women, but the lassie behind the counter was very helpful. "What is your lady's colouring, Sir?" she asked me, like she was used to serving blokes. And I said, "My wife has dark hair and eyes – quite like yours."

'"Then you'll want the colour I am wearing. Flame." It looked fine on her, so I reckon it'll be just right for you. But what is *my* present? A hint, perhaps?'

'Not so much as a whisper till we're home,' she smiled, pink-cheeked. 'But you'll like it. And I do so love you, Bill, and I'm glad you are home.'

'Me, too. I've missed you a lot,' he said softly, wanting desperately to kiss her; knowing that only idiots tried a thing like that when the lady had her hands on the wheel of a car. 'And I'm glad to be home.'

To Tatiana his wife, and to Denniston House. Home was a very good word.

'You'll never guess!' Lyn Carmichael, home from work, laughed.

'So tell me,' said her mother.

'Shoes, that's what! Remember the date, Mum.

The fifteenth of March. No more clothing coupons! I've got my wedding shoes!'

'And not before time, either! Are they comfortable?'

'Yes, and they're in natural satin.' She unwrapped the shoes, offering them for inspection. 'More slightly creamy, than white. They'll go better with the dress. And afterwards, I can have them dyed any colour I want, they said at the shop. Isn't it marvellous – clothes unrationed at last!'

'You'll be getting yourself a decent trousseau, then – some pretty undies.'

'There's a shopping trip going to Liverpool on Thursday; a cheap day ticket on the train. I didn't think I'd be given the time off, since I'm working my notice, but they said it was okay. Are you coming with me?'

'No, *cariad*! I brought my wedding outfit with me. I'll have a quiet day, here. Shall you buy a going-away suit? Now you can buy all the clothes you want, how about pushing the boat out, get something really smart; long, like the New Look.'

'No. I shall wear my grey pinstripe; maybe get a new blouse, if I see anything I like. But I shall buy a couple of nice nighties and loads and loads of silk stockings! And some panties.'

'Ooooh – do you remember?' Blodwen began to laugh. 'Those terrible navy blue knickers you had to wear in the Wrens? They were real bloomers; came down to your knees.'

'We used to call them blackouts – or passion stranglers. I mean – one glimpse of those would put any red-blooded man off! Any news from Dad?'

'There is. He's got the price he wanted for the house; only got to wait for the legalities to go through. He's seen a shipping firm. They're going to crate up the things we want brought here; by sea they'll take at least two weeks. Once that's done, he's having the remainder sent to the sale room. Glad it's all starting to come right. Is it coming all right for you, our Lyn?'

'Of course it is. Only two more weeks to work; wedding dress and veil sorted; Catchpole says he reckons I'll be able to have my tawny orchids, even though I didn't give him a lot of notice! Drew's mother has got the marquee ordered, and you've got the invitations in hand. Gracie will be decorating the church. She'll be here, soon. They're sailing over on the *Mauretania*. I'm longing to see her children. She's so lucky.'

'Luck doesn't have a lot to do with it – I reckoned you'd know that. All it takes is –'

'Yes, I do know! No need to draw diagrams! And what's for supper – I'm starving!'

'It's toad-in-the-hole and onion gravy. And tinned peaches for afters. Thank heaven we brought that food with us! Mind, Jack is flying back, so he won't be able to bring a lot with him.'

'So tell him to buy more tins and have them packed in the crate with the rest of your belongings.'

'Well! There's clever. I hadn't thought of that! I'll put a PS on the bottom of my letter, in case he hasn't thought of it either. So get your hands washed. Supper's ready when you are – and Lyndis, love . . .'

'Yes, Mum?' She turned, hand on the staircase door.

'Nothing, really. Only be happy, eh? Don't let fool-ish thoughts spoil things between you and Drew. You know what I mean?'

'I know what you mean and we'll be happy, I promise.'

'You took my advice, then – got things straight in your mind between you and Kitty?'

'Everything will be fine, Mum, so stop your worry-ing – okay?'

And with that she clattered up the stairs into the bathroom. And the bathroom door shut with what could only be called a defiant slam.

'Young ones,' Blodwen sighed. 'Can't tell them anything . . .'

But Lyn would be happy with Drew. Any girl could be happy with Drew Sutton – unless, of course, she was stupid enough to let another woman come between them.

Trouble was, Blodwen Carmichael was bound to admit, her daughter could be very short-sighted when the mood was on her, and stubborn with it!

She gave the gravy a stir, poured it into a jug and set it on the table. Then she took the toad-in-the-hole from the oven and sliced it into two pieces.

'Stubborn and stupid!' she whispered, tight-lipped, to the crisp, light batter as she manoeuvred it onto hot plates. 'Just you take care, girl, and don't say your mother hasn't warned you!'

'Holdenby 195.' Alice Dwerryhouse picked up the phone.

'Mam. Can you be an absolute angel? Can you –'

'Yes of course I can.' Alice was already smiling. 'When do you want me to have her?'

'Tomorrow morning. I asked Polly but she's promised to put in a few extra hours at the Bothy for Aunt Julia – still some tea chests to unpack. I want to go to Creesby. There's a cheque book burning a hole in my pocket and I want to do some shopping. I really need silk stockings. I think, of all clothes rationed, that stockings were the worst.'

'There'll be plenty, now. And you might get me a pair of lisle stockings whilst you're about it, size nine. You know the shade I like. The ones I'm wearing won't take another darn, and that's for sure! I thought about going to Creesby myself on market day – get some sock wool and vests for your dad. The ones he's wearing now I'm ashamed to hang out to dry! But see you in the morning if I don't see you before. Must go, love! Got onions frying . . .'

Alice hurried to the kitchen, thinking it would have made a lot more sense to have taken butter or lard or margarine off the ration, instead of clothing.

Mind, the young ones would be having the time of their lives, buying shoes and stockings and dresses and coats and not having to worry about coupons any more. And if she were fair, she had to admit that at least *something* was no longer rationed. What next? Petrol, maybe?

She wondered how many black market petrol coupons Keth had been able to come by; Polly was so looking forward to the trip. Sad to think she had not seen Dickon's grave for more than twenty years. Not long to go, Alice calculated. Less than two weeks.

She filled an earthenware dish with a small amount of beef, a generous amount of fried onions and potatoes, thinly sliced, then slid it into the bottom of the fire oven to cook slowly, pushing shortages of butter, lard and margarine to the back of her mind. Because tomorrow she was having Mary Natasha whilst Daisy went shopping. Seven months old, and sitting up in her pram and smiling often to show her two front teeth. Dark-eyed and dark-haired like Keth, the most beautiful baby Alice had ever set eyes on.

Life was good and very soon, when Drew and Lyn were married, she could ask for nothing more. Life could not get any better. She stood quite still, closed her eyes and said a silent thank you to whoever Up There was listening, because she was so happy, so smug and contented that sometimes she was afraid.

Then, because she was Alice and as down-to-earth as they came, she straightened her shoulders, opened her eyes and smiled at the photographs on the mantelpiece.

She had learned to live life one day at a time, and this afternoon she would put the finishing touches to Julia's wedding two-piece, and tomorrow, Mary Natasha, complete with a bottle of milk, several nappies and a teddy called Wilf, was coming to Keeper's. And further than that she would not, dare not go, not even to think of Drew's wedding. Because happiness should be savoured slowly then tucked safely away, in the deeps of remembering, so it was there to give comfort, if sad times came.

'And that,' she said out loud to the photograph of a girl who looked much too young to be in uniform, 'will be enough of the soliloquizing, if you don't mind, Alice Dwerryhouse!'

Because there were turnips and carrots to be peeled and a pudding to be thought about. She wondered if Tom would mind if it was bottled gooseberries and custard – *again*!

Tatty and Bill sat in the conservatory which, because the sun had been on it, was comfortably warm and green-smelling.

'Thank you for the lipstick, darling, but would you mind if I gave one of the petrol coupons to Keth? Last time I saw him he was still in need of three. For the Hampshire trip, I mean.'

'Fine by me. But when do I get *my* present?'

'We-e-ll – you already half know about it.' She put her hands to her cheeks, closed her eyes and took a deep, deep breath. 'Ewart phoned, yesterday afternoon . . .'

'And?' Bill's voice was husky.

'The tests came back. We – you and me – are going to –'

'Have a baby? But darling, that's wonderful! At least I *think* it is. Are you all right?'

'Of course I am. And we've been half hoping it was on the cards, now haven't we? Say you're glad, darling?'

'Glad? I'll say I'm glad!' He held wide his arms. 'Tatty – no one's going to harm this bairn; no one will give it away when it's a week old! This wee thing is going to have everything it could want! Oh hell! I don't know what to say!'

'This child, Bill Benson, is *not* going to have everything it wants! It will *not* be spoiled! And come here, you old softie!' She dabbed with her handkerchief at the tears that filled his eyes, then laid her head on his chest, hugging him closer. 'Do you know, I'm so happy it hurts.'

'When is it to be?' he whispered.

'Late October. I'm not quite sure. Ewart will tell me, though.'

'Your mother will be thrilled . . .'

'She will, but I told Ewart absolutely no one was to know until I'd told you. I'll tell Mother, of course, but only her. I think we should keep our news until after the wedding. I'm still going to be a bridesmaid.'

'But mightn't you be sick, Tatty?'

'You mean am I going to throw up in the middle of the I-wills? Of course I'm not. I'm only sick mornings. After I've had a water biscuit and a drink of cocoa, I'm fine. I read about the water biscuit and cocoa in the baby book I bought.'

'And what else does the book say?'

'It says that this little thing is all of two inches long! But let's keep it a secret a bit longer? I wouldn't want to upstage Drew's big day. Gracie's baby is being christened the day after the wedding – let's tell everyone then – and book Uncle Nathan for *our* christening at the same time?'

'Whatever you say.' Smiling, he shook his head. 'Oh, I know we thought you might be, but knowing it's really going to happen takes a bit of getting used to.'

'Then repeat after me, "Bill and Tatty are having a baby in October." You'll soon get used to being a father.'

'Aye, but right now, I'd rather kiss you.'

'Mmm.' She closed her eyes and searched with her lips for his. 'I love you, Bill Benson.'

'Well, I must say you kept it very quiet, Ewart Pryce,' Anna scolded, when Tatiana and Bill had left. 'How long have you known?'

'Patient confidentiality, darling,' he teased. 'And Tatty came to see me a fortnight ago. The results came this morning. Shall you like being a grandmother?'

'D'you know, I rather think I will. Will you mind going to bed with a grandmother, Ewart?'

'You know I won't!'

'I do hope everything will be all right for her.'

'Stop worrying, Anna. Tatiana's a strong, healthy young woman.'

'Stop talking like a doctor. What I meant was that I hope her first pregnancy is happier than mine was.'

'It will be. Bill will take good care of her. We all will.'

'Is it all right for you to look after her, Ewart – medical etiquette, I mean?'

'Tatty asked me the same thing. No problem. She isn't my daughter. But you are glad about the baby, Anna? And you've never regretted marrying me – *joining the meedle classes*? You were born the daughter of a count, don't forget.'

'And I am now the wife of a country GP and very happy; happy about the baby, too. As for being born the daughter of a count – I was once a near-penniless refugee, don't forget, who was expected to make a good marriage. And look where it got me!

But that's all in the past and right now, I'd settle for a glass of sherry to drink to the future.'

So they clinked glasses and she said, 'Cheers, Doctor darling, and here's to Tatty and Bill's baby. It's going to be awful, keeping it a secret until after the wedding.'

And he said, 'Cheers! And do you know something, Anastasia Aleksandrina Pryce? You're going to be a very glamorous grandmother!'

'Well, that's absolutely it! Everything unpacked and found a place for! Are you going to like living here, Nathan? After all, you were born in Pendenys Place, such a grand house. How does it feel to be living in a bothy?'

'It suits me nicely, Julia love. It is small but cosy, and I'm looking forward to taking the garden in hand. Think I'll have a word with Jack Catchpole – ask him where best to start. The garden hasn't been touched since the Land Army left the place.'

'Jack will like that. He'll probably offer to lend a hand.'

'That's what I was hoping!'

'Well, I think we have made a good move and at just the right time. When we decided to come here to live, Drew hadn't even asked Lyn to marry him. We must have known.'

'I must say it's quite a relief not to be constantly on call. Nice to be almost-retired.'

'We sound quite smug, Nathan. Actually, I think this is the moment for a toast. Shall we have a snifter of brandy, to celebrate?'

'You sounded just like Aunt Sutton, then. She enjoyed her snifters of brandy.'

'Dear Aunt. She'd be happy to know that Drew is having his honeymoon in her little house.' She stopped and stared into the fire and then, as if finding no answer there she said, 'You're happy about Drew and Lyn, Nathan? You haven't got any forebodings, I mean?'

'Julia – I'm a priest, not a clairvoyant! But why do you ask? Have you had *feelings*, about them? Or is it that, having got us moved into the Bothy you have nothing else left to worry about? Drew and Lyndis are going to be fine. They'll be happy at Rowangarth and have children, too.'

'You think so, Nathan? I do so want grandchildren. Of my own, I mean. The Clan were absolutely wonderful when they all congregated here; made me feel I wasn't quite childless. But Drew's child will be really mine. A blood link.'

'No, Julia,' he said gently. 'Not a blood link. A maternal one.'

'You're right. Drew is Alice's,' she said harshly. 'Alice's, and *his*.'

'I seem to remember, darling, that in our war I married Alice and Giles in the hospital chapel, which made the child Alice carried Giles's. And I'm sorry I said what I did. Drew became your son the moment Alice went to Hampshire, and left him with you and Aunt Helen.'

'No, Nathan. Drew was mine from the minute he was born. Alice was sick and there was no doctor there to help. I birthed Drew, then fought to keep him alive because Alice was lying there, with raging 'flu. And let's not be reminded of *him*, please.'

'I agree. Drew is morally yours and when push comes to shove, morals beat legalities into a cocked hat. Now do we have that snifter, or have you gone off it?'

'When did you ever know me refuse,' she laughed, dark thoughts gone. 'And make mine a big one!'

She bent to lay logs on the fire, then raised the glass her husband placed in her hand.

'I declare this house open,' she smiled, 'and lang may its lumb reek!'

'And may God bless her, and all who sail in her!' Nathan drank deeply from his glass. 'This is a very good brandy.'

'It's the bottle Tatiana gave you at Christmas.'

'Now there you are, Julia. Tatiana is very happy, so why shouldn't Drew be?'

'No reason at all, so drink up, darling, and then we can have another to toast Tatiana and Bill. And Tatty is not very happy; she's *radiantly* happy. I saw her yesterday and she was positively glowing. And by the way, I got an RSVP from Cheyne Walk. Olga Maria, Countess Petrovska, regrets that she and Count Igor Petrovsky will be unable to attend the marriage of Sir Andrew Sutton to Miss Lyndis Carmichael. Straight and to the point. Formal invitation, formal reply. And I suppose it is a bit of a drag for her, coming all the way up north. I hope she sends a present, for all that. Like a Fabergé Easter egg, or some other Russian trinket.'

'If the Countess had managed to get a Fabergé egg

out of Russia, I very much doubt she would be in such genteel poverty now. What a pity she has never thought to sell Cheyne Walk and come to live up here. It would be nice for her to have Anna and Tatty so near. Surely between us Drew and I could fix them up with a place, when one comes empty.'

'The Countess would not live in an estate worker's cottage. I believe she had a big house in Leningrad; couldn't consider a two-up, two-down. They lost so much when the Tzar abdicated. Anna once told me her father had money in an account in Paris – just in case – but I think that is long gone. And they had hidden things – jewellery, gold and the deeds of their properties in Leningrad. That's when her father and elder brother were killed – trying to get them back.'

'And they never did, Julia?'

'No. Igor made it to London. He had the deeds and jewellery – a tiara, I believe. But they never got their hands on their rainy day hoard. For all I know, it's still hidden there unless the Bolsheviks and Mensheviks got to it first. Wonder if there was a Fabergé egg among it.'

'There might have been – who knows. I think the Countess has accepted she will never see Leningrad again. She would be glad, I shouldn't wonder, just to hear it called St Petersburg like it used to be.'

'No hopes of that. Come to think of it, the Soviets were on our side during the war – why have they gone all cold on us again?'

'Stalin is annoyed, I shouldn't wonder, that we beat his blockade on Berlin – managed to get supplies to our sector.'

'And we've been flying in food and fuel to them for just over eight months. More than a million flights, it said in the paper. Why should we take it on ourselves to keep them alive? Not so very long ago, we were knocking the hell out of Berlin with damn great bombs.'

'Julia, love, this war will never be over whilst people want to keep it alive.'

'People like me, you mean, who have good cause to hate everything Teutonic? The Kaiser's lot took my brother and Andrew, and Hitler's mob killed Kitty.'

'You won't ever change, will you, darling? Your joys are so brilliant and your sorrows so deep and dark. I don't think I've ever known you on an even keel.'

'Well, hard luck, Reverend, because I'm too old to change now,' she smiled, making for the decanter. 'Have I been an awful disappointment to you?'

'No, Julia. I've known you all your life, don't forget. I was happy to take on your sorrows and joys. They're part of what you are. Don't change?'

'I won't, old love.' She held up the decanter. 'And I reckon there's enough left here for a couple more snifters each, so let's drink to Tatty and Bill then to Drew and Lyn?'

'You mean, let's get tiddly?'

And Julia, on almost an even keel again, said, 'Why not!'

Jack Catchpole sat on the little green wooden chair in the orchid house and fixed two pots marked *Cymbidium tracyanum* – tawny-green poor man's orchids to the uninitiated – with a look of affection, willing them to behave themselves and flower in ten more days. Which they would, of course. He had counted nine stems and all of them well-budded. A little more heat and humidity and he would have enough flowers for a headdress and bouquet for the bride. And to make his life even more perfect, Gracie Fielding – he had never got around to calling her Gracie Sutton – would soon be here, in this very garden. The lass had arrived at Denniston House last night, late on, with Bas, young Adam, and a bairn asleep in her arms, he had been told.

News travelled fast, in Holdenby, and such good news had put the crusty old gardener into a state of high elation. Not that he was head gardener any longer, but Sidney Willis, who had taken over from him, often asked his opinion on gardening matters and made him so welcome that Jack had never felt entirely separated from Rowangarth kitchen garden. The upturned apple box on which he had always taken his drinkings – made by Gracie, of course – was still considered to be Mr Catchpole's seat and never used by any other. And the two enamelled mugs from which they drank their weak, wartime tea, still stood on the top shelf of the potting shed beside the bottle marked *Poison*. Sidney Willis had had the good sense to retain most of the old ways, which had served to foster friendship and trust between the two gardeners.

Jack squinted sideways at the clanging shut of the high iron gate, expecting to see Sidney back early from his midday break, but it was someone entirely different who smiled and waved.

'By the 'eck, she's comed!'

He was on his feet and hurrying to greet his ex-land girl who was having trouble with a pushchair.

'Eh, Gracie lass. Let me give you a hand. Them perambulators are awkward to push on gravel. You take the handle, if it isn't too heavy for you, and I'll take t'other end.'

'Of course it isn't too heavy for me! I could push a barrow load of manure from one end of this garden to the other, don't forget. And how are you, Mr C?' She hugged him tightly, then kissed his cheek.

'The better for seeing you, lass,' he said huskily as they manoeuvred the pushchair to firmer ground. 'And this is Miss Eleanor Sutton, eh, comed all the way from Kentucky for her christening.' He peered inside the hood. 'And her's the spitting image of you, lass.'

'No, Mr C. She's more like mother-in-law. And Bas says she's going to have good hands – for reins, I mean.'

'Ar? Then I hope you told him that good hands can handle a spade, an' all! Is she going to be a horsy lass, then?'

'We'll have to wait and see. Adam is following in the family tradition. He's to have a pony for his third birthday.'

'And you, lass? Have you taken up horse riding?'

'No. You'll be pleased to know that I have taken charge of the gardens at the stud, and though I says it as shouldn't, they're looking pretty good.'

'And why shouldn't they? You're a time-served gardener, don't forget. Have you taken up orchid growing, yet?'

'No, but Bas says I'm to have a greenhouse for

263

our wedding anniversary – our fifth – so I just might try my hand at it. And since we are sailing back, we won't be so restricted for baggage, and I intend taking a few rowan saplings with me – remind me of Rowangarth.'

'Then you plant them like I taught you, and they'll do well. Mind, they'd have been better planted at the back end of last year, but not to worry. That clump you and me planted in the war are over six feet high, and doing well – be sure you have a look at them.'

'I shall have a look at everything. Oh, Mr Catchpole, it's so good to be back. I think of this kitchen garden a lot; just close my eyes and I'm here again.'

'Ar, lass.' He got out two apple boxes, upending them. 'Then lets you and me sit here like we used to.'

'Fine by me, provided you aren't expecting me to make tea. Is the little black kettle still around?'

'It is.' He nodded in the direction of the iron grate in the potting shed. 'Stands there, on the hearth, but only as an ornament. It sprung a leak not long after you left for Kentucky and I was of a mind to keep it, for old times' sake. But where's young Adam, and what does he think to his new sister?'

'He's at the Bothy, with Aunt Julia. He was a bit disappointed, I think, when he first saw her. I think he'd expected a miniature playmate who could walk and talk. And he couldn't pronounce her name. Called her *Nellor*, and now I'm afraid he's shortened it to Nell. So it looks as if she's stuck with it. Reckon it'll only be Eleanor when she's being scolded!'

'Aye, I remember well Mrs Amelia giving young Kitty a telling off. "Now don't you give back answers, Kathryn Sutton," her said. "Don't get sassy with me, young lady!" She were a rare one, that Kitty . . .'

'Do you still talk about her at Rowangarth?'

'Of course we do. Her isn't really gone. Her's around, still, and she'll get her wedding bouquet like always, in June. But young Drew will be all right. The Welsh lass will do very nicely at Rowangarth. Her's having a bouquet of the tawnies.'

'Not the white orchids, Mr C?'

'No. Her asked specially for the tawnies and any road, we couldn't have brought the white ones along in time. Would have been asking too much. I'd thought maybe there'd be roses ready on the greenhouse wall, and she'd like them, but no, it was the tawny-green cymbidiums she fancied.

'But you'll be decorating the church for the wedding, Gracie? You got very proficient at it, and Drew would want you to. There'll be plenty of cherry blossom about, and white and apricot roses, an' all.'

'It might be nice if Uncle Nathan would let me use the silver vases. Roses would look lovely in them, on the altar. Oh, Mr Catchpole,' she smiled tremulously, 'it's just like old times, isn't it? And aren't I lucky that Bas promised Mum and Dad he'd make sure I got home to England every year. My folks would come to see us, of course, but they can't leave Gran, and she's getting a little frail, now, to be crossing the Atlantic. I left a part of me in this garden, y'know. If you ever get lonely, Mr C, the best place to find me is beside the manure heap. In spirit, of course. I often think of the day I met Bas. I'd been barrowing it, was covered in the stuff. My boots smelled awful!'

'Awful? How often do I have to tell you, Gracie Fielding, that there isn't a smell in the world so uplifting as a heap of well-rotted manure – especially in the early morning, with a cloud of white steam rising from it. And tell me why your Bas should have worried about the smell of it? That young man had to muck out stables as soon as he could hold a shovel, don't forget.'

They laughed, and it was wartime all over again, and Jack Catchpole was a very happy old man.

'Can you put up with Adam for just a few more minutes, Aunt Julia?' asked Bas. 'I want to pop up the lane, to have a word with Keth. He's going away tomorrow, didn't you say?'

'Yes, but only for a couple of days. He'll be back long before the wedding. Taking his mother to see Dickon's grave.'

'Dickon was Keth's pa, wasn't he? But I'd like a minute with Keth before he goes – and I want to have a look at the baby. Haven't seen her since she was christened. My, but she set up a hollering over the font, didn't she? Didn't like that holy water one bit.'

'Mm. That was the Dwerryhouse temper coming out. But off you go, Bas. You can leave Adam with me any time at all, surely you know that?'

Julia thought, when he had gone, that going to see Keth was almost the first thing Bas did. There was a great fondness between them, because not only had Keth been a part of the Kentucky Suttons' life whilst he was at university in America, but because Keth had saved Bas's life.

Foolishly, impetuously and with amazing courage, he had got Bas out of the blazing tower at Pendenys Place when Clementina Sutton, the worse for brandy, had set it alight. Bas still carried the scars on his hands to this day; scars to remind him how good it was to be alive – and why he and Keth were almost like brothers.

'So what shall we do now, Adam?' She lifted the small boy into her arms and hugged him close. 'Tell you what – shall we go down to the kitchen to see Mary and Tilda? It's almost tea time and I happen to know,' she whispered, 'that Tilda has made cherry scones especially for you!'

And as they walked carefully down the wooden stairs, Julia wondered how long it would be until she could steal down to the kitchen for cherry scones with Drew's son.

Just to think of it made her glow with happiness.

FOURTEEN

'You're quiet, Mam. Everything all right?'

'Everything's fine, son.'

'I thought perhaps you had a headache.'

'No, but since you ask, I was thinking of all that money the hotel cost. We didn't have to have an evening meal, there.'

'So you didn't like it?'

'Of course I liked it, Keth. I'd thought, you see, that we were doing bed and breakfast on the way down. Didn't think we'd end up in a hotel.'

Keth looked in his driving mirror, keeping the car at a steady forty-five miles an hour to eke out the petrol.

'If I can't treat you to a bit of luxury once in a while, it's a poor look-out, Mam.'

They had stayed the night at a small, comfortable hotel ten miles south of Leicester. Paying the bill had been no problem because Daisy, as he bent to kiss her goodbye, had pushed something into the top pocket of his jacket. And because his mother was sitting in the car, he had been unable to protest.

'For Polly,' she had whispered. 'Stay somewhere decent.'

Three five-pound notes. More than enough. Daisy had been determined all along to help with the cost of the trip.

'And anyway, Mam, small stopover places couldn't have given us food. They aren't allowed catering rations like hotels. Wouldn't have been a lot of fun, would it, hunting for a fish-and-chip shop?

'You've waited a long time to go back to Hampshire. At first we couldn't afford to go and see Dad, then the war stopped us going. So now Daisy and I are determined you'll do it in style. It isn't going to be too upsetting for you, is it – now that we're on our way, I mean?'

'No, son. It's right we should let your dad know how well we've both done; how comfortable we are. And at least he's got a stone . . .'

Before they left Hampshire, Polly had spent half of Mr Hillier's money on it. A hundred pounds each he'd left to staff in his will. And because Dickon had died the same afternoon as Mr Hillier, his solicitors deemed it only right his widow should benefit. A godsend, that money had been. Without it, she and Keth could have faced the shame of Parish Relief, or even ended up in the workhouse.

Yet now they were going to stand beside that gravestone and say a last goodbye. Take a photograph, too, with the camera Keth had brought back with him from America. A colour picture it would be, and maybe they would take a snap of the little house they once lived in. Willow End. She wondered who lived there now.

'You've gone quiet again . . .'

'Just thinking, Keth, about your dad's stone. Hope it isn't in need of a scrub.'

'The Mothers' Union said they'd keep the grave tidy. It was fine when Daisy and I visited; flowers on it – well-kept.'

'Ah, yes. I was thinking about Willow End, an' all. It'll be funny walking down Beck Lane and someone else living in it.'

'It might be empty, Mam, then you can peep through the windows.'

It *was* empty. When he and Daisy went there both Keeper's Cottage and Willow End were in a sorry state, though they had told the mothers that everything was fine; the dogs' grave, too.

'I loved that little house.'

'So you don't like where you are now?'

'Of course I do. Comfortable beyond my wildest dreams, and money regular now, from Mrs Julia. And still being near Alice and Tom, like it used to be when you were little. Life has treated me better than it treated your dad.'

'Do you believe in heaven, Mam?'

'I – well, I don't rightly know,' Polly faltered. 'Why do you ask, son?'

'Well, if you do, then Dad will know you and I have been to see him, that's all I meant.'

'He'll know, anyway. When two people are as close as Dickon and I were, there's a bond between them that can't be broken. Heaven or not, he'll be glad we came.'

'How do you cope, Mam – losing someone you love, I mean?'

'You manage. You've got to. I had you to bring up – couldn't sit there feeling sorry for myself; had to get on with things. The sadness gets less, though; there comes a time when remembering doesn't hurt so much. That's when you know you are coping, though you don't for the life of you know how you did it. I won't make a fuss at the graveyard, Keth, don't worry.'

'I know you won't. And had you thought, Mam, that next week at this time we'll all be getting into our glad rags for the wedding.'

And Polly smiled, and looked around her as if she were used to riding in cars, and wished that Dickon could have seen Keth's fine new motor.

'Mm, and my son best man to a baronet, eh.'

'Don't be such a snob, Mrs Purvis. It's me, returning the compliment. Drew was my best man, don't forget. And we'll stop at Banbury – stretch our legs and have a coffee. Then it'll be all systems go for Salisbury – and West Welby. We should be there around noon, if I don't lose my way, that is.'

They arrived with no trouble at all, and Keth parked the car on the wide grass verge at the end of the village.

'All right?' he asked of Polly who stood quite still, looking around her not quite believing she was here at last.

'Seems nothing much has changed, son.'

Ahead of them, the village pump and trough; the shop where Alice bought knitting wool and paper patterns and cotton and thread. There, too, the Post

Office where Alice went to ring Julia in Yorkshire, and the school, next to the church. And if she turned round, she would see the narrow road that led to Windrush Hall and to Beck Lane.

'Things seem farther on than at home,' she said softly. 'The trees, I mean, are leafing up nicely, and the apple blossom is full out. Warmer, down here . . .'

'Would you like to walk the village, Mam?'

'Afterwards, maybe. Let's say hullo to your dad, first. After all, it's why we came – and to see Beck Lane again.'

Head high, a small smile on her lips, she walked towards the church and Keth took her hand and pulled it into his arm, wishing she did not want to see Beck Lane quite so much, knowing what would greet her when she did.

'Ah.' Polly stood beside the headstone of polished granite, gentling her fingers over the name as if to say hullo to her husband. 'Richard Purvis. And me christened Mary, yet we were always Polly and Dickon. It all looks very well.'

She looked at the headstone which was not in need of cleaning and the stone vase filled with white jonquils and was glad her man had not been forgotten.

'Would you like me to leave you for a few minutes, Mam? I want to go to the Post Office – see if they know who's in charge of the Mothers' Union, now.' They always knew, at the Post Office.

'Yes, son. I'd like to know who the lady is and where she lives; would like to write, and thank her.'

She waited until the sound of Keth's footsteps grew

272

less, then knelt on the grass, her hand still on the stone, and closed her eyes to remember how Dickon had tramped the roads looking for work and found it at Windrush Hall. Met the gamekeeper, who caught him with a poached rabbit, who instead of hauling him off to the lock-up, had shown him kindness.

Poor, limping Dickon. Half his foot shot away in the Great War. Done it himself, the Army had accused. Soldiers who could take no more of the trenches were known to shoot themselves in the foot. The only way to get back home.

Yet Dickon had done no such thing. Dickon could handle a rifle; wouldn't have made such a mess of it, he'd always said, if he'd really done it. But the Army discharged him as a coward so they didn't have to pay him a pension.

Thank God Dickon poached that rabbit, and thank God Tom Dwerryhouse caught him. For Tom it had been who got him work at Windrush; not as a game-keeper, though Dickon had been a good one, before he enlisted. A dog boy, her husband had ended up, for who wanted a lame keeper? Yet grateful, for all that, for fifteen shillings a week and a roof over their heads, wood for their fires. Sad he'd had to die so unfairly.

'Hullo, my handsome. It's Polly,' she whispered, 'come to let you know that me and Keth are fine and that Keth has done so well I know I'll never want for a thing.

'But you'll know that, Dickon. I've sent my thoughts to you so often over the years that you are bound to know that Keth married Daisy and they have a little girl – so you'll know about Mary Natasha an' all.'

She smiled, and thought with love about the good times; of meeting Dickon as a young soldier and them having fine dreams about when the war was over, and what they would do. But the dreams turned to dust and they had been grateful for the cottage at the end of Beck Lane and good neighbours like Alice and Tom.

'You'll know, Dickon, that Keth did real well; went to university then joined the Army and ended up a Captain. I told you all that, didn't I?'

Told him with her heart and sent it to him with love, so he would never feel lonely in that graveyard in Hampshire; never so far away that her love could not reach him.

'You'll know that Keth came to see you, long before the war ended. Married Daisy Dwerryhouse and had their honeymoon in Winchester. And then they went to Beck Lane to have a look at your Beth. She's there, with that soft old Morgan, and a little stone so folk will know, and respect where they lay.

'Keth and I are going to see Beck Lane, soon, and I'll remember how you and me used to sit outside Willow End on warm summer evenings, and how glad we were to be a family again.

'I came to say a last goodbye, Dickon. Keth will be back, soon, but rest easy, for you'll never be forgotten . . .'

She knelt there, until she heard footsteps on the gravel path, then rose to her feet to smile a greeting at her son.

'There you are, Keth. I've had a chat with your dad, and he's fine. He knows about Daisy and Mary Natasha and your new motor. And I've said goodbye, and he knows he'll never be forgotten. So shall we make our way to Beck Lane then; have a look at Willow End?'

'Things might have changed, Mam.'

'I hope not. We were happy there. The three of us together at last and your dad not having to tramp the roads for work nor sleep rough, nights. I want to say goodbye to Willow End, too. Seems daft to come all this way and not see the place. Do you remember the rose I planted? Was it there, when you and Daisy went to Beck Lane?'

'The yellow climber? It was doing fine.'

Climbing so high it was blocking the light from the bedroom window and disturbing the roof tiles, its stems gnarled and woody. Keth hoped his mother would not be too upset.

'And the grave . . . ?'

'It was there. Mind, the bluebells won't be out, just yet. When Daisy and I visited, the beech wood was a carpet of blue . . .'

'Never mind. Shall we leave the car – walk there, Keth?'

'It's a fair step, and I should know. I walked it twice a day, to and from school.'

'With Daisy,' Polly smiled fondly. 'You couldn't wait to get out, mornings, to take her to school.'

'I couldn't wait because I knew that if I got there early, there'd be toast for me.'

'So didn't I feed you enough, son? I know there

were times we lived from hand-to-mouth, but –'

'Of course you fed me! But I was a growing lad, had hollow legs!' He offered his arm. 'Okay, then. If you're determined . . .'

He knew she was, without asking. The set of her chin told him so.

The afternoon was pleasantly warm; much warmer for the time of year, than in Yorkshire. Beneath the hedges were primroses and wild white violets. And in the fields either side, cowslips and milkmaids grew, and the lambs were sturdy and already half their mother's size.

'When I went to the Post Office, I saw a swallow,' Keth said. 'First one of the year.'

'Then I hope you made a wish. And look, Keth, there's a butterfly. Didn't realize how much colder it is, back home.'

Home, Keth thought. She had called Holdenby home, yet was eager as a child to see Willow End, the first home she and Dad ever had.

'Mam – you won't be disappointed if it isn't – well – isn't as you remember? Things change . . .'

'But why should they? West Welby hadn't changed one iota, except for a red phone box outside the Post Office. Once, you had to go inside if you wanted to ring up. The phone was on the counter and everybody heard what you said! But Beck Lane will be lovely, I know it.'

Keth closed his eyes, latching on to his swallow-wish, and as he opened them they were turning the corner into Beck Lane.

'Ah,' Polly said fondly. 'Dear old Keeper's Cottage and Willow End. I knew someone would be caring for them.'

Disbelieving, Keth looked at the white-painted windows of Keeper's Cottage, the dark green front door with its shining doorknob and knocker. Then he looked again at the carefully tended garden, at the shed, repaired and re-roofed. And at the end of the lane, Willow End too had been painted, its windows shining, the front door a bright red. And the climbing rose; a tamed rose, now, with freshly green leaves and buds opening yellow.

'Well now, that's a fine seat they've got outside,' Polly beamed. Far grander, she had to admit, than the wooden bench Dickon had made. 'And the grave, Keth. Someone is looking after it!' The little stone, a foot high and bearing the inscription B & M 1926 had cowslips in a jam jar beside it, the grass around it cut short. 'I wish I'd known. Could have told your dad. He loved that bitch, you know.'

The clicking of a gate made them turn. A girl walked towards them.

'Hullo. Are you visiting, or just out for a walk?'

'We once lived here,' Polly said tremulously, 'in Willow End. It's looking grand. Just as I remember it.'

'But not as my wife and I remember it,' Keth smiled at the fair-haired, blue-eyed child. Ten, was she? Maybe eleven? 'We visited during the war. It was so run-down, I didn't want Mother to see it. I'm Keth Purvis, by the way, and this is my mother. Everything looks so cared for. That climbing rose, for one thing. It looks good.'

'Well, when we came here it had grown over the roof and was attacking the chimney stack. Gone wild, so Grandad cut it right down and look at it now. Grown again. Grandad says it's going to be a picture in a couple of weeks.

'But I saw you looking at the little grave – do you know anything about it? I look after it and I'd love to know who B and M were. I'm Sally, by the way. Mother is a nurse at Windrush – it's a convalescent home, for miners. My gran and grandad live in Keeper's Cottage. Gran has gone to Southampton, window shopping, and mother is at work. Grandad is supposed to be in charge, but he's asleep in the chair,' she giggled.

'Then I'd like to thank you for looking after this grave,' Polly said softly.

'You know about it?'

'Oh my word, yes. There's Morgan buried there. He was a spaniel and never left Daisy's side. Daisy was born in Keeper's Cottage, and now she's married to this gentleman here – my son, Keth.

'And with Morgan is Beth. Beth was a Labrador bitch my husband had trained for the gun. She was a beauty and he was real proud of her. She belonged to Mr Hillier who used to live at Windrush Hall, but my Dickon always felt that Beth was his. Had her right from being a puppy, see.'

'And how did they die?' The blue eyes were troubled.

'Well, Morgan died in his sleep, peacefully, of old age. A gentle end for the old fellow, but Daisy was very upset, for all that. We had a little service for him – said Our Father and sang "All Things Bright and Beautiful".'

'And Beth?'

'For Beth, it wasn't so good. She drowned, poor creature.'

'But dogs can swim. Why didn't Beth swim out?'

'Because she went into the river after a pheasant. The river was in flood, and flowing fast. But Beth was a good 'un. In she went, and her collar caught on a willow branch, under the water level. My husband and Mr Hillier went into the river,' her voice dropped to a whisper. 'Went in after her, and both got swept away.'

The blue eyes filled with tears and Polly bent to hug the child.

'There now, sweetheart, don't get yourself upset. Beth and Morgan are together and did you know dogs can hear sounds so fine that us humans can never hear. And when the bluebells are out in the wood, there – and it won't be long, now – Beth and Morgan will hear them chiming.'

'Will they really? I've never heard a bluebell chime.'

'No more have I, but you and me are humans, see? Dogs have wondrous keen hearing. So dry your eyes. Beth and Morgan will be right grand, with you to care for them.'

'I wasn't crying just because of Beth; it made me think of my daddy. He was killed in the war, you see, when I was four,' she said softly. 'It's why we're here. Mummy is a nurse and got a job at Windrush. It was how we found these cottages. They were very neglected, so Grandad didn't have to pay a lot for them. He said they were solid built, and would do up fine.'

'And they have. Are you happy here, Sally?'

'I love it. We all do. It has been good for Mummy, especially. Getting a job at Windrush has helped her get over Daddy, a bit.'

'Then can my son take a snap of the two cottages? Alice, who lived in Keeper's, would be real pleased to see the old place – and Willow End, too. We had some happy times, here, till the accident made us have to leave.'

'And will he take one of Beth and Morgan's grave, so she'll know I'm looking after it?' the child asked.

'Of course he will, little lass. And I know where I can lay hands on two photos you'd really like. Only in old-fashioned black and white, mind, but one is of your house and has my Dickon standing there with Beth, and the other is of Daisy in her pram outside Keeper's Cottage, with Keth beside it, and Morgan standing guard.'

'But can you spare them, Mrs Purvis? Aren't they precious?'

'They are indeed, but I've got other snaps, and you deserve to know what Beth and Morgan looked like, and where they once lived. I'll send them as a thank you, because I'm grateful to you. And my husband, if he had lived, would be grateful, too.'

Gently, she kissed the girl's cheek.

'And I'm sorry about your daddy. And will you tell your mother that I know she'll find contentment at Willow End. It is a good place to live – takes care of you, sort of. We are going back to the North Riding, now, and I'll send you the snaps, as soon as I'm home. Are you going to walk to the top of the lane with us, Sally?'

It had been, Polly said as they drove towards Leicester, a very satisfactory trip, which had left her much comforted. And Keth said a silent thank you for a swallow-wish and the small miracle in Beck Lane. He smiled sideways at his mother, and wondered if life could get any better.

'It's a very small cake.' Mary Stubbs shook her head sadly. 'Just imagine, if there was no food rationing you could have done four tiers like a wedding cake ought to be.'

'Yes, an' if the bride's mother hadn't brought tinned butter and dried fruit with her from Kenya, Drew would have had to make do with a sponge cake like Daisy had to, and Bas. My, but that lad of his enjoyed the cherry scones. Remember when Drew used to come down here and sweetheart cherry scones out of Mrs Shaw, God rest her.'

'Aye, but do you remember what a martinet she could be? A stickler for the rules of the kitchen. When staff sat down to eat, no one dare start until Mrs Shaw had picked up her knife and fork.'

'True. Mind, we had a real staff, then. Now there's only you and me, Mary. But I miss Mabel Shaw. There's hardly a day goes by but what I think of her. She left me her book of recipes, y'see, and there's hardly a day I don't open it. Mind, it's good that people can buy as many clothes as they want, now.

Shall you be buying new for the wedding?'

'Indeed I will not, Tilda. My own wedding dress hasn't had half enough wear, yet. Nor my wedding hat. I'll be off to Creesby to buy silk stockings. You hardly dare kneel down in church, once, for fear the hassocks would snag them. Then it was *ping*! and a ladder running up your leg like greased lightning. Thanks be for unrationed fully-fashioned silk stockings again. I shall buy five pairs!'

'Will you, Mary Stubbs? Well, if everyone starts buying stockings greedy like that, they'll be back on the ration again!'

'Only joking. Five pairs would cost nigh on ten shillings. I'm not made of money. But I was talking to Jack Catchpole. He's back in the kitchen garden again, fussing over the wedding flowers. Said he'd make you and me a little spray, Tilda. Any road, Jack said there was a new moon last night, and laying flat on its back.'

'Oh?' A new moon like that meant no water could spill out of it as it could when it stood on end. With luck, that meant good weather for Saturday. 'Then let's hope it stays dry, though there'll be the conservatory and the marquee if it clouds over. Wish it could be a right slap-up affair. We don't seem to have had a decent do at Rowangarth for years and years.'

'That's because we're still stuck with food rationing, Tilda. More'n three years this war has been over, yet still we are treated like every mouthful we eat has had to be brought across the Atlantic by convoy, like it used to be!'

'Ah, but it isn't as sinful, nowadays, doing a bit

of dealing on the black market. No seamen are getting torpedoed, now.' Once, it would have been unforgivable to have risked a sailor's life for a bag of sugar, for that's what it had amounted to.

'Miss Julia didn't have any scruples when she got hold of a black market tin of ham, the other day. "Another contribution to the wedding breakfast!" And she tapped her nose and winked and told me to shove it in the back of the cupboard, till required. I reckon we'll be able to provide Drew and his intended with a fair-to-middling buffet, one way or another. You got the rations from the Food Office, yet?'

The Ministry of Food made an allowance for occasions such as weddings. It was a fiddling, bothersome job filling in forms, but Tilda was bound to admit that every little helped. It would go against the grain to make puff pastry for the vol-au-vents with margarine, mind, but if Tilda Willis and Mrs Shaw's recipe book between them couldn't rise to the occasion, then it was a poor look-out!

'I've got the coupons. Will be taking them to the grocer's tomorrow. See if he's got anything under the counter. Let's hope nobody takes more'n their fair share, that's all.'

'They won't. Ellen will be here, don't forget, giving a hand.'

Mary had reason to be grateful for the training Ellen had given her. Taught her everything there was to know about parlour maiding, before she left to marry the farmer's son, at Home Farm.

Yet Ellen was always glad to oblige; could always be relied upon to help out whenever Rowangarth needed an extra pair of hands. Ellen knew the place inside out, where every plate and serving dish was kept, for nothing changed, in Rowangarth kitchen. And Ellen was very experienced, Mary thought, at manoeuvring trays of sandwiches and the like, so no one had time to grab a handful. It wouldn't be a Rowangarth do without her, even though she wasn't as slender as she used to be, Ellen being a grandmother, now.

Yet she would appear, early Saturday, her best serving dress let out and her broderie anglaise serving apron and headdress starched and pressed, her loyalty to Rowangarth undiminished. And her knowledge of how things were done on *all* occasions undeniable.

'Wonder if Polly Purvis is back from her jaunt?'

'I wouldn't call a sentimental journey to her husband's grave a jaunt,' Tilda sniffed. 'Keth always promised he would take her, one day. She would enjoy being driven in the new car.'

'Well, she'll be back by now. Sunday about noon, she told me. She'll be busy doing extra for Miss Julia at the bothy, this week, what with guests and everything. The bride's parents will be staying here, of course, and Tatiana has got Bas and Gracie up at Denniston, as usual, but Mrs Amelia will be staying with Miss Julia and the Reverend.'

'*Mrs Amelia?* Coming to the wedding?' Tilda felt quite peculiar. 'Is that fair on Drew?'

'Is it fair on the lass Drew'll be marrying, don't you mean?'

'I don't know what I mean, I'm that flabbergasted. And who thought to tell you, and not me?'

'Nobody told me.' Mary was uneasy, now. 'As a

matter of fact, I heard it by chance. Miss Julia was talking to the Reverend last night when they came for supper with Drew. "Of course, Amelia will be staying with us, Drew," she said, and that's all I heard. I wasn't going to tell you. It just slipped out. Parlour maids don't repeat what they hear said at table, as well you know. Reckon Miss Julia will tell us both, when she thinks on about it.'

'That's all well and good, Mary, but whatever possessed Miss Julia to invite her?'

'More to the point, whatever possessed Mrs Amelia to accept? Won't be easy for her, seeing Drew getting wed to someone else, when it should have been her daughter.'

'And what is Lyn Carmichael going to think, an' all, knowing Kitty's mother is there? I wonder if anyone thought to mention it to the lass?'

'None of our business, Tilda. Miss Julia knows what she's doing – I hope. And maybe Mrs Amelia isn't coming specially for the wedding. Maybe she really wants to see that little Eleanor christened, on the Sunday. After all, it's her grandchild. She's got every right.'

'Well, if there's a bust-up when Lyn gets here on Tuesday, we'll know what it's about. Her father is due back from Kenya, today, then him and her mother will be arriving here on Thursday. I know that for a fact, 'cos Miss Julia told me. They're to sleep in the guest bedroom with the bathroom attached.'

'I know. She told me, an' all! And happen things will be all right. Mrs Amelia is a lovely lady. Her wouldn't want to make trouble.'

'Not on purpose, she wouldn't. But all I can say,' Tilda quivered, 'is that it's a queer carry-on, and no mistake. I'm beginning to wish,' she whispered chokily, 'that the wedding was over and done with.'

And with that she sat herself in the kitchen rocker and pulled the folds of her white apron over her face, just as Mrs Shaw had done in times of stress.

'There now, love, don't take on so. What we both need is a cup of tea.'

'I'm not taking on. It's just that I'm – well – *confused* . . .'

'Tea,' Mary said firmly, 'is good for confusion.' Then without so much as a blush of shame she reached for the carefully hidden bottle. Tea, with a splash of cooking brandy in it, was even better!

'Men!' said Blodwen Carmichael. 'I haven't seen my Jack in weeks, and he's flat out on the bed, snoring his head off. Poor love. Worn out, with all that flying. Must be his time clock.'

'I think it's to do with time *zones*, Mum. And if Dad doesn't want that cup of tea, I'll have it.' Lyn pushed off her shoes, then, feet tucked beneath her, she said, 'Do you realize that when I leave here on Tuesday, I won't be coming back to this little house.'

'What do you mean, *merchi*! Of course you'll be back. Lots of times. Nothing is going to change.'

'Only that this will be your home again, and I'll be Lady Sutton.'

'So what's wrong with that? Never mind about the handle. It's all part and parcel of the package. What *is* important, though, is that you'll be Lyndis Sutton.'

She looked at her daughter's face. 'You know, *cariad*, for a girl who's going to be married in less than a week, you're very relaxed about everything.'

'Why get myself into a state? I've finished at the hotel, Dad is back home and everything is taken care of at Drew's end. His mother and Lady are having the time of their lives, arranging everything. My dress fits, the veil, too, and I've got my wedding shoes. The wedding flowers are in hand and Gracie Sutton will be decorating the church. Drew has applied to the Board of Trade for petrol coupons for the cars and our hotel is booked in York. So tell me, what is there to worry about?'

'You mentioned Lady – Drew's other mother. Had you realized you'll have two mothers-in-law, in a manner of speaking?'

'And both of them lovely. I've known Daisy's mother for a long time, remember. Drew says I must call her Lady like he does, when we're married.'

'And what will you call Julia Sutton?'

'I'm calling her Mrs Sutton, at the moment. Drew often calls her dearest, but I suppose I'll have to see what mother-in-law sounds like, then take it from there. Kitty always called her Aunt Julia, I believe.'

'Which she was, really, once Julia married Nathan.'

'No. If you want to be nit-picky, Nathan was Julia's cousin. Her second husband.'

'A bit confusing, eh?'

'Not really, Mum. Drew told me he was adopted when he was little by his grandmother Lady Helen, though his inheritance would have been all right even if she hadn't.'

'Suppose Lady Helen just wanted it all cut and dried, as they say. And have you got things cut and dried, our Lyndis?'

'Of course I have. I can't wait to marry Drew, if that is what's bothering you, Mum. Like I said, everything is taken care of. It's only a matter of counting the days, now.'

'No it isn't. What I want to know is have you sorted things out with Kitty?'

'How can I, Mum! I'm not like you. I can't pick up vibrations and all that jazz. And anyway, what do I have to prove?'

'That you can accept Drew's first love.'

'I *have* accepted her! What choice do I have when Kitty is fact. They talk about her at Holdenby. If her name comes up, no one bothers. There's only you seems upset about her.'

'And you aren't, I suppose, yet you ask what else you can do. You can go to her grave, like I told you. Stand there quietly, and open up your mind to her, and your heart. Maybe then you'll get that muddle in your head sorted out. Maybe you'll come to realize that your blood is as Celtic as mine, Lyn.'

'I can't go to her grave. I tried, but I couldn't. If I have to walk down the path to the church, I look away as I pass.'

'You'll have to pass her on your way to your wedding, girl. Or are you afraid to look at her name? Kathryn Sutton she was and Kathryn Sutton she would have remained if she and Drew had been married.'

'She was buried in her wedding dress, Mum. And every June the wedding bouquet she should have carried is laid on her grave. No one round there thinks it's mawkish. White orchids. They're Kitty's flowers, that's all. Nothing more complicated than that!'

'Yet you're making a big thing of it. *Why?*'

'Because . . .' Lyn laid down her cup, then tilted her head, looking into her mother's eyes. 'Because it's as if Kitty never left Rowangarth. It's a feeling I have. She's still there, waiting . . .'

'A feeling, our Lyndis? Then is there more of the Celt in you than you think?'

'What do you mean?' she whispered.

'I'm saying that if you try, be still inside you, you'll be able to talk to her – with your heart and thoughts, I mean.'

'So I might be right? She could still be there?'

'She *is* there, and I don't have to stand at her grave-side to know it. And I think it's you she's waiting for.'

'*Mother*, for God's sake!'

'Don't blaspheme, *merchi*,' Blodwen said softly. 'Meet her halfway, eh?'

'But *how?*'

'She'll tell you, if only you'll let her.'

'So I go there? I stand in All Souls graveyard and I have a chat to a girl who everybody knows was killed nearly five years ago? What are people going to think?'

'I suppose they'd think – supposing they were to hear you – that the red-headed Welsh girl is a bit gaga. But just as you sense that she's around, wait-ing, so can you sense what's troubling her.

'In the old days, our Lyn, people were shriven as they were dying. The priest forgave their sins, so their souls could rest peacefully. Death came slowly, sometimes gently, to most. They had time to prepare for passing on, but a lot didn't. You went through a war. You should know. And in the Great War, men went to their death almost without knowing it; were gone as quickly as the blowing out of a candle flame. No one there to help their passing.'

'But they were blessed when they were buried. Nathan took Kitty's funeral service, and blessed her with love. Kitty's soul *is* at rest, Mum.'

'It will be, finally, when you hear what she has to tell you. Hear with your heart, I mean.'

'I can't do it, Mum.' Her voice was flat, and fear-filled.

'Yes you can, *merchi*. The dead never harmed anyone, haven't I always told you? It's the living you've got to look out for.'

'So I just go there, and then what?'

'You go there, that's all. Surely you can do that much for her – for yourself? Say you'll do it, Lyn? Promise?'

'All right, then. I'll go to her grave.'

'That's my girl. She won't harm you. She might even give you a sign.'

'Can you be sure?'

'Sure as I can be. And we've had enough of the soul-searching for one day. Your dad is back home, our girl is going to be married, and summer is on the way. So why don't we celebrate? Pour us a couple of gins, eh, and we'll drink to – what shall it be, lovely girl?'

'I – I think it should be to love. To old loves and new loves.'

'And to love that never dies. Because real love never dies. It just goes on, but in a different direction, sort of. It's always around, though, ready to be called back to give comfort.'

'What if I can't deal with it, Mum?'

'You're expecting trouble, then?'

'I don't know. When people talk about Kitty, they say she was always the naughty one, always up to mischief. She used to mimic people, was a show-off. At least, that's the impression I got. And she was very beautiful. Big violet-blue eyes you noticed, and black curls.'

'And you've got green eyes and chestnut hair. Shall you put it up for the wedding, Lyn?'

'Don't try to change the subject, Mum. It's Kitty we're talking about.'

'*Were* talking about. Now I'm waiting for that drink. I'll have it with sugar and a drop of hot water, I think.'

'Okay. I'll get it.' Lyn knew when she was beaten; knew, too, that she had promised her mother she would visit Kitty's grave. And she didn't want to, wished she had never given her word. She reached for the bottle. 'How much . . . ?'

'You know how much, lovely girl. Two fingers, one sugar and don't forget to put the spoon in the glass so the hot water won't crack it.'

'I won't – forget, I mean.'

And oh, Drew, I do so love you. I can't believe we'll be married on Saturday . . .

She couldn't; couldn't imagine the church and everyone there being so happy and a blue and pink bridesmaid and Drew, turning to smile as she walked towards him. And she could no longer feel the float and swish of her dress, Daisy's dress, as it billowed with every step she took. Saturday seemed a long way away, a lifetime away; a day that might not even happen if she didn't make her peace with Kitty.

Because Kitty was as real as she had ever been; was there, still, one of the Clan. Drew and Daisy, Bas and Kitty, Tatty and Keth, who had come together twice each year at midsummer and Christmas and were bonded by their love of Rowangarth and of each other. They were special, and fun loving, and each time they met it was as if they had never been apart.

It was the Clan, dammit, who would not let Kitty go; the Clan who kept her close, talked about her, laughed at memories of her. She, Lyn, had always been envious of the Clan. From that first glimpse of the sepia photograph on Daisy's locker, she had known they were special and that no one could divide them; no one else could be a part of them.

Gracie, the land girl, years at Rowangarth, yet never one of the Clan, even though she had married Bas. Nor would Bill Benson be, nor she, Lyndis. Even married to Drew, she would not.

Married to Drew. But would she ever be? Wasn't Kitty coming between them and wasn't it Lyn Carmichael's fault for letting her?

'What's happening to the drinks?' Blodwen demanded, from the sitting room.

'Coming, Mum. Kettle took a long time . . .'

'Then you'd better make a pot of tea, whilst you're about it. I can hear your dad stirring upstairs.'

Back to reality. Tea for Dad and hot gin for Mum and don't forget to put the spoon in the glass, first. No more stupid thoughts. She was going to be married on Saturday. At All Souls, Holdenby, by the Reverend Nathan Sutton. Andrew Robert Giles to Lyndis. Drew to Lyn. It would happen because Drew was worth fighting for; worth risking a confrontation at a white marble headstone for, and be damned to bouquets of white orchids!

'I love you, Drew Sutton,' she whispered to the small brown teapot. 'See you on Tuesday, my darling . . .'

FIFTEEN

Drew was waiting at Holdenby Halt and at the sight of him, it was their first meeting all over again. Lyn's stomach gave a skip and a squeeze, just as it did at the Pierhead stop of the Overhead Railway, so long ago. A gusty day. The wind had blown his cap off.

'Darling!' He reached for her case, kissing her gently. 'This all you've got? I thought you'd be bringing loads.'

'Only essentials, like – well, wait and see.' She offered her mouth to be kissed again. 'Well, this is it – *almost* it. Four days from now, we'll be married. How do you feel about it?' She handed her ticket – not a return, this time – to the station master at the barrier.

'How do you expect me to feel? Six months is one heck of a wait.'

'I know,' she smiled. 'Thanks, Drew, for not – well – rushing me.'

'Think nothing of it,' he said dryly. 'And how do *you* feel about four days from now?'

'Like you said, darling – six months has been a long time to wait.'

It was the only answer – the only *truthful* answer she could give him, because her feelings about Saturday were still in a muddle. Would be, until she had walked down the path at All Souls, to where Kitty lay.

At the station exit, Drew looked right, then took the Holdenby road. Then he cleared his throat so that Lyn looked up, met his eyes in the rear view mirror.

'There's something I have to tell you . . .'

'Serious, is it?' Why she asked it, she did not know, because it *was* serious. The tone of his voice, the look in his eyes told her so.

'It's anything or nothing. Up to you, really . . .'

'I think you'd better pull over, Drew.'

Without speaking he drove on until the grass verge at the side of the road widened then pulled onto it, and the few seconds it took gave Lyn time to take deep breaths and tell her thudding heart to behave.

'Okay.' He pulled on the handbrake, then turned to face her. 'Like I said, it's up to you. Mother sent the invitation as a matter of courtesy. I don't think she expected her to accept, but she has. Kitty's mother, I mean . . .'

'*Amelia Sutton?* Coming to the wedding?' All at once there was a jerking in her throat and she wanted to be sick.

'Yes. We only heard a couple of days ago. Uncle Albert – her husband – won't be coming, though.'

'I see.' She didn't see at all, but it was all she could think of to say.

'But *do* you see, Lyn? In a quirky kind of way I can understand her wanting to be there. And she wants to see her granddaughter christened, too. It will be the last time she comes to Rowangarth, Mother said. Perhaps she wants to say goodbye to Kitty, sort of. But Bas and Gracie will come over every year just the same, of course.'

Lyn let go a little huff of breath, then staring at the road ahead she said, 'That's fine, Drew. Absolutely fine. I – I'm looking forward to meeting her. Where will she be staying? At Rowangarth with Mum and Dad?'

'At the Bothy, with Mother and Nathan. She's a very nice person, Lyn.'

'I'm sure she is. And I suppose I can understand her wanting to come. It was a bit of a shock, for all that.'

'It must have been, darling. But I promise you'll like her. I think she's just about the wisest woman I've ever met. And I've never heard her raise her voice . . .'

'Yes. Fine. But let's get to Daisy's, Drew? I'd kill for a cup of tea.'

She wouldn't. She didn't need tea nor want it. All she wanted was to stop the shaking that had taken her. Amelia Sutton, coming to the wedding. Wise, was she? Who was Drew trying to kid?

'If you're sure you're all right, Lyn . . .'

'Of course I'm all right. Why on earth shouldn't Amelia Sutton come to your – *our* – wedding? She's family, after all.'

'She's married to a Pendenys Sutton but yes, Mother looks on her as family. She's very fond of her.'

'Drew – *please*? I've said it's all right, and it is.

Don't make so much of it, or I'll think you're worried.'

'Only because I thought *you* might be . . .'

'Oh, don't start it all again! Amelia Sutton will be welcome. Now, please – can we get going!'

There was a flush to her cheeks, a sharpness to her words that warned Drew into silence. He was glad, when they arrived at Foxgloves, to see Daisy waiting at the gate, baby on hip.

'Hi, Daiz.'

'Hi, each. What kept you? Had a petting session on the way?'

'No, but Lyn is desperate for a cup of tea? Can do, old love?'

'Kettle's on.' She put an arm round her friend's shoulders, kissing her cheek. 'Here, Lyn – take the baby. She's one heck of a weight, these days. Come on inside.'

Something was wrong. Daisy could sense it. Lyn's mouth was set tight and it seemed Drew could not wait to give all his attention to the luggage.

'So?' Daisy asked. 'Before Drew gets in – what's up, Carmichael? You've got a mouth on you like a trap and Drew's in a right tizzy. Mrs Amelia, is it? He's told you?'

'Yes.' It was all she had time to say.

'Want this lot upstairs, Lyn?' Drew asked from the kitchen doorway. 'And put a cup out for me, Daisy?'

'Okay. Later, then,' Daisy hissed. 'And can you give Mary her juice? She has it from a spouty-cup, now, but watch her, will you? She's very fond of waving it about and spattering everyone. And we'll talk later – okay?'

'Nothing to talk about, actually.' Lyn put on her brightest smile, then snuggled the baby to her, offering the cup. 'Everything's just fine.'

'I said *later*. And isn't it marvellous about clothes coming off the ration? Mam had Mary whilst I went to Creesby shops. No more bare legs. Stockings were the very devil, weren't they?'

'Do you suppose we'll be expected to wear gloves and hats again, when we go out?' Lyn had enjoyed the freedom of bare legs, in summer.

'Don't suppose so. The war stopped a lot of the formality, I'll say that for it. Had you noticed that not so many men wear hats, now?'

Small talk, trivia to relax her friend who was acting anything but bridal.

'Can't say I had.' Lyn bent to pick up the cup Mary had dropped on the floor. 'Is this a new game?'

'It is – good for my waistline, though. Hi, Drew. Take a pew. And by the way, Lyn, the wedding dresses are staying at Rowangarth until Friday night – that okay with you? And you know that you and the bridesmaids are leaving from Foxgloves, don't you? The taxi will drop your father off here, then collect Mam and Polly.'

'And my mother and your mother, Lyn, will arrive together from Rowangarth – Nathan will be at the church already. And Dr Pryce has offered a folding wheelchair for Miss Clitherow,' Drew smiled. 'Will Stubbs is going to push it and Tilda and Mary will walk to the church with them. Everything's close-up.'

Lyn smiled at the expression, so often used in their Navy days. Close-up. Organized. It relaxed her a little.

'Then it seems there'll be nothing for me to do but get myself to the church. And I'm grateful to everyone here – for doing all the hard work, I mean.'

'Hard work? Mother and Lady are having the time of their lives. Nathan and Tom are threatening to join the Foreign Legion, though I think they'll last out until Saturday.'

'It's a pity there won't be a lot of wedding presents,' Daisy said matter-of-factly, stirring the tea, covering it with a cosy. 'It was the same when Keth and I were married. Nothing at all in the shops – and things aren't a lot better, now.'

'But we don't expect presents. I'm going to a home ready furnished – there's nothing Drew and I are in need of. I just want people to come, and wish us well. Dad got a couple of bottles of sherry through Customs in his hand luggage, so that will be a help.'

'And Rowangarth has enough champagne for the toasts, so what more do we want?' Drew demanded.

'A fine, sunny day since you ask, and you'll have to have saccharin in your tea. I gave Tilda a pound of sugar as my contribution to the wedding feast and I'm a bit short, till Friday. And isn't everything just lovely – you two getting hitched, at last. Just four more days,' Daisy beamed.

It was then that Mary Natasha dropped her mug on the floor again, snuggled closer, thumb in mouth.

'I think she's going to sleep,' Lyn whispered, smiling at Drew.

And Drew smiled back, and winked, relieved that things seemed to be returning to normal.

* * *

'So what do you think – Mrs Amelia, I mean?' Lyn demanded the minute Drew had left. 'Drew just sprang it on me.'

'No he didn't, old love. Aunt Julia only heard two days ago that she was coming. Amelia arrived not long after her letter. She flew over. Bas went to Ringway Airport to meet her. It was a bit of a surprise to me, too, but you can understand her wanting to be here. I think she'd like to see Gracie's baby christened, then say goodbye to Rowangarth – and Pendenys Place, an' all. My, but she used to have her work cut out with Clementina Sutton, especially after the old girl took to the brandy when Elliot was killed. An unlucky house, that was. Always cold and forbidding. I only went in it once. Peculiar Place it should have been called.'

'Look, Daisy, I'm not trying to make trouble. I don't want any unhappiness on my wedding day, but I do want to talk.'

'Then I'll put Mary in her pram. A little sleep won't hurt her. She was restless, last night. Another tooth, I think. And Keth will be home in half an hour, so get it off your chest, Lyn – wedding nerves, is it?'

'No. I only wish I had them. It's as if I can't realize it's only four days away. I said as much to Mum – told her I felt – well – *uneasy*, sort of, and she said I'd have to make my peace with Kitty. Mum's like that. It's the Celt in her that makes her a bit – we-e-ll –'

'Like Jinny Dobb? A touch of clairvoyance – second sight? Does your mum tell fortunes?'

'No. But she can pick up vibes. She said I'd have

to have it out with Kitty and I said how could I? "Go to her grave," she said. Seems I won't hear voices. I'm just to open up my mind and my heart to her – because she is still at Rowangarth – in spirit, sort of. Does that sound a bit daft?'

'Not to me, it doesn't. And maybe your mum has got a point. Maybe Kitty is still around because we don't want to let her go – the Clan, I mean. And why should we? If we can't remember someone we loved . . .'

'I agree. But I've got to admit I'm a bit jealous of the Clan – not being able to be a part of it, I mean. I used to look at that photo on your locker, Daisy, and envy you all. It was your closeness, I think. When I was young, things weren't like that for me. I sensed, even then, that something was wrong – between my mother and father, kind of, and between me and my mother – the one I *thought* was my mother. It was such a relief when Auntie Blod told me. Imagine, a grown woman before I felt I belonged to someone.'

'I remember. You got a letter from Kenya from your father. Your mother was dead, you said, and you were so calm about it I thought you were in deep shock.'

'Well, I felt that way about that Clan. And Kitty still belongs to it.'

'Of course she does. The Clan was our childhood and our growing up. It was special, and Kitty was – *is* – a part of it and nothing will change it. Not ever. But there's more to it than that, isn't there?'

'Wedding night nerves, I suppose – will I match up to Kitty?'

'Lyn Carmichael, that's a load of bloody nonsense and you know it! How can you even *think* such a thing! Keth and I were lovers before we were married, you know that, but I think both of us wished we'd been a bit better at it, the first time. Or at least that one of us knew what we were doing. Can't you just accept things for what they are or are you really determined to make things difficult for yourself – and for Drew?'

'Daisy, I love Drew till it hurts. I've always loved him. But if you want the truth, I'm more worried about Kitty. I can't get her out of my mind.'

'Jealous of a ghost, Lyn?'

'She's more than a ghost. And now her mother will be at the wedding. I can't seem to be free of her.'

'Then why try? If you can't beat 'em, join 'em. Do as your mother said; go to Kitty's grave with an open mind. You might be surprised to find that Kitty wants to be free of *you*.'

'I don't know what you mean.'

'Yes you do, so think about it. Don't make a drama out of it. There's sense in what your mother says, even if it's kind of weird. After all, there are more things in heaven and earth than we ever dreamed of – or words to that effect. So while Mary is asleep let's go upstairs, and unpack you. I'm longing to see the glam undies. And Lyn – it's going to be smashing, having you so near again. I missed you a lot, after we were demobbed.'

'Me, too. And I'm glad we had our chat. I'll go to the grave, tomorrow – when I can slip away on my own, I mean. I promised Mum I would and something just might happen, there . . .'

'Mm. There isn't one drop of Celtic blood in me, but I'm as sure as I can be that something *will*. So let's have a look at those sexy undies – or will you be wearing your navy knickers with long legs, Carmichael?'

They both giggled and hurried upstairs, and for just a little while it was Cabin 4A again, in a billet called Hellas House, across the road from Sefton Park, in Liverpool. There was a war on and she hadn't even known, Lyn thought wonderingly, that Daisy Dwerryhouse had a half-brother who, a lot of tears and heartache and eight years later, she would marry. Four days from now.

'Darling – I've got to go to York. Want to come with me,' Drew asked of Lyn on the phone.

'Why York?'

'Want to go to the bank – and see the solicitors,' he added offhandedly.

'Why the solicitors . . . ?'

'To sign my new will. Young Carver advised it. *In anticipation of marriage* I think he called it. Nothing for you to worry about, Lyn.'

'Then would you mind if I didn't come? I want to see Gracie, and the new baby. And I want to look in on the kitchen garden, see how the flowers are coming along. All right, Drew?'

'Sure. I'm not going on the train – blowing a petrol coupon. Should be back some time between twelve and one. See you then – if you're sure, Lyn . . .'

She was sure. She had decided it must be today, and Drew being in York couldn't have been better. What the outcome would be, she did not know. A waste of time, though she desperately hoped not.

This morning, when she awoke, her thoughts went immediately to the graveyard at All Souls, and for just a little time she wished she had not made the promise to her mother. Then she thought of Drew and how much she loved him and how much Kitty had loved him, and knew she would go there. Now it was as if Drew's phone call had set the seal on it, made it possible.

'I'm going out,' she said to Daisy, washing up the breakfast things. 'Mind if I don't help you?'

'*Go*, Carmichael,' Daisy hissed without even looking up. 'You'll be glad you did.'

So now that she was more than halfway there and it would be foolish of her to turn back, she took a deep breath and held her face to the sun. Three days to go, and everything around her so beautiful that it hurt. It was as if Rowangarth was putting on a show for a bride; the grass so green, the wild plum blossom thickly white in the hedgerows. Daisy was right. April was the most beautiful month for a wedding.

She walked past Home Farm. Ellen, who lived there, would be at Rowangarth on Saturday. To look after the place and see to things, she had said, so everything would be as ready as it would ever be by the time the bride and groom got back from the church.

The bride. Lyndis Sutton. She had said her new name so many times, but not once had she written it. Bad luck, people said, to write it before it was truly yours. When you signed the register in church should be the first time.

She waved to the curate's wife who was hanging

out washing, glancing ahead to the cupola of Rowangarth stableyard, pale green above the tree-tops. Around the corner, now, and she would be there. Nothing to worry about. Just be still inside, Mum had said, and something would happen.

She pushed open the iron gate, then lifted her chin to gaze ahead to the marble stone beside the path. A woman stood there; someone she had never met. Older than Julia, and not so tall. Warm brown hair, touched with grey.

Lyn stepped onto the grass verge. To walk on the gravel would give her presence away and she wanted time to calm her thoughts, to relax her clenched fingers before the woman looked up and saw her.

Was that woman, hand on the headstone, head bowed, Amelia Sutton? How terrible when all you had left of your child was a piece of white marble, lettered in gold.

She stopped, not able to go on; unable to turn back. Nervously she coughed and the woman looked up.

There was a moment of complete silence. Lyn began to walk again, and when she was nearer and able to look into the woman's eyes, she knew that here was Amelia Sutton.

'Hullo. You must be Lyndis.' She smiled gently.

It gave Lyn the courage to say, 'Yes. And you are Mrs Amelia from Kentucky. I knew you at once – your eyes . . .' The words came in a whisper.

'And I saw your hair – such a beautiful colour. Gracie told me what you looked like.'

'Gracie – yes. I – I was going to the church. She's decorating it, you know.'

'I don't think she'll be there, just yet. For one thing, it's nearly ten, and Nell's feeding time. And I don't think she'll be doing it until Friday night.'

'Stupid of me. Should have realized.' She took a calming breath, then looked into the violet-blue eyes. 'And I wasn't going to the church. I came here to see Kitty.'

'Something is troubling you, Lyndis?' She asked it gently, as if she understood.

'Yes. You see, I'll never be able to match up to Kitty, but I love Drew very much and I wanted her to know.'

'See here, Lyndis – no sense in us standing here. Why don't you and I have a walk? I don't figure on coming to England again. Bertie – that's Albert, my husband – flatly refused to come with me, even for Nell's christening. He's become very American, you see. It's me who's the Anglophile.

'So I'm staying with Nathan and Julia at Bothy House, and I want to make the most of this visit – take in Rowangarth gardens. So beautiful, in spring. One of my favourite places is the Linden Walk. Shall we go there?'

'Yes. Anywhere. Do you like Rowangarth, Mrs Sutton?' They were walking the gravel path, towards the iron gates. 'I – I find it rather grand, but my parents were there for New Year, and my mother loves it.'

'And so do I. It's so lived in, and enduring. Kitty loved it, too. I think we're going to have to talk about Kitty. Do you mind?'

'No. Anyway, everyone does – talk about her, I mean. Like she was still one of the Clan.' Lyn stopped, wondering if she had said something best left unsaid. 'I'm sorry. Didn't mean that in a disparaging way. It's just that – oh, I don't know what I'm trying to say . . .'

She was making a mess of things. Things were going wrong, but she hadn't bargained on meeting Amelia Sutton.

They had come to the stile at the end of the wild garden, and she climbed it first, then offered a hand to the older woman.

'I believe the Clan used to meet there, under the trees in the wild garden,' Lyn said, lost for words.

'They did so! Not for anything would Bas and Kitty play at Pendenys Place. Kitty rather liked the house, but only because it was spooky and had lots of hidey-holes in it. She and Bas always slept in Pendenys nursery, on the top floor. It had narrow wooden stairs leading down to the kitchens, and that made it bearable.

'Bas couldn't stand Pendenys, though. He says it still makes his teeth water to think one day it'll be his. He had an awful experience there; could have lost his life, but for Keth. But you'll know about it?'

'The fire, and Keth getting Bas out – Daisy told me.'

'Well, the entail ends with Bas, so it'll be his one day, to do what he wants with. I guess if you offered him ten dollars for the place, he'd grab your hand off! But here we are. And the lindens are starting to break bud. Soon be green. Shall we sit on the seat, Lyndis? The sun is on it. It won't be too cold.'

The long walk of linden trees stretched precisely

ahead of them; fifty in all, Drew once said, planted by his grandfather John Sutton, and now at their best.

'Aaaah. It's times like this that I wish Bertie had been a Rowangarth Sutton; understand so well why Kitty loved this place, though I can't imagine her being *Lady* Sutton. Too much of a tomboy. But we came here because you need to talk . . .'

'Yes, I do. About Kitty, and how much she and Drew loved each other and will I ever be as good for Drew as she would have been. And could you call me Lyn, please? Everyone does.'

'So you feel you have to compete with her? But she was Drew's first love, dear child; she'll always be special. But you, Lyn, are his last love, his abiding love. Can't you look at it like that?'

'I never have, even though that was what Drew said when he asked me to marry him – if I'd be his last love, that was.'

'If you had been in Kitty's shoes, been Drew's first love, would you have wanted him to forget you, even though he'd found someone new?'

'No, I wouldn't. Not ever.'

'There you are, then. Now take Julia. Her first love was passionate and wild. They were both young and fighting in a terrible war, and tomorrow might never come. Yet now she is married to Nathan, and happy. First love and last love are vastly different, but equally good, it would seem.'

'Yes, but Kitty was so special . . .'

'Oh, I'll grant you that. She had my blue eyes and the Mary Anne Pendennis hair. Mary Anne was a fishwife, you know. She followed the fishing boats from port to port, gutting herrings. She took in washing, between times; was the backbone of that family. Earned the money that gave her husband – another Albert – the chance to set up on his own.

'Elliot Sutton inherited Mary Anne's darkness and he hated it. It reminded him that he'd come from a washerwoman, he once said to my Bertie, the ungrateful young beast. I'd have been proud to have had someone like that as an ancestress.

'But I'm wandering. Kitty was like Elliot; a throwback from Mary Anne. She was beautiful, but she knew it. Could twist her father round her little finger. Would be the same with Drew, I shouldn't wonder. She was a firecracker, a tomboy. And she was a show-off, liked being centre stage. She asked Tatiana to teach her to swear – in Russian, would you believe – so she could use bad language and get away with it. A little madam, for want of a better word. I couldn't believe that anyone as ordinary as me could have birthed so special a child.'

'You'll never be ordinary, with those eyes. All my mother ever gave me was carroty hair.'

'*Chestnut* hair, Lyn. There's a big difference. And like Kitty you are beautiful, but differently so. You and Drew will be happy together, I know it. I can't for the life of me understand why you should have doubts.'

'Nor me. I should be high on a pretty pink cloud, I know, but I'm not. I feel, you see, that Kitty is still here.'

There was a small silence as Amelia Sutton watched the hovering of a kestrel. Then, eyes still on the bird, she said, 'So you feel it, too? Y'know, back home, she was never far from my thoughts. Oh, the pain of losing her got less, but still I'd sometimes wish to turn a corner and see her there. But whenever I come to Rowangarth, it's like she's taking control of my mind. Her presence is so strong, here, that at times it's suffocating. I think she wants to tell me something, but I'm not sure what it is.

'I have stood before, at her graveside, touched her name with my fingertips to join us, kind of, but still I couldn't be sure what she wanted to tell me. At least, not until a little while ago, when I saw you. All at once it was clear to me. Kitty likes people. She's lonely, even with Lady Helen beside her. And this might be a terrible thing to say, but I think she loved Drew so much that she can't rest until she knows he's happy again. With you, Lyn. She doesn't want to come between you, take him from you. I'm as sure as I can be that Kitty wants you to make him happy.

'She died very suddenly. I think that for a time, some of her lived on. Some might say it was her soul, others – sceptics – would call it her ectoplasm. But some bewildered part of her came back here, that day, to a place she knew and loved.'

'Do you believe that, Mrs Sutton; truly believe it?'

'Yes. All at once, things are clear in my mind. Kitty knows she must go, soon. She isn't waiting for Drew – just waiting to give him into your keeping, your loving. Will you do that for her, Lyn? Will you be her friend? When I say goodbye to her for the last time, will you be there for her – please?'

'I don't know what to say. How can you be so generous, so understanding?' Lyn whispered, gazing at the tightly clenched hands on her lap. 'If I were in your place, I don't think I'd like the woman who will be marrying Drew on Saturday. I would want it to be my daughter, like it should have been.'

'No, Lyn. I had Kitty for almost twenty-four years, and I'm grateful for those years. Once, she was mine completely, then she fell in love and I had to let her go. But she was a will-o'-the-wisp, you see, a wild creature, and not even Drew's love could hold her.'

'You want her to rest, Mrs Sutton?'

'Yes, I do – but I don't think she will. Not completely. It might well be that a part of her will always be here. Could you live with that, Lyn?'

'I – I think so. I can certainly try to be there for her, when she needs a friend. Just her and me, I mean. No telling anyone else . . .'

'Just you and she. In time, maybe, she'll say goodbye to Rowangarth and slip into eternity, or wherever it is she's destined to go.'

'And will I know when that time is?'

'I think you will, and I think she will leave you a sign, when she goes.'

'Can I tell you something? And every word of it is true, though at the time I didn't believe it, couldn't believe it. My mother is pure Welsh; Celtic. And a red-haired Celt is supposed to have mystic powers, though I don't seem to have any.

'But Mum knew how I felt about Kitty, and told me to go to her grave. "Talk to her, with your heart," she said, "and with your mind." My mother seemed to think as you do; said that Kitty might leave a sign. But *when* will she?'

'When she's good and ready, Lyn. So will you do it for me? Talk to my girl with your heart and your mind like your mystic mother says? Bas and Gracie and the children will come over to England every year, I'm sure of it, but this visit will be my last.

'So will you be her friend? Will you try to let her know she is not alone? And will you try not to resent the Clan, and the way they keep Kitty's memory alive. She's a part of their youth, their green years, and they love her just because she was Kitty. But you will come to love her, too. Give her a chance, and you will be as close as can be to her. I give you my word, Lyn.'

'You are so kind.' She took Amelia's hand and laid it against her cheek. 'Drew said you were very wise, and you are. Thank you for talking to me, this morning. It can't have been easy for you. Things are clearer in my mind, now. I was afraid of going to see Kitty. I'm glad you were there. And if we don't have time to talk privately again, will you do something for me? Will you smile at me when I get to the church, on Saturday – wish me well?'

'I shall give you my love and my blessing – Kitty's, too.'

'Thank you. Thank you very much.' Gently she kissed Amelia's cheek.

'That was very kind of you, Lyn.' Amelia laid her fingertips to her cheek.

'Not me, Mrs Sutton. That kiss was from Kitty. I knew she wanted you to have it, you see. And look! There's a swallow. Two of them! Over the stableyard cupola. The first I've seen this year. Make a wish. First-swallow wishes always come true, Daisy said.'

'But do we need to wish? Haven't you and I, Lyn, got just about everything any woman could want?'

'Mm. Except that I want children. I always wish for children.'

'And you'll have them. Of course you will. A boy and a girl!'

'But how can you be so sure?'

'I don't for the life of me know, and that's a fact. Seems I just opened my mouth and the words came out. Guess there must be a touch of the Celt in Amelia Sutton, too.'

And they laughed, companionably, as two women who all at once understood and trusted each other would, and relief wrapped Lyn round like a soft, warm blanket.

'Are you going to Denniston, Mrs Amelia? I'd like to come with you, if you wouldn't mind. I haven't seen the new baby, yet . . .'

SIXTEEN

'What on earth,' Daisy demanded of her father, 'am I supposed to do with *those*?' She gazed, eyebrows raised, at three ladder-back dining chairs.

'Mam's orders,' Tom shrugged. '"Take these over to Foxgloves," she told me. "Will Stubbs will lend you the handcart. And tell Daisy to give them a good clean!" They were in Rowangarth attic, it seems. A bit dusty . . .'

'Leave them there, Dada, and come inside and see the baby. Haven't had sight nor sound of you all week.'

'That's 'cos there's a wedding on – hadn't you heard?' he grinned. 'Been at Rowangarth – helping with the marquee, shifting chairs. And I gave Mary Stubbs a hand cleaning and arranging the conservatory.'

'So sit down.' Daisy scooped the baby from the floor, dumping her without ceremony on Tom's knee. 'And why the chairs?'

'Seems Alice and Julia are coming across, later, with the dresses. Mam wants them laid out careful, and since you have no ceiling hooks to hang them from, nor a bed to drape them over, those old chairs were the next best idea.'

'She's right – as usual. Lyn is in the spare bed, so they'd better go in the front bedroom.'

The spare front bedroom was empty, as was the back one, with no hope of furnishing either until the government once more allowed the manufacture of bedroom suites and carpets and curtains and dining-room suites; indeed, of all manner of household goods people had longed for during six years of war, and were *still* longing for.

'Your Aunt Julia said there's a set of six of those chairs. Solid oak, but they need a bit of attention. She knows where you could get new rush seats on them. Seems you're welcome to them, if they're of any use.'

'Good of her, Dada. They're lovely old chairs. I don't suppose there's an oak table in the attics, too?'

'You'll have to talk to Julia about that – and anyway, she doesn't live at Rowangarth any more. Those chairs are by rights Drew's to give away, now.'

'Dada, they've *always* been Drew's. They were his as soon as he was born, almost. But just let me get the nappies on to boil, then you can carry the chairs in for me. What is Mam doing?'

'She's got Lyn's mother there. Seems the petticoat shows below the skirt of her wedding costume, so Mam is taking it up for her. They're in the kitchen, talking their heads off.'

'Now I wonder what about?' Daisy grinned. 'Lyn has gone to Denniston to see Gracie about the church decorations. She's like a cat on hot bricks, all of a sudden. Think she's realized, at last, that she's getting married tomorrow.'

'So who'll be looking after the bairn while you do your bridesmaiding, then?'

'Polly. She's going to sit at the back of the church with Mrs Amelia and Gracie, and her two. Then they'll be going to Rowangarth in their prams, or whatever, to enjoy the fun. What do you think the weather will be like, Dada?'

'Seems set fair. Sidney Willis thinks the same. Be your own wedding anniversary, soon.'

'Six years next Sunday. Goodness, I'll be thirty next year.'

'And that's *very* old,' Tom teased.

'N-no. But I'd always thought to have my children by the time I was thirty – fault of the war, of course. Suppose we'll be having to think about number two, once Mary Natasha is walking. But not a word to Mam, mind, or she'll be round here, demanding it in writing!'

'Not a word, lass.' Smiling, Tom tapped his nose, all at once seeing a fair-haired little lad in the big fancy pram. 'You and Keth – it's going well for you, then? Things still all right?'

'If you mean do I still love him to pieces – yes, I do. I – I'm so lucky, Dada,' she said softly.

'Reckon you must be, like Mam and me. Mind, they say you get what you deserve, so get those nappies seen to, then I'll be pushing off. Alice has a list a mile long of things she wants done! No rest for the wicked!'

And Daisy sighed, and agreed with him, even though she knew they were both enjoying every minute of the hustle and bustle of a Rowangarth wedding. Drew's wedding. To Lyn. At last!

'Here's your man, Tilda. Come about the vegetables,' Mary Stubbs called.

'Oh, Sidney!' Flush-cheeked, Tilda smiled at her husband. 'The vegetable list. I'm sorry.'

'Aye. In such a hurry to be off to Rowangarth this morning that you clean forgot. Mind, there isn't a lot – not at this time of the year. Pity Sir Andrew didn't stick to June.'

'Well, dinner's here, tonight. There'll be . . .' Tilda counted on her fingers. 'Mrs Amelia, Drew and Lyndis, The Reverend and Miss Julia and Mr and Mrs Carmichael, which will be seven. There'll be pheasant.' Out of season, but who cared? 'Creamed potatoes, roast potatoes and carrots. What else is there?'

'Parsnips, and the last of the apples. And plenty of onions.'

'That's it, then. Roast parsnips, whole onions in caramel, and apple pie and custard.' She would make the custard with eggs, and be blowed to austerity! If that government in London had framed itself and didn't fuss so much about exports, food could have been off the ration long ago and Tilda Willis able to provide a wedding breakfast even Mrs Shaw would have approved of! 'Put the kettle on, Mary. Us needs a sit-down. You'll stay for one, Sidney dear?'

'I will, and by the way, Jack Catchpole wants to know if you'll have room in the bottom of the fridge for the sprays and buttonholes. He's doing the small stuff this afternoon, so he'll have time for the bouquets in the morning.'

'All right, then – provided I can find room. But what won't go in the fridge can go on the floor of the keeping cellar, I suppose. Have you got the flowers cut for Gracie?'

'All ready, but for the roses. I'll leave them till the last minute. There's plum blossom enough to fill the font, and I kept forsythia back so there's enough for the big brass jug, beside the lectern. The greenery she said she would cut for herself, her knowing as much about that garden as I do, and where the best ivy is growing. Has the Reverend left two silver vases, by any chance?'

'That he has, and in need of cleaning!' Mary snorted. 'Not right, locking silver away. It always comes out black, and more work for me! The medium pot, Tilda?'

'Aye, why not? We can all do with a couple of cups.' She dabbed her perspiring brow and thought how grand all the turmoil was, and how worth it. Young Drew getting wed. Tomorrow!

'That was a lovely, lovely meal. And I think I drank too much wine.' Lyn hooked her arm in Drew's. 'Tilda's a wonderful cook. Well, sailor, this is the last time you'll walk Lyn Carmichael home! Remember?'

'Er – *what*, exactly?'

'Don't say you've forgotten the night a certain

Telegraphist said goodnight on the steps of Hellas House, and the Wren said –'

'Said she was a virgin? And the Telegraphist said he was, too.'

'Yep! And then I told him I loved him. Oh, Drew Sutton, if you'd only known how available I was that night . . .'

'I did, darling, only the time wasn't right for us, was it?'

'For me it was, but it takes two to tango.'

'All right, then – kiss me like you did that night and tell me you love me, and I just might . . .'

'Might what?' They had stopped walking, and she turned to him, arms clasping his neck, standing close. 'Tell me, Drew! What would happen?'

'I think I would say sorry, but I'm getting married tomorrow, so no can do.'

'So what is she like, this woman you're marrying tomorrow?' Her voice was husky, her eyes half-closed.

'She is very beautiful, very sexy, and she's a virgin.'

'And will you mind that?' She whispered her lips over his cheek, provocatively.

'Not in the least. I wish you were staying the night at Rowangarth, Lyn.'

'So do I. The way I'm feeling now, I'd put my head round your bedroom door and say, "Are you asleep, Drew?"'

'You couldn't, come to think of it. The floor outside my door creaks. Your mother would hear.'

'Mum wouldn't care.'

'Your father might.'

'Ha! Pots and kettles!' They began to walk again,

and she slipped her arm in his so their thighs touched.

'Is it the wine, Lyn, or are you not quite so jumpy about – *things*?'

'A bit of both. Maybe I've seen the light, at last.'

'Road to Damascus, sort of?'

'Nothing so dramatic, but I talked to Amelia Sutton. And like you said, she's a very wise woman.'

'So what did you talk about?' he asked, very softly.

'Ah, now – that's between me and her. All I can tell you is that I'm not upset any more that she's coming to the wedding. I'm glad, in fact, and I'm sorry for getting het up about it. And we're nearly at Daisy's, and I don't want to leave you. I won't sleep, tonight. I'll look a mess, tomorrow.'

'Well – they say for better or for worse, don't they?' he laughed, and she laughed with him and asked to be kissed again.

'I love you,' she whispered when they stood on Foxgloves' doorstep. 'Say goodnight to me, then go, for heaven's sake!'

They kissed, gently, then without another word, he left her.

'Hey!' she called softly, and he turned. Even in the fading light, she knew he was smiling. 'Night, sailor. See you tomorrow – two-thirty, uh?'

'It's a date. Love you . . .'

'And I love you, Drew Sutton.' She whispered it so softly that he did not hear her. 'I always did. I always will.'

Then, smiling, she knocked gently on Daisy's front window.

* * *

'Mornin', Sidney. You're early.' Jack Catchpole looked up from his work.

'I said I'd call in at the church, spray the flowers for young Mrs Sutton, but it isn't open, yet.'

'At six o'clock in t'mornin, it wouldn't be. What have you got there?' He fixed the brown paper carrier bag with a meaningful gaze.

'A flask of tea and a couple of teacakes, jammed. Tilda thought you might like sustenance, this being a busy morning for you. And if you don't mind, Mr Catchpole, I'd like to stay and watch you work. Me being a parks and gardens man, there's a lot I have to learn about bouquets. And I know now't about headdresses for brides.'

'Then you've comed to the right place to learn.' Jack basked in the compliment. 'Tell me – what do you think to this? Don't want the lass to think she's got a ton weight on her head.'

'I would say,' Sidney balanced the frame on his hand, 'that it is very lightweight. Should be no problem at all.'

'Just a bit of floral tape here and there, then it's ready for the flowers. You'll mind this tiny hook at the back? It's to take hairpins to secure the headdress. Her wants it forward, on her forehead, see? And her's going to wear the veil over her face, till her's wed – or so Gracie told me. Lady Helen's veil, that'll be . . .'

'And for the bridesmaids, Mr Catchpole?'

'Surprising what you can do with an Alice band. Worked fine for Daisy's attendants. White roses and apricot roses they'll have, and finger sprays to match.

321

Which will carry what colour, they can fight out between 'em,' he chuckled. 'And a sup of tea won't come amiss. Tell your good lady it's much appreciated.'

So Sidney rinsed mugs in the rainwater butt and they sat down amicably for tea and jammed teacakes, just as the sun broke through the morning mist.

'They're going to have a good day for it,' said Jack, contentedly. 'Oh, my word, yes!'

'Well, though I says it as shouldn't,' Tilda remarked, relieved, 'I'd never have expected to see such good vol-au-vents; not made with margarine.' The first traybake were nicely browned, light and well-risen. Gently she laid them to cool.

'Skill of the cook.' Mary offered a rare compliment. 'Mrs Shaw couldn't have done better with butter!'

'Well, thank you, I'm sure,' Tilda purred. 'I'll just get the next lot in to bake, then I'll give you a hand with upstairs teas.'

'Sit you down. I can manage. Only Mr and Mrs Carmichael, at eight. Drew said to let him sleep. This place, if you ask me, is a deal too quiet – for a wedding, I mean.'

'That's only because the Reverend and Miss Julia have moved out. I wonder if Polly Purvis is there giving a hand at Bothy House? They've got Mrs Amelia with them, don't forget.'

'Polly will be there till noon, she told me. Then she'll get herself into her finery and look after Mary Natasha – give Daisy a bit more breathing space, at Foxgloves. I wouldn't mind being a fly on the wall, there, this morning. A right old commotion it'll be, what with the bride and bridesmaids leaving from there. And Keth'll have to be here, at Rowangarth, to be with the groom. Remember when it was t'other way round, and Keth was the groom? A long time ago, it seems . . .'

'Six years, if memory serves me correctly.' Tilda always remembered anniversaries and birthdays. 'But today's going to be extra special. I wonder, Mary, if we'll have to call Drew by his rightful name, once he's wed?'

'We can try, but he's answered to Drew for a long time. Sir Andrew is going to take a bit of getting used to. Reckon we'll do as we did when he came back from the war – give him his due, with "Mornin', Sir Andrew", then after that, he's Drew again.'

'But will the new Lady Sutton allow it, Mary? We'll have to go carefully. Remember when Nurse Alice Hawthorn went to France, and came back Lady Alice Sutton? A tricky situation, that was.'

'Granted. But Drew's intended never worked here as sewing maid, did she? But what I think we should do, Tilda, is to ask Miss Clitherow's advice. She knows what's what. Reckon we'll be guided by her.'

'And I'll bet the old lass has been awake since the crack of dawn, all excited. How about making a pot of tea? You can take her one, then – see if she's all right.' Tilda reached for the oven cloth. 'And I'll just have a look and see how this next lot is doing, then I'll have a cup, an' all.'

She opened the heavy door of the iron cooking range, to be met with a gust of hot, pastry-scented

323

air, and thought how good it was to be cook at Rowangarth, and married to Sidney. And how grand it was that the master of Rowangarth – young Drew – was getting wed at last.

'I'm glad you decided to put your hair up, *cariad*. You look really regal,' Blodwen Carmichael said chokily. 'You're wearing those orchids like they're a crown.'

Around Lyndis, Helen Sutton's veil frothed and floated like thistledown, and she thought that only a love child could have been so beautiful. But then, love children were always beautiful.

'Where's Dad?'

'Round the back, having a quick smoke. He's all full up. Shouldn't wonder if he doesn't break down, when he sees you. But see here now, our Lyndis, I only popped in for a quick peep, just to be sure, and I'll have to go. Drew's mum is outside in the car, so I mustn't keep the driver.'

'Didn't she want a quick peep, too?'

'No. Said she'd wait to burst into tears until she saw you walking down the aisle. "Take a look at the veil, will you, Blodwen," was all she said. "Make sure it's firmly fixed." So I'll be off, because if I don't, my mascara is going to be all down my cheeks!

'Now don't forget to walk with your head up, Lyndis. Take it nice and slow, so everyone can see you. I've told your dad he's not to rush down the aisle. So – see you in church, lovely girl.' And with that she was gone in a flurry of pale green chiffon.

'Mum,' Lyn called softly, and when Blodwen

turned, she kissed the tip of her finger, then blew the kiss to her. 'Love you . . .'

'Oh, Julia! Let me get in this car, quick, and compose myself,' Blodwen said shakily, slamming the door shut, flopping into the seat, not caring about crumpling her skirt. 'I only wore mascara today so it would mean I couldn't weep, and now I wish I hadn't, she looks so beautiful.'

'Does she seem nervous?'

'Not a sign of it. Just sitting on a high stool with her skirts spread round her, so as not to crease her dress. Daisy said she wasn't to move a muscle.'

'And the bridesmaids – are they ready?'

'They are, and looking lovely. Daisy's got the white roses and Tatiana is carrying the apricot ones. Married women? Those two look like they're fresh out of the schoolroom. And I'm sorry I'm in such a twitter, but this is a very emotional day for me.'

'For me, as well. I have longed for Drew to marry and I'm so happy about it.'

'Me, too.' Blodwen was calmer, now. 'I'm absolutely delighted, and so is her dad. Wonder what Jack is doing now? I told him to check the windows and doors before they left. Give him something to do. I left him walking up and down in the back garden, nervous as a kitten.'

'Never mind. Not long to go.' Julia looked at her watch. 'Only about fifteen minutes.'

'Purvis – *please* . . .' Lyn held out her hands. 'Help me up? I can't sit here any longer – just got to walk about a bit. This is going to be the longest fifteen minutes of my life!' She wanted to get used to the dress, feel its floatiness as she moved and the soft whisper of silk. 'Y'know, a girl's just got to be happy being married in a dress like this.'

'It did pretty well for me,' Daisy smiled dreamily. 'A lot of love went into the making of it. Some of it's bound to rub off on you, Lyn. And don't we all look beautiful?'

'And the flowers are lovely,' Tatiana sighed. 'In fact, *everything* is lovely.'

It was for Tatiana, high on a cloud of complete happiness, who longed at this special moment to tell Daisy and Lyn about the tiny baby she carried. But she wouldn't. Not until tomorrow with Bill beside her to share the joy of telling.

'Oh, my goodness – I can't believe any of this. Will someone pinch me, please?' Lyn whispered. 'And where has Dad got to?'

'He's in the kitchen, now, looking as if he could do with a cup of tea.' Tatiana grinned. She couldn't stop smiling.

'Or a good stiff Scotch,' Lyn laughed.

'Are you all right, Lyn?' Daisy asked. 'Truly all right? All at once, you're so calm, not a bit worried.'

'Not calm, old love. In a trance, like this is happening to someone else, so let *her* do the worrying. And that, if I'm not mistaken, is your car, girls. Looks like this is it,' she whispered huskily. 'See you at the church, then . . .'

She watched as they got into the car in a flurry and rustle of lace and satin and frilly petticoats, then held up her hand to answer their wave.

Three minutes to the church, and three minutes back. Even timed to a split second, she and Dad would be two minutes late at All Souls. She lifted her train, and walked carefully to the kitchen.

'Dad? You all right? Daisy and Tatty have gone. Just you and me, now. Five more minutes, then –'

'Then it'll be our turn, eh? Sorry I seem a bit quiet, Lyn, but I didn't think I'd feel like this.'

'Like what, Dad?'

'Giving you away, because that's what it's going to amount to. Second time around, too. I gave you away once before when you went to school in England, and all the time knowing I wouldn't see you for a long time.'

'Nearly eighteen years, but all that's behind us, now. You and Mum are together at last and soon we'll be married, Drew and I. And you aren't living miles and miles away any longer.' She laid an arm around his shoulder, then bent to kiss the top of his head. 'Want to know something? Right now, I'm so happy I could burst.

'So what say you do a quick check of the house, then I'll take the clothes brush to your jacket, and straighten your tie. I'm proud of my dad,' she said softly, 'and you and I have got to walk down that aisle with heads high, Mum said, and slowly, so everyone can see us. And Dad, I love you a lot.'

'Goodness, it's packed in there,' Tatty whispered at the church porch. 'All Holdenby's here.'

In the back pew, sat Amelia Sutton with Adam on her knee and beside her, Gracie held the sleeping

Eleanor who tomorrow would be christened at the font behind them. She must remember to empty it of blossom, Gracie thought happily, or Uncle Nathan was going to have trouble. She smiled at Polly and Mary Natasha who, tired of being denied her grandmother's spray of flowers, had gone to sleep, thumb in mouth, clutching Teddy Wilf.

To their right, across the aisle, Miss Clitherow sat straight-backed, her best lace-trimmed handkerchief at the ready for when it would be needed, wishing dear Lady Helen could have been here, knowing that in spirit, she was. And beside her sat Mary and Will Stubbs, who had helped an old lady into the church because not for anything, she declared, was anybody wheeling her in to Sir Andrew's wedding.

And Jack Catchpole was there, splendidly buttonholed, and Lily his wife and beside them sat a flushed Tilda, her hand resting on her husband's.

'What is the matter?' Sidney whispered. 'Something bothering you?'

'Yes. The kettle. I think I left it on the hob and it'll boil dry . . .'

'It'll be all right. Ellen is there. She'll take care of everything. Stop your worrying, Mrs Willis.'

Tilda liked being called Mrs Willis – she would rather he called her Mrs Willis, she had whispered on her wedding night, than Tilda or even Matilda – and the sound of Sidney saying it in church, here at Drew's wedding, banished boiled-dry kettles from her mind.

At the organ sat Winnie Hallam's sister, fingers poised, ready for the bridal music which, over the years and several weddings, she played extremely well.

Winnie, relieved for the afternoon from the telephone exchange, stood on hand to turn pages and give signals. Her sister was well able to turn her own sheet music, but you got a better view of a wedding from the organ, and here Winnie was staying!

Already she had recognized Alice's grand hat from Daisy's wedding; Polly's too. And there was Julia, looking nowhere near her age, in sky blue. And Winnie wondered if she was thinking about her own wedding in this very church, so many years ago. A wedding from another war, and him killed at the very end of it, poor gentleman.

'Almost time,' smiled the curate, who was assisting Nathan.

And there was the vicar, and what must surely be his last wedding, talking to the bridegroom and best man.

'Not long to go, Drew. And I have to ask it, Keth, but . . .'

'Have I got the ring?' Keth grinned, fishing in his pocket for it, holding it on the palm of his hand. 'And she's due in thirty seconds flat.'

'She's late.' Drew pulled a finger round his collar. 'And she said she wouldn't be.'

'All brides are allowed a couple of minutes,' Nathan smiled. 'She'll be on her way, now . . .'

Winnie Hallam caught the pre-arranged flutter of a hymn sheet from the back of the church, and held up a hand to acknowledge it.

'Car's arrived,' she said to her sister in a voice everyone could hear.

There was a hush in the church. Nathan gave a stand-up sign to Drew and Keth. Drew looked anxious; Keth looked cheerful.

Blodwen nervously straightened the net on her hat, but it did nothing to stop the bumping in her throat. She would *not* give way to tears, though. At least not until Julia did!

The driver opened the car door, offering a help, wondering why brides always seemed to wear skirts too big for his car.

'Want a hand, *merchi*?' Jack asked, calmer now.

'No thanks. I'm fine. Just grab the train will you, Dad, while I ease myself out.' She did not feel like Lyn Carmichael. This was some other woman who stepped carefully onto the church path, completely in charge of her emotions. She smiled at the rose pink bridesmaid who hurried towards them. 'Tatty's coming to give me a hand . . .'

'You okay, Lyn?' Tatty whispered.

'Fine. Just fine . . .'

Lyn gazed ahead to the church porch where Daisy waited. Beside it stood a large shiny pram, a pushchair and Miss Clitherow's wheelchair. The very young and the very old, Lyn thought, and all ages in between, come to her wedding. To Drew.

'Ready?' Tatty asked, in control of the train. 'Here we go, then!'

Lyn walked slowly, carefully, head erect, taking small, calming breaths, trying to look ahead of her, yet knowing that beside the path stood a white marble stone.

Kitty. It's Lyn, she said with her heart, pausing for only a second.

The sun, high above the trees, picked out the name lettered in gold, and it was as if Kitty knew, and was sending back a smile.

'Having trouble?' Tatty had sensed the hesitation, felt the need to speak.

'No, Tatty. Everything's under control. Gravel on the path a bit awkward underfoot, though.' Lyn was speaking once more, the unemotional, unconcerned woman banished. From her right hand, the emerald ring she had put there only minutes before, flashed reassurance.

How many more slow steps to the church porch? How many long-drawn-out seconds to where Daisy waited, smiling.

'Hi, Carmichael,' she grinned. 'This is it, then. And aren't you wearing the veil over your face?'

'No, Daisy. Decided not to at the last minute. I like it as it is, and besides, people want to see me . . .'

And she wanted to see people and All Souls, decorated for a bride. And Nathan, waiting, and the mothers looking round, watching every step she took.

She stepped inside the church, Daisy and Tatty satisfied the train was laid rightly; there to take immediate action if it snagged, or dragged.

The organ bellows wheezed, they heard the opening chord of music.

'Ready?' Jack Carmichael smiled.

'Ready, Dad.'

A few steps to the top of the aisle and the back

pew where Mrs Amelia said she would sit. Please let her be there, like she said?

Lyn looked ahead, her smile one of relief. Amelia Sutton smiled back softly, gently, holding up a hand as if in blessing.

Lyn walked on, and there was Drew, Keth beside him. And Nathan was smiling, and Julia and Mum looking at her, wide-eyed.

The silken skirt swung and swished with every slow step. Drew turned and smiled, and she smiled back tremulously.

It was all right! This was her wedding day and she was walking on coloured slants of sunshine to Drew and was glad she had not covered her face; glad Drew could see the happiness in her eyes and in her smile. This was what she had longed for since their first meeting that seemed, now, to have only been yesterday.

I, Andrew Robert Giles, take thee, Lyndis, to my lawful wedded wife.

I love you, her heart whispered as she took her place at his side and his eyes smiled back that he loved her too.

Drew and Lyn, forever. It had come right at last. It *had*!

The front doors of Rowangarth were open wide. Ellen stood at the top of the steps, smiling a welcome.

'Sir Andrew, Milady. My, but this is a grand day. Can I offer Home Farm's good wishes? I only wish Lady Helen could be with us.'

'She'll be with us in spirit, Ellen. And thank you for coming to help. A Rowangarth do wouldn't be the same without you. Where do we receive? Is it to be here at the door, or in the garden?'

'Miss Julia told me it would be on the terrace, and then into the marquee for refreshments. Informal, like . . .'

'Well, we only got a head start. They'll be here, any minute now. Can you direct them, Ellen?' He took Lyn's hand and ran up the steps into the dark cool of the hall.

'Drew! Not so fast! I've got this dress to cope with, and stupid high heels! Give me a hand, will you?'

'Sorry, darling.' He tilted her chin with a forefinger, kissing her gently. 'Lift your skirts. I'll cope with the train. And why ever Daiz wanted such a long one is a mystery to me.'

'She didn't. Her mum wanted it. She'd bought ten yards of silk, Daisy said, and was determined to use every inch of it. And Drew – *receiving*. It sounds terribly posh. Nobody told me about it.'

'Nothing to it. You just smile and say, "Thank you for coming," or something of the sort. In fact, all you need do is smile. You'll knock 'em all for six. Did I tell you how lovely you look?'

'You did. In the vestry and on the way here. But tell me again?'

'You look stunning, wife. Took me by surprise when you walked down the aisle. I'd expected you hidden behind a veil, with your hair down. And instead you'd put up your hair like you had it in the Wrens. And smiled at me. I needed that smile, Lyn. By the way, I think you're beautiful, too!'

'Flattery, Drew Sutton, will get you everywhere,' she laughed. 'And watch what you're doing. I've got to give this dress back in one piece, don't forget.'

Laughing, they made for the drawing room and the windows, wide open, that led onto the terrace.

'Over there, Lyn – beside the tables and chairs, I think.' He raised his head at the sound of tyres crunching the gravel of the drive. 'And that sounds as if they're arriving. Give me a kiss – quickly.'

And when they had kissed, she took his face gently in her hands and whispered, 'I love you, Drew.'

'I know you do,' he whispered. 'The feeling is very mutual . . .'

'This is the most enjoyable day,' said Miss Clitherow, sipping sherry, little finger genteelly extended. 'And I'm grateful to you both for seeing me to the church. It would have been such a disappointment if I'd missed it.'

'No question of that,' Will Stubbs beamed, because praise from Miss Clitherow was praise indeed. 'I must say the gardens look grand. Reminds me of when Mary and me got wed. A lovely day, as I recall.'

'All weddings are lovely, Will Stubbs, and all brides are beautiful, though I must say Miss Lyndis – *ahem*! her ladyship – looked particularly so,' Agnes Clitherow beamed. 'And there is Ellen with refreshments and Tilda, with the sherry decanter. Do you suppose, Will . . .'

She handed over her glass, which was quickly refilled.

'Another for you, Mary?' Tilda smiled.

At which Mary Stubbs made a mental note that when the wedding was over and done with, she would instruct Tilda Willis that when refilling a glass, you never said, '*Another?*' A butler, a footman, even a parlour maid who knew what was what, would have said, 'Sherry, madam?' and that was all. No alluding to how many previous drinks they might have had!

'I think I just might, Tilda dear – in view of the occasion,' Mary smiled. 'And doesn't your wedding hat look grand? I remember you buying that hat on my advice. "Get one," I said, "before some bright spark down in London realizes that hats don't need clothing coupons." Even though you had no hopes, at the time, of wearing it.'

'I remember.' Tilda topped up her own glass – purely for fortifying herself against Mary's verbals. '"Get a good straw – a boater – and the best you can afford," you said. And I was right glad I did, because you'd be lucky to get a hat of this quality, these days, at *any* price.

'But I'll away now and see that Sidney is all right. Last time I saw him he was talking to Jack Catchpole – passing on Drew's compliments on how fine the gardens look, I shouldn't wonder.'

And with that she whisked off, leaving Ellen, the soul of tact, to dispense with silver serving tongs and never so much as the raising of an eyebrow, mushroom vol-au-vonts; cucumber sandwiches; salmon vol-au-vonts; egg-mayonnaise finger rolls and small cheese biscuits, one of each to every plate; did it with such aplomb and grace that no one realized they were being carefully rationed.

'Be back, soon, with cherry scones and cream,' she smiled.

'*Cream* . . .' Mary squeaked.

'Ssssh! Courtesy Home Farm, and not a word to a soul!'

Still smiling, she walked sedately to the next group, leaving Miss Clitherow and Mary Stubbs both, to remember cherry scone days of old, and how sad it was that Mabel Shaw was not here to share this special day.

Blodwen Carmichael bumped – literally – into Julia Sutton at the turning of a corner outside the library door.

'*Duw!* There's sorry, Julia. Was just sneaking off for a sit-down. My feet are killing me! Never was one for smart shoes!'

'Think I'll join you. Just let me lay this veil on a bed. They've taken all the snaps and photos they want, now, so I asked Lyndis if she would like to take it off. Could do with a cigarette, actually. In there.' She pushed open the library door with an elegant toe. 'Won't be a tick!'

'Well then, Julia,' Blodwen kicked off her shoes then inspected her mascara. 'What did you think of it all?'

'*Think?*' Julia drew deeply on the cigarette she had vowed to give up the minute Drew was married. 'I could go down on my knees and thank heaven fasting, for this day! I am so pleased. Aren't they a good-looking couple? Aren't you proud of them?'

'That I am. And pleased and happy; so pleased

and happy I can't believe it. She's loved Drew a long time, you know. Thought she'd end up an old maid.'

'Well, she hasn't and I'm glad, and I think we should drink a special toast – just you and me – to future happiness. Fancy a snifter of brandy, Blodwen?'

'No, but I'd do justice to a drop of gin!'

Smiling, and on tiptoe, they crept to the dining room and the decanters, then closed the door quietly behind them.

'Y'know, darling,' Lyn sat down almost elegantly on the seat beneath the linden trees, 'just when I'm getting control of this dress, it's almost time to take it off. And I'll bet these are a mess.' She bent to take off a shoe. 'Wouldn't you know it, all grass stains and mud on the heels! I'd intended having them dyed – but they're ruined, now. I don't suppose they'll even clean.'

'Don't do either, sweetheart. I want you to leave them as they are. Your wedding shoes. Very precious!'

'Idiot! Y'know, I'm getting to like this Linden Walk. I shall even be around to smell the blossom. June or July, didn't you say?'

'Mm. So tell me – why all at once a liking for this particular spot?'

'Because things seem to happen, here. The night we decided to get married we were sitting on this seat, remember? I'd got so cheesed off I told you I was going to Kenya to live.'

'You shocked me, Lyn.'

'Shocked you into proposing to me, more like,' she laughed. 'And then there was Mrs Amelia. We sat here for a talk, and all at once I seemed to get things straight in my mind.'

'So what did you talk about, or aren't I to know?'

'Not yet, darling, but I will tell you – when the time is right. Promise.'

'Okay. So let's always come here when there's special news for the telling? Let's kiss on it, darling?'

'Drew! People will see us!'

'I know. So let's make their day?'

He tilted her chin with a finger and she closed her eyes and said, 'Want to know something, sailor? I could get really fond of this old marble seat.'

'Where is my daughter?' Daisy asked of Keth. 'I haven't seen her for ages.'

'I have. She's on the terrace with the two grans, smiling for everybody who says "Oh, aren't you a beautiful baby?" She's a real little actress, that one. You were the same, if I remember rightly.'

'Keth! You didn't know me when I was eight months old!'

'I did, you know. I was nearly four. As a matter of fact, I saw a photograph of you and me only the other day. Mam was sending it to the little girl at Willow End. There's one of Dad and Beth, and another of you in your pram outside Keeper's Cottage – with me and Morgan beside you. Long time ago . . .'

'Mm. Come to think of it, you've been around as far back as I can remember. You took me to school every day, wet or shine. It was quite a walk.'

'Half a mile.'

'It was two miles when you've only got little legs!

Oh, Keth! This is a lovely day. Everyone here who matters. Almost as good as our wedding. Goodness, had you thought – only one more year to go then we'll hit the seven-year itch!'

'Never mind that. Let's celebrate the sixth, first. Shall we go somewhere, next week? How about the dinner-dance in Creesby?'

'I'd love that. It's ages since we danced together. Do you think Mam will baby-sit?'

'Can a duck swim? And look over there – the Linden Walk?'

'Oooh! Lyn and Drew, having a crafty kiss. Come on – let's break it up. Anyway, it's almost time for the cake and champagne.'

She lifted her satin skirts and ran, Keth thought, as if she were still a schoolgirl, and he hadn't yet told her he loved her. Loved her like she wasn't his sister, that was. He smiled as she called, 'Hey, you two! Behave!'

'Tatiana!' Bill yelled. 'What on earth do you think you're doing, woman! That tray is too heavy for you to carry!'

'It isn't. I'm giving Ellen a hand.'

'Then don't. By rights, you should put your feet up for an hour afternoons, not be charging about with a tray of crockery. Give it to me!'

'Sssh, darling. Someone will hear you and I'm not officially pregnant until after the christening, don't forget. Isn't this the most marvellous afternoon? Are you enjoying yourself?'

'I've got to admit I am. But let me get rid of these

crocks, then we'll find somewhere sunny so you can take the weight off your feet.'

'A pregnancy isn't an illness, Ewart said, so why are you acting like an old woman, all of a sudden?'

'Because you're carrying my bairn, Tatty, and I happen to love you.'

'Then let's grab a couple of chairs and find somewhere quiet, so you can kiss me – because I'll bet a pound to a penny that that's what Bas and Gracie are doing now. I saw them sneaking off to the kitchen garden. That's where they met, you know, when Gracie was Rowangarth's land girl.'

'Yes. You said. And careful how you go. Don't want you tripping over those skirts!'

But Tatiana laughed, and mouthed, 'I love you,' and ran ahead in search of chairs like she was dancing-on-air happy. Which she was, of course.

'Well, Sidney,' Jack Catchpole beamed. 'I must say that between us, we've done Rowangarth proud.'

'The florals, Mr Catchpole, were magnificent.'

'Aye. And the gardens, thanks to you, came up to my strictest expectations. Rowangarth is a grand place for a wedding. Nowhere like it. But I wanted a word. About the bouquets.'

'Miss Julia did tell me . . .'

'Ar, and I'm checking to make sure her's got it right. You'll collect the bride and bridesmaids' flowers later on this afternoon. We want no bouquet throwing, nor now't like that. 'Tis traditional that Rowangarth bouquets are put on Rowangarth graves. Afterwards.

'So the bride's tawnies are to go on Lady Helen's

grave, Daisy's white roses are for Reuben Pickersgill and Tatiana wants hers to go to her grandfather. Not to Elliot nor Mrs Clementina. Very insistent her was about that. For Grandfather Edward, her said.'

'I shall see it's done,' Sidney said gravely. 'I'll give 'em all a good spraying to freshen 'em up. Leave it to me, Mr Catchpole.'

And Jack Catchpole was content to leave it to Sidney Willis, and went in search of a quiet corner in which to have a pipe of tobacco out of sight of his wife, who had warned him about smoking that smelly old thing on an occasion such as this.

He chuckled. Lily would never see him. He knew *all* Rowangarth's quiet corners!

'Do you realize, Miss Eleanor Sutton,' Bas whispered to his sleeping daughter, 'that it was on this very spot your Mom and I met?'

'No,' Gracie smiled. 'Sorry, but it was just here.' She pointed to a spot outside the potting shed. 'I was sitting on an apple box with my shoes off.'

'And your shirt delightfully unbuttoned. That was when I said to myself, "Sebastian Sutton – *she* is the one!"'

'Then I can't imagine why you thought that. I was hot, my hands were filthy and my boots stank to high heaven. I'd been barrowing manure all afternoon. Don't tell me you didn't smell it!'

'No. Roses, it was – or maybe the scent of jasmine . . .'

'You're an idiot, and I love you.'

'And you're not sorry you gave up home and country to live in faraway Kentucky?'

'Not one bit sorry. And we'll be going to Rochdale on Monday to show off Nell to her English grandparents, and her great-gran. Guess I've got the best of both worlds, Bas.'

'And you still love me every bit as much. In this very special kitchen garden, do you swear it?'

'As much? No. I love you even *more*. I'm truly, truly happy, darling.'

'Me too, Gracie Fielding. But let's get back to the do, before we get sloppy and sentimental. Must be nearly time for cake cutting and toasts.'

'Must be.' She reached on tiptoe to kiss him gently. 'And I'll just take a look at the orchid house – make sure everything's all right. Won't be a minute.'

'Well now, Tom, isn't this a grand day?'

'And today is special for you, isn't it, Alice?'

'It is. My boy got married, and I was so proud of him. Couldn't believe that once I'd resented him inside me.'

'Hush, now. You left him with Lady Helen and Julia, and came to me; left him at Rowangarth – his inheritance, after all.'

'Yes. And I came to love him, didn't I? A little fair-haired boy of two, who couldn't pronounce my name. Mrs Lady, he called me. That's when I knew I could love him – because he was Julia's . . .'

'Her reason for living, poor lass. Helped her get over Andrew. So don't get yourself upset, love. We've just had a nice tea, and champagne and wedding

cake to come. And there's Daisy and Keth, waving
to us – over there see – by the Linden Walk, with
Drew and Lyn. A sight to make your heart happy,
eh, Alice?'

And Alice said that it was, and thought that
weddings always did things to people; brought out
memories – almost always good – and left happiness
trailing behind them. Come to think of it, it didn't
seem like thirty years since she and Tom were married.
Quietly, of course, as befitted a widow, at a little
church in faraway Hampshire.

'Can you believe, Tom love,' she whispered, laying
a hand on his, 'that it'll be thirty years in August –
you and me, wed?'

'Good years, bonny lass.'

'A pity, though, we didn't have more bairns.'

'We decided to take what the good Lord sent,
Alice, and He only had one for us. Mind, we got the
quality, if not the quantity. And we had a share in
Drew, don't forget.'

'Mm. You and Nathan were the men in Drew's
life. Nathan taught him until he was old enough for
grammar school, and you taught him the ways of the
country.'

'Aye, and how to handle a gun safely. Told him
there'd be ructions if he broke any of the rules. And
now he's wed.'

'At last.' Alice beamed. 'So I'll just away and have
a word with Miss Clitherow, then I'll take the baby
off Polly and let her circulate a bit. Tom?' she frowned.

'Aye, lass?' Tom recognized the look on her face,
the set of her mouth, and gave her his full attention.

'They'll have children, won't they – Drew and Lyn, I mean?'

'Well of course they will! Whatever made you say such a thing?'

'You and me. We only had Daisy.'

'Then stop your fretting and put that smug smile back on your face, Mrs Dwerryhouse. Drew and Lyn will have children. I'd bet on it!'

'Aaah.' She smiled, then went in search of Miss Clitherow, who had had two sherries to Alice's certain knowledge and could well be happily asleep! My, she beamed, but this was the third most precious day of her entire life! Her son – hers and *Giles's*, never forget – wed at last!

'There you all are!' Amelia Sutton carrying Adam, thumb in mouth. 'He's almost asleep. Too much excitement. I'm going to take him to Bothy House – let him have a snooze on Julia's sofa.'

'You're going to miss the champagne,' Drew teased.

'Sadly, yes, but I'm sure you understand. It was a lovely wedding – you looked very beautiful, Lyn. Take care of her, Drew. This is goodbye, you see. I'm flying back to Kentucky after Nell's christening tomorrow, so I want to give you both a special hug and ask you to remember me, and the times we've shared at Rowangarth.'

She held out her arms to Drew, laying her cheek on his, closing her eyes briefly, wishing him happiness. Then she smiled as Lyn held wide her arms, hugging her close, whispering chokily, 'Thank you, Mrs Amelia – for everything . . .'

'And thank *you*, my dear. I won't wish you happiness – it's shining all around you. So I hope you and Drew have children – lots of them – and you *will*. Bless you both.

'I'll see you two – and Mary Natasha – at the christening, tomorrow,' she smiled to Keth and Daisy. Then she turned and walked away, her grandson's cheek close to hers, her arm laid protectively on his back.

'What an absolute love she is,' Daisy smiled. 'Sad she won't ever come to Rowangarth again.'

'Perhaps we'll be able to persuade her. She loves Rowangarth so,' Drew said softly.

'No. I know her too well,' Keth said softly. 'I was a part of that family for a long time, don't forget. She won't be back.'

'No, but Gracie and Bas will,' Drew urged. 'Maybe even twice a year, like in the old days. Gracie will want to see her folks, in Rochdale.'

'Let's wait and see,' Daisy said brightly. 'We might even go over to visit them in Kentucky, so don't look so glum, Keth Purvis. And there's Aunt Julia waving like mad. Time to cut the cake, bruv.'

She gathered up her skirts and ran towards the terrace, her hand in Keth's.

'Just a minute,' Lyn whispered, pushing her little finger through the loop inside her train, lifting it over her arm. 'And don't forget my flowers, darling.' She turned her head to wipe away a tear, but Drew saw it at once.

'Lyn, love – what is it?'

'Nothing, really. Maybe one that just squeezed out. A girl can only take so much happiness, you know.'

Yet she knew the tear was for Kitty, whose day this might have been, and for Amelia Sutton, who was leaving her daughter's memory in Lyndis Sutton's care.

'And I *am* happy, Drew . . .'

The bride and groom took the Holdenby Flyer to York station, because that was the way they wanted it to be. No bridal cars with fluttering white ribbons, or Just Marrieds or old boots trailing behind them. Julia was to drive them to the station, after goodbyes had been said on Rowangarth's front steps.

But the Clan thought otherwise, and arrived shortly afterwards, calling and laughing and throwing confetti, waving as the engine slipped and jerked and left the station, calling, 'Good luck! Byee. Have fun!'

'Might have known they wouldn't let us get away with it!' Drew laughed, pulling up the window. 'There's confetti all over the station. And Lyn – let's look out at Brattocks Wood. It wouldn't surprise me at all, if someone wasn't there, too.'

And true to tradition, Tom stood at the waving place, and Ellen with two of her grandchildren, and Will Stubbs, whistling through his fingers so loudly they could hear it above the din of the engine.

'Isn't everyone lovely?' Lyn whispered chokily. 'I think I'm going to have to squeeze another tear out. I can't believe any of it.'

'No tears on your wedding day, Lyn. I forbid it.' He sat on the seat, pulling her beside him. 'And now we're really alone at last, I'd like a kiss, please.'

'Not until you've looked under the seats and searched the luggage rack. I wouldn't put anything past that mad lot!'

'Well, you're a part of that lot now, so you'll have to learn to put up with it!' He tilted her chin, yet even as he kissed her, Lyn knew she would never wholly belong – not to the Clan. She and Gracie and Bill would never quite be allowed in; could never join Keth and Daisy, Drew and Tatiana and Bas, because there were no vacancies for the offering. Not when Kitty was still a part of it.

'Wasn't Mrs Amelia kind, today? She's such a lovely lady, once you get to know her, Drew.'

'I told you she was, didn't I? So what did you and she talk about? Are you going to tell me?'

'Yes. One day – when the time is right.'

'Not now, darling?' he coaxed.

'Not now. But I will tell you. I promise. And Drew – I've just thought! What if someone has got at our cases – stuffed them with confetti, I mean?'

'Well they won't have. I gave them to Mother with the strict instructions to hide them from mischief makers. They'll be all right. No one will know we're honeymooners. We'll get rid of this stuff before we get to York, then act as if we're an old married couple, staying the night en route to London. And Lyn, darling, I'm so very happy about us. Do you realize how much I love you?'

And she said yes, she was almost sure she did, and closed her eyes and tilted her chin, the better for him to kiss her, and prayed silently she might be allowed to keep this amazing, shining happiness. Not until death did them part, but on and on past forever and into eternity.

Then she pushed him gently from her and said, as matter-of-factly as she was able, 'Give me your comb for heaven's sake. Your hair is full of confetti, Drew Sutton!'

No more lovely happy tears. Please, no more . . .

'Aaaah.' Lyn pushed off her shoes, took off her grey pinstripe jacket, then sat at the dressing table to gaze wonderingly into the gilt-framed mirror.

She was dreaming, of course. This wasn't happening to Lyn Carmichael; it couldn't be. People didn't get that lucky – well *did* they? The two of them, signing the hotel register A and L Sutton, and she with never a blush, as if she had been Lyndis Sutton for ages and ages, and was used to smart hotels and bridal suites.

There was champagne, too, shining crystal glasses and a posy of white rosebuds on either bedside table. Bedside. Such a huge, four-poster bed that she dropped her eyes to her hands and the emerald that fitted snugly against her wedding ring.

'Do you want anything, Lyn? Tea, maybe . . . ?'

'No thanks. I'd just like to sit here for a minute or two and look at that smug woman in the mirror. Is she really me?'

'No. Not quite. The girl I'm truly in love with has long hair; hair I want to stroke, it's so beautiful. The one in the mirror reminds me of a Wren I used to take out, in Liverpool. She had her hair in a pleat.'

'King's Regulations and Admiralty Instructions. Cut it short, or roll it up!'

'Then shall we let it down?' He came to stand behind her, feeling for the pins in her hair, taking them out one by one until the shining hair slipped and slid through his fingers, down to her shoulders. 'Where is your hairbrush?'

'In my case at the top – with my nightie and sponge bag.' She fished in her handbag for the key. 'Be a love and get them out for me?'

She watched indulgently through the mirror as he fitted the tiny key into the lock then spun round, surprised, as he yelled, 'Oh, *dammit*! Wouldn't you just know?' He held up a lace-trimmed nightgown and confetti showered from it, covering the carpet. 'And your sponge bag is full of the stuff, Lyn.'

'But who could have done it?' she laughed, completely undismayed. 'You said the cases were safe with your mother.'

'Yes! And she calls herself a vicar's wife. "Promise, Drew, hand on heart. Not a soul shall touch these cases but me," she said. The crafty so-and-so!'

He began to laugh as Lyn emptied her sponge bag, sending rose petals floating to the floor.

'Drew! What will we do? Do you suppose room service could send us up a brush and pan?'

'Sweep it up? Not on your life! It's all over the place, so what the heck. In fact, I'll just add my two-penn'orth!' Still laughing, he opened the door, taking the Do Not Disturb sign, hanging it on the door-knob. 'There now. The cat is out of the bag. We're honeymooners! Let's be hanged for sheep, eh?' He closed the door, sliding home the bolt. 'Now, what was I about to do?'

'I think – I *hope* – you were going to brush my hair.'

'For starters, yes. Put your nightie on, darling.'

For just a moment she hesitated, then looked in the mirror to meet eyes that said, 'Six months is a long time to wait . . .'

Then slowly, her eyes not leaving his, she began to unfasten the buttons of her blouse.

SEVENTEEN

Lyn was sitting at the kitchen table in the little white house eating toast and jam, when Drew returned with the morning papers.

'Hi, there. You've surfaced.' He kissed the back of her neck.

'Why didn't you waken me?'

'Decided not to. You looked so full of sleep, that I left you. Y'know, each morning I buy a paper I think that it's one more day of our week gone. Only two days left. Why didn't we decide on *two* weeks?'

'Never mind. We can come here often. And we've seen so many things. Westminster Abbey and –'

'Made love . . .'

'And Parliament and the Tower of London, then –'

'Made love in the afternoon . . .'

'Drew! Stop it! You'd think we'd –'

'Made love in every room in the house, almost? Of course we have!'

'Yes, and what your Aunt Sutton would think if she knew – and she a devout maiden lady!'

'She was unmarried because that was the way she

wanted to be. Her great love was horses – and Rowangarth, of course, which she left when her brother married my gran. She spent a lot of time in France, too. Died there.'

'Yes, and now she's with the Rowangarth Suttons. Anne Lavinia Sutton. Spinster. 1857 – 1920. Your mother told me she was an absolute love. Liked a drop of brandy – a snifter, didn't she call it?'

'As we all seem to call it, even yet. Are you going to be happy at Rowangarth, Lyn? All the generations glaring down from the staircase. Majors and colonels and one of them a general, even.'

'Mm. All the men with fair hair. And shall you be painted and hung there in your fore and afts, Leading-Telegraphist Sutton, the equivalent of a corporal,' she teased.

'Only if you are painted in your wedding dress with your hair down.'

'Goodness. Lyn Carmichael's portrait in oils! I seem to have come a long way, don't I? From Auntie Blod's love child, to lady of the manor.'

'So? I asked if you are going to be happy.'

'*Very* happy, darling. I think the nicest part of it is going to sleep in your bed, and wakening with you still there. Except, of course, when you sneak out to buy papers. So what are we going to do, today?'

'Tonight, I've got us a table at the Ritz so this afternoon, we'll do the shops and buy you a gorgeous dress – one of the long ones everyone seems to be talking about.'

'The New Look, you mean. Long, full skirts –

absolutely wonderful after clothing rationing. But I think I'd like a short dinner dress. I'd get more use out of it.'

'Whatever you want. I'll have to try to get an off-the-peg dinner jacket. Nothing I had before the war fits me and – now who the heck is that?' He frowned as the phone in the sitting room rang. 'I'll get it . . .'

Lyn smiled dreamily. A new dress. Dinner at the Ritz and tomorrow, a walk in Hyde Park to the very spot where Drew's mother and Daisy's mother got into a fight with police. Drew was very proud of his mother and Lady, who had sent a constable flying. Then home to Rowangarth. Her home, now. Could life get any better?

'So who was that?' she asked of a smiling Drew.

'It was Mother. She apologized for ringing but she couldn't sit on the news any longer. It's Tatty. She's pregnant. Bill announced it after the christening on Sunday. Some time in October. Isn't it great?'

'Marvellous. I'm so pleased for them, even though Tatty's beaten me to it.'

'For Pete's sake, darling, they had a head start on us. I'm trying my best,' he laughed.

'Mm. I know you are.' Her smile was dreamy. Being loved by Drew was wonderful; far better than she had ever imagined. And he hadn't spoiled it for them, because Drew had been tender and very sweet – their first time. Their second loving was something she wanted never to forget, so passionate and uninhibited that she had asked him, huskily, if it would always be like that between them and he had said, no. It would get better and better.

'What are you thinking about, Lyn? You've got a look on your face like the cat that got at the cream.'

'I was thinking,' she lied without a second thought, 'that now I come to look back on it, Tatty did have a kind of smugness about her, at the wedding. How did she manage to keep it quiet for so long? I don't think I'd be able to.'

'You want children very much, don't you, darling?'

'I want *your* children, Drew, but not this very minute if you don't mind.'

'And you're happy about you and me, sweetheart. No more – *hang-ups*?'

'Doubts and hang-ups all sorted, Drew. Want some breakfast?'

'Please. I'm ravenous. What is there?'

'No eggs, no bacon, no butter. Only toast and jam, and I'm afraid I've eaten most of the jam . . .'

'Did I ever tell you, Lyn Sutton, how much I love you, even though you are a greedy gannet and have scoffed my jam ration? Reckon we'll have to go out and try to find another Charlie.'

'You still remember Charlie at Liverpool Pierhead, with his rusty old van,' she gasped, delighted. 'And those cheese sarnies he sold?'

'Black market cheese sarnies, thick as doorsteps, and tea so strong you could stand a spoon up in it.'

'If he trusted you with his spoon!'

'Happy days, Lyn.'

'Mm.' She took his face in her hands, kissing him urgently. And he gathered her close, whispering, 'Behave, woman! It's only nine in the morning.'

'That late?' she murmured, lips on his. 'Let's go upstairs . . .'

The station master at Holdenby Halt said they were welcome to leave their cases in his left-luggage office – which was really the small cubbyhole in which the lady cleaner stored her mops and brushes. The left-luggage, he said, would be open until the last train to York had departed (which was nine-thirty p.m.) after which it would be closed until six-fifteen on Monday morning, there being no Sunday trains, now the war was over.

'If you'd phoned your mother, she'd have been only too glad to meet us,' Lyn complained. 'Why must we walk?'

'Because I want you to see Rowangarth as I saw it, every time I came home on leave. I used to feel excited inside, the minute I passed the gate lodge. And then, when I turned the corner to the straight sweep and saw the house, I could have happily wept. It's your home, now, and I want you to see it as I did. I'll nip down, before the last train, and pick up the cases, but I do want your first homecoming to be special, Lyn.'

So she smiled and said she understood, and took his hand in hers, wondering what she had done to deserve such happiness, aching inside even to think of ever losing it.

'I see exactly what you mean,' she said, when they had passed the little gate lodge where Tilda and Sidney Willis lived, and turned the sweeping bend to the long, tree-lined drive. 'It's beautiful, Drew. So – so *enduring*.'

The house of rose-red bricks and shining leaded windows stood there four square and safe, as if it had never seen death nor sadness nor half a dozen wars; as though it had known only good times and happiness and serenity.

'I used to think about it in the war, Lyn. Times when there were no letters or we were being slapped about in a force-eight gale. Times when I was so tired from split-watches that all I could ever ask of life was to walk the last few hundred yards of this drive and get my head down, in my own bed.

'And when I did get leave, Mother always seemed to sense I was getting near. I'd see her, waiting at the high window, then all at once the doors would fly open and she'd be there with Gran at the top of the steps, all smiles the pair of them.'

'Did you know, Drew, that we Welsh have a word for that feeling? *Hiraeth*. It's a sort of yearning when you're far from home, that calls you back to where you want to be – to your own people and your own hearth.'

They were standing, still, at the top of the drive, hands clasped, happy just to be there together. It made her almost sorry, Lyn thought, that she said, 'Drew – is it my imagination, or does the roof sag in the middle? Is it safe?'

'It has sagged like that since ever I can remember. Old roofs always sag. Of course it's safe – I hope!'

And laughing, hand in hand, they ran towards Rowangarth, and home.

'So how was it, Carmichael? Had a good time?'

'What a stupid question to ask! Of course we had

356

a good time. London was wonderful. And just to remind you, the name is Sutton!'

'Sorry, milady,' Daisy grinned. 'And I wasn't asking how London was. This is Purvis-from-the-bottom-bunk you're talking to, so how did it go?'

'You mean, did I mess things up like I thought? Actually, I didn't. In fact I wondered why I'd worried so much about – we-e-ll – *that*.'

'Good. That's all I wanted to know. At least that's your boring virginity taken care of, thanks be! Where's Drew, by the way?'

'We called at Bothy House but they were out, so Drew carried on to the station to pick up the cases. We left them there, and walked home.'

'Mm. He always left his kit at the lodge and walked the last bit when he used to come on leave. Always said that those last two hundred yards were the longest part of the journey home.'

'Funny you should say that, because I've had an idea for Bill to do a watercolour of the view for me to give to Drew. Think he will?'

'Don't see why not. But how about Tatty's baby? She's thrilled to bits.'

'Wish it were me, Daisy.'

'Hey! Give it time. Or do you think you might be?'

'I could be. We decided not to be careful.'

'Then fingers crossed!' She peered through the kitchen window. 'And that's Drew come to collect you. Where are you eating tonight, by the way? You're welcome at ours . . .'

'Thanks but Tilda has left us something. There was

a note, signed T. Willis. *Salad in fridge. Cherry scones in tin. Don't let on about the illegal cream.*'

But Daisy was halfway down the path, arms wide, calling, 'Welcome home, bruv. Come to collect your missus? My, but you look well on married life!'

Then they hugged and kissed as they always did, and Lyndis stood there and wondered soberly how much happier it was possible to be.

'Mother and Nathan have gone to York to the theatre – her way of being tactful, I suppose, and leaving us to settle in.' Drew piled salad on his plate, then helped himself to sliced Spam. 'How was Mary Natasha, by the way?'

'I didn't see her. Out in her pram with Granny Polly. Daisy is tickled pink about Tatty's baby. Wondered if I might be pregnant, but that's too much to hope for, I told her.'

'But you *could* be, Lyn. Would you mind if you were?'

'You know I wouldn't, but I think I couldn't take much more happiness – not right now. So let's have a quiet night in – go through the post, then get unpacked. I noticed there were a couple of letters for me – one from Wales. Mum did so enjoy the wedding, Drew.'

'Everyone did. Even the weather behaved. But let's get supper eaten, then we'd better wash the dishes, I suppose.'

'Of course we'd better. Tilda and Mary are off, tomorrow. Can't leave dirty dishes for them. But let's get settled in? No ringing round saying "Hi!" to all and sundry. We'll see everyone at church, tomorrow.

After all, this is the last of my honeymoon and I won't be The Bride any more.'

'No. As from tomorrow, you'll be Lady Sutton.'

'I know. It's going to take a bit of getting used to. I could have hugged Daisy when she asked if you'd come to collect your missus.'

'Oh, Daiz is like that. I don't think she's once called me Sir Andrew – even in sarcasm. Don't worry. You'll be Lyn to most people. The Rowangarth Suttons aren't grand people, or rich. We came from yeoman stock, and that's really what we are. We've been around these parts since the year dot, but it wasn't until 1604 that we got the title.'

'How come?'

'Oh, from James the First of England, Sixth of Scotland. Legend has it that he made a triumphant procession from Scotland to collect the English throne, threw titles around like nobody's business at every house he stayed in on the way down, almost. I believe he even knighted a loin of beef he'd particularly enjoyed. So we're very ordinary people, really. And don't ever mention the roof again, if you don't mind, because where I'd find the money for a new one, I truly don't know! Okay?'

'Message received and understood, sailor. And pass the cream, will you – and I love you, Drew. I know I keep saying it, but I truly do.'

'Mm. So what would you give me for a dish of cream,' he asked, eyes narrowed.

'Anything at all – but later. When we've done the washing up . . .'

* * *

'You've missed Lyn and Drew by half an hour, Keth.' Daisy closed her eyes and offered her lips. 'And you've missed your mum by minutes. She's just brought the baby back. Be a love and give her her tea? It's all ready, then I can get on with dishing up the supper. How did the cricket go? Oh, and wash your hands, first!'

'Yes, miss. And we won – by twenty runs. First time we've beaten Creesby. Mind, the umpire was a Holdenby man. He let a couple of leg-befores go. So, how were the bride and groom?'

'Fine. They enjoyed being at Aunt Sutton's house. Carmichael's got a smile on her face like the Cheshire cat. And there's something I forgot. The government is graciously to allow Brits to go abroad again. That's the good news. The bad news is that no one will be allowed to take more than fifty pounds with them. Isn't it awful? There'll be the poor Brits, wondering if they can afford a cup of coffee!'

'Who told you?' Keth aimed the spoon at Mary's wide-open mouth.

'It was on the one o'clock news. Noble of them, isn't it? I mean, our lot will be standing out like sore thumbs. Penniless. And who won the blasted war, anyway?'

'It was definitely us, darling. Trouble is that now we're having to pick up the tab for it and it seems the money isn't there. But are we talking about me?'

'If you still intend going to Clissy – yes.'

'I'd like to, Daisy. Make the effort, at least.'

'Then yes, we *are* talking about you going to Clissy, and how far you're going to get with fifty pounds in your pocket! Anyway, when were you aiming to go?'

'Whilst the weather is still decent. No later than the August holidays, if that's all right with you?'

'You know it is, Keth.' She looked fondly at their child, eating her supper; a little girl who had not been given away nor whose parents would be killed in gas chambers. And Mary Natasha Purvis would not work for the French Underground. Over her mother's dead body would she! 'Oh, who's a clever little girl, then? All gone,' she smiled. 'I got two bananas, yesterday. She can have one of them, for her pudding. Mash it well, Keth. No sugar on it. And darling, I'm on your side. You know I am. It's just that you aren't going to get far on fifty quid!'

'We'll talk about it after supper, love. Surely there'll be a way? If only petrol was a bit easier to come by, there'd be no problem at all. But thanks, sweetheart, for being on my side – for understanding, I mean.'

'You said the little French girl was dark, just like Mary Natasha is. That's one good reason for understanding. And sixteen is no age to die. The child had hardly got a hold on life. That you must go isn't up for discussion. How you'll get there is another matter entirely.

'And you're loving that banana, aren't you, darling?' she asked of the dark-haired, dark-eyed baby in the highchair. 'Well, don't get too fond of them, sweetie pie. They don't grow on trees, you know. Granny Alice had to queue half an hour in Creesby market for that one!'

'We'll think of something, Daisy love. And we'll have to think, too, about why I'm suddenly taking off for France and leaving my wife and child at home.'

'Hmm. Just had a thought. If Mary and I came with you, that would mean we'd be entitled to take a hundred and fifty pounds with us. Maybe, come to think of it, we *should* go with you, if only to say a thank you. After all, we wouldn't have Mary now – we wouldn't have been married, even – if you hadn't got out of France.'

'If Natasha-Hannah-Elise hadn't stopped the bullet that was intended for me,' he said, harshly. 'But I'll get there, if I have to work my passage across on a Channel ferry. I did it once before, remember?'

'Yes. On a transatlantic liner in 'thirty-eight, when you thought there was going to be a war. I remember, Keth.'

'And there *was* a war a year later and you and I were two of the lucky ones. We made it home.'

'That being the case, you don't have much of a choice, do you? You've got to go back to France, and even if you can't find Natasha's grave, at least she might know you've been there, Keth. To send her your love and thoughts, I mean, and to say thank you.'

She had only to look, she knew, at the child that was hers and Keth's, to know that what she said was right.

'Yes, I shall go. I'll manage it, somehow. I could drive south then get one of the car ferries over. It's petrol that's the problem.'

'Ten bob each for a coupon in London on the black market, Bill said. But we'll talk about it later. Supper's ready.' She offered a rusk to Mary Natasha, which could usually be relied upon to occupy her attention for ten minutes before it was thrown, soggy, to the floor. 'Shepherd's pie, and baked custard for pudding.'

And why, oh *why*, had the government announced that as from next week, chocolates and sweets were no longer to be rationed? Wouldn't it have been so much more sensible to have allowed just a little more meat and butter, instead?

But governments were never sensible, were they? It was as Mam said. If there had been a few more women at Westminster, rationing would have been over and done with long ago. Stood to sense, didn't it?

'We can't ask Bill, can we, where he got the coupons in London – not without letting the cat out of the bag?' Daisy frowned.

'Eat your supper,' Keth said softly. 'We'll talk about it later, but bless you for understanding.'

'So what are you two doing today?' Julia asked of Lyn and Drew when Eucharist at All Souls was over. 'Care to pop over for a pot-luck supper?'

'Love to,' Lyn accepted eagerly. 'We're going to Denniston this afternoon to catch up with the news.'

'I wonder what about,' Drew grinned. 'Shouldn't wonder if Bill and I don't shove off to his studio.'

'Drew – a word of advice. Let it all flow over your head. You can, you know, if you try hard enough.' Nathan smiled ruefully. 'Just when I thought we'd seen the end of the wedding talk, Tatiana's news breaks and we're back to square one. All part and parcel of being a married man, I'm afraid. Given time, you'll learn how to cope.

'Meanwhile, see you tonight at Bothy House. Come at half-six, will you, then we can have a drink beforehand and a walk in the garden – I've made a start on it, y'know.'

'And so has Jack Catchpole, would you believe?' Julia offered. '"Just want a word of advice from Jack," didn't he say? "About where to site the compost heap and where best to put up a little greenhouse." Crafty move, that was. I can just see the pair of them sitting there, theorizing and puffing their pipes. There'll be more putting-the-world-to-rights than digging done in that garden! And there's Alice, at Reuben's grave. Want a word with her, if you don't mind. 'Bye. See you later!'

Karl set the tea tray on the low table in the conservatory, then left without a word. Tatiana, beaming, said she would be mother and set about pouring.

'I'm so pleased about tea. Even to look at a teapot made me feel sick not so long ago, but now everything's coming right. I can drink it again. Haven't been sick once since the day before the wedding. And aren't we lucky, never having to worry about how much of it we drink?'

'Shillong,' Drew said to Lyn. 'I told you about it – remember? We once had a tea plantation – we-e-ll, tea *garden*, actually – Gran sold it, but we still get a complimentary chest of Sutton Premier every year. Even in the war it got through, safely. Mother still dishes it out to friends and family. Supposed to be very good tea, isn't it, Tatty?'

'The Petrovska says so. Took some back to London

last December. Pass the cups round, Bill, there's a love?' she beamed. She seemed, Drew thought, to do a lot of beaming, these days.

'So you're feeling well?' he asked solicitously. 'How long did the morning sickness last?'

'It stopped at three months. Like I said, just before your wedding. But I think I was so sky-high happy that day that I just forgot – to be sick, I mean. I'm eating well again, now. Just get the urge to crunch. At the moment, it's raw carrots. Crazy, isn't it?'

'Are you taking note, Drew?' Bill asked mournfully. 'Women get peculiar, it seems, once they're pregnant. Get all sorts of likes and dislikes. Would drive a bloke mad!'

'Take no notice,' Tatiana laughed. 'He's loving every minute of it. Fusses like an old woman!'

'And what do you want?' Lyn asked, sipping her tea, noting she didn't feel in the least sick. 'Boy, or girl?'

'We neither of us mind. Bill says as long as mother and baby are well, that's all that matters. We've decided that I'm to name a girl, and Bill will choose his son's name. And we're neither of us telling, so don't ask.'

It was not until cups were collected and Tatiana said she felt like a walk in the garden, that Lyn said, 'Off you go, then. Walk with her, Drew, and I'll give Bill a hand with the dishes. I wanted to get you alone,' she said, when the door banged. 'I've got a favour to ask, Bill. A big favour.'

'Ask away, hennie. Anything – *almost* – anything, 'cept money. Mind, I'm no' doing so bad, these days. Selling quite a few paintings . . .'

'It's paintings I want to talk to you about. Will you do one for me? I want it for Drew, you see. A view of Rowangarth from the top of the drive, looking down the avenue of trees.'

'But I don't usually do landscapes. It's flowers and suchlike I do best.'

'You did one of Leningrad for the Countess. Tatty said it was brilliant.'

'Aye?' He inspected a cup for lipstick marks. 'She's biased.'

'Please, Bill? That view is special. It always pleased Drew to stand at the top of the drive, when he came home on leave. Used to think about it if things got a bit bad, when he was away at sea.'

'Aye. We all had our fantasies. Mine was a blonde parachute packer – a WAAF corporal. I'd think about her when a searchlight found us, or the flak got a bit too near.'

'I – I didn't know,' Lyn said, surprised.

'No, you wouldn't. She was a married woman, but I always thought about getting back in one piece – handing my 'chute back to her. There wasn't anyone, till Tatty. I knew she was beautiful, but I wasn't prepared for just how beautiful till I could see again. But I'll do the picture for you, Lyn. How do you want it – winter or summer?'

'Not winter, Bill. It was December when Drew came back from the Pacific, coming home to life without Kitty. A winter picture might remind him of sadness.'

'Then why not now? Rowangarth in April. Tell you what, I'll go to the top of the drive – do a pencil sketch – then try to fix the colours in my mind. How about that? Mind, Tatty'll have to know. She often comes to watch me paint.'

'No bother. Just as long as it's a surprise for Drew. And it's strictly business, Bill. No discount for family,' she laughed.

'We'll talk money, later. And what is the picture to be called – and is it to be morning or evening? Makes a difference, you know.'

'Mm. I suppose it must. Mellow, perhaps? Late afternoon, the time we got back from our honeymoon. I'd like it to be called *Homecoming*.'

'Then I shall put my fancy label on the back. *Homecoming*, by William Benson. In celebration of the marriage of Sir Andrew and Lady Lyndis Sutton. Jings, but I've come up in the world!'

'Oh, Bill, you're such an old love.' She hugged him tightly, cheek against his. 'And I'm so happy that sometimes I think I'll die of it!'

'Aye, lassie. You and me, both. I know the feeling well.'

EIGHTEEN

'What's news?' Daisy asked of Lyn. 'At a loose end, are you? Where's Drew?'

'In the village, with a decorator from Creesby. Some of the houses need painting again. Seems it's got to be now, or September.'

'Big decisions. You'll have to take up a hobby, or something. Mary Stubbs and Tilda can run the house easily – things aren't like they were in the old days when Mam worked there. For one thing, there was no electricity in Rowangarth, then. Everything had to be done the hard way, sort of.'

'When Drew isn't there, I feel like a spare part, Daisy.'

'So get yourself interested in something. Mind, when Mam was Lady Sutton it was worse for her. She went to France a sewing maid and came back lady of the house. The people she had once worked with didn't know whether to treat her as Alice Hawthorn, or call her milady.

'But if you really want something to occupy your time, you can give me a hand with the housework –

or take the baby out for a walk, get used to pram pushing.'

'Ha! I'm not pregnant, by the way.'

'Sorry, old love. Did you expect to be?'

'As a matter of fact, I did – at least I hoped. Got the curse this morning.'

'Like I said – sorry. Shouldn't have made inane remarks about pram pushing to someone who wants a baby as much as you do. But it takes time, Lyn, and I should know. When we finally decided to have Mary, I thought it wasn't ever going to happen.'

'You're right, of course. Mum rang last night. They've got the phone in, at last. Llangollen 611. Things must be getting back to normal.'

'*Normal?* The war over nearly four years, and you call getting a phone in normal? And it's the same with petrol rationing. Should have ended long ago. Keth says now the good weather is here, he's going to ride his bike to school – save his petrol coupons.'

'Whatever for?'

'Well we – er – might want to go somewhere on holiday, this year. You never know. And besides, biking is good for him.'

Daisy took a deep breath, reminding herself to be more careful, though why he wasn't supposed to tell anyone he had been in France in the war was plain stupid, when everybody knew, now, about secret agents and suchlike.

'So – are you going to take Mary out of her playpen and wipe her face and hands? She gets filthy on the floor. She's about ready for a sleep. And are you sure you wouldn't like to push her down the lane for a few minutes – get her to sleep for me? I'll have the kettle on for when you get back – okay?'

'Okay. And of course I want to take her out,' Lyn smiled.

'That's better,' Daisy said of the smile. 'And don't worry. The Suttons are a prolific lot. It only took the once to get Drew – did you know that?'

'*Once*, Purvis. Are you sure?'

'Sure. Mam told me.' Damn! She'd let it slip! Fool, Daisy! 'Aunt Julia knew, and Lady Helen,' she hedged.

'You mean that when she was Lady Sutton it only took – once?'

'No, I don't. And you're not to talk about this to anyone – even though Drew knows. Mam was pregnant when she married Giles Sutton.'

'Honestly?' Drew a love child, like herself?

'Yes, but it wasn't like you think, Lyn. It was when Mam and Aunt Julia were nursing in France. Mam had heard that Dada had been killed in action and there was no one for her to turn to. Aunt Julia was in Paris on leave with Andrew – her first husband – and Mam was out of her mind.

'Anyway Giles turned up. He was a stretcher-bearer – been carrying wounded to the hospital Mam worked at. A coincidence, really. They'd known each other a long time and Mam opened her heart to him. I don't know quite how it came about, but Giles comforted her – took her in his arms – and that was when it happened. Just the once between them.'

'So he married her when Drew was on the way – the decent thing to do?'

'No. Not exactly. And you've got to give me your

word you won't say anything about this,' Daisy glared, 'or Drew will think we've been scandalizing – and it wasn't a scandal at all.'

'My word, old love. Hand on heart.'

'We-e-ll, a few weeks later, Giles was brought to Mam's ward, very badly wounded. He was so ill he had to have special nursing – night and day. Aunt Julia wasn't allowed to – him being her brother and the ward sister thinking she might get upset. So Mam and another nurse did it – I think she was called Staff Nurse Ruth Love.

'Anyway, Aunt Julia knew that Nathan was in the area – he was an army padre, then – so they sent for him. Giles Sutton pulled through, but his injuries were so bad he was told he'd never have a child – never have a son, for Rowangarth.'

'Oh, the poor man.' Lyn's eyes filled with tears. 'But your mother was already pregnant . . . ?'

'Yes. What you might call a miracle. Nathan married Giles and Mam in the little chapel at the convent – where Mam and Aunt Julia were billeted.'

'And your mother and Giles came home to Rowangarth to face the music?'

'No. Nothing like that. They told the truth to Lady Helen and she treated it like an act of God, didn't blame either of them. She was overjoyed, in fact.'

'Sad that Giles should survive his war wounds, yet die of 'flu,' Lyn sniffed, dabbing her eyes. 'Yet everything came right, in the end.'

'If you mean that Dada turned up, after being a prisoner of war and not dead after all – and that Mam was willing to leave Drew at Rowangarth for

Julia and Lady Helen to bring up – yes. Dada was her real love.'

'I – I suppose she could have taken Drew with her when she went to your father, in Hampshire. After all, she was his mother . . .'

'Yes, but Drew belonged at Rowangarth. Mam said Aunt Julia looked after him from the night he was born. Mam was too ill. She'd caught 'flu from Giles. She couldn't have taken Drew away from his inheritance or from Aunt Julia, either. And don't forget it was only weeks earlier that Andrew was killed. Drew was all Julia had to love.'

She scooped up Mary Natasha, who had begun to demand attention.

'And it *was* an act of God, Drew getting conceived, because if he hadn't been born, the title would have passed to the Pendenys Suttons, and that would never have done, because Elliot would have got it, in time. A title was the one thing his mother couldn't buy for him. Imagine – Sir Elliot Sutton. Would have been unthinkable.'

'Daisy,' Lyn frowned. 'Will you tell me why you get *that* look on your face whenever Elliot Sutton's name is mentioned. You're just like your mother and Drew's mother. Like you've put too much vinegar on your chips.'

'Because I – I – well because he was Elliot. His mother spoiled him and he was very rude to most people. He joined the Army in the Great War, but his mother saw to it he never went anywhere near the trenches.

'Aunt Julia hates him, I think, because Andrew was

killed and Elliot wasn't, though I don't know why Mam goes all tight-lipped when people mention him. Tatty hasn't actually said so, but I don't think she was overfond of him either even though he was her father, though Mam says Tatty was too young to remember him because he died when she was nearly four. So maybe Tatty's found something out. I don't know,' she shrugged, tiring of the subject.

'Anyway, mum's the word, don't forget. Nobody talks about Mam being pregnant when she and Giles were married, like nobody mentions Elliot Sutton, if they can help it. Water under the bridge, sort of. Mind, everyone knows Drew has two mothers, but not many know the ins and outs of it.

'I knew Drew was my half-brother when I was quite young – when we were still living in Hampshire, but Mam didn't tell me the whole of it until much later. But let's make Mary Natasha comfy, shall we?'

'But why,' Lyn demanded, still puzzled, 'didn't you tell me before this? We were best friends – we always shared secrets.'

'Yes, but you weren't family then, were you? It's all right now, because you're entitled to be told. You and I are sisters-in-law, sort of. And don't be too long, Lyn? When she puts her thumb in her mouth, just lay her down and she'll be asleep in no time. See you, old love!'

And when Lyn was out of sight and sound of Foxgloves, she wrinkled her nose at the baby in the pram and said, 'My word, Mary Purvis, but it's a funny old world, isn't it?'

Only it wasn't a funny old world at all to Lyn

Sutton's way of thinking. It was a wonderful, unbelievable, completely amazing world in which to be and it wouldn't be long, she thought fondly, before the pram she pushed was her own!

And thanks be, she thought, all at once serious, that a Wren, too young to be away from her mother, should have arrived at Cabin 4A, WRNS Quarters, Hellas House, with an infected arm and a raging temperature.

And that she should have a half-brother called Drew . . .

'What's news?' demanded Julia Sutton of her husband when he folded the morning paper and laid it on the table beside him. 'Anything interesting in it?'

'Not really. Seems the prime minister is to have a royal commission set up on capital punishment.'

'About hanging?'

'About abolishing the death penalty.'

'Let murderers get away with it, you mean? But you are a priest, Nathan, and your Bible says an eye for an eye, doesn't it?'

'I'm a *retired* priest, and it isn't *my* Bible, and before you go any further, love, I didn't mean murder should go unpunished; rather that hanging is a brutal and frightening form of retribution. In the twentieth century, it's a bit mediaeval.'

'You're entitled to your own opinion. It's a free world, I reckon. But royal commissions never come to anything. Anything else worth talking about?'

'Yes. That we're negotiating with Russia about the Berlin airlift. About time it ended. We've been flying supplies to the West Berliners for nearly a year! Must have cost a pretty penny.'

'Ha! We're told to tighten our belts because the country is badly in debt, food is still rationed but we spend millions just calling Stalin's bluff,' Julia snorted. 'But I refuse to get upset about things I can do nothing about. It was such a beautiful morning when I awoke, that I didn't want to waste it. Got up and walked the garden and Brattocks Wood.'

'Yes. You banged the bedroom door at five forty-five . . .'

'Sorry, love. I'll try to be a bit more quiet, early on.'

'Julia, you have *always* banged doors! It's too late to ask you to close them like other people do. Oh, and by the way. Petrol is to go up again. Two and thruppence a gallon as from Monday.'

'Now isn't that just typical, and nobody can buy before the increase because it's the end of the month and nobody has any petrol coupons left. Do you remember the days, darling, when you could drive up to the pumps and say, "Fill her up." I used to be able to do that with my first little car for half-a-crown. But I absolutely refuse to whinge about the state the country's in; not when I've got grandchildren to look forward to.'

'Hm.' Nathan picked up the paper again and retreated behind it. Now the wedding was over, there were grandchildren to worry about. Darling Julia. He decided not to tell her that, in a very few lines, he had read that the National Health Service was causing concern; that instead of costing an estimated one-and-tuppence per person per week, it now seemed to be costing two shillings and sixpence per person per week. More than double. Oops! Someone at Whitehall had got his sums wrong!

The mantel clock chimed eleven. Nathan looked over the top of his paper. 'Any chance of a coffee, darling?'

Tom Dwerryhouse always contrived to be in the vicinity of Keeper's Cottage between ten-thirty and eleven because Alice – if she was in, these days – generally had the kettle on the boil at that time. And it *was* on, because she had seen her husband come in by the back gate and put the dogs in the kennel.

'You can smell a teapot from a hundred paces,' she smiled when he pulled out a chair at the kitchen table. 'Everything all right?'

'Aye. Growers coming on a treat. No poachers about, either.'

Tom would have known had someone been taking game birds or snaring rabbits. Gamekeepers could see footsteps in the grass that hadn't been there the night before; steps that usually led to a carefully placed snare. 'And that vixen up the Pike seems to be leaving us alone – getting her food somewhere else.'

Tom knew about the vixen, could have taken her out with a single shot if she hadn't had young to suckle, but as long as she left his pheasants alone, he was willing to live and let live.

Foxes, though, didn't take food enough. One that got into a hen run would savage the lot, snapping off heads, yet only take away one hen. Bloodlust. The killer instinct. But he would leave the vixen alone until her cubs could fend for themselves – or let the hunt take care of her, happen.

'Saw Lyn, pushing our Mary,' he offered, 'along Creesby Lane. Going to be a bit awkward, at times, remembering who she is. I still look on her as the lass Daisy used to bring home from the Wrens.'

'And that's who she still is, Tom. She's Daisy's friend and as far as I'm concerned, that's who she'll stay. Lyn Carmichael isn't going to put on airs and graces if I'm any judge of character.'

'But there'll be times I shall have to be careful. When there are folk from the estate about, and suchlike.'

'Happen you might, Tom – sometimes. But most people round here knew Lyn was Daisy's friend ever before Drew met her. And you can't have sugar in it,' she sniffed, pushing Tom's cup towards him. 'Went a bit mad – gave Tilda my hoarded sugar for the wedding breakfast. You'll have to use saccharin. I wonder,' she frowned, 'if Lyn will use the family christening gown, like Drew did, or if she'd like to have a new one. I'd love to make another, like Mary's.'

'Christening gown? The lass has only been wed three weeks!'

'I know. But christenings come in the natural order of things, after weddings. Best give it thought.'

'Alice love, what am I to do with you,' he said fondly, getting to his feet as she passed, gathering her to him.

'Do? You're to stop your nonsense for a start,

carrying on at eleven in the morning, and get from under my feet!'

Tom smiled and kissed the tip of her nose, because there was a smile in her voice as she ordered him out, and love in her eyes as she said it. And he thought that her nose, pert as it had been the day they met, was still very kissable.

'See you, missus,' he grinned, a very contented man, in spite of Alice's new-found concern. Christening gowns was it to be, now!

'Don't think,' said Drew with mock severity, 'that I can take afternoons off willy-nilly, because I can't. Don't get used to it!'

'I'm sure being a country squire is a very demanding occupation. So how did you spend this morning?'

'Visiting two tenant farmers to tell them their rent will be going up as from next quarter day.'

'Is that fair, darling?'

'It is, considering one of them is a richer man than I am – and as for the other, he was warned to mend his ways!'

'But is it right for you to have to do such things, Drew? Isn't that up to the agent, in York?'

'If he were a full-time agent, yes, but he's more of an accountant-cum-financial adviser, really. The estate can't run to a full-time bod. Couldn't afford a gamekeeper, either, if Tom didn't let out shoots – make the job pay.'

He held out a hand to her, because the climb was getting steeper and because he couldn't bear not to touch her. And this afternoon she looked more touchable than ever, with her windblown hair and lovely smile.

'So how must the farmer mend his ways, Drew?'

'By shifting his manure heap. It's too near the village and there have been complaints – especially when there's heavy rain. Holdenby is a pretty little place. Can't have muck running down the street, stinking everybody out.'

'You can be very bossy when the mood is on you, Drew Sutton!'

'Bossy? No. I just gave him a week to shift it. Am I walking too quickly for you?'

'No, but tell me why we're walking to the top of the Pike.'

'Because I suddenly realized you've never been to the top with me, and because it's our anniversary – by the date, at least. We've been married a month,' he looked down at his watch, 'any minute now.'

'You remembered, Drew!' She took his face in her hands and kissed him gently. 'Has it been a good month?'

'You know it has,' he smiled, and all at once he became the sailor she first met on a blustery Liverpool day, and not the owner of an estate who had to sort out rent rises and muck heaps. 'And we'd better get going again or I'll be very tempted to make love to you here and now!'

'Not here, darling. Daisy said she and Keth once made love in the bushes at the top – before they were married, would you believe!'

'Now there's a thought! See what we've been missing!' He took her in his arms, kissing her, then said, 'Race you to the top, Lyn Sutton!'

* * *

'I phoned, but Mary Stubbs said you were out,' Julia handed Lyn a glass of sherry. 'She never said where you'd gone, but then, she wouldn't.'

'No. Miss Clitherow trained her staff well,' Drew grinned. 'Actually, we were up the Pike.'

'Was it worth the effort, Lyn?' Julia raised her glass.

'Oooh, yes.' Lyn's cheeks pinked. 'You can see all Rowangarth land from up there. I never imagined there was so much of it. We saw Pendenys, too. They don't have a lot of fields, do they?'

'No. The Rowangarth Suttons began as farmers, way back. The Pendenys Suttons – I'm one of them – came many years later,' Nathan supplied. 'They had a grand house and a deer park around the house and gardens, but nothing else.'

'Only money,' Julia wrinkled her nose, 'of which my husband got a goodly share when Aunt Clementina and – and her heir died.'

'That would be Elliot, wouldn't it?'

'That's right, Lyn. My brother was killed when his car went out of control and crashed into a tree. A bit more family history for you.'

'But we hardly ever talk about Uncle Elliot. He was rather spoiled by his mother,' Drew said, offhandedly.

'No, we don't, Lyn,' Julia snapped, 'because it isn't right to speak ill of the dead. Anyway,' she drew in a steadying breath, 'I married his brother who was, and is, totally different, aren't you, darling?'

It was her way of saying sorry to Nathan for being so forthright; for being so capable of hating, even yet, the man who inflicted so much pain on Rowangarth.

'Modesty forbids,' Nathan acknowledged, 'and I must say this is a decent sherry, love. How did you come by it?'

'I called in at Creesby off-licence, just by chance, and didn't the nice man produce it from under the counter. Probably hoping to get a few more orders from us when things get back to normal and people can buy wines by the case, again.'

'We always seem to have got our supplies from London,' Nathan said, 'but I don't suppose it would do any harm to give the local man an order or two – when he gets stocked up again.'

'*When*,' Julia said briefly, still angry with herself for her slip of the tongue – and in front of Lyn, too.

'Talking about family history,' Lyn ventured, 'I'm learning quite a lot from Miss Clitherow. It's surprising how far back she can remember. She could describe exactly, the ball gown Lady Helen wore the night she met Sir John, and the posy she carried.

'I pop in every morning. I got the history of cherry scone days, yesterday, and Mrs Shaw, who left her book of secret recipes to Tilda, when she died.'

'There's nothing wrong with her memory,' Julia sighed. 'It's just her body that's getting older and slower. And I'm glad you have chats with her, Lyn. I'll try to pop in myself, tomorrow – see how she is.

'So do you want to see the house, my dear, now that I'm more or less straight? I felt quite sad, leaving Rowangarth, but now we are so comfortable here, especially in the cold months, that I'm beginning to wonder why we didn't up sticks long ago.'

'So you didn't leave Rowangarth because of me,' Lyn asked, 'when Drew and I got engaged, I mean?'

'Not at all. We'd planned to move into the Bothy when Nathan retired. It was a coincidence, that's all. And there's one thing I'm getting to love about Bothy House – it doesn't echo like Rowangarth does. And this far, smoke doesn't blow down the chimneys when the wind is in the southeast.'

'Is it official then? You're calling it Bothy House?'

'I suppose we might as well. Amelia named it when she was over, and it seems to have stuck. But what do you think of this?' With a flourish she opened a bedroom door. 'Once, it was terrible; disgraceful yellow and black wallpaper and the ceiling ready to fall in. Now, though, it has made a beautiful guest bedroom.'

'It has.' Lyn took in the matching bedspreads and curtains, the off-white walls, the armchair and small table beside the window. 'It's so uncluttered – shows off the lovely old furniture. Rowangarth seems to have furniture wherever you turn. A bit crowded . . .' She stopped, her cheeks flushing. 'I – I don't mean to criticize, but –'

'Lyn, dear girl, it's your home now. If there's anything you don't like throw it out – well, we usually put things in the attics. But feel free. And if you want new chair covers and curtains just order them, if the shops have material, that is. Drew isn't as hard up as he sometimes makes out!

'And whilst we're alone, do you mind if I ask you something – about Kitty. You know Jack Catchpole is taking an interest in the garden here, I suppose?'

'I did. I noticed they've cleared all the paths. It looks tidier already. And I don't mind if you talk about Kitty, Mrs Sutton.'

'Now, before we go any further, young lady! You've been married to my son over a month, and I really don't want you to call me Mrs Sutton.'

'I – I was waiting . . .' Lyn hesitated, eyes down.

'Waiting to be asked, you mean? All right – so is it to be Mother, like Drew calls me, or would you prefer Julia?'

'Oh, I couldn't call you Julia!'

'Then what?'

'W-e-ell, a girl I knew in the Wrens called her mother-in-law Mil, but that, or even Milly, doesn't suit you. Nor does Mummy, so would you mind if we tried Mother, like Drew?'

'Anything at all but Mrs Sutton. It sounds so formal – as if we don't get on, and we do. And to get back to Jack Catchpole,' Julia went on with her usual directness, 'and Kitty. He was talking about her, you see, and wondering if it would be all right for him to give her her orchids, next month. And I said I thought it would be, but it rested entirely with you, Lyn.'

'Why with me? And why should things change? Kitty would want her orchids. She would miss them if they weren't there.'

'That's very understanding of you, and generous, too.'

'No. I had a talk with Mrs Amelia, you see. We sat on the seat in the Linden Walk, and things seemed to straighten themselves out. Or at least, I saw things differently. I haven't told anyone what we talked about

– not even Drew – but I was grateful for what she said. She's a very understanding lady. I feel sad, now, that she won't be coming to England any more.'

'I wouldn't bet on it, Lyn. She loves a lot of things about this country, even though she's thoroughly American. It's Uncle Albert who flatly refuses to visit any more. He never liked living at Pendenys Place and has taken to life in America like a duck to water. He was grumbling, even before war started, about their twice-yearly migrations here.

'But Bas and Gracie will still visit, and there's nothing to stop any of us from going to Kentucky to stay. Amelia and Gracie would love it. As a matter of fact, now that overseas travel is on the cards again, I think we should all consider it seriously.

'And maybe you should have a word with Jack about the flowers for Kitty. It would be better, coming from you. And can I say, whilst we seem to be in a confiding mood, that I'm so relieved you don't seem in awe of Kitty's memory any more, because you were.'

'I know I was. She seemed so perfect in every way and everyone talked about her so much I began to get the jitters. I wondered if I'd measure up to her. I was so nervous that first night in York, but Drew understood.'

'And did you measure up?' Julia smiled.

'Oh, yes. Stupid of me to worry. Things are great for Drew and me.'

'Only *great*, Lyn?' Julia's eyes sparked mischief.

'No, Mother. Things are absolutely marvellous! Sometimes I go around wondering when I'm going to wake up.'

At which, Julia held wide her arms, then wrapped Lyn in them and whispered, 'Oh, let's have a hug and a kiss, Lyn, because I'm really, really happy about you and Drew. Only one thing could possibly make me happier, and that's for you to give me a grandchild.'

And Lyn's cheeks pinked again as she remembered the Pike, and she said softly, 'I don't think you'll be disappointed. Drew and I want children very much – two, or maybe three.'

That was when Nathan called up the stairs to ask them what they were doing, and wasn't it time for supper?

And Julia called back that Polly had left cold meat and salad in the pantry, and would it be too much to expect them to carry it to the table?

'Men!' she snorted.

'Mm,' Lyn laughed. 'Bless 'em all!'

It was late in May when it happened, and though anyone with an iota of sense must have expected it, it came as a bitter shock.

It began as an ordinary twenty-sixth day of May. Lyn had looked at her diary, checking the date circled in red, then decided to rummage in the attics for the chairs Daisy had been promised; in need of repair, true, but exactly what she would have bought herself, Daisy said, had there been any like them in the furniture shops. If there had been *any* chairs at all, come to think of it.

It was when Lyn had found one and was hoping the other three were close by, that there was a clattering on the wooden stairs and a white-faced Mary Stubbs stood wide-eyed at the doorway.

'Milady, come quick! Tilda's with her now, but I think we're going to have to send for Doctor Pryce!'

'Miss Clitherow?' Lyn sucked in her breath. 'Not well . . . ?'

She hurried to where Tilda knelt beside the old woman, rubbing her hands.

'Lady Lyndis.' She rose slowly to her feet. 'I – I think she's . . .' Tilda found it impossible to say the word.

'Miss Clitherow?' Lyn took her hand, feeling for a pulse, but finding one was useless because her heart was beating far too quickly and every small pulse in her own body adding to the clamour of fear inside. 'Can you try, Tilda?'

'I have, Miss. There was – nothing.'

Agnes Clitherow looked peaceful; in one of her little dozes, Mary had thought when she laid a tea tray at her side and tried, gently, to waken her.

'I think she's gone. Hadn't you best ring the surgery, milady?'

'Yes. Of course. And I think they should be told at Bothy House.'

Her mouth had gone dry and her tongue made little clicking sounds as she spoke.

'I'll go over there,' Tilda seemed eager to be out of the room, 'whilst you ring Doctor Pryce.'

Lyn's hand shook as she lifted the receiver; was grateful to hear a familiar voice.

'I'm ever so sorry, Lady Sutton. Surgery's engaged.' It had not taken long for Winnie Hallam to familiarize herself with Lyn's voice. 'I'll ring you the minute they're free.'

'Thank you. I'd be grateful . . .'

She stood for a moment, wishing Drew had not gone to the timberyard the other side of Creesby, deciding against trying to get in touch with him until she had phoned Ewart Pryce.

She returned to the little room, looking down at the relaxed face, the thin, unmoving, blue-veined hands. 'Miss Clitherow?' she whispered, then took the crocheted shawl that had slipped to the floor, tucking it round her protectively.

She heard the back door bang, and hurrying footsteps. Julia had come.

'Is she . . . ?' Julia Sutton, who had seen many deaths, felt gently for a pulse beat. 'I think she's slipped away, Lyn.' Slipped softly away and in her sleep, most likely. Gone quickly, Julia thought sadly, like dearest Mother, without a goodbye. 'Have you told Ewart?'

'The surgery was engaged. The exchange is calling back.' To give strength to her words, the phone began to ring, and she looked at Julia questioningly.

'You answer it, Lyn . . .'

'Yes. Of course.' She was lady of the house, now. Julia was making it plain. She hurried to still the persistent ringing.

'Thank you, Mrs Hallam,' she said before Winnie could tell her the doctor was on the line, now.

'Doctor Pryce? It's Lyndis Sutton. Can you come to Rowangarth? I think Miss Clitherow has – has died . . .'

* * *

The ambulance came quickly from Creesby, yet it seemed a very long time before Lyn said, 'Do you think we should go to the kitchen? They'll be upset – Mary Stubbs, especially. She got the worst of it.'

'Fine by me. Nathan's in York, anyway.' Julia would rather be in Rowangarth's warm, familiar kitchen. 'Tilda will have the kettle on.'

'Will there have to be a postmortem?' Lyn asked diffidently. 'Is that why the ambulance came?'

'No. It will be a formality, at the hospital. Ewart said he knew about her heart condition. She had pills for it. He'll call later, with the – the certificate. This is your first experience of death, isn't it, Lyn?'

'Apart from – well – Kenya, yes it is. I went through the war and the Blitz. Death happened all the time, I suppose, yet never to anyone close, like now. I haven't had your – well, *experience* . . .'

'Then let's hope you never do, nor anyone else, ever. Come on. Let's see how they're managing downstairs.'

Mary Stubbs and Tilda Willis sat at the kitchen table on which stood the teapot covered with a cosy, and four cups and saucers.

'You'll have a cup, Miss Julia – milady?'

'Please.' Lyn pulled out a chair. 'Are you both all right?'

'Aye. Just about.' Tilda poured two more cups of tea. 'A shock, for all that. How old was she, Miss Julia?'

'Older than Mother. Her papers and personal things are in the safe in one of the cellars. She gave Nathan an envelope for safekeeping a long time ago. He'll know all about it,' she said, relieved. 'Has anyone got a cigarette? Left mine at home . . .'

'Sorry.' Mary hesitated. 'Us never smoked, down here. Mrs Shaw didn't allow it and us never got into the habit.'

'And nor should I have done, but they were such a comfort in the war – in *my* war.' Julia pulled down the corners of her mouth. 'Anyway, I'm supposed to be giving it up, but what's a cigarette after what's happened? Ewart Pryce knew she had angina, he said, but she absolutely forbade him to tell a soul. Miss Clitherow could be like that. Very intimidating.'

'You're right, Miss Julia. She could put the fear of death into you, but she was a good one to have on your side when things were going wrong. And a fairer woman never walked this earth.'

'Aye. She promoted me from scullery maid to kitchen maid to cook,' Tilda sighed. 'With cook's full agreement, mind. She always did things right and proper; the way things should be done in a gentleman's household. And would it be all right, milady,' she addressed Lyn directly, 'if we all had another cup with a teaspoon of brandy in it, for the shock? Mrs Shaw would have allowed it, and –'

'A snifter?' Lyn smiled. 'Of course, Tilda. But there's a drop of decent stuff in the dining room. I'll pop up and get it. And if you both don't mind, I'd rather you dropped the *milady*. It's so formal – makes me feel a bit out of it, kind of . . .'

'Then what *are* we to call you?'

'Lady Lyndis?' Julia offered.

'No, Mother. But I think Lady Lyn would do for

a start – and maybe Lyn, sometimes, when no one is around? Now – I'll just nip up for the bottle. Won't be a tick.'

'Snifter, eh? She's learning,' Mary Stubbs said softly.

'Learning,' Tilda nodded. 'Oh, I know she suits Sir Andrew down to the ground, but the lass is going to do well for Rowangarth, an' all.'

And Julia said she was sure of it, because hadn't Miss Clitherow taken to Lyn right from the start, and wasn't dear Agnes Clitherow, God rest her, a perfect judge of the way things should be – in a gentleman's household?

'Sad, isn't it?' Alice said to Tom as they ate dinner at midday. 'I know she's been in retirement for a long time, but she was always there, to remind us of Lady Helen, and the old days.' ·

'Aye, but if what we're led to believe is true, they'll be together again now. I mind that time in Brattocks. The old lass came up trumps, that day.'

'You mean when Elliot Sutton –' Alice's cheeks flamed, her mouth tightened. Then she lifted her chin and whispered, 'I was a lass of seventeen, then. It was a long time ago and anyway, it's not right we should mention Miss Clitherow and him in the same breath, nor rake up the past that's best forgotten. No harm was done, that day. I had Morgan with me, never forget, so eat up your dinner. There's gooseberry pie, for pudding.'

'And how did you come by lard for piecrust?' Tom teased, knowing he should not have talked about Elliot Sutton, trying to make amends.

'Ask no questions, but if you come across a nice young pheasant in the not too distant future I'll have it, if you don't mind, for the grocer's wife. Worth it, wouldn't you say, for half a pound of lard and a bag of sugar?'

'You'll never go to heaven, Alice Dwerryhouse.'

'And you'll never go hungry, either! Any road, it's different now. Sailors aren't having to risk life and limb to bring food to us. Was wrong, in the war. They'd have sent you to prison for it. Anyway, if you don't agree with a bit of black market lard, you'd best not eat the pie!'

'That's more like my lass,' Tom smiled, glad to be rid of all talk of Elliot Sutton. 'And be sure of it, Agnes Clitherow'll never be forgotten while you and me draw breath.'

And Alice agreed, and took the pie from the oven, all brown and sugary on top, with thick syrupy juice oozing from the hole in the crust.

'Think on,' she said, 'about that pheasant . . .'

'Leave it all to me. I'll see to things,' Nathan said, when supper had been cleared away at Bothy House. Best he should. Parsons were more used to the paraphernalia of death than most.

'But it was so sudden,' Julia whispered. 'No time for a goodbye, or a blessing. It was the same when Mother died.'

'Sweetheart – I'll be assisting at the service. Arthur Reid won't mind. It'll be his first funeral since he was ordained. He'll be glad to have me there. Be sure that Miss Clitherow will be well blessed, Julia. And if I know this parish, there'll be a lot of goodbyes.'

'You're right. You usually are,' she sighed. 'By the way, didn't she once give you something to take care of? You put it in the safe, if I remember rightly.'

'An envelope. It's still there. I suppose we'd better read it, fairly soon. There might be some last wishes – about her funeral, I mean.'

'Fine by me. Mind if I smoke, Nathan?'

'I thought you were giving it up, darling. How many is that, today?'

'My fifth, but can you blame me? This has been one pig of a day. I *am* trying, truly I am.'

'I know you are. I think a cigarette would be in order, and maybe a snifter? A small one. Might help us both a bit. I'll have a pipe, to keep you company.'

'You're a very understanding old vicar,' Julia said sniffily, trying to keep her hand steady as she poured two brandies. 'And I'll tell you something else! Now that we've finally handed over the parish to Arthur and Hilary, you and I are going to take a break. We both deserve it.'

'Good idea,' he nodded, as Julia kicked off her shoes and sat on the floor at his feet, her back against the chair arm. 'Anywhere in mind?'

'Yes. London, to Aunt Sutton's. Lyn loved it; right in the heart of London yet so cut off, down an alley. And she's right. Let's do a couple of shows and go somewhere splendid for supper, afterwards?'

'Then I'll leave you to make the arrangements, darling, and ring up about theatre tickets. Go down by train, shall we?'

'Unless you've come by some petrol coupons.'

And Nathan laughed and said that vicars wouldn't dream of doing anything as illegal as dealing in black market petrol coupons, though if he were tempted by one or two, he just might give in, he sighed. Then raising his glass he said softly, 'To Miss Clitherow,' and Julia reached up to clink it with her own.

'To Miss Clitherow, straight-backed spinster of this parish, who'll be much missed at Rowangarth. Thank you, dear lady, for all the years; for everything . . .'

Mary Stubbs said, 'It'll all be in strictest black. Her was a stickler for black, at funerals. Remember when Sir John died, Tilda? All the mourning?'

'I do. I'd not long come here. Two dinner parties, that's all I saw, then now't but black. For three years would you believe, and Lady Helen not receiving nor visiting, either. Not like that, now.'

'No. But she'll expect black, so best I get mine out and give it an airing, get rid of the mothball smell.'

Funerals, she thought, always smelled of mothballs from black suits and coats put away for the next sad occasion.

'Well, it's June, so I shall wear my navy blue walking-out dress, and my leghorn straw – I'll tack a black ribbon round it, mind.'

'Jack Catchpole is doing a wreath from all Rowangarth staff and one for the Reverend and Miss Julia, and for Drew and Lady Lyn. There'll be plenty of flowers for him to go at. He enjoys doing florals. Your Sidney'll be able to pick up a lot from him, Tilda.'

'Aye. And will you tell me, Mary Stubbs, who I'm to consult about refreshments for the mourners, because refreshments will be all it'll run to. Miss Julia, will it be, or her ladyship?'

'I would say,' came the considered reply, 'that you have a problem there, Tilda. By rights, it should be Drew's wife, yet her hardly knew Miss Clitherow. Why not have a word with Miss Julia?'

Julia Sutton, who could be a scatterbrain at times and still went about banging doors for all her age, could be relied upon to do the right thing. Miss Julia was gentry, and would know exactly what was what.

Yet it was Lyn who was to resolve the problem, by knocking on the kitchen door at that very moment, diffidently poking her head around it.

'Can I come in, Tilda?'

'You're welcome, milady.'

'Yes, me and cook were just talking about – well, who would be in charge, as it were, of – *things*,' Mary said.

'My thoughts exactly. Why I came, actually.' Lyn pulled out a chair. 'Mind if I sit down?'

You always asked, Drew's mother had told her. The kitchen is Tilda's domain and the garden is officially Sidney Willis's, though Jack Catchpole still merited recognition. Lady Helen had always asked both the Catchpoles if it would be convenient for her to visit the orchid house, and had never trespassed in Mrs Shaw's kitchen without prior warning. Funny old ways, Lyn thought.

Tilda drew out the chair opposite, nodding her

permission. Mary Stubbs filled the kettle and set it to boil.

'You mean we are to consult you about the arrangements?'

'No, Tilda. I have been thinking that maybe Mrs Sut – er – Miss Julia, would know much better than me how Rowangarth does things. I'm still very much at the learning stage. Your advice and Mary's would be appreciated.'

'Then I think,' said Mary Stubbs, taking three china saucers and cups from the dresser, 'that the Reverend and Miss Julia would be only too pleased to do this one last thing for Miss Clitherow. Miss Clitherow was here at Rowangarth long before Miss Julia was born and I reckon it would be her the old lass would want.'

'Thanks, Mary – and Tilda – you've taken quite a load off my mind. I'll call at Bothy House in the morning. And by the way, Drew agrees with me that his mother would be the best person to see to – er – *things*. Thanks a lot for your advice.'

'You're more than welcome, Lady Lyn,' Tilda beamed.

'Any time,' Mary nodded. 'You'll stay for a cup of tea?'

'There's cherry scones, cooling on the tray,' Tilda coaxed.

'You've twisted my arm,' Lyn laughed, thinking with absolute certainty that Lady Helen would never have taken tea and scones at the kitchen table. But this was 1949 and two wars had changed things, even at Rowangarth. 'Is this a cherry scone day, by the way?'

'Ar. Mrs Shaw alus baked them for glad days to celebrate, and for sad days, to cheer folk up.' Tilda took three scones, halving them, laying them on a china plate. 'Mind, there isn't the butter for them that there used to be in the old days, but I try to keep up the custom.'

And Lyn said the last time she had eaten them was on her return from honeymoon, spread with under-the-counter illegal cream from Home Farm, and that even though this was a sad day, and butter and cream out of the question, one would be very welcome, because hadn't she missed years and years of cherry scones? And didn't she have to make up for lost time?

'She's a grand lass,' Tilda observed when Lyn had left. 'I can see her making a good job of being mistress of Rowangarth – given time.'

'And now that Miss Clitherow has passed on, you and me will alus be here to give her advice,' Mary nodded.

Lyndis Sutton had passed her first test in diplomacy. With flying colours, did she but know it!

'Oh, look, darling!' Julia held up a faded sepia photograph. 'There's Father and Mother and all the staff. See – Miss Clitherow looking stern and Giles, in his pram. And Robert in his first pair of breeches, I shouldn't wonder.'

A photograph from the past, before she was born, even, Julia thought, taken from the large envelope with A Clitherow written small in the top, left-hand corner and FOR THE KIND ATTENTION OF THE REV. NATHAN SUTTON written more boldly.

'Your father looks very pleased with himself. And isn't Aunt Helen beautiful? Mother of two sons, yet she looks like a slip of a girl.'

'She *was* a slip of a girl. I didn't arrive until five years after Giles. Wasn't even a twinkle in Pa's eye, then. I didn't know that photograph existed. Do you think it would be all right if I were to take it, Nathan?'

'More than all right. She would want you to have it. A reminder, I suppose, of the way things were. All the staff there. Two gardeners and four garden lads; two keepers and even a footman.'

'Mm. Mother decided against the footman, after Pa died. And now there's only Mary Stubbs and Tilda Willis and her Sidney. And Mary's William.' She pointed a finger. 'That'll be him. Just a stable lad, then.'

'Hasn't time gone quickly?'

'Too quickly, Nathan. Not much more time for us to gather rosebuds. But are you going to read her letter?'

Another, smaller envelope, sealed with red wax. *WILL & Last Wishes of Agnes Clitherow* written in ink already beginning to fade.

Nathan opened it carefully, then whistled softly as he drew out a fold of white, five-pound notes.

'A hundred pounds, Julia. Must be her entire life savings.'

Nathan laid the single sheet of notepaper on his desk, smoothing it with the flat of his hand, then adjusting his spectacles, and with Julia looking over his shoulder, he began to read.

Dear Reverend Sutton,

The enclosed money is to be used to pay the undertaker for my funeral, for I want no act of charity at my burying.

My silver teapot is to be given to Mary Stubbs (nee Strong) and my rosebud china half tea service to Matilda Willis (nee Tewk) in the hope they may both remember me kindly when using them.

To Rowangarth, and all who live there, I give my unending love, for my days in service here have been happy indeed, and no woman could ask for more.

For myself, I have only one wish. That I be laid in the churchyard at All Souls, and that my grave will lie as near to that of dear Lady Helen as may be seemly and without presuming.

When this letter sees the light of day, I will have left you all, but be sure I will always be there, in spirit and lovingly, to see that Rowangarth comes to no harm.

Yours very truly,
Agnes Clitherow (Miss)

For a moment, neither spoke, then Nathan said, 'Did you read it?'

'Yes.' Julia let go a sigh. 'Oh, dear. I feel quite full up. No charity at her funeral, indeed! Well, I'm sorry, but Rowangarth is going to see to the funeral, don't you agree, darling?'

'Yes. I think we should. And what of the money?'

'That, Nathan, will pay for a headstone. And as

for her being buried near Mother – without presuming, she says – 'well, it goes without saying, doesn't it.'

'There isn't a lot of space left. I can't think of anywhere near.'

'Well I *can*. Of course the churchyard is almost full, and when it is, Drew will give the church some more land, so there's no problem there. But had you thought, Nathan, that there is quite a bit of space, and very, very near to Mother.'

'You mean the Pendenys Place plots?'

'Yes, I do! Aunt Clementina bought up a lot of grave space because she thought there was going to be a lot more Pendenys Suttons to follow. And there won't be. You, husband, are going with me on the Rowangarth side of the path when the time comes, and never forget it!'

'So there'll only ever be Father, Elliot and Mother there . . . ?'

'And little Nicholas.'

Anna's stillborn son, baptized by Nathan and laid with love in the little churchyard. Only the inscription to stand witness to a mother's grief and to bid goodbye to Clementina Sutton's hopes of a Pendenys dynasty.

'We're agreed, then? I'll have a word – I'll get Arthur to have a word – with the grave digger. And look.' He took out a small piece of paper, no more than five inches by four inches. 'Here's her birth certificate.'

Flimsy paper, red on white. Certificate of Registry of Birth, the fee not to exceed three pence.

'One of the early ones. Just giving her name and date of birth – no details of parents or their occupations. Born in 1856.'

'Four years older than mother, then. Ninety-three, that makes her. I don't know of any kin. She had two cousins in Scotland. Elizabeth who died early on in the war and Margaret, who died at the end of it. There's only us, at Rowangarth. We're her next of kin, Nathan.'

'Then we'll do the honours, and glad to. I know one of her favourite hymns was "Onward Christian Soldiers".'

'Yes, and "Abide with Me", so that's the hymns taken care of. Oh dear, Nathan, it all seems to be slipping away from us – the way things were, our friends, our world . . .'

'Chin up, old love. The way things were? Some of it I'm glad *has* slipped away – two wars, for a start.'

'Yes. We must be like Mother and count our blessings, because there is so much to look forward to. Tatty expecting, and fingers crossed for Drew and Lyn. And it *is* rather nice, you and me living in the Bothy. You from the grand Pendenys Place, Nathan, and me a Rowangarth Sutton. Yet now we live where stable lads and garden apprentices lived, looked after by Jin Dobb.'

'And the land girls, looked after by Polly, don't forget, and one of them a Sutton, now. I wonder when next Bas and Gracie will be over.'

'I don't think they'll make the crossing this next Christmas, but I'm sure they'll be here like a shot, for the next big event. They won't need much of an excuse. Probably when Tatty's baby is christened. It's due late October. Isn't it wonderful? I'll be a great-aunt!'

'There you are, Julia. You're looking forward already. Forget what's past – well, *some* of it. And since you mention it, I like living in Bothy House. Roomy enough to be comfortable, yet small enough to be cosy in winter – just you and me.' He bent to kiss the top of her head. 'Growing old does have its perks.'

On the first day of June, they said goodbye to Agnes Clitherow. There was very great respect. Almost the entire population of Holdenby were there in funereal black, or soberly attired.

Her coffin was carried by Tom Dwerryhouse, Will Stubbs, Sidney Willis and Jack Catchpole, and Rowangarth's floral tributes were of the finest, since flowers were carelessly abundant, in June.

Drew and Lyn followed the coffin into church and behind them Julia and Alice then Daisy and Keth, Tatty and Bill, and Tilda and Mary Stubbs.

'Pity she isn't here to see the turnout,' Alice whispered. 'Right pleased, she'd have been.'

'Don't worry. She'll know all about it,' Julia smiled softly. Agnes Clitherow had never missed a trick, in life, and it was hardly likely she would start now – with the benefit of a bird's-eye view, so to speak.

Holdenby's new parish priest Arthur Reid and Nathan Sutton, its almost-retired one, conducted the service and the committal together. No one who stood at the graveside thought it strange that Agnes Clitherow should be laid at Clementina Sutton's feet, or if they did, no one made comment.

This was such a beautiful day on which to go, Drew thought – if go you must. Flowers in hedgerows and gardens and in Brattocks Wood; a blue sky with scarcely a cloud and a gently warm sun, to give comfort.

There now, Miss Clitherow, gently Julia tumbled a handful of earth on the coffin below, *is that near enough to Mother for you?* They had only to reach out hands across the church path and they could touch, had they a mind to. *Goodbye, dear friend. Sleep well . . .*

Goodbye, dear Miss Clitherow. Alice took off a glove, then scooped earth into her hand. *Thank you for all you have done for me, but thank you most of all for giving me work at Rowangarth, all those years ago. Alice Hawthorn has more cause than most to be grateful to you. You'll never be forgotten whilst Tom and me draw breath . . .*

One by one Holdenby said a silent goodbye; some tearfully, some with a small smile for things remembered. Jack Catchpole took the white rose he wore in his buttonhole, and dropped it gently. *From me and Lily, so you'll take a bit of Rowangarth away with you.*

Lyn smiled her thanks. Agnes Clitherow had understood her apprehension; shared memories with her and sometimes a chuckle. *Goodbye. I wish I had known you longer . . .* She stepped aside to find she was standing beside the grave with the white marble headstone.

You knew her too, Kitty; all your life you knew her. Shall I say goodbye from you, too, or will you be here, silently, when everyone else has gone, and will you say it for yourself?

Because she still waited here, at Rowangarth. This was not the time for her to go. Kitty would know, Amelia had said, when the moment came for her to leave Drew.

It will soon be time for Catchpole to make your bouquet, bring your orchids. I have asked him to do it. I want you always to have your flowers . . .

The June sun touched Kitty Sutton's name and made it shine golden; shine a smile. And Lyn smiled back.

'Lyn? We're going, now.'

Julia, ready to leave, touching her arm, Drew reaching for her hand, leading her back to the reality that was Rowangarth.

'It all went very well.' Julia waved a hand at Nathan, who still stood there, saying his own farewell.

I hope you don't mind, Miss Clitherow, but this is the nearest we could think of . . . She wouldn't mind at all. Agnes Clitherow had never let anything upset her in life, coped calmly with good and not-so-good times. Where she rested in death, even amongst the Pendenys Suttons, would matter little if it was beside her beloved Lady Helen.

'All right, Reverend . . . ?' The grave digger waited to finish his task, and Nathan nodded, holding up his hand, tracing a final blessing.

'All right,' he said with a small smile, then turned and hurried after Julia, back to where Mary Stubbs and Tilda would be waiting with tea and biscuits; maybe even cherry scones. To Rowangarth, on a soft June afternoon.

Heaven on earth.

NINETEEN

''Lo, darling. Miss me?' Keth laid a pile of exercise books on the table, then held out his arms for his child.

'Hadn't time. Your daughter has been a right little madam, today. I took her to Keeper's, in the end. Mam gave her a cuddle, and she was as right as rain. That child knows how to play to the gallery. Dada took her to see the new pups. He says we're to have one.

'"A child should have an animal," he said. "That bairn is old enough for one, now. Why don't you have a look at them, Daisy? A bitch, you should have. Very protective of children, Labrador bitches are." Would you like her to have one, Keth – when they're weaned, I mean?'

'I don't see why not, love. You and me both grew up with gun dogs. Seemed part of the furniture and fittings, as I remember. And your dad is right. Bitches are gentler.'

'So I'll tell him yes?'

'Fine by me, only don't forget that you'll get the brunt of the puppy training.'

'Dada will help. Agreed, then?'

'Reckon so.'

'So will I tell Dada – ask him to register her with the Kennel Club as Bethan of Winchester – the *second*, I mean. Or would it upset your mum too much?'

Dickon Purvis had died, trying to save a Labrador bitch called Beth – Bethan of Winchester – from a swollen river.

'No. Think she'd be pleased to think Dad wasn't forgotten. She seems fine, now, when Dad's name is mentioned. Going to Hampshire to see his grave helped – and to see Willow End and Keeper's Cottage with people living there.'

'Good. That's one problem solved, then. When are we going to talk about the other one?'

'About Clissy, you mean? I've got to admit it would be a bit of a bind getting there without the car. I've been looking at routes; I'm pretty *au fait* with getting down south – either to Plymouth or Southampton. Not sure about car ferries, though, to St Malo.'

'Clissy is near there . . . ?'

'No. Farther south. I never actually went into Clissy, though they had a fish pier. Madame Piccard sometimes managed to get fish there. Civilians were allowed to buy it on Fridays. I only left the garden once – the night the Lysander came for me. Had to act the part of a soldier, invalided out of the French Army because shell blast had deafened him. It was good cover when someone spoke too quickly. I could ask him – or her – to repeat it.'

'So you met other people?' Daisy frowned.

'Sometimes. But let's not get too involved with

how it was. Let's talk about ways and means instead.'

'Well the way is up to you; the means I got hold of. Would ten petrol coupons suit you?'

'*Ten!* Where on earth did you get them? You didn't go to the garage in Creesby?'

'No, Keth. I said I wouldn't, didn't I? Bill got them for me. He got some when he was in London. All he did was phone the bloke, and send five pounds.'

'You were taking one hell of a risk!' Keth gasped, still amazed.

'No, but Bill was. Anyway, the coupons arrived in an envelope without even a note.' She reached for the letter rack on the mantelpiece. 'Here they are. And they aren't forgeries. I've checked them, so that's you on your way.'

'But what did you tell Bill?' *Ten* coupons. It took some believing.

'I said you were going down south in the summer holidays on some teacher conference thing and would like to drive down – especially since you've got a new car. Bill's still on cloud nine about the baby. He was glad to do it.'

'Good old Bill. And that's how it's going to be then – me, going down south?'

'Well, down south is very near to France, and it'll save a lot of explanations as to why teachers hold conferences in France – which, things being what they are, I am sure they don't!'

'Crafty lady your mother is.' Keth retrieved the fountain pen Mary Natasha had pulled from his top pocket and put in her mouth. 'And little girls don't eat pens!'

Daisy looked at him fondly. He loved his child so much. It was easy to understand his feelings of guilt about the girl in Clissy; why he felt bound to go there.

'How long have you had the coupons, Daisy?'

'Bill said they came yesterday, but he didn't want to give them to me at the funeral. He brought them over, this morning. He was going to do some sketching at Rowangarth, he said.'

'I'll buy him a pint, next time I see him.' Keth looked at his watch. 'Do you want me to bath Mary, or are we having supper first?'

'Let's get her to bed. She seems tired. Think it's another tooth. We can talk about France in peace, then. And sorry – shouldn't have said that, but you know what I mean . . .'

'Yes. I do. It isn't ever very far from my mind.'

That he and Daisy were married and had a child; a beautiful child who, God willing, would live out more than sixteen years.

'C'mon, darling. Let's get Mary Purvis bathed and fed. And Keth – I do understand. I want you to go to Clissy. And if you find where she is – is buried, will you thank her for me, and tell her about Mary Natasha?'

'I will,' he smiled. 'Promise. And I love you . . .'

'I love you, too, but let's not get sloppy until this terrible child is in her cot. After that, you can have the whole of my attention – and that's a promise, too!'

'Drew. Is there time for a walk before supper – I want to talk to you.'

'Loads of time, Lyn. Brattocks Wood?'

'No. Let's walk right round the house then down the Linden Walk.'

'Fine by me. Why the Linden Walk?'

'Because I want to have a sniff – make sure I don't miss the blossom, and because it's the second of June.'

'Give it a couple of weeks, yet, for the linden blossom. But what is so special about the second of June?'

But she smiled, and wouldn't say another word on the matter until they were sitting on the marble seat, fingers entwined.

'So, Lyn – tell?'

'We-e-ll, the second of June makes me one week late.' She said it matter-of-factly, not looking at him.

'*Whaaat!* The curse, you mean? But you said you're never late!'

'And I never have been – till now. At first I thought it was the shock of Miss Clitherow, but I'm as sure as I can be that it wasn't . . .'

'Oh my lor',' he looked at her, eyes wide with apprehension. 'Are – are you all right?'

'Of course I'm all right. I'm just a week late, that's all. Drew – you're pleased about it, aren't you? If I *am*, I mean.'

'Pleased? Yes, of course. Just a bit surprised, that's all. It didn't take long, did it?'

'Drew Sutton!' Her eyes were bright with mischief, her smile wide. 'You *do* know how babies are made?'

'Of course I do.'

'Then why the surprise? We *have* been doing it rather a lot.'

'Yes. Come to think of it, we have.' He laughed out loud, doubts all at once gone. 'Sweetheart, *could* it be? Honestly?'

'I hope so, but not a word to a soul – all right? Not till we're sure.'

'And when will that be?'

'I'll see Ewart Pryce when I've missed twice. Till then, not a word to anyone.'

'Not even to Mother, and Daiz?'

'No. Not even to Llangollen. Three more weeks to wait, then we'll go to the top of the Pike, and shout it out for all Holdenby to hear. And Drew,' she whispered, pink-cheeked. 'It might just be that it happened there. Remember the top of the Pike?'

'Yes, I do. But what makes you think –'

'Why, the altitude, of course,' she said seriously. 'A funny thing, altitude . . .'

'You're joking, of course.'

He looked at her, seeing her all at once differently. She had always been beautiful, but now she seemed even more so. He reached out for her, wrapping his arms around her, resting his cheek on her head.

'I love you, Lyn Sutton,' he said softly. 'But you know that, don't you?'

'I know it. But a girl likes to be reminded, from time to time.'

'Then on the second of June, at the Linden Walk, I love you, *cariad*.'

'Well, if that doesn't take the plate of biscuits!'

Alice glared at the newspaper as if it were responsible for the announcement that the sugar ration was to be cut to eight ounces and that sweets and confectionery were to be rationed again.

Hard on children especially. They'd only just got used to being able to buy as many sweeties and chocolate bars as they liked – more than was good for them, Alice had to admit – and now that lot in Westminster had spoiled it. Cutting the sugar ration was bad enough; depriving children of the pleasure of sweeties was mean and sneaky.

She heard the clang of the dog house gate and looked through the window to see Tom walking up the garden path.

'See what they've done!' She slammed the flat of her hand on the offending paragraph. 'Sugar's cut to eight ounces a week and sweets back on the ration again!'

'Would that be such a bad thing, Alice? Bad for a bairn's teeth, goodies and chocolates are.'

'Mm. Happen you're right,' she conceded grudgingly, placing a mug of tea on the table beside him and at the same time waving a silent goodbye to jars and jars of home-made jam and marmalade and chutney. The last time she had been able to stock her pantry shelves with such simple luxuries had been in nineteen thirty-nine. Ten years ago! 'But there's something else. Have you read it?'

'Cigarettes? Tobacco imports to be cut, you mean?'

'Aye. Folks'll have to go back to queuing for them again.'

'Happen so, but Julia should be pleased. She's been trying hard to give up smoking.'

'Julia has been trying to give up cigarettes for

years, Tom. Supplies being cut will only make her all the more determined to go on smoking.'

'How do you make that out, lass?'

'Because the scarcer things are, the more people want them. It's a trend of human nature! Oh, sometimes I get real fed up of the way things are! And don't say it's my age, Tom!'

'I wasn't going to. What I was about to remind you of was a night when you and me stood outside Keeper's. August fourteenth, almost four years ago. It was a Tuesday, if I remember rightly.'

'So?' Alice glared.

'You and me saw lights through windows and knew the war was really over. And do you remember what you said, love?'

'Four years ago? Now how do you expect –' She stopped, because she *did* remember that night, even though she was still angry about the sugar. 'We-e-ll, maybe I do. It was the night we knew Daisy was coming home safe from the war, because it was all over.'

'And there was something else, Alice.'

'I know, Tom. I said that never again would I moan and groan over daft little things that were of no consequence; that nothing again could ever be so grand as knowing there was an end to the killing, at last. Sorry, love. And sorry you had to remind me.'

'Not *reminding* you exactly. Just saying, sort of, that a few ounces of sugar doesn't amount to a lot, in the long run. And I'll have to be away. Want to have a look at those growers I let loose last week, to forage. Saw one or two of them in Brattocks, yesterday, getting very close to the railway line. Don't want them frightened. I'll get a few handfuls of barley – coax the silly things back into the open, again. See you at half-twelve. What's for dinner, by the way?'

'This.' Alice opened the oven door, then closed it again.

'Aaaah.' Tom sniffed roast rabbit, stuffed with thyme and parsley. ''Bye, bonny lass.' He kissed her cheek, then was off, leaving Alice to think not of an August evening, four years ago, but of the vow she made so often during those six years of war.

'When this war is over, I swear I shall never cook another rabbit!'

She sighed, because she hadn't known – no one had known – that even though the Emperor of Japan had surrendered unconditionally, it would be a long time before life was back to normal. Nor had their hopes of not only peace, but of plenty, come about.

Foolish of her to think that by the following week-end, she could ring up the butcher and order a shilling's worth of best steak, four lamb chops and a pound of dripping, and would he be so kind as to deliver them to Keeper's Cottage, Holdenby? And more than foolish those who had not stopped to remind themselves that wars cost money and had to be paid for, in the long run! And like Tom said, what did two ounces off the sugar ration amount to?

Two tablespoonfuls, that was all!

'Nathan! Have you seen this?' Julia waved the morning paper angrily. 'Not only is the sugar ration going down, but there's going to be a shortage of tobacco again! Cutting down on unessential imports, that's what! And who, in his wisdom, said that tobacco wasn't essential! Things are just going from bad to worse! We're going to have to start queuing again. Stand there for half an hour, then tip our caps for five measly cigarettes!'

'You *did* say you were cutting down, darling – trying to give them up.' Nathan drove his spade in the ground, and straightened his back. 'Maybe if they aren't quite so easy to come by, it'll be better for you. And there was I, thinking you were coming down the garden to ask me if I wanted a cup of coffee!'

'Nathan! This is serious. It is very, *very* serious. And if that's all the comedians in the government can think of to do, then I find it most unamusing and I, for one, am going to do something about it!'

'You are, darling?' He took her hand and led her to the wooden seat he had repaired only yesterday. 'Let's sit down, and you can tell me about it.'

'Don't mock, Nathan. I really mean it.' She stuck a hand in her jacket pocket and dramatically pulled out a cigarette case. 'Here! One silver cigarette case, three cigarettes! Have them, for all I care! As from now, I have no use for them. I am so angry, I have given them up! Absolutely!'

'You have?' He bit on his bottom lip to stop the smile that threatened. 'Well, good for you, Mrs Sutton!'

'Y-yes. About time. And please shift that holier-than-thou smirk off your face, because I mean it!'

She folded her arms and rounded her lips, then wondered why she had been so utterly stupid. Not ten minutes ago – before she had seen the news in the paper, that was – she had thought how nice it would be to sit in the garden and watch her husband digging over what had once been a vegetable plot, and have a leisurely cigarette, whilst doing so. Maybe to ask him, too, if he would like a mug of coffee. She had not intended, in her anger, to announce her intention to stop smoking.

'Now see here, love.' Nathan took off his gardening hat and hung it over the seat arm. 'Three isn't an awful lot. Why not finish them, and then stop? Weren't you just a little hasty?'

'No.' She pulled in her breath sharply. 'It's now, or never!'

She knew that if she gave in, even to what was a reasonable request, her resolve would falter and fail with the first blissful puff.

'Very well. I'll confess to being too weak to give up my pipe, but from now on I'll only smoke outside – or when you aren't around.'

'Nathan, I wouldn't dream of asking you to. You hardly ever smoke, anyway. I know what it's like, giving up. I was often without a cigarette when they were hard to get, in the war. But if I get snappy, and kick the cat and go around banging doors, you'll bear with me?'

'I will. But we haven't got a cat and Julia – my very dear Julia – you have always banged doors. So what say you pop inside and see if Polly has the percolator on the hob? I could use a coffee. We'll walk round the garden drinking it, and I'll show you what I've done and what I plan. How would that be?'

'Very nice. And might I say, Reverend, you are a very soothing person to have around.'

He watched her striding along the newly excavated path, and hoped she would never change. Not one iota. Cigarettes or not.

Keth knocked on the back door of the middle almshouse, then called, 'Hi, Mam. Only me . . .'

She was reading, so she looked at him over the top of her spectacles and offered her cheek for his kiss.

'Hullo, son. How's the little one? I haven't seen her today.'

'She was a bit fractious, but she's asleep, now.'

'Mm. Teeth. Sit you down, Keth.'

'Mam. I want to ask you – for your thoughts on the matter, I mean. Tom wants the baby to have a dog – well a bitch, actually. And Daisy and I agreed it would be very nice.'

'Mm. One of the new litter? Alice showed me them the other day. Nice little creatures.'

'Yes – we-e-ll – Daisy wanted her called Bethan of Winchester the second. Said it might be nice, but that you would have to approve.'

'I see.' Polly took off her spectacles, folding them, pushing them into the case slowly to give herself a few seconds thinking time. 'Well – I know a dog – or a bitch – has a long fancy name on its certificate of pedigree and a one-syllable name when it's learning to take commands. Bethan – Beth – would suit fine, but if I've got any say in the matter –'

'Of course you've got a say. Daisy was insistent on that.'

'Then could it perhaps be Bethan of Willow End? Or maybe Bethan of Windrush?'

Willow End, where they'd once lived, Keth thought. Windrush Hall, now a convalescent home for miners.

'Up to you, Mam . . .'

'Bethan of Windrush,' Polly said softly, smiling gently.

'Fine. But tell me why?'

'Because I know that is the name your father would have chosen, Keth.'

And Keth said of course it was; that he should have thought of it for himself, and almost told her about the trip south. Instead, he said, 'Why don't you come to supper tomorrow night, Mam? You could have more time with Mary Natasha, then. Daisy's doing pheasant.'

'Out of season, in June?'

'Mm. But according to Tom, this was an old one that threw itself right in his line of fire when he was taking a shot at a carrion. Daisy is casseroling it with baby carrots and little onions.'

'Then I'd love to come, if you're sure I won't be taking your rations.'

'Poached pheasant and onions and carrots aren't rationed, Mam, and neither is baked apples and custard.' He bent to kiss her. 'See you tomorrow, then – as early as you like.'

Polly smiled a goodbye, then put on her spectacles and opened the book she was reading, all the time thinking that life seemed to get better with every month that passed. Here was Polly Purvis with a rent-free cottage, a cart-load of logs every Christmas, a

417

widow's pension and a job at Bothy House with the nicest couple it had ever been her luck to meet.

As if she needed even more blessings for the counting, she thought about her son, who had been a captain in the war and was now a teacher at the grammar school; thought, too, about Daisy and Mary Natasha, and good friends like Alice and Tom.

'Ah, Dickon my old lovely,' she whispered. 'Wish you could have been here, now, to see how well it's all turned out.'

Bethan of Windrush. He'd have liked that.

'Hi, Bill!' Lyn called. 'You've just missed Drew.'

'I know. Saw him going towards Creesby, so I nipped over smartly. It's about the watercolour you wanted. I've brought some pencil sketches for you to have a look at.'

'Come into the house. Want a coffee?'

'No thanks. Just had one.' He tore the sketches from the pad he carried and laid them side by side on the table top.

'That one.' Almost without hesitation, Lyn made her choice.

'Aye. That's the one I like best. You have good taste, milady.'

'Give over, Bill.' She nudged him with her elbow. 'I like it because you've got the cupola in it, and lots of trees. It's the kind of view I'd have liked to come home to.'

'And is it to be autumn – golds and russets – or full-blown and blowsy summer? Or maybe spring – all soft greens?'

'And blossom, and not quite all the trees in leaf – a few bare branches? April, maybe? But I'll leave it to you, Bill. Just surprise me, eh?'

And he beamed and said that he promised that *Homecoming* would be the best yet.

'Oh, and Tatty said I'm to ask you both to Denniston for a meal. OK?'

'Fine. I'll give her a ring, and arrange it. We'll look forward to it.'

'Aye. And so will Mrs Benson. But tell me, Lyn, how is married life treating you? Are you happy?'

'You know I am, Bill,' she said softly.

She only wished there were words to tell him how much.

TWENTY

'Well now, Jack – how does it feel being almost a grandfather?'

'I might ask you the same, Granny.'

'Then it feels –' Blodwen Carmichael took a deep breath. 'It's like that if I had one wish, that's what it would be. I'm so happy for Lyn. A January baby. Wouldn't it be lovely if it came for New Year? I had a word with Drew after Lyn had told me and he said he's very pleased about it. I was the first to be told, you know. Bet they're telling Julia and Nathan this very minute. Wonder what they'll call it.'

'I should think, Blod darling, that they'll be waiting to see whether it's a boy or a girl, first.'

'You know what I mean, clever clogs. A Welsh name, do you think?'

'Haven't a clue. Let's wait and see how things turn out?'

'Suppose you're right. Wait and see. It's part of the fun about babies. You never quite know. Boy or girl? Early or late? Fair-haired like Drew, or another redhead in the family? Y'know what, Jack? This news

420

has bowled me over. I'll have to have a cup of tea.'

'*Tea*, woman? This baby's head is going to be properly wet! Whisky or gin?'

'We-e-ll – gin, if you insist. And use the best crystal glasses – start the way we mean to go on. Nothing but the best for our grandchild!'

'Will I tell you something, *cariad*? With your cheeks flushed and your eyes full of happiness, you're like a slip of a girl again.'

'Like the girl you fell in love with, Jack?'

'Like the girl I'm still in love with.' He held up his glass. 'Here's to our first grandchild!'

'Our Lyn's baby.' Her voice shook. 'God love the little thing.'

'Hullo, you two.' Alice smiled. 'Just calling in, are you? I'd ask you if you'd like a cup of tea, but I'm just going to Daisy's. Baby-sitting.'

'Yes. We know. But could you stand still for just long enough, Lady, for me to tell you that Lyn and I are having a baby. Due January.' His smile was wide and happy.

'Lyn!' Alice let go a cry of pure joy. 'Oh, my goodness! Oh, come here, lass, and give me a hug! And you, too, Drew.'

She put an arm around each, eyes brimming with tears, happy beyond telling that a baby was on the way for Rowangarth.

'And what does Julia say? Isn't she just as pleased as Punch?'

'They're opening a bottle of champagne. She said you were to go over, but I said you were baby-sitting at Foxgloves. Shouldn't wonder if she doesn't arrive there with bottle and glasses. In fact,' he grinned as the phone began to ring, 'I wouldn't be at all surprised if that isn't her, now.'

Tom held out a hand, kissing Lyn's cheek, smiling broadly.

'You've no idea just how much Alice wanted to hear that news. Congratulations, Drew. I'm real pleased there'll be bairns at Rowangarth again. A boy or a girl do you want?'

'A baby in my arms,' Lyn laughed. 'That's all I want. Doesn't matter which – I won't even care if it has red hair, I'm so happy.'

'That was Julia,' Alice beamed. 'Said she'd be round at Daisy's house at about eight. She and I have a lot to talk about! And she says I'm not to tell Daisy and Keth – best to wait till they're all together, at Denniston.'

'Oh, dear.' Alice dabbed her eyes when Lyn and Drew had left. 'Isn't everything wonderful? Daisy married, you and me with a granddaughter, and now a baby at Rowangarth. And Tatty expecting, an' all. Oh, Tom – we aren't having too much happiness, are we?'

'No, love. I reckon folk get what they deserve – good or bad – and you know how much you've wanted Drew to be wed and have bairns of his own. So get your coat and hat on, and I'll walk you to Foxgloves. And before you say you're well able to walk there on your own, I'm coming with you tonight, if only to make sure you don't tell Daisy about Lyn's baby!'

'As if I would! And ooooh.' A look of dismay crossed her face. 'I clean forgot!'

'Forgot?' Tom locked the back door behind them.

'To ask Lyn – about the christening gown. Whether she was intending using the one Drew had, or if she would like me to make a nice new one, like I did for Mary Natasha.'

'There's plenty of time for that, lass. I'm sure that when Lyn gets around to thinking about christenings, you'll be the first she'll come to if she decides on a new gown.'

Babies! Tom closed his eyes briefly as realization hit him. They'd got weddings over and done with and peace and quiet established again, but now it looked as if it was going to be nothing but baby talk from morning till night!

He wondered, with heartfelt compassion, just how Nathan Sutton was going to cope with the latest news.

They walked home in a July evening that was soft and warm and shadowy; honeysuckle threw scent on the air, and from the far meadow came the smell of new-cut hay.

'Isn't everything beautiful, Drew? And wasn't Daisy amazed to hear about the baby?' Lyn sighed pure contentment.

'It isn't every night of the year you drop such a bombshell, darling. Tatty was pleased, too.'

'Tatty was a bit miffed because I haven't been sick. Think she wanted to give me the benefit of her advice. And I'm sorry to disappoint everybody, but I feel one hundred per cent! Ewart told me that morning sickness didn't happen to every woman, and to count myself lucky – this far.

'And if you were to ask me if there's anything in the entire world I want, then I'd say there was nothing. I've got you and the baby and lovely family and friends. The folks don't live miles away in Kenya any longer, and after waiting years and years, I finally got to smell the linden blossom.'

'Was it worth the wait?'

'Yes, it was. Pity the flowers don't last more than a week, though. And oh, Drew, wasn't your mother funny tonight?'

'Mother was so shocked at the news that she completely forgot she was about to light a cigarette; giving in, after almost three weeks doing without, would you believe.'

'That's it!' Julia had said when she was able to speak. 'Do you both realize that I was within seconds of lighting this dratted thing! I begged Nathan to give me my cigarette case back – couldn't go on any longer – then the two of you arrive with such wonderful news that smoking seems rather stupid, if you get what I mean.'

'I think she's over the worst, now,' Lyn smiled. 'It won't be long before she's glaring at people who smoke, and wafting her hand in front of her nose like most converts do.'

And they laughed and linked arms and walked towards the wild garden and the stile you climbed to get onto Rowangarth's lawn.

'Do you think I should tell this to the rooks, Drew?

Aren't you supposed to, when something wonderful happens?'

'I wouldn't bother. Lady will be there first thing tomorrow, giving them chapter and verse. Leave it to her, eh?'

And Lyn smiled and nodded, because telling things to rooks wasn't half as important as standing beside a white marble stone in the churchyard. Because Kitty was still there, waiting, and anyway, she had the right to know.

Well, hadn't she?

'Do you have to go so early in the holidays, Keth? Can't you have the first week at home, unwinding a bit?'

'I want to get it over with. I've got it all worked out – route, francs and the address of a couple of *gîtes* in case the ferry is delayed. Better to do an overnight stop than drive on the wrong side of the road in the dark.'

'You said "Get it over with," Keth, as if you're going for a filling, or something. How much do you want to go and how much of the trip is a penance, a duty . . . ?'

'I want to go, Daisy. I *need* to go. Every time I look at Mary Natasha, I know I must.'

'But things might have changed, there. Where, in Clissy, will you make a start?'

'If there's no one at Tante Clara's house, you mean? I suppose it would have to be the bread shop. Madame went there every day, and at first I didn't think it peculiar. I mean, for someone who was very domesticated – she even knitted her long black stockings – it took a while for it to sink in that people like her usually baked their own bread.'

'The bread shop people were in it, then?'

'With the benefit of hindsight, they must have been. I suppose a lot of Clissy people worked for the Resistance in some way or other. But I wasn't told a lot. Only what was good for me to know. Sensible, really. If I'd been taken that night, I would only have known that Madame Piccard and Natasha were involved – I could have kept quiet about Denys and Bernadette next door. After all, I wasn't sure if they were in on things. The less you knew, you see, the less people you could get into trouble.'

'You'll be careful, Keth?'

'Careful? But what could happen? Even in the war I was safer than most. It wasn't Keth Purvis taking the risks.'

'But hadn't you thought? They're closely knit, those little French communities. What if you were to find Madame Piccard and she held you responsible for Natasha's death?'

'I don't think she would. Tante Clara ran the local Resistance, though it wasn't till I got back that I was told. I'd never have known. She was very level-headed. She wouldn't hold it against me, I hope.

'But if something like that happened, Daisy, then at least I could humbly apologize for my part in it, and hope she would understand. She didn't hate the Allies like she hated the Nazis. Her husband was killed in the Great War, don't forget. I don't think she ever forgave them for it.'

'It must have been a lousy war for people in occupied countries. I often used to wonder – when we were expecting to be invaded in 'forty – how I'd have felt to see Nazis jackbooting it all over the place. And I do understand, Keth, why you must go.

'Only be careful not to be caught at Customs, because I've got some money for you to take – over and above what you're legally allowed. We'll have to find a way of hiding it when you do your packing.'

'How much, Daisy?'

'Only twenty-five pounds, but on the miserable fifty you're allowed to take, you'll hardly be able to afford to eat. Not if you had to stay there longer than you'd thought. I can think of lots of ways to hide a few fivers.'

'And will you come and visit me when I'm in prison on Devil's Island?'

'You know I will, darling,' she teased. 'But you'd better let me know in good time when you'll be going down south to your conference, so I can mention it a time or two – get people used to it. You know what a nosy lot they can be round here.'

'Not nosy, sweetheart. Just interested in what's going on around them. I wonder what Holdenby would think if they really knew what I'd been up to in the war. "What did he want to go and do a madbrained thing like that for?" they'd say.'

'Then I'd tell them it was the only way you could get home from Washington to marry me. But no one will know, Keth. Not even Mam and Dada. Only you and I know.'

'And Nathan Sutton, don't forget.'

'What you tell to a priest is sacrosanct, but I'll be glad when you've been there and squared your conscience, Keth.'

'So will I, love. So will I!'

How much, even Daisy couldn't know.

Lyn lay, head on Drew's shoulder, waiting for sleep to come, happy to go over this day in her mind. It had begun with Ewart Pryce telling her what she so wanted to hear.

'Well, Lyndis, I think we can safely assume late January . . .'

'I'm pregnant then,' she whispered chokily. 'You're certain?'

'As certain as makes no matter. I can see you're pleased. Congratulations to you both.'

Then the delight of phoning Llangollen, then telling Drew's mother and Daisy's mother and oh, *everybody*!

Drew grunted and turned over, so she swung her legs carefully out of bed and padded to the window to look at the round bright moon. It had been low in the sky, and pale, when they left Denniston House, but now it was high and glinted golden.

She looked towards Brattocks Wood, dark against it, and to the squat, square tower of All Souls. She couldn't see the churchyard clearly, but she knew that as soon as she was able to go there alone, she would stand beside Kitty's grave and tell her, too. Not with words, nor in whispers, but with her heart and from her heart. Perhaps when Kitty knew Drew was truly happy, she would cease to watch over him; go, as

Mrs Amelia had said, to wherever the bright spirit that was Kathryn Norma Clementina Sutton wanted to be.

Lyn sat on the window seat, pulling her knees to her chin, wrapping her arms around them, looking now towards the jutting bulk of the Pike, wondering if it really had been there they made this tiny baby inside her.

But did it matter? She was carrying a child, Drew's child. It was wanted, and already loved. In her heart, in her mind, she called it Little Thing but soon, if Tatty was anything to go by, she would have to call it Nicely Rounded Bump.

She wanted to creep downstairs and run barefoot across the lawn in the moonlight, arms wide, laughing with joy. She wanted to shout out that she was pregnant; shout so loudly that the rooks at the far end of Brattocks Wood heard it. But instead she got carefully into bed again, sliding in sideways so as not to disturb Drew, who turned over again, and laid an arm across her.

''Night,' she whispered softly, but he did not hear her.

Jack Catchpole was standing beside Kitty's stone when Lyn got there. He had looked up at the first sound of her footsteps on the gravel path, so she could not turn, and walk away.

'Mornin', milady. Just taking a look at the flowers.' In his hand was a brass sprayer. 'Came to give 'em a freshener, but they'm past it, now. Now't so dead as dead flowers . . .' He bent to pick up the

429

bouquet, now wilted and brown. 'You didn't mind about the flowers?'

'I didn't mind at all. Of course Kitty must have her flowers, every June. Haven't they lasted well?'

'Orchids alus last. I'll take this with me, Lady Lyn. Can use the frame again – er – next year, if that'll be all right?'

'Of course it will.' Lyn wondered how she could feel so calm. 'Next year. Every year.'

They would never be her orchids, Lyn thought. Lady Helen's, of course, and now Kitty's. But never Lady Lyn's orchids. She had broken the chain.

'I'll be on my way, then.' Jack Catchpole fingered the peak of his cap. 'Nice to have a chat, milady. You'm welcome to look at the glasshouses any time you want. And if you don't think it presumptuous, me and Lily is right glad about your little babby. Us wishes you well.'

'Thank you, Jack. I appreciate it. And please thank Mrs Catchpole, too, and give her my regards.'

She wondered, as the old gardener walked away, footsteps crunching the gravel, if she had got it right; done it as Lady Helen would have done, as Julia did, now; hoped she had sounded neither familiar nor condescending. It was hard, sometimes, crossing the divide from employed to employer; from being Lyn Carmichael from Wales to being mistress of Rowangarth.

To real gentry, it was no problem. To someone like herself, it was something to be worked at until she was as sure as she could be that she had got it right. And even when she did, she would still be Lyn

Carmichael. Not unlike the Colonel's Lady an' Judy O'Grady, she supposed.

Hullo, Kitty, she said softly with her heart. *It's Lyn. We're having a baby, Drew and me, and I wanted you to know. Be glad for us . . . ?*

She raised her eyes to the gilded name, which seemed to glow as she looked at it, and she knew Kitty was still there; still at Rowangarth and in Brattocks Wood and in the conservatory. Kitty was still only a thought away, still unwilling to go to wherever it was decreed she belonged, because the time was not yet right. Maybe, Lyn thought, Kitty would never leave. Perhaps Rowangarth would hold her forever.

I'll come again to see you. Hope you liked your flowers.

She touched the name with her fingertips, and gentled her hand across the cool smoothness of the stone. Then she turned and walked away as Catchpole had done; feet crunching the gravel, as mortal feet did. At the church gate she turned and lifted a hand.

''Bye,' she whispered.

Keth wound down his window as his car bumped off the ferry at St Malo, watching the movements of the gendarme, whistle between his teeth, who pointed and gesticulated left and right.

Keth indicated right, telling himself to take it easy for the first few miles; that he had driven on the wrong side of the road before, in Kentucky.

He drove carefully, eyes in the rear-view mirror, glad that most cars had taken the left turn towards the town. Taking the easier coast route, he checked the road sign with the bold figures on the sheet of paper beside him. Forty kilometres to Treguier. Twenty-four miles near as dammit, his mathematical mind supplied. Settle down, Purvis. You're on your way. You're doing fine.

Of course he was. Driving on the right of the road was no problem; never had been. It wasn't the getting to Clissy-sur-Mer that bothered him. It was what he would find – or wouldn't find – when he got there, that was going to take some thinking out. Best he should concentrate on finding someplace to stay, first, then have a wash and a meal. Food was good and, unlike England, plentiful, he had heard. And cheap, if you ate where the locals ate. He should be able to manage on the fifty pounds' worth of francs in his pocket and if not, the banks would exchange the twenty-five pounds Daisy had hidden inside the wrapper of his soap, and taped into the middle pages of a book entitled *Mathematics for Higher Grades* in his holdall.

He was overtaken by a truck, horn blaring, realizing his speed had dropped to twenty miles per hour which made him a nuisance on the road. Pressing down his right foot, shaking all unnecessary thoughts from his head, he looked at the long, dusty road ahead. He would worry about Clissy when he got there, and not a moment before.

He dropped his speed because he was coming to a gated railway crossing and a scatter of half a dozen houses, most of which were small; all of which had immaculate front gardens and shutters closed against the afternoon sun.

Twenty-nine kilometres to Treguier, the roadside sign indicated as he left the houses behind him. Eighteen miles. He wound down the window, enjoying the sudden gush of cooler air, and began to relax.

'Mum says can she and Dad visit next weekend.' Lyn folded the sheet of notepaper and slipped it back in its envelope. 'And if it's convenient, can they have the room they last had, as she likes the view from the window.'

'Up to you, darling. It's your home. And of course they can visit – any time they want. They don't have to ask.'

'Good. I'll ring them tonight. Er – would you mind if I had lunch with Daisy? I mentioned I'd be out to Tilda and she said she would rustle something up for you. I still feel like a spare part, sometimes. Mary Stubbs and Tilda have things so organized between them that I feel I'm in the way.'

'Don't worry yourself. Those two downstairs have been running things for as long as I can remember. You'll get the hang of it, bit by bit. And as for feeling like a spare part – you'll have all your work cut out when the baby arrives. We'll have to think about extra help.'

'A nanny, you mean? But why? Daisy manages all right and does her own housework, too. And washes nappies every day. What's so special about me? And anyway, I don't think I'll want to share the baby with anyone.'

'I never for one moment thought you would,' Drew laughed. 'Did you have a chat to Ewart about where, by the way? I believe you can go to hospital into a maternity ward. Everything provided by the National Health Service.'

'Don't think I'd like that. Daisy had Mary Natasha at home, and Tatty intends to do the same. Daisy said the district nurse is a trained midwife and Doctor Pryce was in on Mary's birth, at the end. And you were born at Rowangarth, don't forget . . .'

'In the middle of the world's worst 'flu epidemic ever. Old Doctor James was run off his feet. He arrived here just as I was born. Mother said she almost panicked, then remembered her training as a nurse.'

'There you are, then. If your mother could manage on her own, almost, then I shall be just fine, here at home. It's a long way off. When I see myself in the mirror I can't believe I'm expecting. I'm eating like a horse and not feeling sick at all – fingers crossed. By the way, Keth says he'll start teaching Daisy to drive, when he's back from his conference.'

She crossed the room to sit on the arm of his chair, then laid an arm across his shoulders, because she couldn't bear not to be near him, touch him.

'Pity Daiz didn't get a driving licence in the war. You could just apply for one, then, and start driving on your own as soon as you wanted. Driving tests were suspended for the duration, remember?'

'Yes. And now they've been started again, she'll have to have L plates, and take a test. Never mind. Purvis isn't thick. She'll pass, all right. What will you be doing with yourself today, darling?'

'I'm meeting Tom at Keeper's. Lady usually brews up around ten. Then we'll walk the beat, and see how the birds are coming along. There's a bod who runs a shooting syndicate coming over from Leeds and I'd like to meet him. Tom said the bloke was interested in regular monthly shoots once the season starts so I'd better stand him a pint at the pub. But to get back to Keth. How long does this conference of his last and where is it? Are you sure he isn't off on a dirty weekend to Brighton?'

'Idiot! They don't come much more faithful than Keth. Those two have been together, if Polly is to be believed, since Daisy was in her pram. Not like you sailors with one in every port. Oh lor'! Sorry, Drew. I didn't mean – I shouldn't have said – Kitty, I mean. Sorry . . .'

'Don't keep saying sorry.' He got to his feet, laying his hand on her shoulder, holding her at arm's length. 'It's all right, Lyn. Truly it is. I thought you were – well – coming to terms with things. Since you spoke to Amelia, you seemed just fine. What is it, darling?' He gathered her into his arms and she laid her head on his chest.

'Nothing, Drew. Just a slip on my part. And I *am* coming to terms with things. I accept you loved Kitty and that now you love me. You love us both differently. Why I made a mountain out of a molehill, I don't know, because they don't come any luckier than me.'

'Lucky? Happy, don't you mean? As happy as I am, Lyn? Look – why don't you walk with me as far as Keeper's, have a word with Lady and ask her if she has any messages for Daisy?'

And Lyn said, 'Good idea,' and that she would go

and powder her nose and be with him in a couple of ticks.

'And don't ever,' she whispered softly to her reflection in the dressing-table mirror, 'do anything like that again.'

Because Drew thought things had settled down; that she had come to terms with his first love and was content to be his last love – and, if you wanted a great big bonus – the mother of his child.

But things hadn't settled down. She had come to terms with the way things were, because she had accepted that Kitty was in the air around them, still; that she wasn't ready to leave her earthly place just yet.

She was so sure of it, Lyn frowned as she tied back her hair with a green ribbon, that she had even accepted Kitty's right to be there – one of the Clan, still. Perhaps, she thought, there might just be a little of her mother's Celtic clairvoyance in her.

'Want me to take you to Daisy's in the car?' Drew asked as she linked her arm in his.

'Of course not. It's no distance at all and anyway, walking is good for me. I'm expecting, Drew, not ill. Tatty still rides her bike. Says she's going to ride it until her bump gets in the way of the handlebars!'

'Good old Tatty. She was such a brat, once. Completely spoiled. Wrapped in cotton wool and not allowed out without her nanny or governess. She really cramped the Clan's style until Kitty said we'd have to find ways and means of getting rid of the escort so Tatty could do all the things we did.'

'Like . . .'

'Oh, general mischief. Climbing trees and having picnics in the wild garden. And, would you believe, spitting contests. Kitty always won those.'

'But why should she stick up for Tatty if she was such a whinge?'

'Because she owed her one. Tatty taught her to swear, in Russian. Aunt Amelia was very strict, you see. She once gated Kitty for a week for saying bloody hell.'

'But who,' Lyn frowned, 'taught Tatty the Russian swear words?'

'Karl, of course. Those two were always hand in glove. Yet for all that, not even Tatty knows Karl's real name – just that he was once a Cossack and loyal to the Tzar. But those days are over, sweetheart. Seems the Clan has turned into parents, all of a sudden.'

'Which is very right and proper and to be expected,' Lyn smiled. 'I wonder how many children we'll have, Drew. I'd like two, at least. I didn't much like being an only child.'

'Nor me. We were all only children when we were young, except Bas and Kitty. Gracie, too, and Bill, for that matter. But Daiz and Keth and Tatty and I grew up pretty close, so it wasn't too bad. I'm pretty sure Bill and Tatty will have loads of kids. She wasn't wanted – by her father, that was – and Bill never knew either of his parents. Bill is good for Tatty. They'll do just fine. And there's Lady, hanging out the washing.'

He waved, smiling, and Alice waved back and called, 'Kettle's on. Be with you in a minute . . .'

* * *

The road sign indicated that Keth was less than four miles from Clissy-sur-Mer. Already the sun was high and bright. Last evening he had stayed at a *gîte* outside Treguier; had slept well and eaten a good breakfast, yet now, as every second took him nearer, the feeling of uncertainty was returning. Why had he come here? Shouldn't he have let well alone? Did he really have the right to straighten his conscience?

He thought about Daisy, and a dark-eyed child called Mary, and knew he didn't have a choice. Natasha hadn't had one. He breathed deeply as he saw, on the skyline ahead, the towers of a large house. Clissy-sur-Mer. He'd made it and anyway, hadn't he passed the point of no return the minute he drove onto the St Malo ferry? No going back, now.

'I remember,' Alice said, 'when Tom lived in this bothy, yet I can't recall what the garden was like.'

'Pretty overgrown even then, if I remember rightly. After all, it was only used for sleeping quarters in those days,' Julia shrugged.

'More than thirty years ago. We're both grandparents now, Julia, yet it seems . . .'

'Hey! They say that when you start wondering where all the years have gone, you're truly feeling old! And I'm not a grandmother, yet, though the waiting is awful. But we came here to admire Nathan's garden. He's really enjoying getting some order into it.'

'He's doing well.'

'With a little help from Catchpole,' Julia grimaced. 'Jack couldn't wait to cut back those ramblers on the walls, and tie them in. I thought he'd been a bit savage, but he says we should have a fine show of roses next year, so who am I to argue with an expert? Nathan has opened up all the paths now, and ordered a load of gravel for them. Catchpole was right. Once the paths are in order, he can take the digging bit by bit. We should grow potatoes, he said – clean the soil – but we've found an old asparagus bed that Nathan is keen to sort out. Mm. Imagine asparagus tips and butter sauce . . .'

'Imagine having butter to spare for sauce!' Alice said dryly. 'Weren't we the stupid ones, thinking that when we got peace there'd be plenty, too? Shouldn't have had that dratted war if they'd thought on how much it would cost! But there'll be a general election in time. Let's see how food rationing fares when they're after our votes, eh?'

They went to sit on the newly repaired seat, each content to gaze across the garden, Alice thinking how grand it would be with its new gravelled paths and maybe a pot or two of flowers around the seat that faced west. Be nice for Julia and Nathan to sit here, summer evenings, and watch the sun go down over Brattocks Wood and the rooks fly home to roost.

Julia thought not of the garden but of Drew and Lyndis and the baby she carried. A boy, perhaps, for Rowangarth? But no! A healthy baby was all anyone could ask. A grandchild. Life could be pretty good, even though Nathan had severely rationed baby talk. None at meal times, for instance, or when he had lit a pipe and opened the evening paper. And did it matter? There was always Alice . . .

'Lyn's looking very well,' she remarked.

'Aye. She's fairly blooming. Motherhood suits her. She was desperate for a bairn of her own. I'd see her looking at Mary Natasha with such longing, but it's all right, now. Tatty looks well, an' all. I reckon she's carrying a lad.'

'What makes you say that, Alice?'

'Well, to my way of thinking, she's neat at the back. No bottom on her at all. But she's well rounded, at the front.'

'So . . . ?'

'It was Jin Dobb told me, and she was never wrong. A boy you carried up front; a girl you carried all round, and lower, if you see what I mean.'

'No, I don't. But if you're so good at it, what will Lyn and Drew have?'

'Oh, I can't tell yet. Lyn's hardly showing. But there'll be a lad at Denniston House, mark my words. Shouldn't wonder if it doesn't start that Mrs Clementina turning in her grave. Tatty with a son, yet Elliot couldn't get one – not one he could own,' she added soberly.

'The way Elliot Sutton rampaged around, it wouldn't surprise me if somewhere there is a son of his. Not one with his name, though. But let's not talk about him? He should have been buried with a stake through his heart!'

'Julia Sutton! That's a terrible thing for a vicar's wife to say – but I can understand the way you feel. And he wasn't entirely wicked, you know. He gave us Drew . . .'

'Yes. And he never knew. God bless Drew for being born Sutton fair, is all I can say.'

For a moment she was silent, staring ahead as if thanking the Almighty, Alice thought, that some good had come out of evil. Then she laughed and said, 'Do you know, Alice Dwerryhouse, that I haven't had a cigarette for four weeks and one day.'

'So you're over it, thanks be.'

'N-no. Sometimes I feel like lighting up. Odd times after a nice meal with the coffee, and sometimes when I have a sherry, evenings. But I shall make it, now. Do you think I'll get fat? They say you do.'

'If you're nibbling bits and pieces to help you get over the craving, yes, you might. But once you've got cigarettes well and truly sorted, then you can lose the weight – if any. The way I see it is that if you can give up smoking, then you'll have the willpower to lose a few pounds. I'm glad for you, Julia. If I had a ten-shilling note for every time I've begged you to give it up, I'd be rich! Don't know why you started the habit. Lady Helen never smoked.'

'Oh, it was the war, I suppose – *our* war, I mean. I used to carry a packet in my apron pocket in case a wounded soldier asked for one. I'd light it for him and – well, I suppose I started to need them, too.'

'Well, you don't need them now. Think of all the money you'll save,' Alice, ever practical, reminded.

'Money? When Nathan inherited half of the Pendenys fortune? Drew's going to be very rich, one day. Hope it doesn't affect him . . .'

'Did suddenly inheriting Pendenys money change Nathan?'

'No, bless him. And if I tell you something, you

441

won't breathe a word, Alice? When the baby comes, he's going to offer Drew the money to have the Rowangarth roof properly fixed. If Drew tries to refuse, Nathan will say that it's a celebration, kind of, for the gift of a child.'

'The gift of a child,' Alice repeated softly, gazing over Brattocks Wood, watching the birds that circled the elm trees at the far end of it. 'We're very lucky, Julia, you and I.'

'Very lucky,' Julia nodded, wondering why, at such moments of utter contentment, she should want to light a cigarette. She put the thought behind her immediately and thought instead of the baby Lyn carried. 'Very lucky indeed.'

It was the yeasty smell of baking bread that guided Keth to the little house that offered bed and breakfast. That, and the fact that it had arum lilies in the tiny front garden.

'How many nights?' asked the plump, grey-haired woman who opened the door to him.

'One, but maybe two,' he answered her in near-perfect French.

'One single room and breakfast – payment in advance. Two nights, eh?'

Keth nodded and hoped it would be only one; hoped, foolishly, that he would quickly find what he had come here to find and would soon be driving back to Foxgloves and sanity.

The room was small and smelled of cleanliness. Through the open window came village sounds. Madame told him that breakfast was included, but that if he wanted to eat, Justin Blanc on the corner gave good value for money.

Keth thanked her, then kicked off his shoes and lay back on the bed, all at once recalling that night. Two minutes on the ground was all the Lysander pilot was allowed, so you got the hell out of it, pretty damn quick!

He had tried often to blot it out, but the memory would not leave him. They'd left Natasha. He had protested; called the pilot a pitiless bastard and more besides, but it made no difference. They were heading for England and safety, and what became of those left behind was nothing to do with them, the pilot said. There was a war on. The Resistance knew what they were about, the risks they took.

Keth remembered wanting to vomit, but whether from fear or disgust he had never been sure. He only knew that a young girl had been gunned down by a bullet meant for him, yet he had made it home and married Daisy; had a little girl with dark hair and brown eyes. Like Natasha's. Or had they put her real name on her gravestone? Was it Hannah Kominski or Elise Josef, the name on her false passport? Did she even have a grave?

He frowned, because Clissy-sur-Mer seemed so normal, now. No more fighting. No more agents slipping ashore or parachuting from a plane. No more waiting for a Lysander to collect a man called Gaston Martin, who carried a precious package.

There had been a row of poplars at the chateau that separated the house from the stables and outbuildings – and the paddock, of course. Usually that paddock was littered with jumps and obstacles which would be cleared, Clara Piccard said, so the plane from England could land.

But who had cleared it? Someone from the chateau or some of the people who came mysteriously out of the undergrowth – the Resistance – to whom Clara Piccard, Denys and Bernadette and Hirondelle belonged? Had the owner of the chateau known, and turned a blind eye?

Yet whatever happened that night was long gone; water under the bridge, an act of war – and the war was over. Until now, that was, because now Keth Purvis had chosen to step back into that war; say a thank you for his life. If anyone he had known in Clissy was there to say thank you to.

Keth called to the woman in the kitchen that he was going out. He had intended finding somewhere to eat, but he wasn't hungry and common sense told him that the longer he left it, the harder it would become to find the little house. It was why he had come, so why had his misgivings returned? And why was he here? What good was it going to do? Why had he been so stupid as to think that this act of remembrance could turn back the clock, put everything to rights?

Blinking in the sudden glare of sun he crossed to the shady side of the street then turned a corner to see the chateau in the distance to remind him that once they knew that the package he had come to collect was on its way to Clissy and that a plane from England would land the following night, Madame and Natasha had not hesitated. It had not been an option, even though they already knew that one man – Hirondelle – had been taken by soldiers for questioning. Yet Hirondelle would tell nothing until he had given that precious package time to arrive at the paddock behind the big house. Twenty-four hours had he been able to hold out? A little longer, perhaps, until he was forced to break, or take the cyanide pill all agents carried.

The people at the Stone House in Argyll had given him a pill, Keth thought with distaste. He had hidden it in the frayed cuff of his working shirt. They told him it would be quick, yet he still wondered if he would have had the courage to swallow it, knowing that in less than a minute . . .

He straightened his shoulders and began to walk towards the towers of the chateau.

Natasha – wherever you are, please understand . . . ?

TWENTY-ONE

'Hi, Mother.'

'Hullo, darling.' Anna offered her cheek for Tatiana's kiss. 'I didn't hear you come in.'

'No, you wouldn't. I've been in the surgery for my checkup. The new district nurse is nice – very young.'

'Sister Fletcher. Ewart thinks highly of her. And is everything all right?'

'Fine. Blood pressure normal. Baby behaving itself. I'm to stop riding my bike, though, since I'm feeling the baby, now. I thought they kicked, but mine is very ladylike.'

'It'll have a kick like a mule before long if it's anything like you were. I'm glad about the bike, though. I always thought cycling too strenuous – in your condition.'

'Mother! My *condition*! I was always careful, never rode up hills, but if Sister says I must stop, then stop I must. You wouldn't have anything to eat? I'm ravenous.'

'I – er – I came by some cheese, yesterday . . .'

'Smashing! A black market cheese sandwich, please, with blackcurrant jam. Mm.'

'Good Wensleydale cheese with blackcurrant *jam*? Whatever next?'

'Heaven only knows, in my condition. Kippers and custard, I shouldn't wonder,' she giggled.

'You're happy, aren't you, Tatiana?' Anna asked, getting out bread board and knife.

'I'm very happy, Mother. I like being married, and pregnant.'

'That's all right, then. Where's Bill?'

'Gone to Creesby, to the picture-framing place. He's done a watercolour of Rowangarth. Lyn asked him to do it – a surprise for Drew.'

'These thick enough for you?' Anna held up two hefty slices of bread. 'And how is Lyn?'

'Goes for her first checkup in a couple of weeks. She's fine. She hasn't been sick, yet, would you believe?'

'Then I'm very pleased for her. Are you going to sit down and take the weight off your feet?'

'Sorry. Said I'd be at Daisy's by three. Think I'll eat this on the way there.' She bit into the sandwich. 'Ten out of ten, Mother. This isn't half good! 'Bye. See you. Love to Ewart.'

And she was gone, holding the sandwich in two hands, sighing blissfully, and Anna Pryce laughed, and whispered, 'Oh, Tatiana. If only your Grandmother Petrovska could see you now!'

Daisy carried two ancient deck chairs into the shade of the apple tree in the back garden.

'There, now. Careful how you sit down, Tatty. Don't want you wobbling over, or anything. I'll nip back for the tea tray. Sorry I can't offer you anything to eat.'

''S all right. Mother gave me a sarnie. Think I'll last out now till supper. A cuppa will be fine. It's great to drink tea again, without heaving. Are you missing Keth?'

'Strangely enough, I am. I thought that I'd got used to us being apart during the war, and that two or three days was nothing at all. Mary misses him, too.' She smiled at the sleeping baby. 'Now that she's crawling, she's ready for a nap, afternoons. I need eyes in the back of my head, these days. Yesterday, I heard such a howl and she'd got herself stuck under a dining chair. Doesn't seem five minutes since –'

'Since she was a bump like I've got? Nice, isn't it, to think that all the Clan are parents now – or will be. Where's Lyn, by the way?'

'Gone to York to meet her folks. They're staying at Rowangarth for a week. Drew's in York, too, on estate business.'

'And Keth – have you heard from him, yet?'

'No. Don't expect to. Phoning from abroad is – I mean – from down south – is still a bit hit and miss.'

'You said from abroad, then went the colour of a turkey cock. *Is* Keth abroad, Daisy?'

'No, of course not.' Tatiana was too sharp for her own good! 'What I meant to say is some of the bods at the conference might take a day extra and do a quick trip across the Channel . . .'

Lies, lies, lies! But she couldn't tell Tatty; couldn't

tell anyone, not even Mam, where Keth really was. Which was stupid, when you came to think of it, because everyone knew, now, about agents who went to France in the war – about agents who had died, too. She said, 'I wonder what he's doing, now?' She did. She really wondered, and hoped that when he got back, things wouldn't have been too awful for him.

Keth walked slowly, looking to left and right, trying to work out which side street would take him nearer to the chateau; which one would end in another small square of houses. It would be trial and error until he had cleared the village and found himself amongst fields again, and the leafy lane he was looking for.

He turned left and was glad to see a farmhouse ahead, and fields opposite. Amazing, he thought, that he'd lived in Clissy for two weeks, yet all he knew now was the nearer he got to the chateau, the sooner he would find Tante Clara's house.

Would he hear the dogs bark? Would the two grey-hounds still be there? In October, it would be six years since he'd been paddled ashore in an inflatable dinghy; six years since he had felt dismay because a child had been sent to meet him.

He tried to focus his thoughts on a house called Foxgloves, and Mary and Daisy, but they were a long way away; six years away, really, and would be, until he had done what he had come to Clissy to do.

The road began to narrow, and led towards trees. Through them, he could see the top of a high-pitched roof, with a chimney pot on each gable end. It was the house of Denys and Bernadette Roche. A few more seconds, a few more strides, and he would be there.

Clara Piccard's house had not changed. Lilies still grew in clumps, and someone had planted vegetables in straight rows in the garden he once dug. No smoke came from the chimney – but then, it was high summer.

He pulled down the iron latch of the gate with a click, but no dogs barked. Slowly, he walked down the path and stood quite still until the thudding in his chest had lessened. Then he lifted the knocker and brought it down three times.

No one answered. No one was in. Should he walk round to the front or should he go to the house with the high-pitched roof and ask there if they knew if Clara Piccard still lived next door, or where she had gone? And would they recognize him, and slam the door in his face?

The front of the house looked onto fields. The grass outside it was neatly cut. Still no one answered his knock. And why, he demanded of himself, suddenly angry, had it never once occurred to him that he might never find the women he sought? Yet someone, surely, must be able to help him? The people at the bread shop, or the local gendarme? He turned to make for the gate again, then stopped in his tracks as he heard a sharp click, and footsteps. He hurried to the back door, then stood stock-still.

A woman was standing beside the woodshed, her hair thick and dark, her brown eyes questioning; a woman who, six years ago could have been – Then she smiled, and he knew.

He tried to say her name, but could not. His stomach lurched and he could feel a tingling in his cheeks as the blood in them drained away. She was still smiling.

'Hibou?' she said.

'Natasha?' Her name came in a gasp of disbelief.

'No. Hannah Kominski, now.' She grinned mischievously. 'So, Hibou, you are back? Sorry, but I am not in need of a gardener.' She spoke in perfect English.

'Natasha!' He held out his arms, not to this beautiful young woman, but to a child of sixteen and three months. Briefly, their cheeks touched. 'I – I thought – that night when the Lysander came . . .'

His heart still thudded. He could feel it, and every small pulse in his body, fluttering in unison. He ran his tongue round lips gone suddenly dry.

'You thought I was dead, Hibou?'

'I did. All these years I've thought it, and that I just took off, and left you lying there . . .'

'It is a long time ago,' she shrugged, 'and you look in need of a drink.' She took a key from her pocket and opened the back door and he followed her inside, wonderingly.

Nothing had changed save for new curtains at the window, a different hearthrug. Tante Clara's chair stood to the left of the fireplace, facing the door. On the small table beside it lay knitting. Black yarn on four needles. She still knitted her own stockings . . .

'Tante Clara?' he whispered.

'They came for her that night. And Bernadette.

They had already taken Denys. When I came back to this house, her knitting was as she left it. I haven't moved it, nor will I. It is her – her – memorial,' she whispered, head high. 'But please to sit down, Hibou. You are needing a cognac – as I am.' She cleared her throat, and laughed shakily. 'We have cognac, now the war is over.'

She offered him a glass, then sat in the chair opposite, gazing thoughtfully into the empty hearth before she asked, 'Why did you come back to Clissy, Hibou?'

'Because I am married, now, and have a child. She has dark hair and brown eyes. We call her Mary.'

He took out his wallet and offered the photograph he always carried with him. His wife and child, taken on a September day, at a christening.

'She is very beautiful, but I remember you said you preferred blondes.'

'There would have been no christening – no wedding, even – had it not been for you.'

'So you wanted me to know, Hibou?'

'Like I said, I thought you were dead. I wanted – *needed* – to find your grave. A pilgrimage, sort of. A penance. A thank you.' He looked down into his glass, still shocked and shaken. 'We – Daisy and I – called the baby after you. She's Mary Natasha. I told Daisy – eventually – why I had chosen your name; told her I wanted, someday, to come back here and she agreed with me. I – I'm sorry about your aunt, and about Denys and Bernadette.'

'I know you are. And I am glad to know that you made it back to England with the package. Were they pleased? And I can't still call you Hibou. You never told me your real name.'

'We never told anything to anyone, come to think of it.' He felt a small smile on his lips. The brandy was doing its work. 'My name is Keth Purvis.' He spelled out his Christian name from force of habit. 'When I had taken the package – it was a naval-type Enigma machine – I went back to Bletchley Park. A secret place. No one – not even Hitler's lot – knew what we did there. You'll know, now, about Enigmas?'

'I know a lot, now.' She leaned over to pour more cognac in his glass. 'Yet I do not know for certain what happened to Tante Clara and Denys and Bernadette. And Hirondelle, too. Mass is said in church, still, for the souls of those who have no grave. You remember I used to go to church with Tante Clara, even though I was reared in the Jewish faith?'

'By the people who adopted you,' he nodded.

'I remember them in my Catholic prayers, too. I became familiar with Tante Clara's religion. I have taken it as my own. My name is Jewish, but I say my prayers in Latin. It is best I do. But will you call me Hannah, now? For the sake of my parents, will you, Keth Purvis?'

'I will. And I'm feeling a little light-headed. Brandy on an empty stomach, I suppose – and shock.' Tears filled his eyes and he brushed them impatiently away with the back of his hand.

'You have not eaten? Good. Nor have I. Will soup be all right?' She busied herself at the electric cooker Madame Piccard had only used when necessary. Then she laid a cloth on the table, and spoons and knives.

'I still buy bread from the *boulangerie*, but now we have butter to eat with it.'

'The people at the bread shop – were they arrested, too?'

'No. They were lucky, were left alone. I think Tante Clara once told you that the less anyone knew, the less they could tell, if they were taken. How true it turned out to be. But drink your soup, and then we will start at the beginning and I will tell you what happened in Clissy that night, and why I am here, still. And Hibou – Keth – don't look so sad. I think you came here because your conscience troubled you, and it should not.'

'You were sixteen. I thought you were dead, and all because you came with me to the chateau that night. People in Clissy might hold it against me, I thought.'

'It was the fault of the Nazis. If they had not invaded our country, we would not have had to fight them! But eat up, then we will sit in the shade on the bench outside – as we used to do when you were Gaston Martin, who dug our garden and chopped our logs.'

She smiled. She was very beautiful, he thought.

'You are not married, yet?'

'Not married. I have been too busy. I've been at university. I am to teach languages. Already I have a position – in England. I start in six weeks. At a city school, in Birmingham.'

'But why England, Natasha?' To Keth, she would always be Natasha.

'Why not? There is a big world out there, and

sadly I have no one to please but myself. Why should I not go there?'

'But what will you teach?'

'French and Russian.'

'*Russian?*'

'Of course. There is great need for Russian in these uncertain times. And what else would I teach? Russian is my mother tongue.'

'Sorry. I forgot your parents – your adoptive parents – came from Moscow.' He wiped his bowl with the last of the bread, feeling less tense.

'Finished? Then you shall sit outside and I will make coffee. We have coffee, now. All we wish to buy.'

'Yes, but you once shared what little you had with me.'

'You do too much remembering! Here, take your glass. Finish your cognac. I will be out, soon.'

So Keth sat on the wooden bench, gazing up the path towards the gate that opened onto the lane, and remembered pruning bushes and digging over the garden, and all the time wondering when a package would arrive; *if* it would arrive. And who would bring it to Clissy.

'So!' Natasha laid a tray at their feet. 'I shall begin the night we went to the chateau – you and me and Denys.'

'When we went to wait for the plane from England. The jumps the chatelaine used to school her horses had all been removed, and you and Denys stuck torches in the ground to mark where the pilot should land.'

'I remember. And the army patrols were out, looking for the second man; the one who escaped when Hirondelle was taken. A pity, that. Had they not been near the chateau when the plane touched down, you would have been up and away and Denys and I heading for home.'

'I wasn't very proud of myself, leaving you there.'

'What else could you have done? We knew the pilot had very little time on the ground. What would you have done, then – risked capture and lost the package that was so important,' she shrugged, 'as well as a plane?'

'But what happened to you? What miracle happened?'

'The patrol – six or seven of them – left me lying there and went after Denys. They caught him, took a look at his identity papers, then went to his home. Sadly, Tante Clara was there, with Bernadette. They didn't have time to hide the transmitter. How do you say it – they were caught red-handed. I don't know why Tante Clara had gone to Bernadette's. Maybe to tell her that the plane had taken off – or maybe she had heard the firing.'

'But what happened to you, Natasha?'

'Ha! When the patrol ran down the paddock, I was hurried into the chateau without a word. Someone wrapped his jacket around my legs. I was hit in the leg, you see, and bleeding badly. They dare not leave a blood trail.'

'But I thought the people at the big house fraternized with the Nazis. Why should they help you?'

'Because really they were part of a cell – not ours – in the Resistance. Inviting the officers to the chateau for a meal, giving them wine and cognac, made them look like collaborators, but everyone at the chateau was loyal to France. As soon as the doctor could, he visited me, and took out the bullet. They said I was very ill – delirious – but they looked after me.'

'And where did you go, when you were well?'

'Certainly not to this house – it was watched for a long time, I was told. Then padlocks were put on the doors and shutters so no one could use it. I don't know what happened to the dogs. Maybe the soldiers took them. At least the Nazis were kind to animals. I didn't come back here until the Allies liberated the village. More coffee?' she asked matter-of-factly.

'Please.' Keth offered his cup. 'So you stayed at the chateau? For more than a year? How did you manage it?'

'It is a big house and they had many servants – or people who passed as servants. A lot of them were really in the Resistance. I know for certain that the head groom was one of them. I just joined in – as a servant. I helped in the house, helped with the grape harvest, earned my shelter and keep. No one remarked on my being there. As long as I never went into the village, I was safe enough.'

'And how soon did you know about Madame Piccard and Bernadette and Denys?'

'Not until I was well enough – when the fever had left me. They told me they had been taken away by the Gestapo – Hirondelle, too. I think they must have been very brave,' she whispered. 'They can't have informed on us, because we were left alone, in Clissy, after that.'

'How terrible for you, Natasha, and you just a child.'

'*Tiens!* Still I am a child! You forget, Hibou, that one of the last things Tante Clara said to me was that after that night, she would never call me child again. Sadly, she did not have the chance.'

'She was very brave. And so are you – and so alone. You have no family at all, now.'

'No one. Except perhaps my mother – my *natural* mother. I don't know what happened to her. She would have had a hard time during the occupation, if the Nazis had known she was Russian. I hope she got out – maybe to Spain or Switzerland. I have no way of knowing, since I never knew her name. Only that she was White Russian, and called Natasha. It was why I chose it for my codename.'

'I still can't believe it,' he said softly. 'And there is so much I want to know.'

'How long have you got? When must you go back?'

'I'd planned to get the ferry from St Malo tomorrow. I have a bed, in the village . . .'

'But why not stay here – for old times' sake? You can have your old one back, in the attic.'

'Are you sure? What might people think?'

'Keth-Hibou, this is the middle of the twentieth century! And anyway, who will know? Bernadette's house is empty, at the moment. A nephew from Paris inherited it, but rarely uses it.'

'Then if you don't mind . . .'

'Of course I do not mind. And in return, you shall take me to the village for a meal, tonight. There is an excellent restaurant; fish so fresh it was only landed this morning. We can eat, and talk, and maybe have a bottle of wine, yes?'

And Keth said it was fine by him, wondering how much of his paltry allowance the meal would use, all at once glad of the extra money Daisy had hidden in his luggage.

'Then hurry back to the *gîte* for your things whilst I make a fresh pot of coffee. As you say, we have so much to talk about. Your little girl; your wife. Now it is possible to ask questions, I want to know all about you.'

'And I about you, Hannah-Elise-Natasha,' he smiled. 'Six years to catch up on . . .'

'Where on earth have you been? I expected you yesterday.' Daisy lifted her mouth to be kissed.

'Just a day adrift, darling, and there's so much to tell!' He went to stand beside the pram where his daughter slept, cheeks flushed, eyelashes fanning her cheek. 'I've missed you both. Could do with a cup of tea.'

'You look quite pleased with yourself, Keth Purvis. Did everything go to plan?'

'Better, much better, than I'd ever hoped. I found Natasha. *Alive.*'

'But you thought – you were so sure,' Daisy whispered.

'Oh, it wasn't all good news, but she wasn't dead as I'd always thought. Someone was on the ball, though. They got her into the chateau without the soldiers knowing. She was very ill, but she made it.

She's coming to visit us – oh, and by the way, I stayed overnight at her place,' he grinned.

'Philanderer!' She took his face in her hands, and kissed him provocatively. 'Your French lady friend will be welcome. But come inside and I'll put the kettle on. And darling – I've missed you.'

'I've missed you too. And by the way, Mrs Purvis – I love you.'

'Do you like it, Drew?'

'Lyn, it's marvellous, and I know just where we'll hang it. Aunt Sutton's painting of Rowangarth – Mother took it with her to Bothy House, remember? This can hang in its place.'

'Look on the back. *Homecoming*, by William Benson. Remember you telling me that when you were away at sea, that view was what you always thought about, and coming home to it. And I know your last homecoming was a sad one, but that was in winter, wasn't it?'

'Yes. Christmas 'forty-five. I'd just got my demob . . .'

'That's why I asked Bill to paint an April homecoming; because that was when Rowangarth became my home, too.'

'Want to know something, Lady Sutton?' Drew bent to kiss the tip of her nose. 'You're a very nice girl.'

'Mm, I know,' Lyn said with exaggerated nonchalance. 'But let's get this hung over the fireplace, the hook is still there. Then I'll ring Daisy and Tatty, ask them all over to admire it – any excuse for a party.'

'Good idea. We might learn what Keth got up to in Brighton.'

'Up to? What on earth can you get up to at a teachers' conference?'

'I don't know, but he stayed an extra night, Daiz told me.'

'If we're meant to know we'll be told, so don't ask, Drew. In a place like Holdenby, that's how rumours start.' Lyn folded her arms and gazed at the watercolour of an old house with an April sky behind it, and everywhere spring-fresh. 'I must say, that for someone who specializes in florals, Bill's made a pretty good job of it. Rowangarth looks marvellous.'

'I know. Even the roof. Did he have to make it sag quite so much?'

'That roof has sagged ever since your mother can remember, so stop worrying about it and pour me a sherry, please.'

'Are you allowed alcohol, Lyn?'

'Tonight, I am!'

'I love you,' he said softly, 'but you know that, don't you?'

'Yes I do, sailor, but don't ever stop telling me, will you?'

'There's just one thing I don't understand, Keth.' They sat on the settee, shoulders touching. 'How, when you were so sure Natasha had been shot, did the people at the chateau manage to get her to safety?'

'A chance in a million, I'd say. But Natasha found out later that they were in the Resistance, too, but in a different set-up.'

'But didn't the soldiers look for her?'

'They did. They searched the chateau twice, but didn't find her. It seems there are a couple of tiny rooms there that few people know about. The doctor couldn't get to her, at first. He had no reason to go to the chateau and everyone in Clissy-sur-Mer was being watched. They eventually managed to get him there at two in the morning.'

'It sounds like a spy novel, doesn't it?'

'It was a spy novel, but for real. And before you tell me again that I was a fool for getting mixed up in it, remember it was my own choice. I wanted to get home to marry my girl.'

'Yes, and I'll tell you again that you should have sat pretty in Washington in your safe job. Taking risks like that!'

'You were worth it, sweetheart. And anyway, I didn't take any risks. I was taken there, looked after, then flown out.'

'Yes, but four people lost their lives getting you and that Enigma back to England. Was it worth it, Keth?'

'It isn't for me to say. I only know that once that Enigma was set up and working, losses in the Atlantic dropped dramatically. We sank a lot of U-boats, too, which made a nice change. But I'm home from my conference in Brighton and no one need know anything about Clissy. Forgotten – okay?'

'Fine by me, but tell me something? How, when I smell like a million dollars, will I tell people where you got the French perfume? And how, when Natasha comes to stay, will I explain her away, too?'

462

'The perfume was bought for me by a delegate who went on a day trip to France, and I've thought it all out about Natasha, too. She worked with me at Bletchley Park, during the war.'

'You're very quick on the uptake, Keth Purvis!'

'I can be very devious, when I set my mind to it. But it *was* all right, to ask her here?'

'Of course. I want to meet her – thank her. It might be nice if she came during one of the holidays. You've got her address?'

'Got the name of the school she's going to teach at, and the address of the digs they've found for her, outside Birmingham. She promised to write, as soon as she arrives there.'

'So. All's well that ends well. Kiss me, Keth?'

'With the greatest pleasure,' he said huskily. 'And you owe me for the perfume but I'll take it in kind, if that's all right with you?'

And Daisy said it was, and snuggled closer, then said, 'Damn and blast!' when the phone rang.

'That was Lyn,' Keth said on his return, 'and your daughter is crying, Mrs Purvis.'

'Mm. She might as well have her ten o'clock feed now. What did Lyn want?'

'Drinks at Rowangarth tomorrow night, to celebrate the watercolour Bill painted. I'll ask Mum if she'll baby-sit. Go and pick Mary up, love. I'll make her a bottle.'

'No, Keth. *I'll* make the feed, *you* see to her. And her nappy'll need changing.'

'Back to the old routine,' he called over his shoulder as he hurried upstairs. Then he looked at his daughter and thought about where he had been these last few days, and that the old routine wasn't all that bad, come to think of it.

August 5 1949, and Mary Natasha Purvis a year old. Celebrations lasted all day long, with birthday cards at breakfast and presents and visits from half of Holdenby, or so it seemed to Daisy.

Granny Alice was the first to arrive, with a birthday sponge, decorated with white icing, a pink candle and scattered with dolly mixtures.

'I've made her a birthday dress, too,' Alice confided. 'She can wear it tonight, when her dad comes home from school. A little buttercup print and two pairs of matching knickers – and before you say it! – yes, big enough to go over her nappies.'

Then Great-Aunt Julia arrived with a savings bond for ten pounds and, when the little girl had got thoroughly excited and Daisy feared she would burst into tears, there was a knock on the back door.

'Go answer it,' Alice urged. 'I know who it is . . .'

So Daisy opened the door to a smiling Tom and a fat Labrador puppy.

'Where's my birthday girl, then?' Tom grinned. 'Come and say hullo to Bethan of Windrush, eh?'

Daisy lowered the child to the floor; the puppy, whose fat stomach wobbled from side to side as it scrambled to greet her, licked her face. Mary Natasha laughed with delight and landed Bethan a slap.

'No, Mary, no!' Daisy scolded. 'Poor little puppy.'

'Oh, don't be bothering,' Tom laughed. 'Beth'll soon learn to get out of the baby's way. They'll grow up grand together. A little lass should have a dog of her own. And any road, it'll grow quicker'n she will. You'll soon be able to hold your own, won't you, little pup?'

He bent to stroke her, then she ran into the kitchen, skidding to a halt on the tiled floor against the table leg. Mary, on all fours, followed, and Bethan licked her face in approval. Mary chuckled and closed her eyes as the licking became more frantic.

'Er – should that be allowed?' Julia murmured.

'Of course,' Alice chuckled. 'You should know as well as I do, Julia, that puppy spittle won't harm her. Clean as clean, it is.'

'Well, Daisy, how are you feeling, then? Proud, I'll be bound.'

'Yes, and much less tired and weary than I was a year ago, Dada. You'll be coming tonight, Aunt Julia? Just a little celebration for the grown-ups, when Mary is in bed.'

'Sorry. Got a previous engagement. Dinner, tonight, with Nathan's bishop. He's retiring, too.'

'Never mind. I'll save you a piece of cake. Mum and Dada can't make it, either, but Tatty and Bill and Lyn and Drew are coming. I've got champagne on the cellar floor, cooling. Oh, isn't this nice, and had you thought that on Mary Natasha's next birthday, there'll be two more babies around?'

'Aye, and that pup'll be almost fully grown,' Tom said. 'A little beauty, if I says it as shouldn't.' He fished into the large pocket of his keeping jacket. 'Now here's her collar and lead. She'll walk nicely for you, on it, though she doesn't always come to heel when she should. And here's a list of what she should be eating for the next few weeks. Only one meat meal a day, and don't give her butcher's bones to chew on, unless you've well-boiled them.'

'Dada! I know what to give her! I've walked more pups than most people! Don't worry. Beth will be well looked after. And thanks. She's a little beauty. It'll be nice having a dog in the house again.'

'Aye – well. And that dog is a bitch, don't forget.' Tom Dwerryhouse was very particular about gender. 'An' I'll be off.' He bent to kiss Mary and tickle Beth, then left without another word.

'Take no notice,' Alice smiled. 'He never likes parting with a pup, even to his own granddaughter, and I think it's just got to him – being a grandfather for a year, I mean. Sentimental old softie! And sorry we won't be with you tonight, Daisy love. Polly and I are going to Creesby, to the pictures. A granny celebration, sort of. Walk with me to Keeper's, Julia?'

It was all too much, Daisy thought when she and Mary Natasha – and Beth – were alone. There wouldn't be a lot of work done today. She took the drinking bowl her father had left on the table and filled it at the tap, putting it down at the back door. Then tucking Beth under her arm, and carrying Mary on her hip, they went to sit on the doorstep.

Tears pricked her eyes, but if a girl couldn't have a little happy weep on her daughter's first birthday, then when could she?

'Oh, Mary Natasha Purvis, your mummy is so lucky,' she sniffed. She really was. Everything that any right-minded woman could want, Daisy Purvis had in abundance. It made her think about Clissy-sur-Mer, and Natasha, so alone in the world. Given away as a baby, her adoptive parents sent to a death camp and the woman who befriended her dead, too.

They had heard a lot, when the war was over, about the agents – a lot of them women – who had been sent into occupied Europe. Many were captured, few had survived, and a grateful country posthumously decorated them for their bravery. Medals for dead heroines. Ironic, really.

Keth knew about such things. Keth had been lucky, yet he still insisted that no one should know about what had happened in Clissy-sur-Mer, and still she couldn't think why it should be so. The war was over now. Everyone knew about Enigma and Bletchley Park, and safe houses where agents were trained, so why was Keth so touchy about it?

Was it because he had left a safe posting in the war, volunteering to go into danger in order to get back home? Was it because people would think him a fool to have done so, or was his part in that secret, underground war so small that he felt embarrassed even to mention it? Or was it because people had died, helping him to freedom, and he was ashamed?

She closed her eyes, shaking such thoughts out of her head, and when she opened them she yelled, 'Oh, *no*!'

The puppy was sniffing its way to the open gate and Mary Natasha on all fours, following it across the grass. Now she not only had a baby who crawled with the speed of lightning, who opened cupboard doors, broke ornaments and found the coal bucket irresistible, but a puppy, too, who seemed determined to find its way back to Keeper's Cottage, leaving a trail of puddles behind it!

She scooped them up, scolding and laughing, and for just a little while Clissy-sur-Mer was pushed to the back of her mind, and only today and the joy of Mary's first birthday mattered.

'So how has the first year been, Daisy?' Tatiana wanted to know. 'Frantic, was it?'

'She's been worth every sleepless night. I can recommend motherhood.'

'Can't wait.' Complacently, Tatiana patted her abdomen. 'Eleven weeks to go. I think it's a boy,' she smiled.

'What makes you think that?' Daisy offered birthday cake.

'No reason at all – except that when it kicks, it's like it's wearing football boots. Mother warned me it would get worse. Mother wanted a boy, but she got me. My father wasn't best pleased.'

'How do you know?' Carefully Bill picked the dolly mixtures from his slice of cake, giving them to her. 'Any bairn of ours is welcome and wanted, and I'll not mind if it's a girl!'

'So what will you call her?'

'I haven't made up my mind, yet, but I'm almost sure it won't be anything Russian. I choose for a girl, by the way; Bill chooses if it's a boy.'

'Aye. His name's decided on already, but not even Tatty knows. But what made you choose a Russian name for your wee girl, Keth? Might prove a bit awkward, these days – especially as Stalin seems set on making trouble in Europe.'

'It was a name we both liked,' Keth said shortly, and then, because it mattered so much he said, 'Anyway, Bill, your wife has a Russian name and your mother-in-law, too.'

'Only joking,' Bill grinned. 'Have you decided yet, Drew, on a name for your wee one?'

'Afraid not. We're only now getting used to Lyn being pregnant. But like you two, I shall choose if we have a son and Lyn will choose if it's a girl. Bas and Gracie didn't have family names for their two, and I don't suppose we will, either. And this cake is good, Daiz. I suppose Lady made it.'

'She did. Not so fussy these days about the odd spot of black market dealing. She says she doesn't care and it's the government's fault for not doing away with food rationing. Keth said that in France, they eat a lot better than we do; food isn't such a problem, there.' She stopped, horrified and wide-eyed. 'What I mean is –'

'What she means,' Keth said without so much as a blush, 'is that you can get Chanel perfume in France. Some of the delegates' wives did a day trip over, and brought all sorts of things back with them.'

'Perfume?' Tatty gasped. 'Chanel? Keth got some for you?'

'He asked one of the ladies to try to get some for me. Remind me to let you both have a sniff, next time you're here,' Daisy said shakily, relieved that Keth's quick thinking had saved her making an awful blunder. 'And you'll never guess what Mary did, tonight? She wanted to take the pup to bed with her. Flatly refused to have Teddy Wilf in her cot! Anyone else for more tea? Cake?'

And Lyn said she would love more cake – and wasn't it that nice that pregnancy was the perfect excuse for being a pig?

And Daisy smiled, and cut another slice, and told herself sternly to be more careful in the future.

'I'm sorry about tonight,' Daisy said as they undressed for bed. 'Me and my big mouth – nearly let the cat out of the bag, didn't I?'

''S all right, darling. We got away with it – this time.'

'Meaning there better hadn't be a next time? Keth – does it really matter about you going to Clissy? The war has been over four years, and there's often articles in the paper and on the wireless about secret agents going to occupied Europe in the war. Why must you be so cagey about it? And anyway, Natasha wasn't dead after all. Why the secrecy?'

'Because I was told not to say anything – ever. Look, love – for all I know, Castle McLeish and the Stone House in Argyll might still be hush-hush places. Okay – so the war is over, but like Bill said, the Russians are making trouble all over Europe. There might be all sorts of things going on that we don't know about. And as for Natasha not being dead – it turned out that three people I knew *were* killed. There's still a mystery over Bletchley Park, too. Do you know that as soon as war ended, everything they could lay hands on was thrown on bonfires – orders from very high up. I know that for a fact.'

'You're right, I suppose.' Daisy turned back the quilt, then got into bed. 'And if it were all to come out now, your mother and Mam and Dada would feel a bit put out, not being told.'

'That would only be the half of it, Daisy love. Only Nathan Sutton and you and I know. Let's leave it that way, uh?'

'Fine by me. But don't forget that Natasha knows, too, and that she's coming here, probably at half term, in October.'

'Natasha? Her name is Hannah Kominski, now, though it's going to take a bit of remembering. But she knows better than most how to watch what she says. And shift over, woman! You're in my half!'

'I love you,' she whispered, reaching to turn out the light, searching for his lips in the darkness.

'How much?' he asked huskily.

'A baby daughter and a bottle of Chanel,' she said softly, kissing him again, wondering why their marriage seemed still new and every bit as marvellous as it was on an April day, six years ago. Wondering, yet not knowing why. Not really caring, either, but thankful beyond telling, for all that.

TWENTY-TWO

No one thought that October 'forty-nine would be such an extraordinary month; not Tatiana Benson nor Lyndis Sutton, nor Keth and Daisy Purvis, who were all to have reason to remember the tenth month of that year; but Hannah Kominski, too. Especially Hannah.

It all began with Keth and Daisy awaiting the arrival of the Birmingham train.

'I must remember to call her Hannah.' Daisy's cheeks were pink with pleasure.

'Me too.' Keth remembered the undisguised joy with which their invitation had been accepted.

. . . It will be good, when everyone is talking about where they will be spending half term that I, too, will be spending it with friends . . .

'I feel a bit choked,' Daisy had said. 'Friends. She deserves friends, after all she's been through. So much trauma, and she so young. How old, exactly, do you know?'

472

'She's seven years younger than you, give or take a month. Your birthday is in June; hers is July. When I was first at Clissy, she said she was sixteen and three months. The three months was important. That makes her –'

'Twenty-two. And beautiful, didn't you say?'

'She is. *Very* beautiful if you're partial to brunettes.'

'Then we'll take good care of her – keep the wolves away – and make her very welcome,' Daisy laughed, sure in her husband's love. 'And ssssh! Listen . . .'

But the voice of the station announcer was lost in the noise of the arriving train; Hannah's train, from Birmingham.

Windows were let down, hands reached out to open doors. They were standing near the ticket barrier so they should not miss her. And no one would miss her, Daisy thought; not even on a crowded platform in busy York station.

She was wearing a grey suit and was hatless and she walked like a mannequin, slim and tall and straight.

'Hannah!' they called in unison, and she raised a black-gloved hand and hurried towards them.

'Keth, *mon ami*!' She was in his arms, kissing his cheeks, right and left – the way, Daisy supposed, they did it in France.

'Hannah – my wife, Daisy.'

Smiling, Keth introduced them and was glad they hugged each other, then kissed, and that Daisy laughed with pleasure when Hannah said, 'You are more beautiful than your photograph, Mrs Purvis.'

'The christening photo,' Keth supplied.

'Of course, and thank you, Hannah. But will you call me Daisy?'

It was going to be all right, Keth thought as he hurried to where his car was parked. There had been instant liking, he knew it at once, and he had left them chatting at the station entrance. They were still chatting when he drew up beside them.

'You sit in the front, Hannah.' Daisy tilted the front seat forward and wriggled into the back of the car. 'You and Keth will have a lot to talk about.'

'Not really. I think we said it all when Hibou – when *Keth* – arrived at Clissy in August. We talked and talked, then. Nothing is new, except that the nephew of Denys and Bernadette no longer wanted their house. He has sold it, and the new owners are busy making it good. It stood empty for three years, almost, and needed many repairs. The young couple have a child and now that the weather is getting cold, they asked if they might rent my own house until theirs is ready – by Christmas, they hope.'

'That's good. They'll keep it aired for you, Hannah. But if they aren't able to move out in time, where will you go for the Christmas holidays?'

'I have already thought. I shall go to London or to Edinburgh – treat myself. I have heard much about Edinburgh and bagpipes and kilts and tartans. I will be fine.'

'Look – there is the Minster.' Keth pointed to the right. 'You must see it before you go back to Birmingham. We'll leave Mary Natasha with one of the grannies – and make a day of it.'

'I should like that – and to see the old city. One

of my colleagues told me I must not miss it.'

She turned in her seat to smile at Daisy, who smiled back and thought of the week ahead, and how she had borrowed rugs and an armchair from Rowangarth to make Hannah's bedroom more comfortable; thought how delighted she would be to meet Mary Natasha, her namesake. And she knew with absolute certainty that she and Keth and Mary must be Hannah's family, for there was no one Daisy knew of who was so alone in the world, yet who seemed so happy, in spite of it. From now on, they would draw her to them and she would be an honorary member of the Clan as Bill and Gracie and Lyn were. Daisy Purvis, above all, owed that to Hannah Kominski.

'Tomorrow, when you have settled in, Hannah, the Clan will be coming to meet you.'

'*Clan*, Daisy?'

'The gang Keth and I grew up with. We've been together since ever I can remember. There's Drew and his wife Lyndis – she's having a baby – and Bill and Tatty – she's having a baby, too – and Bas and Gracie, though they won't be coming. They live in Kentucky, now, and have two babies – Adam and Nell. They come over, though, quite regularly.'

'So many babies? I must be careful not to catch one,' Hannah laughed.

'There's a rash of babies in this country,' Keth supplied. 'Couples separated by the war are making up for lost time. We call it the baby boom. Tatty's is due in about a week.'

'Tatty? It is an unusual name . . .'

'Short for Tatiana. It's Russian.'

'Indeed it is. Once, there was a Grand Duchess called Tatiana. My mother told me about her.'

'But of course – you came from Russia, Keth said.'

'No, Daisy. My parents came from Moscow. They left, because of the Revolution. My mother was a milliner, my father was a musician, but they are not my blood parents.'

'Do you remember them, Hannah?'

'I remember a lot. I remember our apartment in Paris and going to the synagogue. I was almost twelve years old, you see, when my parents took me to Tante Clara's house, at Clissy. Already the Nazi party was making trouble for Jews in Germany and they feared for my safety, if war broke out.'

'And it did . . .' Daisy prompted gently.

'Yes. Soon the Nazis were marching through Paris, and my father and mother knew they had done the right thing in getting me false papers and sending me away. The last letter I had from them was on my fifteenth birthday. They were good people . . .'

'I'm so sorry,' Daisy whispered. 'And I haven't thanked you properly for helping Keth get out of France, that night the plane came for him. But I do know that if it hadn't been for you, he and I would never have married, nor had Mary.

'There are no words to thank you enough, but I want you to promise, Hannah, that you will look on Keth and me as close friends, and come to see us as often as you want to. Say you will?'

'I would like that very much. And perhaps we will write letters?'

'Of course we will,' Keth beamed, 'and ring each

other up. There's just one thing I must tell you, Hannah. I told no one that I had been sent to France, to Clissy, during the war. I think it's better no one knows, because I still might be breaking the Official Secrets Act, if I do.

'So would you mind if I introduce you as someone I worked with, in the war? People round here know I was in something to do with signals at Bletchley Park – at least, that's what I told them – so could you have worked there, too?'

'*Mais oui!* And the place was so secret that you and I cannot talk about it, eh?' She smiled mischievously. 'And what did I do at your Bletchley Park, Hibou?'

'You – er – you decoded signals – okay? That's all you need tell them if they get nosy.'

'I think I am going to enjoy telling so many fibs,' she giggled.

And in that moment, she was a young girl of sixteen and three months again, and Keth knew that he and Daisy would never allow her to be alone in the world again.

'I'm glad you have come to Foxgloves, Hannah-Elise-Natasha,' he said softly.

'Now – are you sure you'll be all right, Lyn?' Ewart Pryce asked. 'Why don't you let me ring Drew and get him to pick you up?'

'No. I'm fine, thanks. Just fine.'

'I still think –'

'No, Ewart. I'll tell him. And I'll take it easy – truly I will!'

She was out of the surgery door and was opening the front gate before Holdenby's doctor could call, 'Careful, Lyn!'

At Daisy's house, Lyn hesitated, then hurried on. Drew was going out at eleven – the first shoot of the season, and he liked always to be there. If she hurried . . .

She pushed back the iron gate at the end of the Linden Walk, easing through carefully. Another month and she would be too big to use the kissing gate any more.

She caught up with Drew, shotgun over his arm, on the front steps.

'Oooh!' she puffed. 'Thought I was going to miss you!'

'What is it?' She was flush-cheeked and gasping. 'You've been running, Lyn. Why? Come inside?'

'No, darling.' She took a deep, steadying breath. 'Just hurrying. No one can run with this great lump to contend with!' Carefully she lowered herself onto the top step. 'But do you know something, Sir Andrew – your wife is having twins!'

'*Whaat!*' He was on his knees beside her. '*Twins?* Are you sure?'

'Ewart said I am – and it makes sense.' She held out a hand. 'Help me up, there's a love? My bottom's cold. And don't look so horrified.'

'I'm not. It's just that I can't believe it. *Two*. How on earth will we manage?'

'The same way most people with twins manage, I suppose. Drew – you *are* pleased?'

'Y-yes. Now that it's beginning to sink in, I'm

pleased. But you're being very matter-of-fact about it, Lyn.'

'That's because I've had time to get used to it. I've thought for a long time that I might be. For one thing, I'm not quite six months, but I'm as big as Tatty is, and she's due any day now. And for another, had you forgotten – my mother is a twin.'

'Lordy, yes! Look, Lyn. Go and take the weight off your feet whilst I ring Tom, tell him I won't be there.'

'No! This is the first shoot of the season and you've got to be there! And besides, you know they'll expect you to put in an appearance. Just call in at Bothy House and tell them, and ask your mother to tell Daisy's mother, will you? I'll ring Daisy, then nip down to the kitchen, and tell Mary Stubbs and Tilda. Should be worth a cup of tea – and a cherry scone. So *go*, please!'

'Then why don't you ask Daisy to pop over?'

'Because she's got a house guest and anyway, your mother'll be over like a shot, once you've told her. Now get yourself down to Keeper's Cottage, for goodness' sake. You're holding things up. And by the way, isn't twins worth a kiss?'

And he laughed and took her very gently in his arms, and kissed her twice, then said, 'Ewart *was* sure, Lyn?'

'I reckon he knows what he's doing. Besides, he could hear two heartbeats. He says next time I'm in the surgery – and when I'm a little less excited – he'll let me listen to them.' She held open the door, 'Out! I've got things to do. Can't wait to ring Purvis. 'Bye, sailor. See you!'

She closed the door behind him and flopped down on the bottom step of the staircase, smiling, wondering why her eyes were filling with tears, and why anyone should dare to be so happy. Then she sniffed inelegantly, picked up the phone and said, 'Hullo, Winnie. Can you get me Foxgloves, please?'

They heard the back door bang, then Julia calling, 'Cooee. Lyn . . .'

'That's Miss Julia.' Mary Stubbs took another cup and saucer from the kitchen dresser. 'Hasn't taken her long to get over here.'

'In the kitchen, Mother,' Lyn called.

'You'll have a cup of tea?' Tilda asked. 'I've just mashed a pot.'

'Tea!' Julia gasped. 'Champagne, more like.' Laughing, she gathered Lyn into her arms. 'Two! What a clever girl you are!'

'Remind me of that when we're pacing the floor, nights! And Tilda must have known – she's just taken a batch of scones from the oven.'

'Sit you down, Miss Julia.' Mary Stubbs pulled out a chair. 'My, but I wouldn't like to count the times you've sat at this table, over the years.'

'Yes. Good times and not so good times. But it's a cherry scone day today, so here's to my grandchildren.' She lifted her cup. 'And what do you want, Lyn? Boys? Girls – or one of each?'

'One of each would be lovely, but I'll be happy with what the good Lord sends.'

'That's the right attitude to take, Lady Lyn,' Mary said smugly. 'Two healthy babies will be just the ticket.'

'And what will you do about a pram, milady?' asked Tilda, ever practical. 'Well, it's hard enough coming by prams at the best of times.'

'I got my name on three lists,' Lyn said ruefully. 'Thought I'd hit lucky with one of them. Now I'll have to change it to a twin pram. Wonder how long I'll have to wait?'

'Wouldn't worry, if I were you.' Julia selected a scone. 'One will turn up, and there's always Hilary Reid at the vicarage. She had *two* sets of twins, don't forget. I'm sure she'll loan you her pram till you get one of your own.'

'Then let's hope she hasn't got rid of it,' said Mary Stubbs tartly.

'She won't have,' Julia said. 'Bet you a pound to a penny it's there in the attic, Lyn. I might pop over and see her, later. It's all right, is it, for me to tell people? And what did Blodwen say when you told her?'

'I rang, but Winnie said there was no reply. Shouldn't wonder if they aren't out for the day. She'll be pleased, though.'

'Of course she will. And Hilary once told me that twins aren't a lot more trouble than singles – that's once they're past the crying stage and the six o'clock colic. They amuse each other, she says. Shall you consider a nanny now, Lyn?'

'Not if I can help it! But everything has happened so suddenly. Last year about this time, Drew had only just asked me to marry him – after Mary Natasha's christening, actually – yet now I'm only a few months away from *two* children. How lucky can you get?'

'Luck don't come into it,' Mary Stubbs sniffed. 'I

am of the firm opinion that you get what you deserve, Lady Lyn. And you and Sir Andrew are the right people to be having bairns, if you'll pardon the familiarity. Bairns born to Rowangarth are twice blessed.'

'So they are,' Tilda nodded in rare agreement. 'Now why don't you have another scone, milady? Don't forget you're eating for three, now. And that's the phone!'

Mary rose quickly to her feet, because after all it was her job to answer phones. And answering phones this morning was very interesting!

'Pound to a penny it'll be Alice Dwerryhouse,' Tilda grinned. 'Better put the kettle on, make a fresh pot. She'll be coming round, I shouldn't wonder.'

And Lyn smiled, and thought how special it was to be sitting in Rowangarth kitchen, eating cherry scones and drinking tea and feeling very smug about life in general and her two babies – *two*, mark you – in particular.

Lord, this is Lyn Sutton. She sent up a silent prayer. *Thank you with all my heart, but no more good luck for me, if you don't mind, or I'll take off like a big fat rocket and disappear forever – and that would never do!*

'That was Alice. She's coming round now the shooting party has moved off. I told her you were here, Miss Julia. Hope I did right?'

'Of course you did. And get another cup and saucer, Mary. Having twins in the family is very serious business. Mind, in the old days, there'd have been a snifter of cooking brandy in the tea, but best not, eh, Lyn? And here she is!'

482

'Well, now! And who's a clever girl, then?' Soundly Alice kissed Lyn's cheek. 'And Drew was so delighted telling all the guns about it, that everything got a bit disorganized, and they've only now got themselves off! And before I forget, Lyn – there's the matter of a christening gown.

'I know you'll want to use Drew's – tradition – but you'll be needing two now, so how about me making one for you? We can have a chat later about how you'd like it to be. Maybe I could make one to match Drew's, or maybe I could do a real bobby-dazzler, like Mary Natasha had. And all hand sewn, mind.'

'Mrs D, you're an angel, if you're sure it won't make a lot of work for you?'

'Nonsense. And now that knitting wool isn't rationed any more, I'll do you three more first-size vests and one or two pairs of bootees, an' all. You'll have to be thinking about another layette, don't forget.'

'Lordy, yes! I hadn't thought! I'm in such a tizzy that I haven't got around to thinking about more baby clothes.' Her eyes filled with tears. 'And will you tell me why everyone is being so marvellous? I'm quite full up.'

'There, there, milady.' Gently Tilda dabbed Lyn's eyes. 'Don't you get upset, none. Being marvellous comes easy where babies are concerned.'

'Sorry,' Lyn sniffed. 'I'm a bit emotional. Such a lovely surprise you see.' She forced a smile.

And lovely to be sitting in Rowangarth kitchen, she thought tremulously, being accepted as she had so longed to be, and never thought she would.

'Surprise? Bet Drew is still in shock,' Alice said wryly. 'He'll be missing a few birds, this morning.'

'Poor Drew. Here's me being made a fuss of, guzzling scones and loving every minute of it, and Drew will be thinking, *two*, for Pete's sake! How are we going to cope with *two*?' Lyn said softly, tears gone.

'Well, that's what you'll have to talk about later, when you've both come down to earth again. And I've just thought,' Julia laughed with delight. 'Nathan doesn't know, yet. Poor old love. First it was wedding talk, then baby talk and now, it's going to be *twins* talk! He'll be leaving home!'

'Aye, and Tom Dwerryhouse'll be going with him! Come to think of it, he had a glazed look about him when Drew arrived at Keeper's with the news,' Alice grinned wickedly. 'And don't fret none, Lyn. You'll have plenty of willing helpers. Me and Julia, for a start.'

'And you can rely on the staff, milady,' Tilda said primly. 'Us two are pleased as can be.'

'Just ask.' Twice in the space of an hour, Mary Stubbs and Tilda were in agreement. 'Any time. Day or night.'

'We just might hold you to that.' Lyn got to her feet, hands in the small of her back. 'I believe Drew cried a lot as a baby, Mother.'

'He did. Alice was very ill, had no milk for him. He couldn't keep cow's milk down. Threw back every feed.'

'But fair play, Miss Julia. He was as good as gold,

a little angel, once he took to goat's milk,' Tilda defended.

'*Goat's* milk?' Lyn gasped.

'Yes, and it's Jinny Dobb we have to thank for suggesting it,' Alice nodded. 'The poor little mite was beside himself with hunger. But all this baby talk is getting you flummoxed, Lyn. Why don't you put your feet up for half an hour?'

And Lyn agreed, looking down at her swollen abdomen, wondering how much bigger she could possibly get.

'Reckon I might just do that, Mrs D. It's sunny, this morning. It'll be warm in the conservatory.' At the kitchen door she turned. 'And thanks, everybody, for being so marvellous and thanks, Tilda and Mary, for having me.'

'She's learning,' Julia smiled as slow footsteps took the wooden stairs. 'She's going to be just fine for Rowangarth.'

But Lyndis Sutton, euphoria spent, wondered for the first time how she would cope with two babies. Lowering herself into the sturdiest chair in the conservatory, she wished Drew could be beside her this very minute, telling her that of course it would be all right and of course they would cope.

Nor did it end there. Someone else had to know. Kitty, too, had the right.

Lyn closed her eyes. Tomorrow, it would have to be, when she was calmer. Tomorrow, she would go to the churchyard.

She hoped Kitty would be glad for her.

* * *

'Ewart!' Anna Pryce flung open the kitchen door, then made for a chair. 'I – I think I'm going out of my mind!' Her face was pale, her eyes too bright.

'Darling – what is it?'

'I saw her. Was shutting the garden gate behind me, and there she was, pushing the pram.'

'*Whose* pram?'

'Daisy's. Who else down this lane has a pram? Daisy, next door I'm talking about!'

'All right. All right.' Ewart made little shushing sounds. 'Was the baby in the pram?'

'Of course she was. And I know they've got a house guest at Foxgloves and it was probably her I saw. But it was such a shock!'

'So tell me, Anna?' He took his wife's hands in his and was dismayed to find they were shaking. 'The young lady is called Hannah, I believe. Keth knew her in the war. They worked together at some signals place down south.'

'No, Ewart. No! She couldn't have. Not the woman I saw. She looked too young to have worked anywhere in the war. It was frightening. So like her . . .'

'Tell me – so like *who*?' He spoke softly, gently, as if to a frightened child.

'Her walk, Ewart. *She* used to walk like that. Straight-backed, and proud, like a ballerina. And her hair was the same, and her eyes.'

'*She?*' he coaxed.

'She came to London with us when we had to get out of Russia. She was the daughter of our sewing woman. She'd called at our house with a dress that had needed altering. She shouldn't have been out alone. Not with men behaving like animals in the streets. Mother told Igor to see her safely home, but when they got there, there was no trace of her parents and rioters were looting their house.'

'This was in the uprising, in nineteen seventeen?'

'Of course!' She began to pace the floor. 'Igor brought her back to us. He couldn't have left her alone. They were setting fire to houses, the Bolsheviks, I mean. We waited until it was quieter, then we all went to the farm at Peterhof – for safety, you'll understand – and we had to take her with us. She stayed with us, just as Karl did.'

'You're talking about the – the servant in black, Anna?'

'I'm talking about Natasha Yurovska. It was him, Elliot, who called her the servant in black.'

'And you think you saw her – saw someone like her – at the gate?'

'I think I saw what might well have been one of Elliot's sins coming home to roost. Mother of God! All those years ago, and still he won't die!'

'Your husband – your *first* husband – is dead, Anna. He's been dead a long time. You are my wife, now, and I love you very much.' He laid an arm around her shoulders. 'Come on – sit down. Try to tell me why you are so upset?'

'I – I'm upset because – because –' She took a deep, shuddering breath. 'Because I have just seen someone who is the living image of Natasha Yurovska.'

'The one you told me about – the one Elliot . . .'

'The woman he seduced – or raped – when I was eight months gone with his child. I heard them. In

487

her room, they were. I think I went mad, that night. I could have killed him – wanted to!'

'That was the night you lost your son?' he asked, gently.

'The night I behaved like a hoyden and hit him and scratched him – went into premature labour. And yes, I lost my son.'

'But sweetheart – what makes you think Natasha Yurovska had Elliot's child, and that that child is staying next door? Is it feasible?'

'Natasha told me she was pregnant, and that it could only have been his. He had forced himself on her, she said, and I believed her. She went back to London with my mother, and I was never told what happened to her, or the baby. They sent her somewhere to have it, but not even Igor knows where.

'But if you don't believe me, Ewart, why don't you speak to Nathan, and Julia? They both knew Natasha Yurovska, would remember what she looked like. And I told Nathan – as a priest – about it all. I had the death of my son on my conscience, you see. In my rage, I killed him. I felt the need to be given absolution.

'Nathan comforted me; told me he had baptized the child and given him a Christian burial. He called him Nicholas, for Tzar Nicholas, who was murdered by the Bolsheviks. You've seen his tiny stone, in the churchyard.'

'Yes, darling, I have. But tell me why, in this whole wide world, the child of Elliot Sutton's infidelity should be staying next door? Surely the odds against that happening are colossal?'

'I can only tell you what I saw, Ewart, and it was like I was staring into my past; looking into Natasha Yurovska's eyes.'

'Then hadn't we better talk to Nathan and Julia about it? Perhaps they can find out how old the young woman is next door. Because if they can, then maybe it would help prove – or disprove – your fears. Can you remember when it all happened, and when the child would have been born?'

'Yes, I can. I worked it all out. After Elliot was killed, I wondered if somewhere he had a son he would never know about. I remember thinking that the child would be born about June or July in –' She closed her eyes, frowning, counting back. 'In nineteen twenty-seven, it would be. That child would be twenty-two or twenty-three, now.'

'And the young woman you've just seen, Anna . . .'

'Is about that age,' she whispered reluctantly.

'Then do you think I could have a quiet word with Keth, see what I can find out? He seemed quite open about it. Told me last week that someone he'd known in the war was coming to stay with them. Said she teaches in Birmingham, actually. I'm sure Keth would be discreet.'

'No, Ewart! It's Nathan we must talk to, and Julia. They know about it. Julia hated Elliot, too!'

'All right, Anna. I have a good excuse to ring Bothy House. Congratulations are in order. Lyndis is carrying twins. I know I shouldn't tell anyone outside the surgery, but they would expect me to tell you. After all, Nathan was your brother-in-law, once.'

'Twins? Was she pleased?' A small smile gentled her lips.

'She most certainly was – or will be, when it sinks in. So shall I ring Julia – ask if we can pop over after supper? Or better still, if they can come over here for a drink – celebration, sort of?'

'It would be better if they came here, Ewart. Maybe then we might see the young woman next door. Daisy might even bring her round, to introduce her. Sneaky, I know, but if Julia and Nathan could see her, just the once as I did, then I know they would think as I do; that the girl Hannah could be Natasha Yurovska's – and Elliot's.'

'Yes, but before we do anything; before we jump in with both feet, *if* what you think is true, *if*, against all the odds, Elliot Sutton is her father, then do you realize that she and Tatiana are –'

'Sisters. *Half*-sisters, anyway.' Anna covered her face with her hands. 'No, Ewart, I hadn't thought. But now that you've reminded me, I don't think it wise that Tatiana should know. The shock in her condition, and the baby due any day. She mustn't find out – ever.'

'No, Anna. Tatty might have a half-sister and it is right she should know. But not yet. Let's wait till she's safely delivered, eh? And anyway, it may be that you've got it wrong. As far as I'm concerned,' he comforted, 'it's too much of a coincidence.'

'I hope you're right.' She had to force the smile to her lips, because she was still shaking inside. 'And there's the phone, drat it!'

'I'll get it. You put the kettle on, Anna love.' Most

490

times, he thought wryly, their phone rang on medical matters and he hoped it was so, tonight. 'Doctor Pryce,' he said into the receiver.

'Oh, Ewart. Thank goodness!'

'Hullo, Tatiana. How are you?'

'We-e-ll, since you ask, Doctor . . .'

'Something happening, lovely girl?'

'I don't know. Maybe not, but I've had niggles in my back, and what worries me is that the baby hasn't kicked for ages.'

'Mm. Probably having a little rest, before it starts. Want me to pop over?'

'No thanks, Ewart. Probably my own fault, anyway. I've been on the go all day – got myself tired, I expect.'

'That often happens, too. Mother Nature's instinct to clean the nest, sort of. I suppose you've been doing housework?'

'Yes. But don't come over, thanks all the same. Just tell Mother, will you?'

'I'll tell her. She's making a cup of tea. So take a few deep breaths, put your feet up, and ask Bill to do the same for you. And I'll give Sister Fletcher a ring – just in case,' he added hastily. ''Bye, now, and don't worry!'

'That was Tatiana, wasn't it?' Anna stood in the doorway.

'Yes. I think she might be starting.'

'Oh, my goodness! I must go to her!'

'You'll do no such thing! You'll have a cup of tea and then I'll run you over. Or better still, I think you should walk there. If the two of us arrive like the cavalry, it might bother her a bit.'

'But you said –'

'Anna Pryce! You've had babies of your own . . .'

'Yes. It might be a false alarm. After all, it isn't due for a couple of days.'

'Then you'll know that a baby – a first baby especially – arrives when it's good and ready and not when the physician calculates it should. Anyway, what's two days – either way?

'So have that tea, powder your nose, then arrive there as unconcerned as you're able. It's Tatty's first time, remember. She could well be a bit apprehensive and she'll want you with her. And see that Bill has a cup of tea, and something in it! He'll probably be every bit as bothered. It's his first, too.'

'You're right, darling. You usually are.'

'Of course I am! So get yourself over to Denniston and this time tomorrow, you just might find you're a grandmother!'

'So you really think it's happening?' Anna took a deep breath, letting it out slowly, feeling all at once calm.

'I think so. But it'll be a few hours, yet.'

'I know! Like you said. I've had babies of my own. So pour me that tea, there's a dear man.'

Children of her own, she frowned. Four pregnancies in a little over five years; two miscarriages and a stillborn son; only a girl who wasn't wanted by either Elliot or his mother. But it would be different for Tatiana. Her child, be it boy or girl, was wanted and would be loved.

Flicking open her powder compact, Anna smiled impishly into the mirror, hoping that perhaps it just might be a boy and that Elliot's loud mother would be looking down from heaven – if she'd managed to get in there, that was – and wailing in anguish!

All at once, Natasha Yurovska was completely forgotten.

In the kitchen at Denniston House, Karl looked at the mantel clock yet again. Four in the morning, and the little one still not born! Eight hours! How long did it take?

He had set kettles to boil, knowing that at times such as this, hot water was always in demand, not thinking there was hot water enough in the upstairs taps.

And now the doctor was there, and the midwife, and the master and the little countess waiting in the drawing room. He wondered if he should enquire if they needed more logs for the fire, and decided against it. Last time he had opened the kitchen door he had heard the commotion upstairs and Tatiana gasping, 'Dammit, I *am* pushing!' He heard it, because she was speaking in Russian. He wondered, yet again, if he should knock on the door of the drawing room. After all, they might be in need of wood for the fire . . .

'For pity's sake, how long has it been now!'

Bill Benson jumped to his feet yet again and went to stand at the glass doors that opened onto the conservatory, gazing into the darkness and the small, distant pricks of light at Creesby.

'It's normal, Bill,' Anna soothed. 'A first baby does

– sometimes – take a little longer. But Tatiana is in good hands and I'm sure we'll know, soon. Why don't I make us a cup of tea?'

'I've had enough tea this night to float the *Queen Mary*,' he said gruffly, then ran his fingers through his hair, shrugging his shoulders by way of an apology. 'Heck! You know what I mean. And I should be with her. Whose bairn is it, anyway?'

'Bill! You know as well as I do that expectant fathers are not allowed.'

'I'm going upstairs. Tatty might want me there!'

'Yes, but Sister Fletcher *won't*! She'll chase you, if you as much as try it.' Anna opened the door, glancing upwards, then said, 'There's a light in the kitchen. Karl is still up. Why don't we go and see how he is? Anyway, I'm tired of this room.'

'Aye. It'll make a change. And I'm sorry. Didn't mean to be so – so *direct*.'

'I know you didn't.' She laid a hand on his arm. 'I'm worried, too, Bill.'

It was at that moment that the door of the upstairs room opened and the midwife came out and leaned over the banister.

'There now! It's all over! Mother and baby both fine.'

She was smiling, Bill Benson thought through a haze of disbelief. It really *was* over!

'She's all right?'

'She is. And the baby, too, didn't I say? And sssh . . .'

They heard the crying, angry and protesting, and the soft murmur of Tatiana's voice.

'And don't come up!' Sister Fletcher straightened her shoulders and became a midwife again, starchy and straight-faced. 'Another quarter of an hour. I'll tell you when . . .'

'But what *is* it?' Bill called.

'That is not for me to say.' She was smiling again. 'That is Mrs Benson's privilege. After all, she's done all the hard work!'

'Not just a wee hint . . .'

'We-e-ll – it's either a boy or a girl!' And with that she whisked away and closed the door firmly behind her.

'Bill! Congratulations!' Anna held wide her arms.

'And the same to you, too, mother-in-law. You make a gui' bonny granny!'

'Is over? The baby is come?'

Karl, standing there smiling, speaking unashamedly in English.

'It's here, and mother and child both well. Listen. Can you hear it crying?'

Karl could. A lusty, gusty yelling.

'Little Countess, this old man is happy. The baby brings happy with it.'

'Yes, Karl, dear friend. *This* baby brings much happiness with it.'

'*Da.*' He nodded, remembering Anna's confinements, and the anger and tears that followed each one. 'And Mr Bill. I shake hand.'

The old grey-haired Cossack and the young Scot clasped hands. Both were emotional to the point of tears.

'Thanks, Karl,' Bill said huskily. 'I don't know

what it is, yet. The dragon woman wouldn't tell me.'

'We celebrate?' Karl made a drinking motion with his right hand.

'Not yet. Not till I've seen them, then I'll have a dram with you, and gladly. And with you, too, mother-in-law . . .'

Tears that had filled his eyes began to trickle down his cheeks, and Anna made little hushing sounds and took her handkerchief and wiped them away.

'It's all right, Bill. It's all over. For you, too . . .'

In that moment, the unhappiness of the past was wiped out for Anna, and it was as if she had paid in advance and in full for this precious moment of joy.

'And look – there's Sister Fletcher. You can go up, now, Bill.'

'Aye – w-e-ell . . .' He wiped a hand over his eyes, straightened his shoulders then walked slowly up the stairs. 'Lassie . . . ?' He hesitated in the doorway, looking anxiously at his wife. She was pale, and there were dark shadows beneath her eyes. And then she smiled, and he knew everything was all right.

'Bill! I can't believe it! Isn't he just beautiful?' She was nestling the child to her. 'He's seven pounds, ten ounces, and look at all that hair!'

'A boy,' Bill whispered croakily. 'I have a son?'

'*We* have a son! And darling, did I make a noise? I was heaving and shoving and Sister said, "That's right, Mrs Benson. Have a good yell!" So I did. In Russian, because I wasn't feeling very ladylike at the time, I'm afraid.' She grinned, impishly. 'Here – you take him. Give him a cuddle.'

'Hullo, son . . .' He held out his arms, and in that

moment he wanted to laugh and cry, both at the same time, but instead he gentled the tiny cheek with his lips. 'Hullo, Peter Benson.'

'*Peter!*' Tatiana gasped. 'Where the heck did you get Peter from?'

'You said I was to choose.'

'I know I did, but *why* did you choose it?'

'For your grandmother.'

'The Petrovska! What has *she* got to do with it?'

'We-e-ll, I got to thinking I'd like a family name, and since I've got no family – well, none that own me – I thought your granny would like him to be called after her husband. Peter Benson, eh? Mind, Pete Benson sounds better.'

'So it does, darling.' And when, she thought, did the Sutton Clan ever get their right and proper names? Tatty, Drew, Bas, Kitty. Even the new Kentucky baby had got stuck with Nell. 'Mm. I like it, but it's going to make the Petrovska more bossy than ever.'

'She's an old bewildered lady, hen, who spends most of her time in St Petersburg. Besides, I like her, even though her political outlook and mine are on collision course. And I haven't said thank you for this wee laddie. He's beautiful, Mrs Benson.' He kissed her mouth gently. 'I'm glad you offered to take a blind air gunner out on the town.'

'So am I, so give me another kiss, then go and shout Mother and Karl to come up, will you? I want to show him to everybody!'

She did! She wanted to fling wide the window and shout out loud that Bill and Tatty Benson had a son, Peter: born 4.45 a.m. Tuesday, 25 October.

'Come and see your grandson,' she whispered tremulously to her mother. 'Isn't he wonderful? We've called him Peter.'

'Congratulations, both of you. Y'know – he looks the image of you, Tatiana, when you were born. All pugnacious and puffy-faced, like he's been in a fight. And very precious. Look, Karl. Here's our new baby, Peter.'

And the grey-haired Cossack, who had been standing by the door, came to the bed and traced a cross of blessing on the tiny forehead.

'Well done,' he said softly, in Russian, taking Tatiana's hand, kissing it. 'Peter is a good name, little one.'

'For my grandfather. I never knew him, but Grandmother will be very smug about it.'

'I did not know him for long, but when he and your Uncle Vassily left the farm at Peterhof he said to me, "Look after them, Karl. I leave them in your care." And I am still caring . . .'

'What are they blethering about?' Bill demanded of Anna.

'About my father, and how he left us with Karl, bless him. And do you mind, you two? Bill doesn't understand a word you're saying.' Anna bent to kiss her daughter. 'You're tired, Tatiana, and you're getting yourself excited. Ewart and I are going home, now. Try to sleep?'

'I'll close my eyes, and try to. But isn't it a lovely feeling, Mother? Did you feel like this when you had me?'

'I did, darling. It's the best feeling in the world. I'll

be in, first thing in the morning. Take care of her, Bill.'

'Mother sounded quite wobbly when she left,' Tatiana smiled. 'And I think I'd like to try to sleep. Will you stay with us, darling?'

'I will. I'll kip down in the armchair. Shall I put the baby in the cot for you?'

'No. Let me keep him with me. And bring the chair to the bed so I can hold your hand. Night-night, Bill.'

She closed her eyes and lifted her lips to be kissed.

'Goodnight, Mrs Benson, and you too, son. And did I tell you I love you?'

A small smile lifted the corners of Tatiana's mouth, and half-asleep already she whispered, 'Love you too, Bill. A lot.'

'I suppose there wouldn't be a cup of coffee going?' Ewart Pryce flopped into an armchair, then eased off his shoes.

'Coffee? Won't it keep you awake? You'd do better to get a couple of hours' sleep.'

'Mm. Maybe I will. I'll just check with the exchange, first.' He picked up the phone. 'Morning, Winnie. Sorry to disturb you so early. Any calls whilst I was out?'

'Not a one, Doctor.'

'Thanks a lot. Oh, and by the way, they've got a lovely boy at Denniston. Seven pounds, ten ounces. Both well.'

'Well now, isn't that just grand? And congratulations to both of you – having a grandson, I mean. Mrs Pryce'll be tickled pink.'

'She is. We all are. Tatiana especially.'

'I – er – suppose I can pass the good news on, Doctor?'

'Of course you can!' What better way, he smiled, replacing the receiver. 'Think I might nip into bed, Anna. Are you coming, too, darling?'

'No. I'll stay down here till it's a more respectable hour – to ring round with the news, I mean. Off you go, darling. I'd like to be on my own – wallow in being a grandmother.'

Yet when she was alone, Anna Pryce did not think about Tatiana's child, because the moment she closed her eyes she saw Natasha Yurovska's face, lived again the night they had carried her stillborn son away from her and Elliot's look of contempt.

Dear God in heaven, *why* had Natasha Yurovska come back to haunt her; remind her of something she thought she had long ago forgotten. Because the young woman who stayed next door with Keth and Daisy could be no other than her child; hers, and Elliot's. Conceived in sin, had she been, or lust? Or maybe, as the weeping servant had confessed, in rape? She sighed, knowing there would be no peace of mind for her until she had, somehow, got to the truth of it.

And when she had – what then?

TWENTY-THREE

Anna saw the car as it turned into the drive. She was waiting at the door before it had come to a stop.

'Bless you both for coming,' she smiled. 'And I know I should have told you more, but I didn't want to say too much on the phone.'

'Urgent, you said?' Nathan was clearly intrigued.

'We-e-ll – yes and no. I mean that it *might* be, but I hope I'm making a fuss over nothing.'

'And do you think you are?' He settled into a chair.

'No, Nathan, I don't.'

'Nothing wrong with the baby, I hope?'

'No, Julia. Ewart called at Denniston this morning. They're both fine. It's about the young woman who's staying next door, at Foxgloves.'

'Hannah? We haven't met her, yet. Lyn told me she and Daisy are going to see Tatiana, and that they were taking her with them,' Julia nodded.

'Yes. I saw them leave. Lyn was pushing the pram and Daisy had the pup on a lead, and I got another look at her – at Hannah.'

'And . . .' Julia urged.

'She's Elliot's child. Elliot's and Natasha Yurovska's.'

'*What!*' Julia sat bolt upright. 'She *can't* be!'

'Anna, how can you be so sure?' Nathan said softly.

'Because she is so like Natasha. She walks the same way – even holds her head the same. And because she is the image of her mother. I don't know how old she is. If I knew that, I'd be absolutely certain, then.'

'But Anna – out of the millions and millions of people in this world, one of bloody Elliot's indiscretions arrives on your doorstep, almost. It takes a bit of believing,' Julia gasped.

'I know. That's exactly what Ewart said. Too much of a coincidence. But wait until you've seen her, Julia. You'll believe me, then.'

'We aren't doubting you,' Nathan soothed, 'but as Julia says – well, coincidence would have to have a very long arm, don't you think?'

'Daisy rang up to see if they could go and see the new baby and Ewart said they could, but only to stay for a few minutes,' Anna rushed on. 'They shouldn't be long. If you have time, why don't you wait till they come back? You can both remember what Natasha Yurovska looked like?'

'Of course. It was a long time ago, but yes, I'm sure I'd see if there was any resemblance.'

'It was twenty-two years ago, Julia. I've worked it out, to within a couple of months, and she fits.'

'And if we see her – and if we think as you do, Anna,' Nathan said, all at once longing to light his pipe, knowing he must not, 'what do you intend to do about it? Remember that this might concern Tatiana, too.'

'I know. I've been over all that with Ewart and it's one reason for keeping quiet about the girl. I don't know what to do for the best. I suppose that in the end I'll have to square it with my conscience – one way or the other.'

Conscience, Nathan brooded. He was the keeper of quite a few consciences, Keth's included. Keth had felt the need to square things with *his* conscience. They had walked together to the top of the Pike.

'It's about a girl, Sir. I've been to France and I'm hogtied under the Official Secrets Act. But I can't live with it. She was only sixteen and she stopped the bullet intended for me. I'm home and safe, and going to marry Daisy because a young kid is dead. Her codename was Natasha . . .'

Keth had called his child Mary Natasha and only he, Nathan, had known why. Their eyes had met for an instant over the font. He had given a small nod of understanding. And now a young woman called Hannah was staying next door at Foxgloves. Elliot's child, Anna said. His brother, whom no one could quite forget because his soul refused to rest, was tormenting them again.

'Nathan?' It was Julia. 'You're miles away . . .'

'No, not really.' Even retired priests could avail themselves of the odd white lie. 'Trying to keep an open mind, I suppose.'

'You can't be open-minded about this, Nathan,' Anna whispered. 'Not when you've seen her.'

It was then they heard laughter and the excited yap

of a puppy. And without speaking they walked towards the window and saw Lyndis with the pram and a little fat Labrador, its lead wound round Daisy's legs. And someone was picking up a teddy Mary had thrown from the pram, someone with dark hair and eyes and who was tall and slim and very beautiful. Someone who, years ago, could have been Natasha Yurovska.

'*No!*' Julia gasped.

'You see?' Anna urged.

'You're right,' Nathan said gravely. 'We've just seen the most amazing coincidence in the world, or –'

'Your blasted brother's child,' Julia hissed. 'You blessed him when you buried him, Nathan, but he won't rest. There's always something to remind us. What are we going to do?'

'I don't know.' The three had gone now, but there had been no doubt in his mind. The young woman Hannah was somehow connected with Keth, and maybe with France. 'We've got to think about it and leave Elliot out of the equation. If we don't, it'll get us nowhere. I – I think someone should talk to Keth about her, ask where she is from.'

'She's from Birmingham. She teaches languages. French and Russian, I believe, and she speaks near-perfect English, according to Daisy,' Julia offered.

'Then will you both leave it to me?' Nathan asked. 'I'll find a way to bring it up. Keth will be straight with me, I know it.'

'But she's been to Denniston House, to see Tatiana's baby!' Anna gasped.

'Of course she has! They've all been. Hannah won't

have ill-wished the baby, Anna. What do you think she is, then – a wicked witch?'

'She's Elliot's, Julia, so what does that make her?'

'She is, if what we suspect just might be fact, someone who was born in secret, then given up for adoption. There is nothing sinister about her, Anna. And before we jump in at the deep end, we should consider not only Tatiana but Hannah, too,' Nathan said softly.

'I see what you mean.' Julia's mouth was set tight, her cheeks flushed. 'Neither one of us has the divine right to wish Elliot Sutton on her. It wasn't her fault.' She was thinking of Drew's getting. 'She seems a perfectly ordinary young woman to me.'

'And to me, too.' Nathan knew at once Julia had been thinking about Drew. 'Let's all calm down, and as soon as I can I'll have a word with Keth.'

'Sooner than that, if you don't mind,' Julia said soberly. 'We've got to get to the bottom of this as quickly as we can.'

'But why?' Nathan reasoned. 'It isn't really any of our business.'

'It *is* our business, when it concerns Elliot Sutton, don't you agree, Anna?'

But Anna Pryce only nodded vaguely. She already knew what she would do, because the young woman next door *was* her business. Hers, and Tatiana's.

'Anna . . . ?' Julia prompted.

'Yes. I – I think we should leave it to Nathan. And I'll get on the bike and ride over to Denniston. A bit of pedalling will calm me down. And don't worry, Nathan,' she hastened, 'I won't start quizzing Tatiana.'

* * *

Tatiana was sitting up in bed, her hair tied back with a pale blue ribbon. She looked rested and happy, Anna thought.

'Hullo, Gran.' She kissed her mother's cheek. 'I've just fed him and got his wind up. I'm getting quite good at it. Bill's gone down to make tea.'

'Mm. I saw him. How are you feeling now, darling? Not getting too tired?'

'No. In fact, I'm rather cross with Ewart and Sister Fletcher. They say I must stay in bed for a week, at least.'

'It was two weeks, in my day,' Anna smiled.

'Well I feel just fine. And don't tell on me, will you, but I've been out of bed a couple of times, to the window. I didn't feel wobbly at all.'

'So what did your visitors think of Peter?'

'Lyn adored him. She said if she didn't have two of her own tucked away, she'd probably have stolen him. And Daisy got the broody look in her eyes. I reckon they'll be thinking about another, now that Mary Natasha's started to walk.'

'And Daisy's house guest?' Anna hadn't meant to be so direct. 'Hannah, isn't she called? Did she like the little one?'

'She adored him. I let her hold him. And yes, she's called Hannah Kominski; speaks Russian. It's her mother tongue, she said. Her parents were Jewish – got out of Moscow when the uprising started. Ended up in Paris.'

'Ah. And Hannah was born there . . . ?'

'She thinks so. She's adopted, you see. Daisy told me she knows nothing about who she is, or anything, except that her mother's name was Natasha. Isn't she absolutely beautiful, Mother? Bet it won't be long before she's married.'

'Good looks aren't everything, Tatiana. And she has time enough. It's not like before the war. If you weren't spoken for before you were twenty-one, people had consigned you to the shelf. Er – how old is Hannah?'

'Haven't a clue. And here's Bill, with the tea. Are there any biscuits, darling?'

'You know I got a packet at the shop this morning!' He set the tray on a table. 'Those three wee lassies who were here just now scoffed half of them!'

'*Wee?*' Tatiana giggled. 'There's nothing wee about poor Lyn. She said if she hadn't had the pram to hang on to she wouldn't have made it to Denniston. Poor love. And she's got months to go, yet. I told her she'd have to be sure to put her feet up, and rest more.'

'Don't worry, darling. Ewart is keeping an eye on her.' The moment had passed, Anna thought. No more asking about Hannah. And anyway, hadn't she said she wouldn't? 'Mother is delighted the baby is to be called for Papa by the way. She wants to come for the christening, she said.'

'She'll be welcome.' In her present state of euphoria she meant it, too, because didn't she have absolutely everything she'd always dreamed of – and never thought she would get? Didn't she have Bill and Pete and a lovely home and friends who had been to Oh and Ah over the baby? And with a bit of luck, she calculated, Peter could be christened in the Lady Chapel at All

Souls on their first wedding anniversary. Then she forced herself from her smug contentment and said, 'If she isn't in St Petersburg, of course.'

It caused her husband to look at her sternly then say, mildly, 'That was not very nice, Tatiana Benson. She's a poor old body and you should be kind to her.'

'But I *am* being kind to her! Haven't I just said that she and Uncle Igor will be welcome at the christening?' She pretended wide-eyed innocence then giggled. 'And do you think, darling, that I could have that biscuit? It's the last one on the plate, you see, and there's a wish on last biscuits.'

There was no answer to that and anyway, Bill Benson was used to his wife always managing to get the last word. So he passed the plate with a look in his eyes that said, 'I love you.'

And Tatiana winked slowly at him which was her way of saying, 'I love you, too . . .'

Anna saw the look, and was glad for her daughter, and the matter of the young woman staying with Keth and Daisy took second place in her thoughts. For the time being.

Nathan met Keth quite by accident in Creesby High Street.

'Hi, there. Just been taking my jacket to the cleaner. Mary is learning to feed herself and the little madam flung porridge all over it, this morning,' Keth grinned.

'And I,' Nathan sighed, 'have just been to the tobacconist's. He's a decent sort. Always keeps an ounce for me, under the counter. Pipe tobacco is harder to come by, now, than it was during the war. Thank goodness that Julia seems to have given up cigarettes – fingers crossed. But are you in a hurry, Keth? Can you spare me a minute?'

'Sure. I'm on my dinner hour, anyway. How can I help?'

'It's a bit embarrassing, I'm afraid. Can you remember – oh, ages ago, during the war – you and I walked to the top of the Pike?'

'I remember. I was pretty bothered.'

'Look, Keth – I'm not resurrecting something you told me in confidence, because we agreed it was more in the way of the confessional . . .'

'Yes, and I felt better for telling you, but I never forgot that young girl.'

'I know you didn't. You called your little girl after her, and I understood.'

'Then can I unburden again? You've got every right to know, Sir. I was supposed to go to a conference in Brighton, but I went back to France. I reckoned I had so much that the very least I could do was to try to find her grave, and thank her.'

'And did you – find her grave, I mean? Has it made you feel better, Keth?'

'A whole lot better. I found *her*!'

'She hadn't been killed, then? But that's marvellous.'

'Yes. It's a long story, and I *will* tell you, one day, Reverend. I not only found her, but she's staying with us, at Foxgloves. I told Daisy I'd been to France, told her everything and she was fine about it; says that since Natasha – *Hannah* – seems to have no one in the world, she and I and Mary must be her family.'

'Yes, and that's why I'm asking you – in confidence, of course, how much you know about her? Trust me, Keth? I do have a reason.'

'I know nothing about her. She couldn't tell me anything because she only knew she was adopted as a baby by the Kominskis; Russian refugees, of the Jewish faith. They sent Hannah to Clara Piccard in Clissy-sur-Mer. They knew it was only a matter of time, once the Nazis occupied France, before they were deported.'

'Dear God! Auschwitz? Belsen?'

'Some place like that. Hannah never saw them again. It seems that the less you knew in occupied France, the better it was, so her aunt said very little – except what her parents had never told her; that she was adopted. All Hannah knew was that she'd been born in Paris to an unmarried woman whose name was Natasha. It was why she took it as her codename when she worked for the Resistance.'

'And Clara Piccard . . . ?'

'The soldiers took her the night the Lysander got me out of Clissy. No one knows what happened to her. But why do you want to know about Hannah? Who is interested in her?'

'Anna, actually. She – er – remarked that Hannah was too young, in her opinion, to have been in the war with you. Idle curiosity, I suppose.'

'At Bletchley? Working on signals? Why not?'

'Because Anna reckons she's twenty-two or twenty-three; too young.'

'Hannah Kominski was sixteen when I met her,

and she wasn't too young to be in the war – or to get a bullet in her leg!'

'You know what I mean, Keth . . .'

'Yes, I do. But what business is it of Mrs Pryce's where Hannah and I met? Daisy knows, and she's all that matters. As a matter of fact, I haven't even told my mother about Clissy, nor Daisy's parents, so Anna Pryce has no chance at all of finding out – well – whatever it is she wants to know!'

'Keth – I can understand the way you feel, believe me. Maybe I wasn't quizzing you. Perhaps I was warning you, in a roundabout kind of way.'

'About what, for heaven's sake?'

'That Anna seems interested in your house guest, that's all. Just pass the word to Daisy, will you? If Anna asks any questions, be careful what you say, both of you.'

'Like I said, Reverend, it is nothing at all to do with Mrs Pryce, and Daisy and I will have whoever we want to stay with us! It's nothing to do with anybody, come to that, so if Hannah comes up in the conversation – idle curiosity or not – can you and I forget we ever had this talk?'

'We can, Keth. And I'm as much to blame as anybody for even presuming to ask you. Hannah Kominski is entitled to her privacy and in future I will respect it. I'd be glad to forget we ever had this talk; won't even mention I met you.'

'That's fine, then.' Keth had the grace to feel embarrassed. 'I didn't mean to fly off the handle, Sir. It's just that I reckon Hannah's been through enough in her life, and she's nobody's business but mine and Daisy's.'

'Exactly.' They had reached the school gates, now. 'And it wasn't a warning, Keth; not as such. Just thought I'd tell you what had been said, that's all.'

They parted amicably, though Nathan wished he had never brought up the subject of Hannah Kominski. Knowing more than he dare tell Keth, his conscience troubled him. Because there was more than a fair chance that the young woman born to Natasha Yurovska had been fathered by his brother Elliot, then given in adoption.

'My brother's keeper,' he muttered as he got into his car. It seemed he would have Elliot on his conscience for the rest of his days, because now he must lie about having met Keth in Creesby. And he must certainly keep the truth from Tatiana for as long as he could; that she had a half-sister who yesterday had visited her, and held her child.

And as for Anna? Well, as far as he was concerned, she would have to find who Hannah was without *his* help. And Julia, too, for that matter, because being a priest and the keeper of consciences could be a dicey thing, especially when he knew both sides of the story and couldn't admit to knowing either!

It seemed strange, somehow, that if you looked facts in the face, the young woman staying at Foxgloves could well be his niece; blood kin. Yet he was the only one in possession of those facts; to all others, she must remain someone Keth had worked with in the war. Except Julia, perhaps? Anna had told her, many years after, about Natasha Yurovska and Elliot, so didn't that entitle his wife to know?

No! his common sense told him. Julia especially

must not know, because her hatred of Elliot matched Anna's. Julia knew about another rape child, which made telling her impossible.

'Sorry, Nathan. Once a priest, always a priest,' he said to no one in particular. Yet it did not stop him from wondering, for all that, just what Keth Purvis was thinking about their talk, and hoped it was already forgotten.

Yet Keth had not forgotten; had realized that there was more to the strange conversation than met the eye, because why should the Reverend suddenly have reason to ask about Hannah? And why, when he, Keth, had shown annoyance, had he been so eager to forget what had been said? Did he know more than he was prepared to admit? Had Anna Pryce said something, in all innocence, that had set warning bells ringing in his head? But warning bells about *what*?

'Watch out, lad!' he yelled at a boy who almost collided with him. 'Look where you're going!'

He felt, at that moment, like yelling at Anna Pryce, too; telling her to mind her own business, because Hannah Kominski had nothing at all to do with her!

He opened the door of the staff room and, finding it empty, made his way without even realizing it to the pay phone on the opposite wall, fishing in his pocket for a coin, asking for his home number.

'Sweetheart?'

'*Keth?*'

'Of course it is. Who else calls you sweetheart?'

'Idiot! You don't often ring from school, that's all. Anything the matter?'

'N-no. Just felt like speaking to you. Everything all right?'

He took a deep breath, all at once knowing that to tell Daisy what Nathan had said was the very last thing he should do.

'Everything is fine. Hannah is just spooning Mary's dinner into her and then we're going to Denniston to see the baby again. Lyn isn't coming, this time. Says she wants to put her feet up, this afternoon.'

'Enjoy yourselves, then. See you, darling. Love you.'

And his wife's throaty chuckle told him she loved him too; without having to say it. He smiled into the receiver then hung it up, wondering why he was worrying.

Worrying? Not exactly, yet there was still doubt in the back of his mind, and it was all to do with Hannah – and Nathan Sutton.

Perhaps, he frowned, he should try to have a quiet word with the Reverend, ask him what had really prompted his probings. You didn't start asking questions about people without good cause – at least, people like Nathan Sutton didn't. And then Keth shrugged the matter from his mind and hoped that by the time he got home, the matter had been forgotten by the Reverend, too.

'Hullo, darling. Your lunch is ready. Had a good morning in Creesby?'

What she really meant, Nathan knew, was had he been able to get tobacco without actually saying the word because, although Julia was doing very well in her efforts to give up cigarettes, the less said about it, the better.

'I did, Julia. A very good morning.'

'See anyone? Any news . . . ?'

'Not a soul. Creesby seemed very quiet, this morning.'

He was lying to Julia; doing it deliberately, because what Keth Purvis had said made sense. Forget it. None of our business. But Keth hadn't the remotest idea what it really was all about, and what Keth didn't know he couldn't worry over. And the less Julia knew, he brooded as he washed his hands at the kitchen sink, the better.

'Alice and I are going to see the little one tomorrow. Daisy and her guest are going this afternoon.' She laid two bowls of soup on the table, then cut thick slices of bread. 'And the more I think about the girl Hannah, the more curious I am. She is so like Natasha Yurovska, yet why should she turn up here of all places, I ask myself.'

'Exactly. Too much of a coincidence, Julia, though I'm bound to admit there is an uncanny resemblance. Even so, I think we'd be wise to let the matter drop, before it gets out of hand. It was a long time ago, and what good will it do to open up old wounds? We both know that Anna was desperately unhappy when she was married to my brother, but things are better for her, now. If she mentions it again to me, I shall say much the same thing to her.'

'Agreed. But knowing what we do, I do get a bit sniffy when something like this happens. I've every reason to. I'd gladly throttle anyone who got at the truth of Drew's beginnings, so the less we talk about Elliot, the better.'

'My feelings, too,' Nathan nodded, relieved, hoping with all his heart that Anna would be as easily diverted as Julia; knowing she would not. Anna was determined to find out all she could about Hannah Kominski, and with very good cause. It was sad, he thought, that Anna was unable to put the matter behind her; that somehow, still, she needed someone to suffer for his brother's wrongdoings.

She must, Nathan thought, have disliked him to the point of hatred.

Anna Pryce turned into Denniston House drive and saw the large, old-fashioned pram at the front door, knowing that if she had one iota of sense in her head, she would have turned and quietly walked away. But knowing Hannah Kominski was here with Daisy only made her more determined to discover who she really was, and why she was in Holdenby, of all places. Only this morning she had seen the girl again and been surer than ever that this was the child Natasha Yurovska had been sent away in shame to have. It had made angry pulses start their beating again and she knew that no matter what, she would get to the truth of it.

And make the girl so aware of her sordid beginnings that she would never show her face again in Holdenby!

'Hullo, you two! Am I glad to see you! I'm sick and fed up of having to stay in bed, when all I want is to get up and be normal again. I feel fine.'

'You might think you do, but take it easy, Tatty.' Daisy hugged and kissed her. 'Once you're on your feet again –'

'But I've been out of bed lots of times! When there's no one around, I get up and go to the window. And I walk around the room, too. I'm not a bit wobbly. And which lovely person is going to bring a tea tray up? Karl is out, this afternoon. He's had toothache for two days now, so he's plucked up the courage to go and have it seen to. Imagine – a Cossack afraid of a dentist!'

'I will make the tea,' Hannah offered, 'if you will point me in the direction of the kitchen.'

'Down the stairs, turn right at the bottom and at the end of the passage is the kitchen door. Milk in the pantry; cups and saucers on the dresser. Isn't she a lovely person?' she asked of Daisy when Hannah had left the room. 'I'd be very jealous if I thought Bill had had a past with someone like her,' she grinned.

'When Keth and Hannah were together in the war,' Daisy said, choosing her words carefully, 'she was very young indeed. A child, Keth called her, and anyway, he was already engaged to me!' She went to stand beside the sleeping baby. 'He's beautiful, Tatty. It doesn't seem five minutes since Mary was tiny and fragile.' She made a funny face at the little girl who sat beside Tatiana on the bed. 'And now she's walking, and says quite a few words.'

'Getting broody again, Mrs Purvis?'

'We-e-ll, we've always said that when Mary was on her feet would be the best time to think about another. Get the value out of the pram, as Mam keeps hinting. I'd like a boy, I think, and I know Dada would. Ah, well. Change the subject, eh? Where's Bill?'

'Gone to Creesby. I told him you were coming, and maybe Mother, and that I'd be fine on my own. I think the last few days have been a bit traumatic for him, poor love. A trip into town will do him good. And was that the front door, Daisy? Probably Mother. She'll have gone to the kitchen looking for Karl, I shouldn't wonder. She's as jumpy as a kitten about Peter, you know. "Don't do this, Tatiana, and don't do that!" And I mustn't have him in bed with me for a snuggle, and when am I going to see about getting a nanny, or someone to help me?'

'I told her yesterday I'm well able to look after my own child and that if I need any help, Bill will muck in. She's going to have to get used to the idea that things have changed since I was little, and that there'll be no nanny at Denniston House nor a French governess. Goodness! How they fussed and coddled me when I was young.'

'I know. You were such a drip that the rest of the Clan christened you Tatty Anna – it was Kitty, I think. But Mam'selle wasn't all that bad. Keth was very fond of her. She brought his French on in leaps and bounds.'

'Was I such an awful whinge, Daisy?'

'Not for long. You met Tim; did everything you could to get out and meet him. Gracie and I used to alibi you, remember? And I shouldn't be talking about Tim, should I?'

'Why not? If he comes up in the conversation, Bill is all right about it. Tim is like Kitty. They're both

518

gone, but we all remember them. Yet I think what finally put the tin hat on it was after Tim was killed, and I was determined to get away. Mother nearly fainted when I told her I was going to London to be a translator. London's where I met Bill. I sometimes think it was Tim, giving me a gentle shove, bless him. And where is that tea?' The sadness was gone from her eyes. 'Stick your head over the banister and tell Hannah to shift herself, will you?'

'I'll do better than that. Keep hold of Mary and I'll nip down and see if she wants a hand. And maybe it was Karl coming in, not your mother. Perhaps he'll be in need of tea and sympathy,' she giggled.

But Daisy did not reach the kitchen. Instead, she stood on the half-landing, listening to raised voices. Female voices. Turning, she quietly tiptoed back to the bedroom, closing the door behind her.

'It wasn't Karl,' she whispered. 'It was your mother who came and there's a right old carry-on in the kitchen – or it sounds as if there is. Your mother seems very agitated.'

'Agitated! Why? What has Hannah done?'

'How should I know? But whatever Hannah has done, she seems to be getting the worst of it!'

'But what are they going on about? What were they saying, Daisy?'

'I don't know. They were both speaking Russian, I think.'

'Then I'm going to find out! Take hold of Mary, and stay here. I'll soon sort it.' Tatiana threw back the bedclothes. 'And I'm all right, Daisy. Leave me be. I'll be careful . . .'

With the baby on her hip, Daisy watched fearfully. Tatty shouldn't be out of bed till the end of the week. She had no right to be trying to get downstairs.

'*Tatty*,' she hissed.

But Tatiana merely turned, a finger to her lips, and holding on to the banister made her way towards the kitchen. Then standing a little way from the open door, she listened with disbelief to the angry voice of her mother.

'Yes, you *will* go away, Miss! And you'll never come back here if you have any sense at all!'

Her mother, Tatiana frowned. Speaking as if she were the daughter of a count still, and Hannah a servant! Talking to her exactly as Grandmother Clementina once talked to her own servants!

'I have said I am sorry, Mrs Pryce. What more can I do? If I had known, I would never have come here.' Hannah's voice, trembling with sobs. 'And I will go away. I will go at once . . .'

'Mother!' Tatiana flung wide the door, wincing as her bare feet touched the cold flags of the floor, reaching for a chair, sitting heavily.

'Tatiana, child! Are you out of your mind? Go back to bed this instant!'

'No. I will not! Nor will I be ordered about in my own house! What is going on, here?' She glared at her mother. 'What did you say to upset Hannah so? You've made her cry.'

'No. I am all right. Perhaps Mrs Pryce has misunderstood – got me mixed up with someone else. She asked me who I am, and I do not know. I swear I do not know!'

'Then you'd better tell us, Mother, what Hannah is supposed to have done, and why you were telling her to leave.'

The silence hung heavily. Anna, chin in the air, refusing to answer; Hannah, hands tightly clasped, gazing at the floor.

'Tell me!' Tatiana demanded. 'Someone please tell me?'

'I have said I am sorry and that I will leave,' Hannah whispered. 'I will be glad to. Who wants the likes of me . . . ?'

'Go on,' Tatiana urged gently. 'Tell me, Hannah?'

'It seems I am no better than I should be. Your mother she ask who I think I am, and I don't know! I say I don't know. All I am sure about is that my mother was called Natasha, and she gave me up for adoption. I swear I did not know, when I came, that –' She faltered, then raising her eyes, looked pleadingly at Tatiana. 'I swear I did not know that my mother was a loose woman and that she came between your parents.'

'You are shivering with cold.' Anna took off her jacket and laid it around her daughter's shoulders. Petulantly, Tatiana shrugged it off.

'I am not cold, Mother. Just shocked. So will you – one of you – tell me what is going on, why you were yelling at Hannah?'

'Yelling? Nonsense. I never yell.'

'Mother, you were yelling just like Grandmother Clementina used to! And what is more, Hannah is a guest in my house and I will not have it!'

'Mother of God!' Anna gasped. 'Do you know

who your guest is, then? Do Daisy and Keth know what they have taken in?'

'What are you saying, Mrs Pryce?'

They turned to see Daisy standing in the doorway, Mary on her hip and carrying slippers. She tossed them to Tatiana's feet.

'Put them on, and go back to bed, Tatty. And will you all speak in English, please? I don't know what's going on and I'd like very much if someone would put me in the picture.' Protectively, she went to stand beside Hannah. 'And Peter is alone, upstairs, Tatty. Go to him? You're cold. You shouldn't be down here.'

'She should not! But this is not your business, Daisy. I will deal with it. And I will ring Ewart at once,' Anna said, in English. 'You need something to calm you down, Tatiana, or you'll lose your milk.'

'Calm me down? Who started it, Mother? Tell me, because I'm not shifting from here until you do! And don't even *think* of sending for Ewart, because I won't see him! I don't need a sedative, I need the truth.'

'And I, Tatiana, have just learned the truth of who I am,' Hannah whispered. 'It seems that once my mother was a servant, here. Her name was Natasha Yurovska. She was your father's mistress, and was sent away in shame because she was pregnant. Because of what my mother did, a son was stillborn and your mother left your father.'

'But how do you know that this Natasha Yurovska was your mother? Do you believe it?'

'She better had,' Anna hissed. 'She's the living image of the woman, and what's more her age tallies – to a month, I'd calculated, and I'm right. But Ewart must come. You have no right getting out of bed, coming downstairs. And I think you should go, Daisy, and take Miss Kominski with you!'

'No, Mother. *You* will go. And you won't come here again until you have apologized to Hannah!' Tatiana said, wearily.

'Apologize to *her*? I will not!'

'Hannah. Will you help me, please?' Tatiana rose to her feet, grasping the back of the chair. 'I'm going back to bed, and I want you and Daisy to stay with me. And before you leave, Mother, let me tell you something. I've known for a long time how things were between you and my father, so don't twist things and don't blame Hannah – nor Natasha Yurovska, for that matter. You knew the truth of what went on all those years ago, and so do I!'

'You can't know. You were a small child. How can you remember?'

Tatiana, her arm in Hannah's, paused at the foot of the stairs.

'I remembered vaguely, but Uncle Igor told me the truth of it years ago when I was living in London; me and Kitty with Sparrow, in Aunt Julia's house. He told me everything; that the doctor ordered my father to keep away from you and that Grandmother Petrovska took you to London with her, so you could get well again. She took Natasha Yurovska, too, and sent her somewhere to have her baby.

'Uncle Igor hated my father and with good reason, because I'm not overfond of him, either. I'm sorry for Natasha Yurovska. A pound to a penny she was seduced. She knew no English and was alone.

Grandmother Petrovska brought her to England from St Petersburg and she should have taken better care of her!'

'Igor?' Anna gasped, eyes wide with disbelief. 'Igor told you all this and you've never said a word, never asked one question? He should not have told you.'

'Well he did, because I asked him to. Y'know, Mother, I've known for a long time that somewhere there was someone belonging to me – but I never thought I'd meet her. Now will you go, please? I'm tired. Help me, Hannah?'

'Tatiana! I insist Ewart comes at once!' Anna gasped. 'You've taken leave of your senses!'

'No, I haven't. Perhaps I've only just now come to them. And I'm sorry I never told you I knew my father was a lecher who'd take any woman's knickers down, given half a chance!'

'How – how *dare* you. How can you be so – so *vulgar* in public!'

'Because I come from vulgar stock. Goodbye, Mother. And I mean it when I say you should apologize to Hannah.'

She began to walk slowly up the stairs, one hand in Hannah's, the other grasping the banister rail.

'Well!' she said, lying back, eyes closed against the pillows. 'This is a right old to-do.'

'Forgive me, Tatiana? I did not know, I swear it,' Hannah whispered.

'I know you didn't and I'm sorry, Daisy, that you had to hear what it's like when people wash their dirty linen in public.'

''S all right, Tatty. I'm still not quite sure what it

was all about, but I always sort of knew there was something that didn't add up. Both Mam and Aunt Julia have never had a good word to say for your father. Could he really have been such a swine?'

'Of the first water. I believe my mother never shed a tear at his graveside, and I can't say I blame her.'

'Please – this trouble is all because I am here. I should never have come to your home, Daisy.'

'Yes you should,' Tatiana smiled, 'because if Mother *is* right, I might have just found a sister, and that can't be bad. But I could murder a cup of tea.'

'Oh, dear. It will be cold, now. I'll make more?'

'No, Hannah. I'll do it.' Daisy got to her feet. 'Take Mary, will you? Could do with a cup myself. Are you sure you're all right, Tatty?'

'Fine, thanks. But before you make a fresh pot, will you ring Bothy House – see if Aunt Julia is in and ask her to come over. And Uncle Nathan, too. Tell them it's urgent. And then will you both stay with me till they get here – or till Bill gets back?'

'Of course we will. Chin up, Tatty. Won't be long . . .'

'Well – what do you make of it?' Tatiana asked when they were alone. 'Do you believe it, Hannah?'

'I would like to – if you're sure my mother wasn't a bad woman.'

'She wasn't. She was more sinned against than sinning. No one seemed to like my father – except Grandmother Clementina, and even she got mad at him, at times. My father was too rich and too good-looking for his own good. And far too spoilt by his doting mother.

'He drove his car into a tree. Killed instantly. It was a happy release for my mother, I was told, and I can't for the life of me understand why she flew off the handle at you. Nothing that happened was your fault, any more than it was mine.'

'I understand that, but perhaps seeing me reminded her of a time in her life she would rather forget, Tatiana.'

'Then she isn't going to forget it if she starts raking it up again, is she? And don't look so anxious. I'm over it, now. I knew that somewhere you existed but never, ever, thought you'd walk into my life, Hannah.' She leaned over the cot at the bedside. 'And this young man who has slept through it all, will wake up to find he's got a new auntie. He's an angel, isn't he? We'll love him to bits, but neither of us will spoil him.'

'He is beautiful. I would like a child of my own, but first I must find a man to love. And I hope that if I have children, they won't lose their mother as I did.'

'You lost *two* mothers, Hannah, so I reckon it's about time Fate dealt you a better hand. Would you like to be married?'

'Yes I would, when the right man comes along. It would be good to be part of a family. I've almost forgotten what it is like.'

'You *are* part of a family. Daisy and Keth are both very fond of you and now you've got a half-sister to call your own. And as for never coming back to Holdenby again – well, I'm afraid it isn't on. Bill and I have got two godfathers for Pete – Bas from

526

Kentucky and Keth, and I reckon he should have two godmothers, too. Will you be one of them, Hannah?'

And Hannah, who said she was going to weep again, nodded her head and smiled then said, as she heard footsteps on the stairs and the clinking of china, 'I think the tea is coming. And I think Mary Natasha should have some. She has been a very good little girl. Daisy lets her have milky tea, now, but she will only drink it from a saucer!'

They were laughing as Daisy set down the tray, and relieved she said, 'Aunt Julia is coming straight away. I told her it was urgent, but that she wasn't to break the speed limit getting here. And I think she's got an idea what it's all about, because she asked me if it concerned Hannah, and I said it did, sort of.'

'It won't be a shock to her. None of the Clan remember Natasha Yurovska, but your mother and Aunt Julia will; Uncle Nathan, too. Maybe, when they first saw Hannah, they must have known something would come of it. And it's been quite a time for me, hasn't it? A son and a sister in less than a week. How lucky can you get!'

'Will cheese and pickles do for supper, Nathan? Polly left a home-baked loaf for us, so would you mind eating off trays, tonight? I don't think I'm up to cooking.'

'Fine by me. I'll put a match to the sitting-room fire, and we can take it easy and have a good chat about – things.'

'It was bound to come out sooner or later you

know, though I'm a bit disappointed with Anna. If she'd kept quiet about it, things might have blown over.'

'Things wouldn't, Julia. Hannah Kominski is my brother's child. Best we face up to it. Tatty is pleased about it, and she's the one who matters.'

'No, Nathan. Hannah's the one we should worry about. She must have had a rough time, this afternoon. Anyway, she's a Sutton – a *Pendenys* Sutton – as far as I'm concerned. Everything fits. What we've got to ask ourselves is does she *want* to be a Sutton? She was brought up by Jewish parents in Paris, then went to a family friend she looked on as an aunt. There is nothing English about her.'

'Tatty's laid claim to her, for all that. Y'know, I've often thought how proud Elliot would have been of her. She's grown up into a lovely person.'

'Elliot,' said Julia, slicing tight-lipped into the loaf, 'wanted a son.'

'And his son was stillborn, and all because of him. If Anna hadn't caught him with Natasha Yurovska, things might have been different.'

'Y'know, darling, I've more than once thought that your brother might have been a changeling – and don't laugh! You and Albert are fair, like your father.'

'Father was a Rowangarth Sutton . . .'

'Yes, but Elliot was every bit as dark as you two are fair. Maybe he was swapped at birth!'

'Ha! Is that likely? Elliot was a throwback from Mary Anne Pendennis, we all know that.'

'Yes, and he was the only one. And neither of his

daughters take after him – I'm talking about Tatty and Hannah; the ones we know about!'

'You can be very sharp, Julia Sutton, when the mood is on you.' Nathan picked up the tray. 'I'll take this into the sitting room, and light the fire.'

'Fine. And while I'm waiting for the kettle, I'll give Alice a ring. She's bound to know, of course. Daisy will have told her. Maybe, later on, I'll pop over to Keeper's . . .'

'I thought you might,' Nathan smiled over his shoulder, because nothing was more certain than his wife and Alice would want to talk over the happenings at Denniston House, and Anna's behaviour.

'Will you ring Anna?' he asked when the logs had begun to crackle and they were seated either side of the fireplace.

'No. Not just yet, though I'd like to think Ewart might look in at Denniston – just to make sure Tatty is all right. If he doesn't, I'm sure he'll ask Sister Fletcher to call. Someone ought to take Tatty's pulse. She was on a real high when we got there this afternoon. I'm glad we were able to persuade her to keep things within the family, so to speak. When I phoned Alice, she said Daisy had been very matter-of-fact about things, and that she wouldn't be telling anyone, but Keth. Best if Holdenby doesn't find out just yet, though if I know the village some of the older ones will work things out for themselves before very much longer, especially now it seems that Hannah is going to be a regular visitor. Ellen from Home Farm, for one.'

'It'll calm down, given time. I can't help thinking that if Bill had been at home this afternoon, things might have been very different. He's very protective of his family. I don't think Anna would have dared say what she did if he'd been there. But at least we were able to persuade Tatty to draw a deep breath and count to ten before she shouted from the rooftops that she's got a sister!'

Nathan looked into the fire that was beginning to glow red and comforting and thought how very lucky he was, because soon Julia would go to Keeper's Cottage to talk over the afternoon's happenings with Alice, and he would be left alone in the comfort of his armchair, to enjoy a pipe of tobacco and listen to the wireless. Or to think, perhaps, about what Tatiana once said to him.

'You're such a love, Uncle Nathan. I do wish you'd been my father.'

And seeing how wonderfully well she had coped this afternoon and how proud of her he had been, he rather wished he had!

TWENTY-FOUR

Lyn walked slowly down the Linden Walk, knowing she was taking the long way round to the church-yard. It would have been easier by far to climb the fence beside the wild garden, walk past Bothy House and Keeper's Cottage and through the top end of Brattocks Wood.

But she could not climb the fence now, nor the stile, and the wood was thick with fallen leaves which could be very slippery, especially when you couldn't see your feet, and where they were going!

She missed Daisy. On Saturday, of course, Hannah Kominski would be going back to Birmingham, and the way open for her to call at Foxgloves uninvited whenever the mood took her.

Hannah, Lyn pondered, was very attractive. Her native tongue was French, but she also spoke near-perfect Russian and English. Brains and beauty, and she so unaware of it that it made her even more attractive.

At Keth's secret signals place in the war they had met – or so Daisy said – and maybe it was true.

Probably she had been a translator, as Tatty had. A very young translator, for all that. A refugee, had Hannah been? Not that it mattered. Nothing was more important now than the babies she carried and that if she got much bigger she would be in danger of going off pop! She walked clumsily, swaying from side to side, she thought, like a hippopotamus with every step she took. And no matter how hard she tried, sleeping was a problem, now. Poor Drew. He must be tired of her fidgeting in bed beside him.

But the fault was her own, she thought as she walked past Home Farm gate. She had yearned so desperately for a child that she had landed herself with twins which couldn't be bad, she smiled.

The churchyard gate creaked as it always did, and which no amount of oiling could cure. Closing it carefully behind her she walked on the grass verge beside the gravelled path to the grave.

The white marble stone felt cold as she laid her hand on it, though the gold lettering was as bright as ever. Kitty. The name chiselled there shone like a beckoning light.

It's awful *Kitty – having two babies, I mean, and especially when they both decide to have a good old kick*, she said with her heart. *Not that I mind. Drew is very pleased and I want you to know, and be glad for us, too.*

She gentled the name with her fingertips, as though to touch it would draw them even closer. Because Kitty was still here. Her restless spirit had not left the grave in which they had laid her. Mrs Amelia had been right; had known too that her daughter was not yet ready to leave the place she so loved; the place she had thought to live in for the rest of her life. With Drew.

What do you want, Kitty? Lyn whispered with her heart. *What can I do to help you, comfort you?*

Lyn worried about her. Kitty in summer with green leaves above her and flowers, and the air warm with the scent of hay and honeysuckle was altogether different from the young girl who must lie here throughout the cold loneliness of winter.

I love Drew, Kitty; love him as much as you did. Must you stay? What is it that keeps you here? I wish you would tell me.

'Lyn?'

The voice made her start, and turn round.

'Mother. I didn't hear you . . .'

'I'm not surprised, Lyn,' said Julia. 'What are you doing here?'

'I – I'm looking at the graves. There was a frost last night. The flowers have gone limp.'

'So they have. First frost of the year. Winter will soon be here.'

'Yes, and the sooner the better, as far as I'm concerned,' Lyn managed a smile. 'These two are getting to be quite a weight. I haven't seen my feet for ages! Where are you going?'

'Was taking a short cut to the vicarage, as a matter of fact, to ask Hilary if she's still got her twin pram. It won't be in first-class condition, it having coped with two lots of twins, but at least it would do until you can get a new one.'

'I'd be glad of it. I have my name on three pram

lists and yesterday I phoned them all and asked if I could change my order to a twin pram. They said of course I could, but they rarely get one in their allocations. I suppose I could use a single pram for a while – put one each end, till they get bigger, that is.'

'Not in winter you couldn't. They'll both need a hood over them. But not to worry. Something will turn up. It usually does. I think I'll walk you back to Rowangarth, then go see Willis and ask him for fresh flowers for the graves. I suppose there'll only be Michaelmas daisies and chrysanthemums, now.'

'Miss Clitherow likes chrysanths – the pink spray ones. Mr Willis gave her a bunch every year – when she was – was – still alive, I mean.'

'Yes! And this is no place for a young woman in your condition to be standing in the cold! Let's have you home, Lyn, and tucked up on the sofa with your feet up. I'll ring the vicarage, instead. Come on! Pop your arm in. Don't want you slipping and falling over.'

Julia hugged Lyn to her, wondering why on earth she had been standing beside Kitty's grave, and so preoccupied that she hadn't heard her approach.

'You all right, Lyn?' she asked. 'You looked sad, just then.'

'Did I? Perhaps I was feeling sad for Kitty . . .'

'But Lyn – it happened a long time ago. We loved her and we always will, but life has to go on. An old cliché, I know, but it's a fact. You are happy with Drew and Drew is happy about the babies – let Kitty go, Lyn?'

'Yes. Stupid of me, when I didn't even meet her. But she seems everywhere, still.'

'No. She's where she belongs. She's with all the young people whose lives were snuffed out suddenly and viciously. They are very special, those young ones, and Kitty is with them, I know it.

'Soon be at Rowangarth, now. Just take it easy. Before so very much longer you'll be skipping around like a spring lamb again. And don't forget – people *can* love twice; I'm living proof of it. And it's you Drew loves, Lyn, so promise you'll stop worrying about what is past? Kitty has gone from this life . . .'

'Yes. Sorry I said what I did. Maybe it's being pregnant is making me a bit maudlin.'

But Kitty wasn't gone. She was still there, waiting. And it wasn't just herself who thought – *knew* – it. Mrs Amelia knew it, too. Kitty wasn't ready to go to wherever it was decreed she should go. Not yet.

'Well, isn't this just fine – you and me and young Pete Benson sitting beside the fire? Sure you're not tired, darling? Ewart said you were to be sent straight back to bed if getting up was too much for you.'

'Ewart's an old fusspot. He's worse than Mother!'

'Is that so? Then will you tell me why your mother has neither visited nor phoned for three days? And don't tell me I'm imagining it, because I think you two have had words. I'm right, aren't I, Tatty?'

'We-e-ll, yes. She started laying the law down about Pete – it was the day you went to town – and one thing led to another, and . . .'

'Tatiana Benson, what a silly wee lassie you are! I'm sure she meant no harm. She's so pleased about

535

the baby; it must be hard for her not visiting. Are you sure it was only words?'

'Of course I'm sure.' She was lying to Bill, and she knew she shouldn't. Bill had every right to know about Hannah and of course she would tell him – but not just yet. When they got around to talking about the christening would be the best time, she had decided. It would come naturally, then, to explain why Hannah was to be a godmother. 'Let's just enjoy being almost back to normal, darling? Tomorrow I'm going to have a walk round the garden. I seem to have been cooped up for ages.'

'It's only a week. And why don't you ring your mother, tell her you're out of bed and dressed and why doesn't she pop over for a cup of tea, or something?'

'I will, Bill, but tomorrow. Tonight I just want to sit here, snuggled close and Pete sleeping in his basket on the coffee table. It's such a wonderful feeling – having got it over with.'

'So you were worried about it? Why didn't you tell me, Tatty?'

'Not worried, exactly. Just wondering how it would be, and how I would cope. It wasn't as bad as I thought it would be and anyway, Pete is worth every push and shove.'

'And swear word?' he said, teasingly.

'That, too. Handy being able to curse and swear and no one knowing a word of what you're saying. Shall you mind if I teach Pete Russian?'

'Not at all. And while you're about it, you can teach me. Might as well know what the pair of you are nattering on about. I'd be able to talk to Karl, too.'

'And the Petrovska. You're really in her good books, now, calling the baby after my grandpa.' She snuggled closer. 'But give me a kiss, Bill, and tell me you love me and Pete.'

'I love you, wife, and the wee one over there. I've got everything any man could ask for.'

'Mm. Me too, but we both had unhappy childhoods, so we deserve it.'

And Hannah, she thought. The sibling she knew must be somewhere in this big wide world, yet despaired of ever meeting. And Bill should know about her, too. *Now*, whilst they were so very, very happy.

'Sweetheart,' she whispered, lacing her fingers in his. 'There's something I want to tell you. A big secret, but something wonderful . . .'

'Oooh. The things I do in the name of friendship!' Lyndis sank gratefully onto the sofa. 'I've missed you, Daisy. Visitor gone?'

'She went back yesterday, but there was nothing to stop you coming. Hannah wouldn't have minded. She's a lovely person, Lyn. But tell me something, will you? I was talking to Aunt Julia this morning. She said you were at Kitty's grave, yesterday, just looking at it. Why?'

'Looking at the flowers, actually – on all the graves. That frost got them. And are you coming to Auntie Lyn?' she asked of Mary who had climbed up to sit behind her. 'Let's you and me have a snuggle. And heaven only knows, sweetie pie, there's enough of me for you to snuggle into!'

'Don't change the subject, Carmichael! This is

Purvis-from-the-bottom-bunk, don't forget. Something is bothering you.'

'It isn't, Daisy – honest. We-e-ll, apart from you-know-what. I can't even climb the stile, now. And I get tired.'

'Of course you do. Towards the end I got tired, too, and I was only carrying one. But you and I went through a lot together, Lyn. We used to tell each other everything, so why don't you get it off your chest?'

'I'm all right, Daisy. It's come to something if I can't walk down the churchyard path without it causing comment.'

'All right. Have it your own way. And there was I, willing to tell you something that'll make your eyes pop. Still, if you won't trust me, why the heck should I trust you, Lyn?'

'Gossip? Who about?'

'About Hannah, and it isn't gossip. She's going to be godmother to Peter.'

'*Is* she? I'd have thought it would have been someone closer.'

'Hannah *is* – close, I mean. As close as Drew and I.'

'But you and Drew are –' Lyn stopped, confused, then looked into Daisy's eyes. 'Listen, Purvis – are you trying to tell me that there's some connection, like you and Drew having the same mother?'

'That's it, only Hannah and Tatty have the same father. And before I say another word, I want your promise that this isn't going to go any further; not to be mentioned to anyone, even Drew – okay?'

'Okay. But why have you told me about Hannah and Tatty? Why should you trust me, Daisy?'

'Because in return, I want *you* to trust *me*. Will you do that – for old times' sake?'

'Okay. But only if you're sure . . .'

'I'm *not* sure, but you and I have been through a lot, together; good times and bad, bombing and boyfriends and broken hearts and heaven only knows what else. What I'm going to tell you involves Keth, too, so it proves how much I trust you, Lyn.'

'But what do you want me to tell you, in return?'

'Why you seem obsessed with Kitty, and why you don't seem able to stay away from her grave! Anyway, I've told you half the story, so I'll give you the lot, right from when Keth came back from Washington – the second time. Do you remember, Lyn?'

'Of course I do. He phoned you and you nearly took off!'

'Yes, well – he hadn't come back from Washington. He'd come back from France. Occupied France. It was where he met Hannah. She was with the Resistance and her codename was Natasha.'

'Good grief! Are you sure?' Lyn gasped.

'Of course I'm sure. And it's a long story, so make yourself comfortable.'

It *was* a long story, because Daisy left nothing out; told about the submarine Keth had been taken to France on, and about Tante Clara and Hirondelle and Bernadette and Denys. And about the Lysander, too.

'But how did Natasha – er Hannah – and Keth meet again? Such a coincidence, such a shock, and him thinking she was dead.'

'His conscience took him back to Clissy-sur-Mer, Lyn. He felt he had at least to find a grave but he found more than he could ever have hoped for. Mind, we told everyone that he was at a conference in Brighton, but let me tell you how I know that Tatty and Hannah are sisters.'

And when the telling was over, when Daisy paused to draw breath, Lyn whispered, 'Nathan's brother Elliot is Hannah's father? Is there any doubt?'

'No. Like I just told you, Anna Pryce knew at once and so too did Mam and Aunt Julia. I think it'll all turn out for the best that Anna lost her temper and had a go at Hannah. Very volatile, those Russians. We might never have known, but for that.

'Anyway, Tatty is tickled pink and that's why Hannah is going to be one of Pete's godmothers. And not a word to a living soul, okay?'

'But how long do you think it's going to be before it all comes out – because it will, you know. Holdenby is a gossipy little place. How do you know some of the older people in the village won't put two and two together,' Lyn demanded, eyebrows raised.

'I don't know – not for sure. But it was a long time ago, and unless Tatty chooses to tell people she has a half-sister, then we'll just have to keep our fingers crossed. Anyway, it isn't any of Holdenby's business who Tatty chooses to have as a godmother. But it's bound to be a shock for you, at first. Don't forget I've had a couple of days to digest it. Do you feel like a cup of tea? You look a bit shook up.'

'No thanks, but I'd like a glass of water, and you'll want to know about me and Kitty, I suppose?'

'I will. A bargain is a bargain. Won't be a tick.' She was quickly back with water and a feeding cup of orange juice for Mary. 'Right, Lyn. Tell!'

'You'll think I'm a fool, but when you say I don't seem able to keep away from Kitty's grave you wouldn't be far from the truth, Daisy. Because Kitty is still there, and before you say what Drew's mother said, and that it was a long time ago, let me tell you that Kitty's mother thinks as I do. It's why she won't ever be coming back to England.' Eyes closed, she took a deep breath. 'Mrs Amelia told me that the only time she feels close to Kitty is when she's here, at Rowangarth. She thinks Kitty is still watching over Drew, because she loved him so much, but she said that only when Kitty was satisfied that Drew was truly happy, would she leave and go to wherever Fate decreed she should be.

'I'm not bothered so much, now, that she and Drew were so in love. What really worries me is why Kitty is so restless. Is she trying to tell me something, Daisy?'

'Like what?'

'Warn me, perhaps? To be careful, I mean. Might it be something to do with the babies?'

'Well, if that doesn't beat cock fighting! Why on earth should she want to warn you – if she's there as you think, which I'm sure she isn't! Lyn, you can't go on like this, worrying about Kitty. It's you Drew married, you who is carrying his children. But there's more to it than that, isn't there? Has Ewart said anything to make you worried?'

'No, I swear he hasn't. He says the twins are fine,

but that I must rest more – and go into hospital to have them.'

'Hospital? Do you want to?'

'No. I want them to be born at Rowangarth. I've got every faith in Sister Fletcher and I told Ewart so. I worry about Kitty, I suppose, because I know how much she loved Drew. I love him too, don't forget. I want her to be at peace and there's enough of the Celt in me to know she isn't.'

'Oh, Lady Sutton, what am I to do with you?' Daisy chided.

'Walk me back to Rowangarth, old love? Put Mary Natasha in the pram so I can hang on to the handle, eh? Would it be a bother?'

'It wouldn't. Anyway, she's looking a bit sleepy and I don't want her to nod off, now, or she'll take an age to get to sleep tonight. I'll just wipe her hands and face and put her coat on. Want to spend a penny, or anything, before we go?'

'No thanks, old love, I'm fine. But hasn't this been one heck of an afternoon?'

'It has, Lyn. Just like when we were in Cabin 4A at Hellas House – swapping confidences, talking half the night, sometimes. Seems nothing has changed.'

'Nothing at all, Purvis, except that we are both a whole lot happier.'

And she *was* happy, Lyn insisted silently; exquisitely so. *Almost . . .*

'The Petrovska,' Tatiana said flatly, 'says she is coming for Peter's christening, even though it's in the wrong faith. She's never stopped being Orthodox, you know.

542

She's giving me good notice, she says, so I can have her bed well aired, which means she'll expect a fire in her bedroom, as well!'

'Well, it isn't every bairn has a countess at his christening,' Bill grinned, laying down his brush, stretching his arms above his head. 'And didn't I tell you no' to come into my studio without knocking?'

'I know, darling, but I haven't once peeped at the easel, though I'd love to know what you are painting.'

'You know what it is – a thank you present for my son, Tatty. And since I've just now finished it, you can have a look.'

'Bill! It's – it's *wonderful*! Whatever made you think of it?' Blinking back tears she whispered, 'And don't ever say again you can do nothing but flowers, because that painting is the most beautiful, poignant thing I have ever seen!' Tatiana stood, hugging herself tightly, gazing enchanted.

A hand, against a pale blue background; Bill's left hand. She knew it at once because of the shape of the fingernails and the wedding ring she had placed there, almost a year ago. And another hand; Peter's, small and fragile, clutching his father's finger tightly. Tiny, trusting, clinging hand.

'Aye. It's no' bad.' He came to stand behind her, hands on her shoulders. 'Mind, if I tried forever, I'll never get the feeling that came over me, when he grasped my finger. I won't ever let him down, Tatty; no one will give him away.'

'Over my dead body, Bill Benson! Oh, dear. I feel quite sniffy. But what I really came over for was to tell you about the Petrovska, and ask you if you want a coffee. I didn't ever expect such a lovely surprise. How can I thank you?'

'I can think of lots of ways,' he laughed, taking her hand, walking across the cobbled yard towards the house. 'And I'll make sure it's framed in time for the christening. Where's the wee one, by the way?'

'In his basket, on the kitchen table, with Karl watching over him. Shall we have coffee in the kitchen? It's lovely and warm in there. And Bill, I do love you . . .'

'And I love you.' He raised her hand to his lips, kissing it gently. 'I always will. And thanks, hen – for *everything* . . .'

'I'm glad to see,' Alice said, 'that Anna and Tatty have patched up their differences.'

'There was no need for it – Anna flying at Hannah Kominski. If she'd just counted to ten, none of it need have come out. Mind, Nathan knew and Anna told me about it, too, but as far as I was concerned the entire sordid episode was forgotten.' Julia frowned. 'Now, Daisy knows and of course, Tatty.'

'Daisy told me about what went on – in strictest confidence, she said. I was longing to tell her I knew what a disgusting creature Elliot Sutton was, but I held my tongue. Y'know, every so often his ghost walks; something happens to bring it all back. Nathan should do an exorcism over his grave, Julia.'

'The Church wouldn't allow it and anyway, Nathan's retired now. I think it could be done, but only by very special priests. But I always said, didn't I, that he should have been buried with a stake through his heart! That would have held him!'

'Julia Sutton! You sounded just like Jinny Dobb, then.'

'I hope I did! Jin was harmless. She told fortunes, read teacups. She wasn't equipped to deal with *that* kind of wickedness. Do you think it'll get out? My, wouldn't Holdenby go to town on it!'

'I don't think it would worry Tatty if it did. It's only because of her mother she's keeping it quiet. There aren't many left in Holdenby who can remember Natasha Yurovska with any clarity, and they are the kind of people who wouldn't gossip. But I didn't ask you over to talk about *him*, Julia. I've something to show you. Come into the front room.'

'Alice! You've finished it! Lyn will love it.'

The christening robe for Drew and Lyn's surprise child was very beautiful. In fine cotton, frilled with broderie anglaise, it awaited only the threading of fine ribbon at the cuffs and neck – when they knew if it was to be pink, or blue.

'I had a word with Lyn. Told her that since Drew's christening robe was in cotton, I should try to make a replica. And she agreed. What colour ribbon do you want, Julia, if you could choose, that is?'

'I think one blue ribbon – which we already have – and for this one to be threaded pink. A boy and a girl would be wonderful, though all I want is for it to be safely over, and for the children to be healthy be they boys, girls, or one of each!'

'Lyn still wants a home confinement?'

'Insists on it. Drew gets a bit jumpy about it, but Ewart will keep an eye on her, and if he thinks she'll be better in hospital, that's where she will go. Lyn thinks she's carrying boys; got to be. She says it's like they're wearing football boots, when they kick. Drew fusses, so. Only this morning he told her she was to be careful if she went out, and keep off the cobbles in the stableyard. They can get very slippery, you know.'

'I do know, love,' Alice said softly, draping the gown over the back of the chair, making for the warmth of the kitchen. 'Our war was not long over. I saw you coming. It was bitterly cold – the end of November – and you were there, head down into the wind and no luggage with you, or anything. I was carrying Drew, then, but I ran out to meet you and Mother-in-Law – Lady Helen – called to me to be careful on the cobbles.'

'You remember? It was more than thirty years ago.'

'And Andrew's anniversary tomorrow, Julia? November the fifth is hard to forget. Just a few more days to go to the Armistice, and he'd have been safe.'

'We were a fine pair, Alice. Me hating the world because Andrew was dead when I was sure he'd make it to the end of the war and you, carrying a child you didn't want.'

'Didn't want?' Alice whispered. 'It was like a great sin inside me. I hoped I'd die when it was born, God forgive me.'

'But you love him now. He's a lucky young man having two mothers.'

'Yes, and he was born fair, like all the Rowangarth Suttons. Life hasn't been bad, Julia, all things considered. Drew came back from the war, and only right that he should. That war – *our* war – took both your brothers and your husband, too. Fate couldn't have taken Drew.

'But let's not remember things better forgotten. I saw Tatty, this morning. Went to give her a matinee coat for little Peter and she liked it so much she said he would wear it to his christening. On the eighteenth of December, she told me it was to be. She'd have liked Gracie to be the other godmother, but they won't be able to get over from Kentucky, it being in Christmas week.'

'The *other* godmother . . . ?'

'Do I have to spell it out, Julia? She has asked Hannah.'

'Oh, my lor'. And there's you and me talking about keeping things quiet! Hadn't you realized the Countess and Igor are coming for the christening! Had you for one minute thought about what's going to happen when they come face to face with Natasha Yurovska's reincarnation?'

And Alice's eyes opened wide, and she said she hadn't thought. Not for a minute had she!

'Well, all I hope is that Hannah won't be put through it as she was when Anna let fly! It isn't her fault, Julia, that she was fathered by Elliot Sutton, any more than it was Drew's. I think that you and I should be on Hannah's side if the balloon goes up, if only because we've been lucky that no one ever found out about Drew. Not even Elliot.'

'No one we couldn't trust. Nathan knew, of course, and Tom. And Ruth Love and Sister Carbrooke. I wonder where they are, now, Alice.'

'Wonderful women. Sister was a dragon, but good to have on our side when things went wrong. I think Sister at her best could have demolished even Clementina Sutton, if she'd set her mind to it. But I think Tatiana should tell the Countess about Hannah well beforehand, if she doesn't want the christening spoiled.'

'She won't do that, Alice, because the old lady would refuse point blank to attend.'

'The Countess might not even remember Natasha Yurovska.'

'She'll remember, and Igor, too. Don't forget it was the Countess who had Natasha sent away to have the baby and she told no one, not even Igor or Anna where she was, or what happened to her. Just the biggest coincidence in the world that Keth should find Natasha's child. It was as if it was meant to be. Amazing, isn't it, that no one thought about Countess Petrovska and had you realized, Alice, that once the Countess is drawn into it, Tatiana is going to want to know every last detail of it, so Hannah can start looking for her birth mother – if she wants to, that is.'

'Oh my lor', it gets worse and worse.' Alice got to her feet and filled the kettle which seemed to be the only thing to do in situations such as this. 'I think we'd better have a cuppa and work out what's to be done about it, although strictly speaking, Julia, it isn't really our business.'

'Everything is our business when there's even the slightest chance that Drew's getting might come out.' She took down mugs from the dresser, and the glass salt cellar in which Alice kept saccharin tablets. 'And we thought that everything was just fine; that no one would ever know.'

'And they won't know, Julia. Drew is a Rowangarth Sutton, your brother Giles's child. Even Lady Helen, God rest her, thought he was, so if anyone starts getting anywhere near the truth, they'll have me to reckon with!'

'And me, too! But there's nothing so certain that Countess Petrovska and Igor intend coming to Peter's christening and stopping over Christmas, I shouldn't wonder, so someone has to tell both her and Igor about Hannah. I reckon the best person to do it is Bill. He gets on amazingly well with the Countess. If there's anyone she'll take it from, it'll be him.'

'Igor is pretty level-headed. He'll pitch in on Bill's side. And he's very fond of Tatiana, so we'll have at least one ally.'

'So I'll have a quiet word with Bill, next time I go to Denniston?'

'Think you better had, Julia. And let's keep Nathan and Tom out of it for the time being? I have a feeling they'd both tell us that Hannah Kominski is none of our business.'

'I'm not so sure, Alice. Tom loathed Elliot, and with good reason, too. And Nathan wouldn't stand by and see Tatiana upset. But I agree with you. We'll leave them out of it for now – see how things go before we start calling in reinforcements?'

'It's a right old carry-on if you ask me,' Alice sighed, plopping a saccharin tablet into her mug, stirring it noisily.

'I wouldn't argue with you on that score. Heaven only knows what's going to happen once the Countess lays eyes on Hannah. There's only one thing certain about the whole messy business. Anna Pryce might soon be wishing she'd kept quiet and left Hannah alone.'

'That's *her* business, Julia. It becomes *our* business only if Drew is drawn into it – okay?'

'And surely he won't be? Even Elliot never made mention of that night. I think he was too drunk, when it happened, to know what he'd done. So who's going to find out after all these years, will you tell me?'

'No one,' Alice said flatly, because she was as sure as she could be that no one would. How *could* they? She forced all thoughts of the fearful night in Celverte from her mind, then smiled impishly. 'Wish I had some cooking brandy in the cupboard, Julia. Reckon we could both do with one of Aunt Sutton's snifters.'

And they laughed as they had laughed together so many times over the years. After all, what else could they do?

TWENTY-FIVE

'Ten days to go to Christmas and when it's over, I can begin to hope it won't be long before things start to happen, Drew. I'm glad we've got Miss Clitherow's room done. It was brilliant of Sister Fletcher to think about it.'

'I'm afraid, Lady Lyndis,' she had said, 'that your big, low bed isn't going to be very convenient, if you see what I mean?'

And Lyn agreed entirely that for everybody's sake, a more suitable bed would be needed when the time came, and the little sitting room downstairs would be ideal, stripped of its carpet and heavy curtains and the wooden floor scrubbed. And a high, iron single bedstead carried down from the attics and thoroughly disinfected. Heaven bless those attics, Lyn had thought, and how clever of the Suttons never to throw anything away.

So the little bare room, with two wooden chairs and a table, similarly scrubbed, and kindling and wood ready for when the fire needed to be lit awaited the day – or night – when two new Suttons would be born.

'I'll hang around as much as I can, darling, when the time gets nearer.'

'But I won't be alone. Mary Stubbs and Tilda are downstairs and your mother at the end of the phone. You aren't getting jumpy, Drew?'

'Mary and Tilda go home at six don't forget, and yes, I am a bit nervous – if things start happening at night, I mean.'

'Drew Sutton! You'd think there'd never been a baby born in Holdenby before! Lots of husbands are at work when wives go into labour. Keth was. And I'm sure Ewart and Sister Fletcher are often called out in the night. I'm not a bit worried. In fact, I'll be glad when it starts. I just want it over and done with.' She wriggled in her chair, placing a cushion at her head. 'And I shall rest up as much as I can so I can keep on my feet for Pete's christening.'

'But are you sure you should go, Lyn? All that standing around in church. Wouldn't it be better if you just went to the do, afterwards?' Drew bent to place more logs on the fire.

'I'm going to *both*! Do you remember Mary Natasha's christening?'

'I do, sweetheart,' Drew smiled. 'Afterwards, you said you'd marry me. It all started because I asked you why you looked so sad at the font, and you told me it was because you envied Daisy – you longed for a child of your own, you said.'

'Yes, and look where it got me,' she laughed. 'I got landed with *two*!'

'What do you think we'll have?' He went to sit on

the arm of her chair, taking her hand in his, kissing her fingertips.

'I don't mind one bit, but wouldn't it be clever if we managed one of each? Have you had any ideas about names, Drew?'

'Not quite sure, yet. Still open-minded. All I know is that you will choose for a girl, and I'll come up with something for a boy – like Tatty and Bill did.'

'Mm.' Lyn sighed and closed her eyes, thinking how lovely it was to sit, well cushioned, in front of a blazing fire, Drew at her side and the waiting almost over. 'I wonder if Tatty's grandmother has arrived yet? Tatty says she's bound to complain all the time, but Bill insisted on her being there. He gets on well with the old lady. I think it's because he's so direct with her. Tatty told me the Countess once said it was because Bill looked her straight in the eye when he spoke to her – and there's not many dare do that!'

'Well, I'm sorry for her, Lyn. I know she goes on a bit about her house in St Petersburg and the farm they used to go to in summer, but I'd feel the same if someone took Rowangarth off me.'

'No one is going to take Rowangarth, Drew. Things like that couldn't happen in this country.'

'Couldn't they just? Nathan once told me that it wouldn't have surprised him if our soldiers hadn't walked out of the trenches like the Russian soldiers did, on the Eastern Front. He said the tommies were very badly treated. Our war wasn't anywhere near as terrible.'

'Our war is over,' Lyn said softly, 'and there won't be another. Just let's you and me concentrate on these babies – who are being very well behaved at the moment. I think they must be having a little rest.'

She laid her hands on her swollen abdomen, smiling gently, wondering how much longer she must go on looking like a barrage balloon with legs, wishing it would all start soon. Tomorrow, given a choice!

'Penny for them!' A hand passed in front of her face. 'You were miles away!'

'No, Drew. Just thinking about the christening on Sunday and wondering how Tatty is going to cope with the Petrovska,' she lied glibly, because no one, not even Drew, could even begin to understand how she longed for her babies to be born. And both of them healthy, please God.

'Tatty will be fine. She's got the dour dependable Bill to watch over her don't forget. I shouldn't wonder if he isn't charming the Countess right now . . .'

'Was that Peter?' Bill Benson jerked his head in the direction of the door. 'I thought I heard him . . .'

'I'll go and see.' Tatiana got quickly to her feet, because she knew that her mother and Ewart would be arriving as soon as evening surgery was over, and she wanted it to be Bill who broke the news to the Countess. 'And whilst I'm about it, I'll make us a cup of tea – or would you like coffee, Grandmother?'

'I would like coffee, if you please,' the Countess replied and then said, as soon as the door had closed behind her granddaughter, 'I want you to know how happy I am to be here, Sergeant, and how proud you should choose to call your son after my dear husband, God rest him.' She closed her eyes, sighing, crossing herself devoutly. 'And I am pleased that Tatiana and you are happy. You will be good to her? Always, you will be kind to her?'

'You know I will. I give you my word. Nothing shall harm her, nor my boy. But there is something you should know. I've taken it on myself to tell you, and I hope you'll no' be too upset.'

'Something is wrong with the child, with Tatiana?'

'No. They're just fine. What I have to tell you concerns – well – *memories*, I suppose. And I am sorry to be so direct, but there's no other way to do it. Do you remember Natasha Yurovska, Countess?'

For a moment there was silence in the room. Olga Petrovska sat unmoving, hands clasped on her lap, staring into the fire. Then almost reluctantly she said, 'Natasha Yurovska? *Should* I know her?'

'Aye. She was a young girl and came with you to this country when the troubles started in Russia. Herself, and Karl.'

'And if I say I do not remember her?'

'Then I would be inclined not to believe you, Countess.'

He went to sit beside her, taking her hands in his, holding them gently as if to give them both courage. He to say what must be said and she to accept it with dignity.

'You and I, Sergeant, understand each other too well, do we not? What is it then that I must know, and how does it concern Natasha Yurovska?'

'Natasha had a child. Twenty-two years ago. That child will be here, tomorrow. Her name is Hannah.'

'So long ago – how can you be so sure?'

Not by the lifting of an eyebrow, even, did Olga Petrovska show any emotion; neither shock nor disbelief nor anger. Only her eyes challenged him.

'I am not sure, Countess, but Tatiana's mother is. And I believe Tatty's Aunt Julia is sure, and her husband, too. The likeness, you see . . .'

'So they will know that the child Hannah was fathered by my son-in-law, Elliot Sutton?' she said flatly.

'Aye, and Tatiana knows, too. In fact, she has known for a long time that somewhere she had kin. Her Uncle Igor told her, you see, when she lived in London and used to visit him, at Cheyne Walk. Until now, she had never told anyone – not even me.'

'And this Hannah – did she also know?'

'Only that her natural mother – Natasha – gave her up for adoption. Hannah didn't even know her mother's surname, much less her father's.'

'Do you know, Sergeant Bill, that we Russians have a saying. Be sure your sins will find you out . . .'

'Aye. We Scots have a saying, an' all, about sins coming home to roost. Only the sin wasn't Hannah's, Countess.'

'No. I was partly to blame. Natasha came to this house to work for my daughter when she married Elliot Sutton. When he got the girl pregnant, we took her back to London with us; took Anna, too, out of his reach. Igor threatened him with a thrashing if he ever tried to come near his sister until she was ready, of her own free will, to live with him as his wife again. She never did. Only a few days later, Elliot was dead. The devil, you see, had claimed his own. But how did Tatiana find Natasha Yurovska's child?'

'She didn't. It was Keth Purvis – Daisy's husband. But it's a long story, Countess, and I can hear Tatiana making sounds at the door. Is she to come in?'

'If you will tell me – both of you – all you know about this?'

'We'll tell you.' He got to his feet and opened wide the door. 'You can come in, darling. Your grandmother knows.'

'I was expecting to hear ructions, all the way down to the kitchen. You aren't angry, Grandmother?' Tatiana whispered.

'I was a Russian Countess – I still am. And I was reared never to show emotion. Always I have control of my feelings, though inside my heart goes pitty-pat.'

'Well, Mother didn't have control.' Tatiana laid the tray she carried on a low table beside the fire. 'She flew at Hannah like a hoyden! And in Russian, too! Trouble was, that Russian is Hannah's mother tongue.'

'So what did you do, child? And I will take my coffee black.'

'Do, Grandmother? I told Mother that she must apologize or leave. She left. And we've got brandy. Would you like a little – for the shock?'

'I think I would. Just a little. And I hope you will not take a liking to brandy, child. Your grandmother Clementina drank it all the time. It was her ruination.'

'We only have it because it's Christmas – and for the christening. But where shall we start?' Tatiana smiled tremulously, relieved that the worst seemed over, and that from now on surely things could only get better. 'And do you know something, Countess Petrovska?' Tatiana took the lined face in her hands and kissed her grandmother gently, lovingly. 'You aren't such a bad old stick, are you? And I shall give Uncle Igor a hug and a kiss, too, when he gets back from Bothy House. Will you pour, darling?' she smiled sunnily at her husband.

Then she took a cushion and settled herself on the floor at the Countess's feet, thinking how lucky she was, and how very, very happy.

'I sometimes wish, Jack, that we were going to our Lyn's for Christmas,' Blodwen Carmichael sighed.

'But we agreed, lovely girl, that Lyndis would be getting near her time and would want a bit of peace and quiet over the holiday.'

'We did, but her cook and cleaning lady are going to be having time off. It's why Lyn and Drew are going to Julia's for their meals.'

'You'd better not let Mary Stubbs hear you calling her a cleaning lady. Parlour maid she said she really was, but didn't mind helping out with the housework. Those two are part of the furniture and fittings. They were at Rowangarth when Drew was born, Lyndis told me.'

'Hm. I don't know why the girl is being so stubborn about not going into hospital. She ought, you know, with twins.'

'And she will, if the doctor thinks she should. Drew will put his foot down. Lyndis will have the best of attention, so don't you fret, *cariad*.'

Best of attention. Blodwen gazed into the fire, watching small red sparks fly up the chimney. A sign of frost, wasn't it, when the sparks flew? And it was right that

Lyn should have every attention when her babies were born, with a doctor and midwife there. Different when she'd had Lyn. Born in shame, in a home for wayward girls and unmarried mothers.

Yet whose fault had it been? Her own, Blodwen supposed. Stubborn to the end and not telling a soul she was expecting until after her sister and Jack had married. And what else could she have done but give her baby to them so it could be brought up decently, and far away, in Kenya.

'Ah, well . . .' she whispered.

'Well – what?' Jack Carmichael laid his arm around his wife's shoulders, hugging her close.

'I was thinking that our Lyn is going to have a better time of it than I did, when she was born.'

'But it turned out all right for us, in the end?'

'It did, Jack. We're together. Lyn's mam and dad wed at last, all respectable, and her married into the aristocracy. Y'know, Lyn and me are alike, come to think of it. I thought I'd lost you, and Lyn thought she'd lost Drew, but we've both been lucky, in the end.' She jumped to her feet, kissing him teasingly. 'And before you and me get romantic, put the kettle on, there's a lovely man, and I'll go and ring Lyn – make sure everything is all right, at Rowangarth.'

There's posh, Blodwen Carmichael thought as she waited to be put through to Holdenby 102, not only having a telephone, but being well heeled enough to be able to ring your daughter long-distance whenever the mood took you.

As Jack said, it had turned out all right – in the end.

* * *

'So, Anastasia Aleksandrina Pryce, you did not come to greet your mother last night, and it is I who must come to you!'

'I am sorry, Mama. I – I didn't want to cause trouble,' Anna said softly, eyes on her hands. 'And besides, surgery was late finishing. I intended coming to Denniston this morning.'

'So am I not to be asked in!' Olga, Countess Petrovska was not used to being kept standing on doorsteps.

'Y-yes. Of course. If you don't mind the kitchen, that is. I haven't lit the sitting-room fire yet – shortage of coal, you know. And can we please speak in English?'

'I suppose so.' The Countess unbuttoned her sable coat and took a chair at the kitchen table. 'You have become as English, now, as makes no matter, though I never thought the day would come that my daughter ranted and raved like a peasant!'

'Who told you that!' Anna flung. 'Tatiana, I suppose, and she is wrong. I spoke *firmly* to the young woman, asked her why she was there in my daughter's house.'

'That is not the impression I got, Anna. And what was so awful about the girl that you felt obliged to make her weep – your daughter's guest? Have you forgotten all I ever taught you?'

'I'm sorry. Not for what I said, but for the way I said it,' Anna Pryce said contritely.

'Then is it not perhaps the girl Hannah you should be saying sorry to? Tatiana said she insisted you apologize, but you have not. Is the christening of my great-grandson, named for your father Peter Petrovsky, to be spoiled, then, because you are too proud and haughty to admit you were in the wrong?'

'The christening won't be spoiled. Hannah Kominski will be arriving today to stay next door with Daisy and Keth. I will apologize to her, then. But put yourself in my place? How would you have acted if one of *your* husband's by-blows turned up as she did? And I knew at once who she was. When you have seen her you will understand my shock, Mama. It was as if Natasha Yurovska had come back to haunt me.'

'I do not know how I would have acted, Anna, had one of your papa's indiscretions come to light. Your father did not take mistresses – or at least not on his own doorstep. But you should have held your tongue. I believe Daisy Purvis was there when it happened, so now her husband will know and maybe soon, all the village.'

'Daisy's husband knew all along. Keth was responsible for inviting Hannah Kominski to stay with them. It seems they met in the war, though exactly how, I haven't found out.'

'I suppose the Reverend and Julia Sutton know, too?'

'They knew Natasha Yurovska, remember. They don't have any doubts. And to add to my shame, Tatiana looks upon Hannah Kominski as a sister!'

'Which she is! And am I to be offered coffee? It is so cold, up here in your English north!'

'It was cold, too, in St Petersburg.' Anna ventured a small smile.

'Ah, yes. But there we had stoves and fuel enough,

and servants to keep them lit from morning till night! Do you remember your other life, Anna?'

'I do, Mama. And I remember my father and my brother Vassily, God rest them. But I remember, too, that I am alive and happy with my middle-class doctor, as you call him. Ewart is a good man.'

'Any man would be good compared to the brute you first married.'

'Why does Elliot Sutton refuse to die?' Anna sighed. 'Every so often, mention of him comes up to haunt us. Julia hated him, too.'

'Everyone hated him, except his stupid mother. But let us think of tomorrow. I am glad the girl Hannah is to stand godmother to Peter, even though she is not of your faith, nor mine.'

'Nathan will be christening Peter, Mama, and he is a liberal Christian. He knows Hannah Kominski is a Catholic, now, though she was brought up in the Jewish faith.'

'Yes. I know all about that. Sergeant Bill and Tatiana told me everything. And when I said my prayers last night, I asked Our Lady for guidance.'

'And . . . ?' Anna prompted, softly.

'This morning I awoke with charity in my heart. I am prepared to treat Hannah Kominski with courtesy, as Tatiana has done. The young woman is not to blame for who fathered her, any more than Tatiana was. I am getting too old for feuds. There is none of Elliot Sutton's wickedness in my granddaughter; why should there be any in Natasha Yurovska's child?'

'Perhaps you are right,' Anna murmured as she laid a cloth on the tray and set it with her best china cups and saucers. 'But will you tell me one thing? Where did you send Natasha Yurovska to have her baby?'

'She was sent to France, to caring people, and that is all I am prepared to say.'

She set her lips stubbornly so her daughter might know that the matter was closed and not to be mentioned again.

'But what if Hannah Kominski wants to find her?'

'Why should she? The two she looked on as parents, Tatiana told me, were sent to an – an *extermination* camp. Those Nazis,' Olga Petrovska rounded her mouth in disgust, 'were every bit as bad as the Bolsheviks. But if she is determined, she has a name to offer, now – and the whole of France to search in. But it is highly unlikely Natasha Yurovska will ever be found. You have no need to worry.'

'I don't worry, Mama, though if ever I were to meet her, I would feel like apologizing for what happened to her. If Elliot used her as cruelly as he used me, then she has my pity.'

'I do not wish to hear of what happened between man and wife!' The Countess held up a commanding hand. 'Bedrooms should never be discussed. But I hope you thank heaven on your knees every night for your deliverance. Do you still say your prayers, Anastasia Aleksandrina Petrovska?'

'Yes, I do. And Anna Pryce says her prayers, too,' she smiled. 'Would you like a biscuit with your coffee, Mama – your favourites?'

'Shortbreads? Where on earth did you get them?'

'From under the counter – where else?'

She had wheedled them from the grocer last week

and put them on the highest shelf of the cupboard, out of harm's way. To give to Tatiana, she had thought, to help out with the christening tea. Yet wasn't it worth it, she sighed, to make her peace with Mama? And with Hannah Kominski, too?

Almost as soon as her mother had left for Denniston House, Anna saw Hannah. She was holding Mary Natasha's hand, carefully guiding her down the path.

'Please?' she called, running towards her. 'Can I speak to you? It won't take long . . .'

'I – I am taking the baby for a little walk. She has new shoes, Mrs Pryce, and is very proud of them.'

'Shoosh,' Mary said, holding up a foot.

'Mm. Nice shoes,' Anna smiled.

'Shoosh.' Mary held up the other foot.

'*Two* shoes. Pretty new shoes.' For just a moment Anna hesitated, then she said softly, 'I am sorry, Hannah, for speaking to you as I did. It wasn't your fault. You weren't to know . . .'

'And I am sorry, Mrs Pryce, for giving you such a shock. But at least I am forgiven?'

'You are – if I am forgiven, too. And tomorrow, at the christening, I shall introduce you to my mother,' Anna smiled. 'She's on your side, by the way.'

'Ooh! I have never met a countess. Do I curtsey?'

'No you do *not*,' Anna scolded. 'Those days are long past. But thank you for being so nice about – *things*. We'll talk again, perhaps?'

They smiled a goodbye, with Hannah feeling very relieved to have a countess on her side – and a new friend in Mrs Pryce. She had come a long way, she thought, since the night of the Lysander. She had a half-sister, Keth and Daisy and Mary and, somewhere in the world – maybe in France – the mother who had borne her, and who now had a name. But best of all, she was alive. Wonderfully, gloriously alive, when she should not have been. Was it luck, or had she been guarded by angels? Had her dear Kominski parents been watching over her, that night? And was it Tante Clara who guided Keth to her door?

She did not know. Probably she would never know. But of one thing she was very certain. Tomorrow, she was going to be a godmother, which made her very, very happy.

Lyndis opened her eyes, and laid her hands on her abdomen. The babies were very still, and Keth was still, too, at her side. She wondered if she could get out of bed without awakening him, and decided that perhaps she had better not try. The bedside clock with the luminous dial told her it was far too early to get up, yet, even though she desperately needed a cup of tea, strong and sweet and hot.

But the kitchen was a long way away; three flights of stairs away. The stairs to the hall below she could manage, but the steepness of the wooden steps that led to the kitchen made her apprehensive.

She thought of the rocking chair beside the fire, and longed to sit in it, if only to ease her aching back; thought, too, of the old-fashioned hearthrug there, made of clipped cloth, and wanted to sink her feet into it. But mostly she thought of the brown teapot which, in her present mood, she would gladly drink dry.

Go on, Lyn! Put on your slippers, tie your dressing gown around you and make yourself that tea! You can do it, and anything's better than lying here in the dark!

She pulled herself upright and put a leg out of bed, giving a sigh of satisfaction as her foot touched the floor.

'Lyn?' Drew grunted, only half-awake.

'Ssssh.' She laid a hand on his shoulder and he turned on his side and slept again.

She felt for the torch on the bedside table, locating her slippers and dressing gown, gratefully folding it around her. The slippers were altogether another matter because bending down was impossible. She shuffled her feet into them, then quietly opened the door, making for the top of the stairs.

Clever girl, Lyn! Take it easy to the half-landing, and then you can switch on a light, and see what you are doing.

Thoughts of the still-warm kitchen gave her courage. She made the hall and sighed with relief, switching on another light, making for the green baize door that opened onto the kitchen stairs, looking down, calculating that if she could manage to sit down, she could take it step by step, on her bottom.

'Just take it easy. You're almost there . . .'

And that was something else! No more twins! Any more babies must come one at a time and not make their mother look like the back end of a double-decker bus! Still weeks to go. How was she to manage when even now she was so clumsy there were times when walking was difficult? And fastening her own shoelaces and getting into the car!

'Made it!' She snapped on the kitchen light.

There were still glowing embers in the fire grate, and she threw kindling on them, and logs from the stack in the ingle. Then she lit the gas beneath the kettle.

She was fine, just fine, and soon she would sit in cook's rocker and drink a mug of tea! And twins weren't so bad, were they? Nor was looking like a stranded whale, when soon there would be two babies to lay in the two wicker baskets that waited on the scrubbed table top in Miss Clitherow's room.

Mind, her back still hurt and her perilous descent hadn't done anything to ease the ache in it, either, but a mug of tea would soon put things to rights. Lyn Sutton wasn't helpless, could still negotiate three flights of stairs. With difficulty.

The logs in the grate began to snap and flicker, the high back of the rocker brought comfort to her aching body. She sipped tea and thought that Rowangarth kitchen was by far the nicest room in the house – especially at ten minutes past five in the morning.

0510A it had been when she was a Wren. The A, of course, indicated that it was winter. They'd put a B after the time when it was summer.

She closed her eyes and set the chair rocking gently. She was so lucky. She had met Daisy – Wren Dwerryhouse D J – at Hellas House, their quarters; had met Drew, too. And her darling mother, Auntie Blod, was married to the man she had loved all her life.

And she was now Lyn Sutton – Lady Lyndis, if you wanted to be stuffy – and would soon have two babies, even though she hadn't yet got a pram to push them out in!

The babies were very still, but it wasn't their waking-up time yet, she thought, gentling her abdomen. She loved them so much already that probably, when at last she held them to her, she would weep from sheer joy.

'Lyn Sutton! What on earth are you doing?' Drew, standing in the kitchen doorway, hair tousled.

'Having a cup of tea. Want one?' She smiled, glad to see him. 'And stand on the hearthrug. That stone floor is too cold for bare feet.'

'I got the shock of my life when I found you gone and all the lights in the house on, Lyn. Are you all right?'

'I'm fine. Warm the teapot up and pour yourself a cup.'

'You're sure nothing is wrong? I expected to find you pacing up and down, somewhere, in agony. And how did you manage the kitchen stairs?'

'With a little difficulty and a lot of effort, darling. And there's weeks to go before the pacing up and down starts! Actually, this chair is very comfy. Might we have another, in the attics?'

'Most probably,' Drew grinned. 'That was cook's chair – Mrs Shaw's, I mean. She always wore a long white apron, and when she was upset, she would rock in the chair with her apron over her face.' Drew squatted on the hearthrug at Lyn's feet. 'This kitchen could tell a lot of stories, y'know.'

'And most of them with happy endings,' Lyn laughed. 'Actually, I've been sitting here thinking, and

I've almost decided not to go to the christening this afternoon. Would Tatty mind, do you think? There'll be so much standing up and kneeling down and I thought you could nip back here for me when it was over and I could go to the party, afterwards.'

'Tatty wouldn't mind a bit, and I think you're being sensible, Lyn. Mind, you'd be on your own for a couple of hours – Mary Stubbs and Tilda won't be here today. Will you be all right?'

'Of course I will. I'll put my feet up and read the Sunday papers. Might even have a little sleep. And we do have a phone, remember. A wonderful invention, the telephone. If I suddenly wanted you, Drew, I could pick it up and Winnie would be at the other end of it in no time at all,' she teased. 'So that's settled, then?'

'Settled,' Drew smiled. 'I'm glad you've changed your mind. Can't have you tiring yourself out, or getting chilled through, in the church. Now, how about me giving you a hand back into bed?'

'Fine by me, though I'm not too bad climbing *up* stairs. It's going down that's a bit dicey. It'll be lovely seeing my feet again! And darling – leave the fire safe, will you – make sure everything is all right. Don't want to upset Tilda.'

And Drew poked through the fire and pushed in the dampers and said, 'You're learning, Lady Sutton! Now, back upstairs with you, and no more creeping around in the middle of the night!'

Middle of the night, Lyn thought, as she lay in bed. She wondered how many more middle-of-the-nights there would be before the babies came, and wished she had stayed in the kitchen rocking chair, which had been kinder to her back than this soft feather bed. Because now the aches had begun again and she was glad, at least, that she had decided against going to Peter's christening. To sit, well cushioned, in the winter parlour in front of a log fire would be more to her liking, she was bound to admit. And Tatty would understand.

All Souls was decorated with late Michaelmas daisies and jugs of chrysanthemums. Sidney Willis was relieved to cut them. They had been a nuisance, outdoors, and him having to cover them against the frost every night. Mind, the Christmas blooms – the grand ones with incurling petals and heads like mops, almost – had been carefully potted and carried into the shelter of the greenhouse to be cosseted and sprayed so they would be at their very best for the festive season.

At All Souls, the boiler had been lit early, and now warm air was beginning to seep through the iron grilles in the church floor. A large kettle of hot water had been set atop the boiler, so it could be mixed, when the time came, with the icy water already in the font – having previously been blessed by the Reverend Arthur Reid, of course.

All was ready. The Sunday School children, who always attended christenings, were already wriggling in the small pew nearest the font and tenants and villagers seated around. Most of them had watched Tatiana grow up; had silently applauded when she left Holdenby for London, despite being forbidden to do so. Now that she was happily married and bringing her first-born to be christened, they felt it only right and proper they should attend this most happy occasion.

Tatiana had had doubts, though. A year ago, she and Bill had been quietly married in the little Lady Chapel and she would have liked her son's christening to be there, too. But Bill had intervened. For one thing, the chapel was too small for all the folk who would want to be there and for another, it had no font. So unless Tatiana Benson wanted her son to be christened out of a soup tureen, be there holy water in it or not he said, she would have to do the same as everyone else, and have the ceremony in the big church.

'You look very bonny,' he said as they set out for All Souls.

Tatiana was wearing the suit she had been married in and the same apricot silk blouse and matching hat. She *felt* very bonny. She felt so happy she sometimes wondered what she had done to deserve it.

'You really will have to get a driving licence,' she scolded as Bill took the passenger seat, his son in his arms. 'And be careful.' She straightened the folds of the satin and lace christening gown. 'We don't want him arriving at the church all creased. And oh, Bill, isn't he a little love? Not a murmur of protest when we put all that fancy clobber on him. He's a contented little soul.'

'Aye. You've done well, Mrs Benson,' Bill smiled. 'But get in the car and stop your drooling. There'll be folks waiting at the church for this wee laddie.'

He raised a hand to wave to Karl who stood at the head of the steps. Karl had declined his invitation to the ceremony, declaring that he would be of more use

571

guarding the house, looking after the fires and making sure that kettles were on the boil for when the guests returned from the church.

Tatiana tooted the horn and waved as they left. Karl, arms folded, watched them go.

'Isn't this a lovely day?' She looked left and right at the top of the drive.

'It's gui' cold!'

'Yes, but the sky is bright. Just like a year ago when we were married.'

'A whole year, hen. Has it been to your liking?'

'It has, darling. In fact, it has been so perfect I wouldn't mind another just like it.'

'Jings, woman! Not another bairn! We haven't got this one properly launched yet!'

'Not for a couple of years. Y'know, Lyn has been rather crafty, getting a two-for-one pregnancy. She's right not to come to the church. Drew will pick her up, later.'

'Can't say I blame her. She's no' so good on her feet, just now. And here we are at the kirk, young man.'

Bill smiled down at his son, pride flushing his cheeks. Tatty was right. It *had* been a good year!

Lyn tossed the Sunday paper aside, then got carefully to her feet. She felt restless, alone in the house. Not a sound. She looked out of the window, wishing she dare go for a walk, knowing she must not. Cobbles and flagstones were slippery, Drew had warned.

The trees of the Linden Walk stood bare, their trunks and branches wetly black. The leaves had long since yellowed and fallen and been swept up for compost.

Everywhere looked so cold and damp she could hardly believe that once there had been flowers and sunshine and wide blue skies.

Not long ago her mother had phoned, asking if she were all right, telling her how snug and warm she and Jack were in the thick-walled little cottage near Llangollen and how much they were looking forward to Christmas.

'I'm just fine, Mum,' Lyn had said as brightly as she was able, being careful not to mention that she *wasn't* just fine and that the backache that awakened her this morning was hurting like mad.

'You take care of yourself, *merchi*. Chin up. Won't be long, now!'

Lyn was thinking that tomorrow wouldn't be soon enough when the pain hit her. She gasped in surprise, hands in the small of her back. The ache was getting worse.

She sat down on the window seat, telling herself that everything was all right, that the babies weren't due until the New Year, thinking that perhaps Sister Fletcher wouldn't mind if she phoned – just to check that the odd pain was nothing to worry about. The odd *stabbing* pain.

The hall felt very cold when she picked up the phone; dank and comfortless, and the Suttons looking down from the staircase walls. It was a great relief to hear the operator's voice so nice and normal.

'Number, please?'

'Hullo, Mrs Hallam. Can you give me Sister Fletcher?'

'I can try, Lady Lyndis, but she did tell me she was out for the day. Is it urgent?'

'N-no. Not important. Did she – er – say when she would be back?'

'She didn't. Only that she was going over to her parents' house, the other side of Creesby. Taking Christmas presents, she said.'

'Oh, well – thanks . . .'

'Tell you what, Lady Lyndis.' Winnie Hallam hadn't been a telephonist nearly thirty years for nothing. Winnie knew every voice on her switchboard and the mood they were in an' all. And Lady Sutton sounded not a little apprehensive. 'I'll check on Sister's number every now and then – tell her you rang, shall I, when she comes back?'

'Thanks, Mrs Hallam. Kind of you. But I'm all right. And Drew will be back soon, to take me to Denniston.'

'I'll bet he's at the christening. Think everybody must be there 'cept you and me, Lady Lyndis! We-e-ll, I'll go if you're sure you're all right. Take care, now . . .'

'Thanks. I will. 'Bye.'

Lyn put down the receiver, strangely reluctant to let Mrs Hallam go, because she *wasn't* all right, and what was more she felt very alone, now. Tilda and Mary Stubbs on their day off; Drew at the church and not due to collect her for another hour at least.

But what could happen in an hour? she demanded of herself as she made for the winter parlour and the warmth of the fire. She'd had a niggle in her back she had thought so unimportant she hadn't even mentioned it to Drew. And she had felt one pain. Rather a nasty one, but it was gone, now.

And the babies weren't due, yet. Late January Ewart had said.

She sat down on the sofa, taking a cushion, hugging it. Everybody at the church. Even Ewart would be there because wasn't it Anna's grandson who was being christened?

Idiot! Drew would be here in no time at all, so why was she worrying? And she wasn't worrying! It was just that being so alone, she supposed, was making her just a little jumpy.

She sat, eyes fixed on the mantel clock, and hugged the cushion closer.

The vicar and Nathan – who had donned surplice and cassock for the first time in many weeks – the godparents, grandparents and close family, stood round the font and smiled as Bill and Tatiana and a baby, overwhelmed almost by his finery, entered All Souls.

Olga, Countess Petrovska, adjusted her sable hat and stood proudly straight-backed; Anna, who all at once remembered the last time the satin and lace gown had been used, stepped closer to her husband and twined her little finger with his.

Daisy was there with Mary Natasha on her hip, because Keth was a godfather. Drew stood beside his mother, Alice and Tom to his left. Hannah Kominski looked very beautiful in a long blue coat with a matching pillbox hat, and, smiling, held out her arms for the baby.

Julia Sutton gazed at the Countess, wondering what was in her mind; how exactly she felt about the living embodiment of the servant in black who had left Holdenby in shame and disgrace.

But it had nothing to do with Hannah, Julia thought

rebelliously, then smiled across at Drew, sending her silent love, praying he would never know that the young woman who stood between Arthur Reid and Nathan, was half his sister too.

And this holy spot, this happy gathering, was not the right place in which to damn Elliot Sutton to further than Hell. She should be ashamed of her thoughts! She closed her eyes, made a hasty apology to God, then opened them to see Alice gazing at her; dear Alice who knew her so well that surely she must be reading her mind.

She winked and smiled, and Alice winked back, ever understanding, then turned her attention to Nathan who dipped an exploratory finger into the font.

They were ready, Alice thought, for the three splashes; those for the Father, the Son and the Holy Ghost. Most babies cried when the sanctified water touched their heads. Alice hoped Peter would protest, because that would mean he had cried the devil out of him and that all was well. Old-fashioned and stupid, of course, but Alice always welcomed a cry from the font. Daisy, she remembered, had yelled blue murder at her christening, making it plain she was Tom's daughter!

'In the name of the Father,' Nathan said gently. The baby wrinkled his nose. 'And of the Son.' The baby opened his eyes, questioningly. 'And of the Holy Ghost . . .'

Master Peter Benson fixed his tormentor with a bright blue gaze, waved his fists angrily and gave a loud yell.

Everyone smiled, happily. Nathan dabbed dry the

little head. The baby closed his eyes, snuffled, and went back to sleep.

Drew thought that very soon, his own children would be carried to this font. He thought briefly about the name he had chosen, should he have a son, then thought about Lyn, alone at Rowangarth.

'Would you mind, Tatty,' he asked as they stood on the church steps, afterwards, 'if I didn't wait for the photographs? Want to nip back home to Lyn.'

'Not a bit. Uncle Igor gave Peter a fancy flash camera, so we'll be taking more photos indoors. Off you go, old love. See you.'

Drew walked quickly to his car, realizing how much he had missed having Lyn beside him. These days, even a few hours apart seemed a long time.

'Hi, darling – it's me!' he called the minute he closed the front door behind him. 'Ready for the party?'

'In here.' They met at the winter parlour door. 'Oh, Drew, I'm so glad to see you!'

'What is it, Lyn?' The pallor of her face, the tightness of her mouth were at once obvious. 'Aren't you well? Got a headache?' He guided her to a chair.

'Headache? I – I think it's worse than that. I've been having pains. I think I might have started, Drew. I thought it was backache at first.'

'But why didn't you phone me?'

'No phones in the church, love, and besides, I'm still not sure . . .'

'Do they hurt – the pains, I mean?' He dropped to his knees, and took her hands in his. 'And why haven't you rung Sister Fletcher?'

'I did. She's out for the day. Mrs Hallam is going

to keep ringing her for me. And yes, they're starting to hurt . . .'

'Oh, Lordy! Ewart's at the christening, too.'

'I think everyone is, Drew, but me and Mrs Hallam. And answer the phone, will you? It might be her, with a message.'

Drew hurried to the hall. He didn't know what to do. Floating mines, force-eight gales, Zero dive-bombers – he had survived them all, in his time. But Lyn in pain and two babies who looked as if they were coming before they should, was altogether a different matter.

He picked up the phone. 'Rowangarth. Winnie?'

'Hullo, Sir Andrew. It's Sister. Winnie said Lady Sutton might appreciate a visit?'

'Sister Fletcher! I thought you were gone for the day!' Relief wrapped Drew round.

'Thought I'd get back before dark. The roads are getting icy. Is everything all right?'

'Lyn's having pains. Can you come?'

'Ten minutes,' came the brisk reply, then the phone went dead.

'You heard?' Drew leaned on the door jamb. 'Sister Fletcher's coming.'

Lyn closed her eyes and let go a breath of relief. 'Good,' was all she was able to say before another pain took her.

'Well, Lady Lyndis. You seem to have caught us all on the hop. Have you timed your pains?' The sight of the midwife in her pale grey dress and white apron was wonderful to see, Drew thought. 'Can you lay back on the sofa, so I can have a look at you?'

'Sorry to make a fuss,' Lyn whispered.

'You're not making a fuss,' the midwife smiled. 'You're having a baby, that's all – well, *two* babies, which will take just a little longer. I'll ring Dr Pryce – tell him you are in the first stages. I wonder, Sir Andrew, if you could have the fire lit in the little room we got ready?'

'Of course!' Drew hurried to do her bidding, eager to do something – *anything* – to help, because Lyn was going to have the babies and all at once, he didn't know what to do. Except to light the fire, and maybe check that the boiler was stoked. They'd need hot water, wouldn't they?

He crumpled newspaper into balls, laying kindling, wishing he could phone his mother, or Lady. Or maybe Daisy?

He watched as the kindling ignited, then piled on more. The bed in this little room was already made up. Should he put hot bottles in it?

He wished he could ring Denniston House, have a word with Bill, or Keth. They knew about it, didn't they? And why, in heaven's name, did he feel so helpless? Was it because having babies was women's business or was it because, all at once, he was unsure and afraid?

'That's better. Get the room aired,' Sister said from the doorway. 'I've had a word with Dr Pryce. He'll be along later.'

'*How* much later?'

'When I send for him. Don't worry. He'll be here for the deliveries.'

'But my wife is in pain.'

'Yes, but nothing that she and I can't handle together.' Then seeing the downcast face she smiled and let down her midwife's disguise long enough to say, 'Tea, Sir Andrew? Why don't you make a pot? I think we could all do with a cuppa.'

'But Lyn . . . ?'

'She could do with one, too. She's just said so.'

Tea, Drew brooded as he clumped down the kitchen stairs. His wife about to be delivered, and they wanted *tea*! Mind, he'd heard Tom Dwerryhouse say it often enough, and now he knew it to be indisputably true!

Women *were* queer cattle. Very queer cattle indeed!

TWENTY-SIX

Lyn's babies were born in the small cold hours of Monday. Along the passage, sitting in the winter parlour, Drew and Julia had heard the first protesting cry.

'Thanks be. That's one of them here,' Julia murmured.

She had phoned, when the christening was over, to ask if any help was needed at Rowangarth and Drew had gratefully accepted. Not the offer of help, but for someone to be near at hand.

'She *will* be all right, Mother?'

'Of course she will. Hilary Reid had twins twice, don't forget. And by the way, the pram is ready for collection any time you want it. It's been given a good clean and polish, she said. I'm looking forward to seeing a pram standing in the hall at Rowangarth again.'

'What happened to the one I had? It isn't in the attics.' Drew didn't care one iota about his pram, but it gave him something to say; something to briefly think about in the middle of the worrying and listening and aimless pacing.

'No. I gave it away when you were about five. There were a lot of families in those days who couldn't afford food, let alone prams.'

'People couldn't afford to eat, yet they had babies?'

'Babies, as well you know, Drew Sutton, have a habit of happening. And if you get up and pull back those curtains once more, I swear I shall scream! It is still dark, outside. Soon be the shortest day, don't forget. It won't be light for ages.'

'I know. And this is the longest night I've ever spent, Mother.'

'Me too. But shall I tell you what I'd like right now?' she smiled.

'Not another cup of tea!'

'No, Drew. A cigarette. I'd kill for one!'

'But Mother, you've given them up!'

'So I have, but it isn't every cold, dark morning you become a grandmother!'

'Please don't? You've been so good. And anyway, there are no cigarettes here.'

'All right, but maybe a snifter of brandy would calm us both down?'

'No cigarettes, no brandy just yet!' Drew jumped to his feet.

'Okay. But please sit down, Drew? You're making me –' She stopped, hurrying to open the door. 'Listen! That's the other baby! Didn't you hear it?'

'Probably the first one, having another yell.'

Yet for all his studied calm, Drew wished with all his heart it was indeed the second child; that it was all over for Lyn, and that she was all right. They sat unspeaking, eyes fixed on the door, but there was no sound from the little room along the passage. The mantel clock ticked far too loudly in the waiting silence, then with a noise like a pistol shot, a doorknob clicked and there were footsteps. They jumped to their feet, Drew with eyes closed, Julia with breath indrawn. Then Ewart stood there, and he was smiling.

'Congratulations,' he beamed. 'All's well. Mother tired but happy, babies fine. Five pounds, and five pounds three ounces. Good weight, for twins, born early. Just give it five minutes, then you can both have a look.'

'What have we got?' Drew gasped, flush-faced.

But Ewart Pryce knew better than break Sister Fletcher's rule.

'So what do you think they'll be?' Julia flung wide the curtains, opened a window and stood, eyes closed against tears, breathing deeply.

'I don't know and I don't care. We've got two babies, Mother!'

He held wide his arms and Julia went into them, hugging her son, sniffing loudly.

'Old softie.' Drew dabbed dry the tears in her eyes. 'Didn't Ewart say they're all fine?'

'I know, but Alice was so smug getting a grandchild before I did, and now I've got two! And isn't it awful? Four o'clock in the morning, and everybody will still be in bed. We can't ring round, just yet.'

'It doesn't matter. As soon as I've seen Lyn, I'm going to the top of the Pike and I'll yell it out for everybody to hear!'

'Idiot! You'd do better getting some sleep.'

'Don't think I could. I'm as high as a kite, right

now. I'll hang around till Mary and Tilda get here.'

'They'll be disappointed to have missed it all – especially Mary Stubbs,' Julia laughed. 'And I'll bet you anything you like they're both in good and early. The news will have got around, you know. Oh, Drew, I'm shaking like a leaf.'

'Join the club! So what are you going to be – Granny? Grandma?'

'Gran, I think. Blodwen and Jack are going to be *nain* and *taid* – that's Welsh for granny and grandpa, I believe.'

They turned to see Ewart Pryce in the doorway, shrugging into his jacket, winding a muffler round his neck.

'I'll get myself off, then – try to get a few hours' shuteye before surgery. Sister won't be long after me. Sure you can cope?' he grinned. 'You both look shattered!'

'Tired but triumphant. What Lyn must be feeling,' Julia smiled, 'I can't imagine. Can we go in, now?'

'You can, but only for five minutes, Julia. Want me to wait and see you back to Bothy House?'

'Thanks, but no thanks. It's only a cock-stride away. I promise not to stay too long, and Ewart, thanks for – for *everything*.'

'You first,' Drew smiled, when they were alone. 'You've been waiting for this for a long time.'

How long, Julia thought tremulously as she bent over her grandchildren, he would never know.

'Lyn,' she whispered, kissing her daughter-in-law gently. 'Thank you, my dear. Thank you so much . . .'

* * *

When Julia had left, emotional and tearful, still, Drew stood by Lyn's bed. There were patches of red high on her cheekbones, though her face was pale. Beneath her eyes were dark smudges.

'Well, sailor. We did it! Don't I get a kiss?' she said huskily. 'And say hullo to your kids!'

'Darling, I'm so choked, I don't know what to say, to do . . .' Gently he kissed her mouth, then gazed at the babies she held on each arm. 'Goodness! What a mop of hair!'

'That's your daughter, and Sister says it's only baby hair and will soon come out. Take a look at young Master Sutton, though. And sorry, darling, I know you Suttons are always fair, but I've gone and upset the apple cart!'

'A redhead,' he laughed, 'and it doesn't matter a bit! They're here, and that's all that matters. Was it awful, darling?'

'We-e-ll, now I come to think of it, now that it's over, it wasn't all that bad. Mind, I yelled a bit, and I wanted you with me, but Sister won't have fathers around. Fathers, she said, are meant to walk the floor, and worry.

'I was thinking of Tatty, and how she said she swore at the top of her voice, in Russian, so next time I'll have to get a few choice Welsh swear words from Mum! Mind, not so very long ago, there wasn't going to be a next time. Not ever! And if Sister Fletcher told me to push just once more, I vowed I would bite her!'

'But it's all right now, darling?' Drew whispered, hardly able to take his gaze from the black-haired baby who seemed to have fixed him with her eyes. Such very blue eyes.

'We're all fine. Boy is going to take after you, I think. He had a little protest when he was born, but he's slept, since. But madam, here,' she laid a cheek on the dark head in the crook of her arm, 'yelled like mad and is still grizzling. And she won't go to sleep. It's as if she knows she's been born, and is weighing things up, sort of.'

'Ahem.' The midwife coughed. 'I think these babies should be in their baskets, now. And you, Mother, need some sleep.' Deftly she tucked both babies round with blankets. 'I'm leaving now, Sir Andrew, but I'll be in again, this afternoon, and we'll think about getting you upstairs, back to your own bedroom, Lady Lyndis.'

'That would be lovely. This room is a bit spartan, and the mattress is very hard. I'm sure I'd rest better, in my own bed.'

'That's settled, then. I'll see you about three – when *I've* had some sleep,' she laughed. 'You did very well, Lady Lyndis. A born mother. 'Bye. I'll let myself out. Oh, and no visitors except close family until I say so!'

When they heard the closing of the front door, Drew wrapped Lyn in his arms, his cheek on hers.

'I love you, Lyndis Sutton,' he said softly.

'Mm. Love you too. And isn't everything quiet, all of a sudden? Just you and me and the kids in this big old house?'

You and me and the kids. They had a son and a daughter. For Christmas.

* * *

'Thank goodness!' Julia opened the kitchen door at Keeper's Cottage and strode into the kitchen. 'I've been waiting for your light to go on. Tom not up, yet?'

'Out early after poachers. Folks are on the look-out for their Christmas dinners, don't forget. But there's news?' Alice smiled, knowing there was.

'There is! One of each, and mother and babies both well. A bit early, but they're a good weight – for twins.'

'Well, congratulations to the grannies, eh, though I think the little ones should call me Lady, like Drew does. And I've got a drop of brandy in the cupboard. Got it to douse the Christmas cake with, but I reckon you and me should have a snifter in our tea, eh?'

'We should. I deserve one! I never want to spend another night like that for a long time. Drew was like a cat on hot bricks, and I'd have swapped my soul for a cigarette.'

'Julia! You didn't!'

'No. There weren't any in the house, but I'm over it, now. Shall we have mugs, or cups?'

'The best china cups, Julia Sutton! This is a cele-bration! Now, tell me about the babies.'

'The little boy is going to have hair like Lyn's and the little girl is dark. Like Lyn's parents, I suppose. Blodwen is a redhead and Jack is dark-haired.' Julia pulled out a chair and sat at the kitchen table, chin on hands. 'I left a note for Nathan. He was still sleep-ing when I got back so I decided to leave him be.'

'Now why on earth did you go and do a thing like that? You should have wakened him up. Now, he'll wonder where you are!'

'He won't. I wrote, Congratulations, Grandpa. Boy and girl and mother all fine. Father as well as can be expected! Gone to Keeper's, or words to that effect . . .'

'So what's wrong, Julia?' Alice placed the cosy over the teapot and set it in the hearth. 'Either you've tired yourself out stopping up all night, or there's something you aren't telling me! And don't say I'm imagining things, because I know when you're worried!'

'I think I need a cigarette, Alice.'

'Nonsense! You haven't had one for months and you're not starting again – not in this house! You'll have to make do with a drop of brandy in your tea! Heavens, woman, this is an occasion!'

'I know, Alice, and I'm ashamed of myself. And when I've told you, you'll be ashamed of me, too. It – it's the little girl . . .'

'Nothing's wrong with her?' Alice looked up from pouring the tea, eyes concerned. 'You said they were both fine.'

'They are. They're lovely. Only the girl baby is dark. She's got a shock of black hair, but not like Lyn's father. She's Mary Anne Pendennis-dark. At least, I – I think so . . .'

'In heaven's name, Julia Sutton, what are you trying to say?' Alice stood stock-still, teapot still aloft. 'You can't mean what I think you mean?'

'Oh, I'm tired, and maybe I got it wrong. I hope to heaven I did. I suppose I was expecting one of the babies at least to be Sutton-fair, you see.'

'So tell me?' Alice sat down opposite, fixing Julia's eyes with her own. 'Are you trying to say that little

588

girl could be a throwback? From Elliot Sutton?'

'Yes,' Julia said flatly, looking down at her clenched fingers.

'No. Oh, *no*!'

'Look, Alice – I'm sorry and I'd like nothing more than to be proved wrong, but you and I know who Drew's father was.'

'Drew's father was Giles Sutton, your own brother. Drew was born in wedlock and he's Giles's. You and Nathan and me and Tom know different, but no one else does. Not even your mother knew the truth of it, so why are you resurrecting it, now?'

'Because the twins jumped a generation. It happens like that, Alice.'

'And Elliot Sutton's Pendennis darkness has jumped a generation, too, through Drew? Is that what you are trying to say?'

'Yes . . .'

'Well, you can forget it, Julia.' Alice jumped angrily to her feet. 'No matter what Elliot Sutton did to me that night in Celverte, *Giles* is Drew's father! And what's more, I would swear it with my hand on a stack of Bibles! Drew thinks he's Giles's, just as your mother did. Drew won't associate his little girl with Elliot Sutton. Why should he?'

'You're right, Alice. Why on earth should he? Unless some mindless idiot like myself makes such a fuss about a baby with dark hair that he gets a bit sniffy about it. I'm sorry I said what I did. Really sorry. It was just that the little thing had such deep blue eyes.'

'All babies are born with blue eyes, you daft woman!'

'Yes, but that colour eyes usually turn brown in a few weeks, in my experience.'

'All right! And Jack Carmichael has deep brown eyes and black hair – or must have had, before it started getting bits of grey in it! It's him that little girl takes after, so drink up your tea and stop talking like a complete idiot!' Alice sloshed a generous amount of brandy into each cup. 'And then we'll talk about other things – like you have two grandchildren, Julia Sutton, and what they are going to be called, so cheers!'

'Cheers!' Julia raised her cup. 'And what would I do without you, Alice?'

'Sometimes I wonder,' Alice said, matter-of-factly. 'And I'll bet you anything you like that those two babies will be called John and Helen – after Drew's grandparents. Drew never knew his grandfather, but he adored Lady Helen, God love her. So I'm drinking to John and Helen Sutton – two lovely little babies and just in nice time for Christmas!'

A fire burned in the grate, lamps glowed softly and the Sutton babies slept in baskets, either side of the fat double bed.

'Back in my own room,' Lyn sighed. 'Lovely.'

Drew had carried her up the stairs; lifted her in his arms as if she were no weight at all. So romantic, she had thought, her cheek against his chest. It was nice being fussed over by Mary Stubbs and Tilda; nice having two babies; *really* nice to have it all over and done with before even she had time to start worrying – seriously worrying, that was. And absolutely wonderful that in a week it would be Christmas.

'Daiz rang. Wants to know when she can come over,' Drew said. 'Knowing my sister, I'm even surprised she asked! Whenever, I told her.'

'Fine. But before she comes – before anyone else comes – I think it's time these two had names. We can't go on calling them Boy and Girl, can we?'

'Agreed. Actually, Lyn, I've been pretty certain for quite a while about a boy's name.'

'Me, too. I've known for ages and ages. And darling, we promised, didn't we, that whatever the other chose, we'd accept.'

'We promised,' Drew smiled. 'It's okay if you want to call Girl Blodwen, even!'

'There's nothing wrong with Mum's name, except that Blod Sutton doesn't sit well, does it? Anyway, you go first, darling.'

'So, how does Jonathan sound? Even though he'll be bound to get Jon, do you like it?'

'Jonathan Sutton. Jon,' she smiled brilliantly. 'Love it.' She leaned over to where he slept, kissing her fingertip, placing it on the tiny nose. 'Hullo, Jon Sutton. You've got a name . . .'

'Hope he approves.'

'I'm sure he does. One thing is certain, he couldn't care less. He's going to take after you, Drew. Very placid. And now for Madam.' She looked into the other basket to be met with a bright blue stare. 'Wouldn't you know it – she's awake again. She's a very nosy baby – eyes everywhere.'

'Why did you call her Madam, Lyn?'

'Because that's what she's going to be – a right

591

little madam. And I'm her mother, so I know!' Then, all at once serious she said, 'Remember you promised, Drew – *my* choice.'

'*Your* choice, sweetheart.'

'Then she's to be Kathryn . . .' Lyn whispered.

'*Kathryn!* But why . . . ?' Uncertainty showed for only a moment in his eyes. 'There's to be another Kitty Sutton, is that it?'

'No. She'll be Kathryn when she's naughty, but mostly she'll be Kat.'

'Have you always known, Lyn – about the name, I mean?'

'Yes. Every time I saw Kitty's grave I became more and more sure of it. You aren't upset, Drew?'

'N-no. Not upset, darling – just a little curious, that's all. I mean, what do we tell people?'

'*Tell* them? We tell them it's to be Kathryn – Kat. No explanations, no nothing! I want my – *our* – daughter to be Kat Sutton. She isn't taking Kitty's place. She won't be expected to climb trees, or be the best spitter, or always want to be centre stage, you know.'

'No, but I bet she will, for all that!' Drew laughed. Then gentling the little cheek with a forefinger, he returned the so-blue gaze. 'Hullo, Kat Sutton. Do you like your name?'

And Kat Sutton, already running true to prediction, immediately closed her eyes, and slept.

'Well, that's Mary in bed,' Keth Purvis smiled. 'Will you be all right, going to Rowangarth in the dark?'

'Of course I will. I haven't lost my blackout skills.

And I'll take a torch. But darling – before I go, there's something . . .' She reached up, arms around his neck, standing close. 'I didn't tell you before – what with the christening, then Lyn going into labour – but I'm late. Three days.'

'Surely three days late is neither here nor there,' he said, warily.

'With me, it is! I'm always spot on. It should have been Friday, and it hasn't come.'

'Do you mind, Daisy – if it's another baby, I mean? You did say –'

'I said that when Mary was on her feet would be the right time to think about it, and I meant it. I just might be pregnant, and if I am then it's fine by me.'

'Good. It's fine by me, too. What do you think Lyn will say when you tell her?'

'Tell her? Not for anything would I steal her thunder! I'll tell her later, when I'm more sure. And we aren't telling anyone just yet – not even Mam and Dada.'

'Not a soul, but fingers crossed, eh? Give me a ring when you leave Rowangarth and I'll nip out to the gate, and wait for you.'

'Okay.' She buttoned up her long, winter coat. 'Anything else before I go, fusspot?'

'No. Just that I love you, Mrs Purvis. Very much.'

'Lyn, they are *beautiful*!' Daisy laughed with delight. 'What a clever lady you are! Was it awful, old love?'

'No. Thinking back, it wasn't so bad. Now I've had a decent night's sleep, I feel fine. Wish I didn't have to have a week's bed rest. And I'm thinking straight, again. The little room Miss Clitherow had is going to be the day nursery, we've decided. Save a lot of running up and down stairs.

'And Sister Fletcher says I'm to keep the babies warm and snuggled, because she's sure it's going to snow. It makes sense, them arriving early. They aren't big bouncing babies, but they're healthy and there's all the world for them to grow in, she says. And we aren't in any hurry to have them christened. Drew thinks Easter will be soon enough.'

'Couldn't agree more. Wait till the warmer weather comes, then have a bit of a do. Where's Drew, by the way?'

'Nipped down to the pub, with Nathan. I had to practically order him out, poor love. I think he suffered more than I did! A few beers will do him the world of good.'

'Seems you are back to your old bossy self, Lady Sutton. Everything under control again! I suppose you've decided on names?'

'We have. Little copper nob is Jonathan – Jon – and his sister is Kathryn,' Lyn said softly, eyes on her hands.

'*Kathryn!*' Daisy sat bolt upright in her chair. 'Whose idea was that, then?'

'Mine entirely. And she won't get Kitty. We're to call her Kat.'

'We-e-ll, I suppose you know what you're doing . . .'

'Yes, I do. I've given it a lot of thought. Kat Sutton,' Lyn said firmly, chin tilted.

'Right, old love. What you call your daughter is

nothing to do with anyone, so don't look so defensive about it. But you must have had good reason for it?'

'No reason at all, other than I like the name.'

'All right. One more try. This is Purvis-from-the-bottom-bunk, don't forget!'

'All right. I did – *do* have a reason. The answer is simple. I couldn't have called her anything else, you see.'

'Why couldn't you?' Daisy persisted. 'And what does Drew think of the idea?'

'Oh, you know Drew. Nothing bothers him. Fine by him, he said, and I'm sure as I can be that he meant it.'

'So go on, then? Tell me why no other name will do? Mam said she was sure it would be John and Helen.'

'No. It's *got* to be Kathryn. Kitty Sutton has been waiting a long time to come home, you see.'

'Kitty *is* home.' Daisy ran her tongue round suddenly-dry lips. 'Aunt Julia brought her to Rowangarth, because Rowangarth was where she'd have wanted to spend the rest of her life. Kitty *is* at rest, Lyn.'

'She isn't – or *wasn't* – until now. And before you think I've gone off my head, Kitty's mother thinks exactly as I do. She and I met at Kitty's grave, and agreed we should talk.'

Daisy felt distinctly put out. 'What on earth did you talk about?'

'I never told anyone, not even Drew, but she and I agreed Kitty wasn't at rest. Mrs Amelia said she

595

was probably still watching over Drew; said that only in her own good time would she leave that church-yard and go to wherever it was intended she should go.'

'That doesn't sound a bit like Amelia Sutton to me. She's usually so level-headed; was the only one who could handle Clementina Sutton when she'd been at the brandy bottle. Are you sure you didn't get it wrong?' Daisy whispered, heart thudding.

'I didn't. And what's more, I agreed with her and I shall write to her as soon as I can, and let her know Kitty is going to be all right now.'

'All this is a bit much to take in.' Daisy walked to the window and stood, arms folded stubbornly, gazing out at the lights of the village and Brattocks Wood, dark and still. 'Oh, I know you always had a bee in your bonnet about Kitty being Drew's first love and all that, but I never thought you'd go as far as to even think that little girl of yours is Kitty's reincarnation. Because reincarnation is what it boils down to, isn't it? I hope Nathan Sutton never hears you say such a thing!'

'He won't. I've only told you, Daisy, and I shan't ever tell Drew. And it isn't reincarnation. It's just Kitty come home, *really* come home to us, and I'm glad. Don't you see, it's the most wonderful thing that could have happened to me? I don't ever need to feel uneasy about Kitty, now, because she's *mine*, and I adore her.'

'I don't know what to say, old love.' Daisy sat on the edge of the bed. 'You seem so sure about it, so happy. How can you be so – so *positive*?'

'I told you Mrs Amelia agreed with me, didn't I, and she said something else, too – something that makes sense to me, now. She said she felt I would have a girl and a boy. And what's more, she said that when Kitty was ready to move on, she would leave a sign, and I would recognize it at once.'

'And didn't you feel peculiar, Lyn, standing over Kitty's grave, talking about her like it was the most natural thing in the world?'

'We weren't in the churchyard. We went for a walk and ended up on the Linden Walk seat. It's lovely, there; a beautiful, peaceful place to talk about Kitty. And Mrs Amelia told me that she was certain I would come to love her. She gave me her word I would, and I *do* love her.'

'Well, all I can say, Lyn, is that you're right in one thing – never to tell Drew what you've told me tonight. I don't think he would understand.'

'No. He isn't a red-headed Celt, like me. I thought I hadn't inherited any of Mum's kinkiness, but I think I must have. I'm sure, you see, that Jon is going to be just like Drew – very relaxed, and slow to anger. Kat will be a show-off, an attention seeker.'

'That's Kitty to a T,' Daisy smiled fondly. 'But Kitty was a love, for all her precocious ways. If Kat grows up only half as much fun, she'll be all right. But you've given me the shivers, Lyn, because now you've got me believing we've got Kitty back.'

'We have, only she's called Kat and she's my daughter! Mind, Jon is going to be the most angelic, and I adore him, too. I used to wonder if there would be enough love inside me for two babies; worry in case

I cared for one more than the other. But I love them both, every bit as much. It's a good feeling, Daisy.'

'Then I'm happy for you, but should you be talking like this, Lyn? Shouldn't you love that little girl for what she is, and not because you think Kitty has sent her? Are you trying to convince yourself that Kat has somehow got Kitty Sutton's soul?'

'Daisy – listen.' Lyn plumped up her pillows, then lay against them, hands relaxed on the bed quilt. 'It's my belief – it has *always* been my belief, that souls never die. And I believe, too, that someone who died suddenly as Kitty did might be a bit disorientated for a while; that her soul would fly to where it longed to be.'

'To Rowangarth, Lyn? But souls go to heaven.'

'And so they do, eventually. But each time I have stood at Kitty's grave, I knew her soul was waiting there, still. I didn't know what for, but I was as certain as I could be that Kitty knew I was there – just as I knew she hadn't passed on.'

'So you believe in reincarnation, Lyn? That our soul, if it wants to or needs to, can choose to stay on earth? Well, all I can say is that it's a bit much if you think you've got Kitty's soul in your keeping, now. It isn't Christian!'

'Then nor was it Christian that a lovely young girl, who was desperately in love and who had everything to live for, should be killed so wantonly. Kitty deserved better than that, Lyn.'

'It seems you're all at once on her side, yet when Drew asked you to marry him, you had doubts about ever taking her place. It really got to you.'

'Yes, but that was before I realized that if it had been me who Drew loved then, and I'd been just snuffed out by a bomb – in Liverpool, say – then I would have wanted someone to be on my side, too.' She reached for Daisy's hand, holding it tightly, smiling into her eyes. 'I shall never say again to anyone, what I have said to you tonight. We-e-ll, maybe only to Mrs Amelia. But I am so happy, and happy for Kitty, too, that it just came spilling out and you copped the lot, Daisy.'

'Then I promise I won't ever tell a soul – not even Keth – though much as I cared for Kitty, it's going to take a while for me to come round to your way of thinking, Lyn. I'll be glad to try, though.'

'That's all I ask, Purvis old love.' Lyn leaned to kiss Daisy's cheek. 'And it looks as if Kat is awake again, so why don't you give her a cuddle – tell her you're going to be her godmother?'

'Hullo, Kat Sutton.' Gently, Daisy lifted the swaddled little bundle, fondling the baby-soft cheek. 'Your mother has just said you're going to be a show-off, but I won't mind if you are. I'll always be on your side, little thing, because I'm your Aunt Daisy – well, your half-aunt. And I'd love to be your godmother.' Then smiling, she said, 'I think she's going to sleep, Lyn. All she needed was a bit of attention.'

'Attention,' Lyn laughed. 'Told you so, didn't I? And oh, this is just like old times in Cabin 4A. Lyn Carmichael and Purvis-from-the-bottom-bunk, having a heart-to-heart, swapping secrets.'

And Daisy rocked Drew's little girl in her arms and smiled softly, because she was as sure as made no matter, that soon there would be another secret to share.

'Mm. Sharing secrets. But we've come a long way, you and me,' she laughed, 'since Cabin 4A, Carmichael.'

Oh, my word, yes!

TWENTY-SEVEN

1950

Tatiana stood on the steps in front of Denniston House, waving goodbye to her grandmother and uncle, then hurried inside, closing the door against the cold.

'Well, that's them on their way. Mother will see that they get on the London train all right.'

'They've both enjoyed themselves. We had a good night, at Hogmanay. I'm glad Keth let the New Year in for us again. He's a lucky first-foot.'

'So you think we've been lucky?'

'Speaking for myself, I do. I have you and Pete, and I'm beginning to think I'm no' a bad painter, either. If that isn't lucky, I don't know what is!'

'Then speaking for *my*self, I've got a husband I adore, the most beautiful boy *and* a sister! How lucky can you get?'

'You're pleased about Hannah, aren't you? Things could have been a bit sniffy, hadn't you thought?'

'You mean Mother mightn't have apologized for the things she said, and the Petrovska might have got on her high horse. You've got to admire the old girl, y'know,' Tatiana smiled wickedly. 'She took it very well when you told her about Hannah, but I think she knows when she's beaten.'

'She carried it off with great aplomb,' Bill defended. 'I suppose that's where breeding comes in. Mind, she didn't have much choice, all things considered.'

'No, but she seemed to warm to Hannah, in the end. And so she should, considering she couldn't wait to get Natasha Yurovska and her sin bundled off to Paris.'

'So there's no doubt in your mind that Hannah is your blood kin?'

'No doubt at all, Bill. And I also happen to think she's due some compensation. After all, I did very well out of the Pendenys Suttons. Grandmother Clementina left this house to me and, before he died, Grandpa Edward made provision for me, so I'd never want for money. Don't you think Hannah deserves something, too? She's a Pendenys Sutton, after all.'

'Legally she has no claim on you, Tatty, or on Pendenys, though morally I suppose she has. So you and I will always be here for her, and make her welcome whenever she wants to visit Denniston.'

'Mm. I've asked her to spend Easter with us and she said she would love to – and to see young Pete Benson, of course. She's on a year's contract at the Birmingham school. I hope she won't go back to France when it runs out.'

'So what if she does? We can visit her there. Don't worry, you won't lose your precious sister. And here's Karl. I asked him to bring tea.'

The elderly Cossack walked with back ramrod

straight, and laid a tray on the table. Then he said in careful, reluctant English, 'Here for you is tea. And the boy is sleepink on the kitchen table.'

'Well done, Karl,' Tatiana laughed. 'Very good English. And now, between us, we must teach the boy and Bill to speak Russian, eh?'

'*Da*.' He gave one of his rare smiles. 'The babe is safe with Karl,' he said, at the door. 'I look after.'

'Dear Karl,' Tatiana sighed tremulously. 'Oh, darling, do you suppose we could be *too* lucky?'

'Not a bit of it. We all get what we deserve, so stop your blethering, woman, and pour your man a cup of tea!'

'That's a very pleasant district nurse,' Blodwen Carmichael said when Sister Fletcher had left.

'And a very efficient midwife, too. Isn't it great – both babies have gained weight. And she said I could go out, too, if I wrap up warm and don't overdo it,' Lyn beamed.

'Then away you both go, *merchi*. Me and your dad will look after the little ones. A spot of fresh air will do you good, you're a bit pale.'

'That's because I haven't been out since they were born. Wish we could take Jon and Kat. I want the village to see them.'

'You leave them where they are, girl. They're fine, sleeping in the conservatory, and you don't want people coughing and sneezing all over them, now do you? If everything had gone to plan, they'd only just have been born, don't forget. Have you got a woolly hat, and a muffler?'

'I have, Mum.'

'I won't let her get tired,' Drew smiled.

They walked across a lawn white with frost and climbed the stile beside the wild garden into Brattocks Wood. Everywhere was still and cold. Bare trees glistened black and dead, tufted grass looked almost beautiful, sparkling with frost.

'Are you going to tell it to the rooks?' Drew teased.

'I am *not*. In future, I shall leave things like that to those who believe in them! And anyway, they'll know about the twins. Lady will have told them.'

'Careful. The ground is slippery. Keep off the moss.' Drew pulled her arm into his, and she snuggled closer.

'I've got something to tell you, Drew – it's about the christening. I want Mrs Amelia to come.' The words came out in a rush; as if they had been waiting too long to be said.

'But she said she wouldn't be coming back to England again. Uncle Albert dislikes the upheaval, he said, so it's hardly likely Amelia will come alone.'

'I don't think it would be a problem. She went back to Kentucky alone after Nell was christened. I'd really like her here, Drew.'

'Have you any special reason, Lyn?' He stopped walking to draw her close to him. 'She knows about the babies. Mother phoned her. Don't you think that if she'd wanted to come over she would have said so, by now?'

'She was at our wedding, Drew. I want her to see the twins.'

604

Lyn set her mouth stubbornly. It was important that Amelia Sutton should know that Kitty was at peace; that she had truly gone to wherever the Fates had meant her to be.

'Then it's fine by me, Lyn. Bas and Gracie are going to be godparents, so it's certain they'll be over. Maybe Aunt Amelia could travel with them. Ring her, and be blowed to the expense!'

'No, Drew. I shall write.' A letter would be better. 'I'll write tomorrow, in fact. By airmail, she'll have it in four or five days. So will you please kiss me, so we can get on with our walk?'

So they kissed, then hurried hand in hand across the near corner of Home Pasture to the little iron gate at the top of the Linden Walk.

Lyn liked the long avenue of trees. They had been sitting there when Drew's proposal of marriage had begun to take form; were there when she told him she thought she was pregnant. And where she and Amelia Sutton talked about Kitty, and became friends. The Linden Walk was becoming a special place for Lyn Sutton.

Drew pushed back the swinging gate, and Lyn laughed and said that two weeks ago, to get through the kissing gate would have been well-nigh impossible.

'You're happy, Lyn?' Drew asked.

'Very happy, darling. And I'm glad Gracie and Bas will be godparents.'

'Me, too. That way,' he laughed, 'Kentucky will have no excuse for not coming, and we'll get the church decorated by Gracie.'

'They'll come.' Of course they would, Lyn insisted

silently, and Mrs Amelia would come too. When she got the airmail. When she knew about the little girl with dark hair who was to be called Kathryn. 'Mind, there won't be a lot of flowers for Gracie to work with.'

'There'll be daffodils and white narcissi and primroses, and Willis and Catchpole will make sure there's some blossom out, too. Everything will be fine. And look, there's your mother in the window. She's got one of them over her shoulder!'

'Yes, and I wouldn't take bets on which one it is! Kat Sutton, for sure!'

They clasped hands and ran laughing across the grass to the old house, the frosty air pinching Lyn's cheeks to red; ran to Rowangarth's benign shelter and the warmth of its fires. And all at once it seemed to Lyn that it reached out to her in welcome, because she was a Sutton, now; a part of it forever.

She smiled and waved to her mother, holding the little girl who demanded attention. And she knew that little girl would grow up to be like another Kathryn and that Rowangarth's loving arms had reached out to her, too. Kathryn Norma Clementina Sutton was no longer a restless soul, waiting beneath a stone of white marble until the Fates decreed where she should go. Mischievous, beautiful, wilful Kitty had come home to Rowangarth, where she was welcome and loved.

Lyn turned to smile at Drew. There was so much she wanted to say to him; to tell him how completely happy she was and how she adored her babies and how good it was to live at Rowangarth. But in this moment of utter contentment, words were hard to find, so instead she whispered, 'I love you, sailor.'

Julia hung her jacket and long woolly scarf on the peg behind the door at Keeper's Cottage kitchen, then drew out a chair to sit chin on hands at the table.

'It seems an age since we had a good old natter, Alice. And there's so much to talk about!'

'I know, love. I heard it on the early news.'

'About the election? Well, all I can say is that if they carry on the way they are, they'll lose it! Taking tuppence off the meat ration! I read somewhere that if you wanted to buy a small leg of lamb, nowadays, you'd need thirteen ration books!'

'And a small leg of lamb wouldn't go far among thirteen, now would it?' Alice demanded, aggrieved, because only yesterday she had read that the government in Bonn had triumphantly announced that on 1 March, rationing of food would be abolished in West Germany.

'Who won that war?' she had asked angrily of Tom and to soothe her he had said he sometimes wondered.

'Put the kettle on, love,' she asked of Julia. 'I'm just finishing off Kathryn's – *Kat's* – christening gown.' With the aid of a bodkin she threaded narrow pink ribbon at the neck and cuffs. 'And I'm sure I won't be the only one to forget the little one's name. There'll be a lot who'll think of her as Kathryn, you know. I hope I don't do it in front of Lyn.'

'But it was Lyn who chose the name. She insisted on it. Drew isn't a bit bothered about it – leastways, not that it shows. And Lyn is writing to Amelia to ask her to come over for the christening, would you believe? I thought when she told me it was asking a bit too much, though I didn't say anything. I'm trying hard to be a good mother-in-law,' she sighed.

'And you will be! Be there for Lyn if she needs help, and she'll do all right for Rowangarth.'

'I know she will. And whilst we're on the subject, Nathan is having the builders in to have a look at Rowangarth roof – his present to young Jon, he said. And when Drew asked him if he knew how expensive it would be, Nathan said it was only money and that one day young Jon would be glad his roof didn't sag any more. I think inheriting half the Pendenys fortune has always made Nathan uncomfortable, poor love. He's always glad when he can give some of it away.'

'It makes sense to have it seen to, though that roof has sagged as long as I can remember, and I came here forty years ago as kitchen maid to Mrs Shaw.'

'I remember. It was just before Pa died. Where have all the years gone, Alice?'

'Aye. Funny old years, some of them have been. Who'd ever have thought you and me would grow so close.'

Alice shook the folds from the delicate white gown, then held it up for inspection. 'I remember the start of it. You wanted to go to London and young ladies couldn't travel without a chaperon. I went with you, to maid you, and a right dance you led me, Julia Sutton!'

'Oh, my word, yes! You and me going to a Suffragette meeting . . .'

'And getting into trouble with the police. You'd have been arrested if you hadn't fallen and knocked yourself out!'

'Aiming a kick at a policeman whilst wearing a hobble skirt was a silly thing to do, Alice. That was the evening I met Andrew. So long ago,' she sighed, smiling softly.

'Get pouring,' Alice ordered, ever practical. 'I can't abide stewed tea!'

'And then the war came and Andrew and I were married, quietly.'

'Aye. In a blue dress that wasn't even new. And you wore white orchids in your hair. No sugar in mine, Julia . . .'

'So we enrolled as nurses,' Julia smiled, determined to remember. 'The only way we could follow Andrew and Tom to France. We were so determined to be in that war that you lied about your age to get there, Alice.'

'Yes. I went to France as your mother's sewing maid and came back Lady Sutton. I know how Lyn feels, being one of the aristocracy. Mind, she'll learn, and these days a girl can marry above her station. Folk didn't take so kindly to it, when I did it. I was four months pregnant with a rape child the day I came back to Rowangarth.'

'No, Alice. You were carrying my brother's child, never forget! Giles married you, so that made the child *his* – Rowangarth's. And now Drew has two of his own. All in all, life hasn't treated us so badly. Tom came back from the dead and I saw sense at last, and married Nathan.'

'And took your time about it, didn't you, and him in love with you and plain for all to see.'

'Mm. He told me afterwards that he'd always been in love with me, but didn't realize it till I told him I was going to marry Andrew. And because of my shilly-shallying, I left it too late to have children. I shall always be sad that I didn't give Nathan a child.'

'Now stop it, Julia! It's all turned out for the best. And you had the Clan, don't forget.'

'My lovely young Clan . . .' Her eyes took on a dreaming look. 'They always congregated at Rowangarth.'

'Except when they could smell that I was baking bread, then they descended on Keeper's like a swarm of locusts, for bread and honey. Lovely days, Julia, when we were so sure there'd never be another war.'

Six sturdy younglings, Alice thought fondly, and before anyone could blink an eyelid, they were all together again in uniform, because there *was* another war, and it took Kitty.

'This tea is awful! It's gone black and bitter with all our nattering. I'll make another pot.'

'Have you had any more thoughts about – er – Kat?' Julia concentrated too hard on the cups and saucers she was rinsing at the sink.

'You mean about her being so dark? No, I hadn't. You know and I know why there's another Mary Anne Pendennis, but the child can't be held responsible for that, no more than Drew can,' Alice said firmly. 'If blame there must be, then it's –'

'Don't! Don't say that man's name!' Julia flung. 'Kat is my granddaughter. She belongs to Drew and

Lyn and I won't even think of her as anything else. Kat is a Rowangarth Sutton!'

'Good for you, Julia. Just remember there's another Clan growing up – because there is, you know.'

'Oh, I do know. I've thought about it a lot. There'll be Adam and Nell over from Kentucky twice a year, let's hope, and there's Jon and Kat and Mary Natasha, and Pete. We've got six young ones already to watch over, Alice.'

'Yes, and Daisy is bound to have another. She and Keth don't want an only child, as they both were. And Tatty's sure to want more children.'

'Would you like a grandson, Alice? *I've* got one,' Julia teased.

'I'd like another grandchild, I won't deny it, but Tom would like a boy. A fair-haired little lad, he once said. Ah, well – fingers crossed.'

'So let's drink this tea before there's another pot ruined. Let's raise our cups to the new Clan.'

'The new Clan,' Alice said solemnly. 'To those we have already, and to those still to come!'

She thought about a fair-haired boy in the big, old-fashioned pram.

'The new Clan,' Julia said softly.

She thought about six – oh, *at least* six – younglings, running, shouting and laughing across a summer lawn towards the stile and the wild garden. And please God, a girl with a mop of black hair and mischief in her eyes, the leader of the pack. Then she blinked and shook her head and said, 'Any more tea in the pot, Alice?'

* * *

Lyn read through the letter yet again. It had not been an easy one to write for fear of saying too much and at the same time, of saying too little. Except for Daisy, only she and Mrs Amelia knew of their talk at the Linden Walk when each opened her heart to the other; knew it must remain their secret.

'The last time I shall visit Rowangarth, much as I love it,' Amelia Sutton had said, yet it was so important she should know that Kitty's soul was restless no longer; that the Fates had decided it should come home to Rowangarth. She, Lyn, had that soul in her keeping now, gladly and lovingly, yet how to write a letter that would keep that secret safe?

'I think,' she said, 'that it's just about okay, now . . .' Given that Drew would read it and almost certainly add a message of his own, that was.

Dear Mrs Amelia,

*I know you said a fond goodbye to Rowangarth, but will you please, (*she had underlined please*) just once more, visit us at Easter? We plan to have the babies christened then, and I feel the day would not be complete without you.*

They are to be called Jonathan (Jon) and Kathryn (Kat). Jon has my auburn hair and is the most placid child. Kat has a mop of black hair and has already learned to get attention the moment she wants it! There is something very special about her – but I am her mother, and must be forgiven for thinking it!

*Drew and I – indeed everyone here – would
so much like you to come. Please say you will?*

She had gone on to write that the babies were gain-
ing weight steadily and on the next not-so-cold day
would be given their first outing; had written, too,
that Julia was delighted with her grandchildren, and
would do her best to completely spoil them.

*They are so loved, so welcome here at
Rowangarth, and I very much want you to see
them, if only the once.*

She had ended the letter almost satisfied she had
been able to remind Amelia of their talk at the Linden
Walk. In a few days' time, when the letter with its
underlying message was safely there and had been
read and understood, she and Drew would ring
Kentucky, urging that Amelia come with Bas and
Gracie and Adam and Nell.

'See if you think this will do.' Lyn handed the letter
to Drew. 'And a PS from you might be appreciated.
I really want your Aunt Amelia to come.'

'Y'know, darling, I believe you do. Are you going
to tell me why?'

'No reason, really.' Her shrug seemed genuine, her
voice non-committal. 'But she was at our wedding,
and having her at Easter will – well – round it off,
sort of.'

'It's a long way to come to round things off, Lyn.'

'No it isn't. Once they all came twice a year and
now it's much quicker to fly. And do I have to make

excuses? I want the Kentucky Suttons to be here, that's all . . .'

'Fine by me, darling. You don't have to give a reason. It's your show, after all. You did all the hard work.'

Lyn, Drew pondered, had so desperately longed for a child of her own. Of course Amelia must be at their christening. Lyn was so happy he wouldn't be surprised if the entire Riding were asked. There were times, he was bound to admit, that food rationing had its uses.

'Why are you looking at me like that,' Lyn demanded. 'All soft and soggy, I mean.'

'Was I? Actually I was thinking how having the babies has changed you – for the better, I mean. You were a bit of a worrier, once, but now you are getting quite bossy. And you are even prettier. Motherhood must have done something to your hormones.'

'If it's the bags under my eyes and the dark rings you're talking about, it is entirely due to broken sleep and double doses of nappy washing! So are you going to add a little note to the letter?' She stopped, head turned, listening. 'Oh, *no*!' she sighed as a wail from the day nursery confirmed that one small person was not going to sleep, after all. 'Bet you anything you like it'll be Kat!'

'Then hurry and bring her in here before she wakens Jon,' Drew grinned.

Then he picked up the pen, wondering what to write, thinking instead that in the first year of their marriage, he and Lyn had a family of *two*! Some going!

PS to Adam and Nell, he wrote. *Jon and Kat are looking forward to meeting their Kentucky cousins. Please make sure you bring your grandmother with you, at Easter . . .*

'Would you believe it – it's Jon,' Lyn sighed from the doorway, a small boy over her shoulder. 'Think it's a bit of wind. For once, Kat was sleeping like a cherub!'

And they laughed, because life was good, at Rowangarth.

TWENTY-EIGHT

Easter 1950

Rowangarth rose to the occasion as only Rowangarth could. On this sweet spring day, the willows on the edge of the wild garden showed pale green and silky leaves and in the hawthorn hedge, wild sloe blossom frothed white. There were daffodils, too, shining in bright clumps, and primroses and wild white windflowers carpeting Brattocks Wood.

'Well, now – wasn't that a lovely christening?' Alice and Tom sat outside the open conservatory doors, faces to the April sun. 'And wasn't it lovely when Nathan named Kathryn? Seemed right and proper, didn't it?'

'Aye. It seemed to please Amelia. She smiled over at Lyn real contented. Mind, there won't ever be another Kitty . . .'

'There won't, but Kat Sutton gave a good account of herself when Nathan wet her head. Yelled like a good 'un – just like our Daisy did – remember?'

'I do. And now she's having another of her own.

Might be a boy, this time. You'd like a little lad, wouldn't you, Tom?'

'Happen I would, but a healthy baby will fit the bill nicely. Come to think of it, Alice, there's a lot of babies around these days.'

'Well of course there are! People are making up for lost time! Not a lot of chance having bairns with half the husbands overseas in the Forces for years and years. The baby boom they're calling it. There's a right epidemic around these parts!'

'Worse things could happen, love.' Tom knocked out his pipe. 'And I think Ellen is going to start the teas.'

Tilda, too, had risen to the occasion, and no one asked how she had managed to provide so many vol-au-vents, sandwiches, chocolate biscuits and cherry scones dolloped with illegal cream from Home Farm.

'I heard,' Alice said, getting to her feet, smoothing her skirt, 'there's to be chocolate biscuits. Now where did they come from, I wonder?'

'Not from Creesby grocers, that's for sure. Wouldn't surprise me if they haven't crossed the Atlantic on a plane. And talking about Kentucky, there's Gracie waving to you. Away and have a word with the lass – tell her what a grand job she made of the church flowers.'

Gracie Sutton. Such a bonny, happy lass, Alice thought.

'Hullo there!' she smiled. 'I've hardly seen you since you arrived. You made a grand job of the decorations – the church looked lovely.'

'Well – thanks. But I love doing it, though I've had plenty of practice, over the years. Didn't know a thing about gardening, till I came to Rowangarth. Happy days – even if there was a war on, though I think I'm inclined to forget the sad things and remember only the good bits – like meeting Bas, and working with Mr Catchpole.'

'Your two are lovely bairns, Gracie. And Nell, toddling now. Doesn't seem five minutes since you all came over to have her christened at All Souls. Amelia must get great comfort from her grandchildren.'

'She does, and they adore her. They help her, I think, to accept Kitty's death. She had made up her mind, you know, not to come to Rowangarth again. Don't know what made her change it, but I'm glad she did. She seems so much more relaxed, now. And she's very touched that Drew's little girl is called Kathryn. But let's join the others? I think tea is on its way, and I'm famished!'

Gracie looked around her. Dear Rowangarth. To come here was like coming home, even though she was a Lancashire lass. Nothing seemed to change. The lawns had had their first cut – always at Easter, she had been taught – and everything budding and leafing after winter. And the smell of newly turned earth in the kitchen gardens, and Mr Willis starting his sowing and planting out just as Mr Catchpole had done.

She had visited the kitchen garden as soon as she arrived, making for the orchid house, to sit on the little green chair and take in the scent of warm, moist air touched with perfume, gazing at the pots of white orchids. Special, the white ones, and now they were showing tight buds, a sure sign that come June, Jack

Catchpole would make a bridal bouquet to lay on Kitty's grave. Gracie was glad about Kitty's flowers and that Lyn wanted her to have them, still.

'See, Gracie.' Alice broke into her thoughts. 'Over yonder, on the terrace – Bas and Adam and Nell. Think they're looking for you. Away you go, lass, whilst I see if I can find Julia!'

Julia. Smugly contented. Drew married and children at Rowangarth again! Alice smiled gently. Dear bull-at-a-gate, door-banging, straight-talking Julia. May she never change.

'I was thinking, Julia,' Amelia Sutton said, 'that though Jon's eyes have changed colour, Kat's haven't. Jon's have turned hazel, but it looks as if Kat is going to keep her blue eyes.'

'Mm. She's going to grow up very beautiful, like Kitty, I – oh, dear. I'm *so* sorry, Amelia.'

'Now why be sorry? Kitty *was* beautiful, and so will Kat be – nothing so certain. But Kitty's eyes were violet, almost; there's the difference.'

'You – you don't mind talking about Kitty? It doesn't upset you that there's another Kathryn Sutton?'

'No, Julia, it doesn't. I believe Lyn chose the name – kind of her.'

'I'll never know why she did it, but it seems right, doesn't it?'

Right, Julia thought mutinously, that Kat should have blue eyes and not deep brown, Mary Anne Pendennis eyes. Kat Sutton was Drew's, and nothing to do with Elliot! She, Julia, would remember it always; say it in her heart and in her mind so often that one day, she would believe it! *Elliot Sutton did not father Drew!*

'Right, Julia? Of course it does. It's in the – well – in the order of things, isn't it? God gives back, just as He takes.'

'Amelia! You don't think Kat has –'

'No! Of course not!' Amelia felt her cheeks flush red, because she was not in the habit of telling lies – not even white ones if she could help it! 'What I meant was that there is a new baby at Rowangarth who is very beautiful and seems to like attention and who, one day, will have lovely black curls and blue eyes. But she's *Kat* Sutton. That's all I was trying to say – and that Lyn will only call her Kathryn! when she is being a naughty girl.'

'Oh, I see,' Julia said, relieved. 'In the order of things, like you said, I suppose . . .'

'Exactly. But will you tell me, before I run into Lyn's folks again, why they have chosen such strange names for themselves. Not granny and grandpa, but nine and tide? Surely I've got it wrong?'

'No you haven't, Amelia. They are just that. It sounds like nine and tide, but it's spelled *nain* and *taid*. Welsh, you see. Jack isn't Welsh, but Blodwen is – even speaks the Celtic tongue, though Lyn never picked it up. Blod is a darling. I like her.'

'Well, I *don't*!' Amelia laughed. 'How dare a grandmother have such glorious hair! Lyn has it. Thick and lovely . . .'

'And young Jon has got it, too. Oh, Amelia – aren't grandchildren a delight? Look at those two, over there.'

She nodded to where Nell and Mary Natasha

tumbled like puppies on the grass, falling, giggling, legs in air; smiled as Adam, tired of their antics, wandered off to find more grown-up company – preferably one who dispensed biscuits and creamy scones.

'I hear Daisy is expecting another baby. Her little Mary Natasha is so beautiful – dark, like Kat.'

'Mm.' Julia willed herself calm. 'She gets it from Keth; he's of Cornish stock. It's wonderful to think that there's another Clan growing up at Rowangarth. If we can get them all together – with their parents, of course – I want to take a snap or two of them.'

She wanted to take pictures all the time so none of their growing up should go unrecorded. And each time she looked at those pictures she would pray, silently, that the new Clan would never have to face war, and danger. Nor death.

'A good idea. It seems as if Bas and Gracie will come to Rowangarth and Rochdale every year, just as Bertie and I came here. And oh, the joy of staying at Bothy House, Julia, and not that awful Pendenys Place as we were expected to! Bas hated it, but Kitty –' She stopped, pink-cheeked, hoping not to have embarrassed Julia.

'But Kitty loved it,' Julia said, a small smile on her lips and tenderness in her eyes. 'There were so many nooks and hidey-holes. And she swore it was haunted – which it wasn't, of course. No self-respecting ghost would haunt Clementina's vulgar house!'

They were talking about Kitty again and all at once neither seemed to care. Amelia smiled softly, then said, 'You knew I once decided not to come to Rowangarth again?'

'Yes, and I'm glad you changed your mind. Nathan and I have always looked on you as family, and dear to us. Will you, perhaps, come again? Like I said, there's a lovely brood of young ones growing up; it would be such a pity if you were to miss it.'

'I think now, that I might. Before, you see, I always felt such sadness at Kitty's grave that it pained me to stand beside it. There was such an air of despair and unrest there; like her spirit was earthbound and protesting.

'I am a devout Christian, Julia, yet I couldn't accept that her soul was at peace as I should have done. I wanted to ask her, "Darling – what is it? Tell me?" But of course she didn't, couldn't. Am I shocking you, Julia?'

'N-no. After all, you are her mother. The bond between you was strong – will always be. But why, when you were so sure, do you now seem to have accepted that she has gone – because I feel you have, Amelia.'

'I have, though I can't tell you why because I – I don't know myself.' Again, the flush to her cheeks, because she *did* know. 'Yet I feel, now, that her soul has gone to wherever it was ordained it should be. Kitty is at peace at last, and that is all I can be sure of.'

'Then I am glad for you, Amelia, and for her. But if you should decide not to come here again, I promise I will always remember her with love and that she will have her wedding bouquet every June.'

'Thank you, Julia. And being the Anglophile that I am, I would like to visit again, though I have a favour to ask of you.'

'Then granted, soon as asked!'

'Bas and family intend to go to Rochdale on Tuesday, have a few days extra with Gracie's folks, this time, and I will leave with them – but for London. Will you let me stay at Aunt Sutton's house, Julia? I have great need to be there, just the one time.'

'Kitty?' Julia whispered.

'The last goodbye. I want to stay where she stayed and to stand where it was, at the time it was. And I want to know that she is not there, either. Will you give me a key, Julia?'

'Of course I will, if you are sure that is what you want.'

'I do want, and I shall ask Tatty to tell me exactly where. It was near a chapel, I believe?'

'Yes, the Guard's Chapel. A direct hit, but Tatty will know better than I. She'll remember what they wore, that morning – what kind of sandwiches Sparrow had packed for them – what Kitty's last words were. She was posting a letter to Drew.'

'And you don't think I will be making a maudlin pilgrimage?'

'No. Tatty and Bill went to Hyde Park when they honeymooned in London. Tatty hadn't been brave enough, before that, to go back. She told me she was glad she did, so I hope it will be the same for you, Amelia.'

'I think it will be. And here is your Ellen bringing trays, and I can see Mrs Stubbs pouring so-English tea, in the conservatory.' She reached for Julia's hand, squeezing it tightly. 'Bless you for understanding, my dear.'

* * *

623

Blodwen Carmichael sat on the terrace with Jonathan Sutton on her knee, his christening gown spread out for full effect. She was wearing her wedding outfit and hat, and loving every minute of the smiles her grandson gave readily to everyone who stopped to say to him, 'Well, don't you look grand, young Jon?'

Or, 'My, what a lovely boy he is, and how he's growing!'

Because Lyn's boy *was* lovely and had the most friendly nature, giving lopsided grins to all – when he wasn't sucking contentedly on his clenched fist, that was. He had completely stolen her heart, this grandson.

'Hullo, Mum.' Lyndis standing there, looking tired, but so very happy. 'Just checking up. Have you had a cup of tea and something to eat, yet? Shall I take him?'

'No, you leave him with me. I can drink tea and eat scones any time I want, but days like this don't come often. Where's Kat, then?'

'She's with Julia and Amelia. They want to take photos of all the young ones – a memento, sort of, of the day. Then after that, I'm going to get the pair of them out of their fancy clobber, feed them and put them down for a sleep. Oh, it's all go!'

And with that she was gone, leaving Blodwen to shake her head and wonder for how much longer could Lyn stay high on her cloud before she fell off it, and slept for a week.

'Hullo!' they said simultaneously when Lyndis met Amelia Sutton at Bothy House gate.

'Was just going for a stroll in this lovely April

evening,' Amelia supplied. 'I want to sniff the air.'

'And I am trying to get Kat to sleep. Jon is well away, but little Miss Sutton here has different ideas. I thought maybe an outing in the pram would do the trick. I was going down the Creesby road – shall we walk together?'

'Only if I can push,' Amelia laughed. 'And thank you, by the way, for a lovely day. Rowangarth always puts on a splendid show. I suppose everyone has gone, now?'

'Yes, and everything cleared up. Lots of willing helpers. Mum is listening out for Jon, and Drew and Dad are reading the Sunday papers. I'm glad we met. I've hardly had chance to talk to you since you arrived. I'm – *we* – are glad you came. But I'm especially glad. I want to talk to you about Kitty – and about Kat. Do you think as I think?'

'That Kitty is at peace, now? Yes, Lyn, I do. I think that what we talked about that afternoon beneath the lindens has happened.'

'I don't think. I *know*. You see, two things you said have come true. You told me I would come to love Kitty; that one day I would be as close as can be to her. And you said I would have a boy and a girl, yet I hadn't a clue, at the time, that I was carrying twins.'

'So now you believe that Kitty's waiting is over; that she has come home to Rowangarth?'

'Yes, I do,' Lyn said softly, 'and I'm very happy about it.'

'And what does Drew think to it all?'

'Oh my goodness – I haven't told him! Only Daisy knows, and Drew thinks as Daisy and most other people think – that Jon and Kat favour my mother and father.'

'So how come you told your best friend, and not your husband, Lyn?' The question was gently asked.

'It was just after the babies were born and I was on a high, I suppose. I was so sure, you see – I still am. But Daisy wouldn't accept it. She said it smacked of reincarnation and that I'd better keep such thoughts to myself; or words to that effect,' she laughed, shakily. 'It's why I want you to believe as I do, Mrs Amelia, then I won't care what the others think.'

'Sssh. I think she's going to sleep.' Amelia made a rocking motion with the pram, then whispered, 'Don't worry. I'm on your side, Lyn. I want to go back to Kentucky knowing Kitty is safe at Rowangarth, and happy.'

'Bless you. And should we turn back, now?' Lyn tucked the blanket round the dark-haired little baby, then pulled up the pram hood. 'And you *will* come back to visit, once in a while?'

'Of course I will, even though Bertie can't ever understand why I love Rowangarth so much. And I've got good reason to return, now, haven't I? Tell you what! I'll be over again to celebrate the new roof – how about that?'

'You're invited! But it won't be entirely new. They're going to check all the timbers, then re-lay the same tiles – only more securely. Now the better weather is here, I expect they'll start pretty soon. It's going to be a three-month job, at least. Y'know, I don't think anyone has got to the bottom of that roof since the day it was built. It's going to be very exciting – wondering what we might find.' She sighed, feeling all at once contented and relaxed, and whispered, 'I love that funny old house. It's so enduring. Daisy told me that Kitty once said she would marry Drew if only to get her hands on Rowangarth! I know exactly what she meant! Did she always say outrageous things?'

'Always, Lyn, but that's the way she was. And losing her doesn't seem to hurt so much, now. I shall visit London – the place it happened – then everything will be straight in my mind, again.'

'And do you think that Kat will say outrageous things, too?'

'She will, Lyn, and be mischievous and naughty and very, *very* loveable, I promise you. But it's turning a little chilly. Let's go home, shall we?'

'We'd better make the most of this,' Drew laughed. 'The baby-sitters will be going back to Wales tomorrow. No more runs ashore for you and me!'

'Of course there will be! Mother and Lady will be only too glad to oblige.'

'Lady will be taken up with her own new baby before so very much longer! Sure you can cope, Lyn? Twins are more work than I thought.'

'I'll manage. Jon is sleeping most nights, now, and Kat will settle down, soon.'

'So what is it to be – a quick half at the pub, or a stroll?'

'A stroll, please. I want to walk right round the garden, then down the Linden Walk.'

'The seat will be very cold . .'

'It doesn't matter. It's my favourite place, I think.

So many nice things have happened to me, there.'

'Like me proposing to you?'

'Yes, amongst other things. And I like to look to the left and see the stableyard cupola, and Brattocks Wood on the right. But most of all, I like to sit on the cold marble seat and look ahead at Rowangarth.'

'And?'

'And think that there is my home – and your home and Jon's and Kat's. So shall we go to the Linden Walk and shall you kiss me goodnight there, darling?'

'If that's what you want.'

'I *do* want, because goodnight kisses can lead to all sorts of things. Lovely, passionate things . . .'

'Then full speed ahead, Lady Sutton, to the Linden Walk,' he laughed, tucking her arm in his.

And they walked across the grass to where the avenue of trees stood dimly against a darkening April sky and where soon the leaves would open, green and silky, to another summer. And for a few days, give out an unbelievable perfume to those who walked beneath it.

'Hold on a minute! I want to kiss you – *now*.' He folded her in his arms and she closed her eyes and parted her lips. 'I love you, Lyn Carmichael,' he said, huskily.

'Love you too, sailor.' She whispered her lips teasingly across his cheek. 'And let's not bother with goodnight kisses at the Linden Walk, darling? Let's go home?'

Home to Rowangarth, where now she belonged . . .